Praise for Anna Durand's Books

"[In *One Hot Roomie*] Anna Durand adroitly sets the stage for a fun romantic comedy. [...] Durand's two main characters are perfect foils for each other; both are conflicted and for good reason. Seeing as they try to make being roomies for two weeks work is priceless entertainment."
Jack Magnus, Readers' Favorite

" I loved the slow-burn, should we-shouldn't we, what's right, dilemma and desire that built and built until the steam had to escape. [*One Hot Chance*] is equal parts fun, steam, and moral quandary. [...] I am in love with Chance and his brothers already."
MaryLou Hoffman, Page Princess blog

"[*Lethal in a Kilt* is] full of hot sex, adventure, and so much laughter. I found myself laughing-out-loud at the antics of the Witches of Ballachulish (Logan's sisters) and the hilarious flirting and sexy banter between Serena and Logan. [...] Recommend highly! "
Sharon Clayton, The Eclectic Review

"[*Insatiable in a Kilt*] smokes from the very first pages... Durand's characters are a delight and seeing how they mix business with their increasing attraction for each other is entertaining indeed. [...] Durand's Hot Scots family saga just keeps on getting better."
Readers' Favorite

"I loved the Scottish in Ian and the strength of Rae, but the love of one little girl makes [*Notorious in a Kilt*] something to behold."
Coffee Time Romance

"*Gift-Wrapped in a Kilt* is a marvelous continuation of the author's MacTaggart family saga. Durand's story has an entertaining plot, and her steamy interludes are well-written...a celebration of healthy relationships between loving adults written in a tasteful and compelling manner."
Readers' Favorite

"I have enjoyed this whole series, but Emery and Rory [from *Scandalous in a Kilt*] have stolen my heart and are now my favorites!"
The Romance Reviews

Other Books by Anna Durand

One Hot Chance (Hot Brits, Book One)

One Hot Roomie (Hot Brits, Book Two)

One Hot Escape (Hot Brits, Book Four)

Natural Passion (Au Naturel Trilogy, Book One)

Natural Impulse (Au Naturel Trilogy, Book Two)

Natural Satisfaction (Au Naturel Trilogy, Book Three)

Dangerous in a Kilt (Hot Scots, Book One)

Wicked in a Kilt (Hot Scots, Book Two)

Scandalous in a Kilt (Hot Scots, Book Three)

The MacTaggart Brothers Trilogy (Hot Scots, Books 1-3)

Gift-Wrapped in a Kilt (Hot Scots, Book Four)

Notorious in a Kilt (Hot Scots, Book Five)

Insatiable in a Kilt (Hot Scots, Book Six)

Lethal in a Kilt (Hot Scots, Book Seven)

Irresistible in a Kilt (Hot Scots, Book Eight)

Fired Up (standalone romance)

The Mortal Falls (Undercover Elementals, Book One)

The Mortal Fires (Undercover Elementals, Book Two)

The Mortal Tempest (Undercover Elementals, Book Three)

The Janusite Trilogy (Undercover Elementals, Books 1-3)

Obsidian Hunger (Undercover Elementals, Book Four)

Willpower (Psychic Crossroads, Book One)

Intuition (Psychic Crossroads, Book Two)

Kinetic (Psychic Crossroads, Book Three)

Passion Never Dies: The Complete Reborn Series

Reborn to Die (Reborn, Part One)

Reborn to Burn (Reborn, Part Two)

Reborn to Avenge (Reborn, Part Three)

Reborn to Conquer (Reborn, Part Four)

THE DIXON

Dixon Brothers Trilogy

Hot Brits, Books 1-3

ANNA DURAND

JACOBSVILLE BOOKS · MARIETTA, OHIO

THE DIXON BROTHERS TRILOGY

ISBN: 978-1-949406-37-5 (paperback)
ISBN: 978-1-949406-38-2 (audiobook)

Manufactured in the United States.

Jacobsville Books
www.JacobsvilleBooks.com

Publisher's Cataloging-in-Publication Data
provided by Five Rainbows Cataloging Services

Names: Durand, Anna.
Title: The Dixon brothers trilogy : hot Brits, books 1-3 / Anna Durand.
Description: Marietta, OH : Jacobsville Books, 2020. | Series: Hot Brits, bks. 1-3.
Identifiers: ISBN 978-1-949406-37-5 (paperback) | ISBN 978-1-949406-38-2 (audiobook)
Subjects: LCSH: Administrative assistants--Fiction. | Legal assistants--Fiction. | Virgins--Fiction. | Businessmen--Fiction. | Attorneys--Fiction. | British--Fiction. | New York (N.Y.)--Fiction. | Romance fiction. | BISAC: FICTION / Romance / Contemporary. | FICTION / Romance / Romantic Comedy. | FICTION / Romance / Workplace. | FICTION / Romance / New adult. | FICTION / Romance / Collections & Anthologies. | GSAFD: Love stories.
Classification: LCC PS3604.U724 D59 2020 (print) | LCC PS3604.U724 (ebook) | DDC 813/.6--dc23..

Contents

Book 3: One Hot Crush **243**

One Hot CHANCE

Hot Brits, Book One

Chapter One

Elena

I am cursed. Seriously. Since I was born on the thirteenth day of October—Friday the thirteenth, no less—I feel justified in declaring myself to be cursed. Why else would I get my dream job only to discover it's a nightmare? I've admired Raisa Volkov for years and followed her legal career like a true fangirl. Becoming her paralegal seemed like an awesome gift. I get to work alongside the toughest, most successful divorce attorney in New York.

Except she's hated me from day one. She snips at me, snaps at me, barks orders at me, and generally makes me wish I'd taken a job at McDonald's instead. I suppose I should be comforted by the fact she makes everyone feel that way, but it doesn't comfort me at all.

And this is only day two. Thank God it's Friday.

Now I understand why Raisa's former paralegal, Mia, gave her two-week notice sixteen days ago. Her Royal Snippiness tasked Mia with hiring her own replacement.

That would be me. The cursed Elena Linwood.

While I fantasize about murdering my new boss, I raise a hand to get the bartender's attention. I just sat down at the bar a minute ago and desperately need booze. I mean *desperately*. Two days with Raisa have left me drained and depressed. So here I sit, in the swanky hotel across the street from the office, on a Friday night, about to drown my sorrows in a margarita. The bartender takes my order, smiling and calling me "babe," though not in a creepy way. He's cute and sexy, but way too busy to flirt with me. "Sure thing, babe" is all I get out of him.

God, I need a hot guy to flirt with. To dance with. To do all sorts of naughty, naughty things with.

That proverbial light bulb goes off in my head. A bright, flashing, neon-pink bulb. What do I need to lift my spirits? Why, a steamy fling with an anonymous piece of sizzling-hot ass.

You're brilliant, Elena.

I congratulate myself on my awesome idea for about thirty seconds. Then reality slams down on my head as I glance around the bar. It's full of older couples and middle-aged men on their own who look like they probably just got served divorce papers and want to get hammered. I have a feeling a lot of men who get served by Raisa Volkov wind up in this bar after their first meeting with their wives' attorney.

No hot prospects. Looking at these guys makes me want to face-plant on the bar.

So I do. And I moan, like the pathetic wage slave I am.

"You still want the drink?" the bartender asks.

I don't bother to raise my head, instead waving my hand to indicate that yes, I do want that margarita. I plan to guzzle it like a sorority girl at a frat party. As soon as I can peel my face away from the shiny, cool surface of the bar. I hear the cute bartender set my drink down.

Maybe I should've ordered straight-up tequila.

"Are you all right there?"

That voice. It's not the cute bartender. The man who spoke to me has a silky British accent and a husky voice that makes me want to crawl onto his lap without even looking at his face. Since I am cursed, I know if I do look, I'll find out he has the face of a bulldog and the body of a sumo wrestler.

But that voice…

A warm hand touches my arm. Since I'm wearing a sleeveless blouse, I get to feel his skin on mine. Oh, it feels sooo good.

"I said are you all right?" he asks.

"Mm-hm." I finally peel my face away from the bar—and sit up straighter. Blue eyes. Blond hair. A body to die for. *Lucky me.* Everything south of my waist wakes up from its months-long coma and tingles in all the right ways when he smiles at me. I smile back. "I'm fine, but thanks for asking. I love polite British men."

Why did I say that? *Stupid, stupid Elena.*

He lifts one brow and smirks. "How do you know I'm polite? I've barely spoken five words to you."

"Seven, actually. Unless you count the ones you said twice, which would mean eleven words. Not including what you said a second ago."

Oh. My. God. Why do stupid things keep pouring out of my mouth? It's not like I've never seen a hot guy before.

He leans against the bar, his beautiful blue eyes twinkling in the subdued lighting. "It's comforting to know you're intelligent enough to count to at least eleven."

"I can count to twelve in German."

"Can you?" He's still smirking, but damn, that expression makes me start to tingle above the waist too. His voice gets even deeper, even sexier, when he says, "Let me hear it."

What the hell. I slant toward him a little, enough that I can smell his spicy cologne, or maybe it's aftershave. Either way, the scent makes me want to lick him from head to toe. *"Eins, zwei, drei, vier, fünf, sechs, sieben, acht, neun, zehn, elf, zwölf."*

"Say *zwölf* again. I love the way you pronounce it."

He loves my pronunciation? I really hope he isn't making fun of me.

The sexy Brit leans in to brush hair away from my face, his fingers grazing my skin. "Say it again, please."

I grin. "See, you are polite."

"For the moment." He trails his fingertips down my cheek to the corner of my mouth. "Say *zwölf* again, and I'll kiss you."

"What if I don't want to kiss you?"

He drags one finger across my mouth, slowly, sensuously. "You do."

Yeah, okay, I do. My fling idea sounds better and better every second.

I lick his finger and say, *"Zwölf."*

He slides his hand into my hair, pulls my face closer, and kisses me.

Oh God, his lips. They're soft and warm, and taste faintly of caramel. Maybe he had a decadent dessert a few minutes ago. I don't care, because all I want is for his lips to tease mine for the rest of eternity. His breaths tickle my skin, and my nipples go hard. When he slips his tongue between my lips, I melt. I'm floating on a warm, silken cloud of desire, my body pure liquid and the only thing keeping me from collapsing into a puddle at his feet is his mouth.

He pulls away, but only a few inches. "Come to my room with me."

"What?" Sure, it's exactly what I wanted, but my brain can't quite catch up to his words.

"Come with me, upstairs, to my room." He catches my bottom lip with his teeth, swipes his tongue over it, and releases my flesh with a slowness that makes me ache in all the best ways. "You're the most adorable creature I've ever seen, and I want to make love to you all night long."

"Oh God, yes." Did I say that out loud? *Ugh, Elena, stop doing that.* "Let's go to your room."

"Do you want to finish your drink first?"

I glance sideways at the untouched margarita. Suddenly, my scorching Brit sounds like a much better cocktail than the drink I ordered. "No, I'm done with it."

He slings an arm around my waist as I ooze off my stool, slinging my too-big purse over my shoulder. We walk across the lobby to the elevator with me hugged to his hard body and his hand on my hip.

The elevator doors open. Three people hurry out, leaving the car empty.

My Brit and I get in, and the doors glide shut.

He turns toward me, still hugging me to him, and I suddenly find myself plastered to the hottest body I've ever seen—and the stiffest hard-on I've ever felt.

"Can't wait," he almost growls. "I'm on the nineteenth floor, which means we have time."

"Time for what?"

He backs me up to the wall and crushes his mouth to mine. His tongue thrusts deep, making me moan and latch my arms around his neck. I'm helpless to resist his hungry swipes, helpless to do anything except let him ravage me and mash me to the wall with every inch of his delicious body. I moan again, rougher, needier.

And he shoves my skirt up.

I gasp, but then grin like an idiot. My purse slides off my shoulder, thumping on the floor.

He tears my panties off, his expression tight with need and a craving so intense it seems to bleed into me, making me slicker and hotter and achier. He unzips his slacks while he seals his mouth over my nipple, soaking my blouse and bra, and suckles the tip. My back arches. I clutch his head to my chest, loving the softness of his hair and the sharp sting of his teeth scraping my hard peak.

I barely notice when the sound of foil ripping fills the elevator.

My Brit pulls away only long enough to sheath himself with a condom, then he hoists one of my legs and thrusts into me.

A cry bursts out of me, surprise and lust and sheer ecstasy rushing through me like high tide on a full moon night.

He pushes inside me again and again, every thrust strong and purposeful, his cock penetrating me so deeply it's like our bodies were made for each other. He consumes me, unrelenting in his passion, and soon his movements grow wilder, greedier, like he can't get enough of me and never wants this to end. I want it to go on and on and on. The slapping of our bodies as they collide becomes a frantic rhythm, while I bounce and he grunts every time he slams me into the wall.

I come like a fireworks display on New Year's Eve, every burst of pleasure bigger and hotter and brighter, blinding me to everything except the look on his face. No man has ever looked at me that way, like he can't bear to give up being inside me but can't wait a second longer to let go.

His climax pulsates deep inside me, and I come harder.

We both go limp. I sag against the wall. Luckily, he has enough strength left to keep us both from falling into a lump on the floor. He nuzzles my neck, then peppers soft kisses on my skin as he makes his way up to my ear.

A phone rings.

Not mine.

My Brit digs his phone out of his pocket and answers it. "What do you want?"

He sounds irritated.

I'm kind of irritated too. I mean, he's still inside me, and he takes a call? What the hell? So much for politeness.

"I'm busy," he says curtly, his mouth pinched. "We can talk about this Monday."

While he chats with somebody else, I wriggle away from him, fix my dress, and stuff my wrecked panties into my purse.

The elevator stops. The doors open.

I don't have a room on the nineteenth floor, or anywhere in this hotel, but I suddenly need to get away from him. My plan to cheer myself up with a fling started out so hot, but now I'm feeling weird about the whole thing. So I stumble out into the hall.

"Wait," he calls out to me.

I turn toward him, hoping my expression conveys how much I don't like being screwed and then forgotten about.

He's holding his phone to his chest and giving me the sweetest look of regret. "Please wait. I'm sorry about this."

Being a total sucker for a pitiful, hot man—not to mention a sucker for a British accent—I chew my lip and try to decide what to do. I can hear the person he's been talking to shouting at him, demanding his attention.

"Not now," he hisses into the phone.

I hear more tinny shouting. My shoulders sag, because obviously, this is the end of my hot night of sin with a stranger. Like I said, I'm cursed. I get one good bang in an elevator, and then it's over.

He looks at me again, his expression pleading for me to stay.

I shake my head and march toward the stairs. I do my dramatic exit thing, then schlep down one flight of stairs before I realize I can't walk down eighteen more flights. Groaning at my sucky luck, I sit down on the steps and face-plant in my own hands this time.

The clapping of shoes echoes in the stairwell, coming down the steps from the floor above.

Someone sighs right beside me.

I peek through my fingers at the person.

My sexy Brit is kneeling beside me, looking a little embarrassed. "I'm sorry about that. I shouldn't have answered my phone."

A shrug is all I can manage in response. I'm still covering my face with my hands and watching through the gaps between my fingers.

He gently pries my hands away, clasping them in his bigger ones. "Please come to my room. I'd love to spend all night with you. You're the most enchanting woman I've ever met."

Enchanting? No one has ever called me that before. He'd also said I'm adorable. He is definitely adorable, enchanting, sexy, beautiful, and all sorts of other adjectives.

I open my mouth to accept his offer when my phone chimes, alerting me to a new text. Since I got annoyed when my Brit took a call, I can't check my text. I clutch my purse to my stomach, chewing on my lip.

"You can check that," he says. "It's all right."

"Sorry," I say as I pull out my phone and read the text.

It's from my brother, Kyle. He says, "Where R U?"

Oh crap. I forgot I'm supposed to spend the evening with him, hanging out, before he and his girlfriend leave for their spring break vacation tomorrow morning.

"You need to go," my Brit says.

Wincing, I say, "Yeah. It's, um, a family thing I forgot about."

"May I know your name?"

"Elena." I get an idea, and rummage in my purse until I find an old Starbucks receipt and a pen. I scribble numbers on the back, then hand the paper to him. "Here's my number."

He smiles. "Thank you, Elena. I'm Chance, by the way."

The man I just had sex with is called Chance. Maybe my luck is changing. I try not to read too much into his name, since chance is a roll of the dice, not a good omen.

We both get up.

He kisses my cheek. "I'll ring you tomorrow, if that's all right."

"Yes, I'd like that."

I allow myself one last look at his blue eyes, then I walk out of the stairwell and take the elevator to the lobby. When I get home, Kyle is waiting for me with two pizzas and a six-pack of beer. We have fun watching action movies until two o'clock, but when I fall asleep, I dream of the sexy Brit.

Will he call me?

As it turns out, no. My luck hasn't changed at all.

Chapter Two

Elena

I arrive at the offices of Raisa Volkov & Associates on Monday morning feeling surprisingly good, despite having spent the weekend at the office working overtime without the overtime pay. This is the life of a paralegal. I no longer feel like a loser who had a quickie in an elevator and never got a callback. Definitely not like the girl who had face-planted on the bar, or the girl who counted to twelve in German. No, I'd left that idiot behind. Locked her in the hotel basement, actually.

Still, my sexy Brit had liked the silly things I'd said. At least, he seemed to like them. Maybe he was pretending to, so I'd have sex with him. Whatever. I'd wanted a fling, and I'd had one. Yay, me.

I sit down at my desk in the cubicle zone and resolve to never think of Friday night again. My large, steaming latte from Starbucks calls to me, so I take a swig. Mm, yummy goodness.

A memory of the sexy Brit's face pops into my mind. Oh yeah, yummy goodness there.

Stop that, I command myself. *You're a strong, capable woman who has a freaking job to do.*

Yes, I do. My job sucks in every way imaginable, but I will do it anyway. Straightening in my chair, I take another sip of my latte and log on to my computer. Like the other paralegals and the interns, I have a crummy chair inside a crummy cubicle. My coworkers named all of us the plebs, a term taken from ancient Rome, which means we're the dirt Empress Raisa scrapes off her shoes. Other attorneys work here, but she has no partners. That would give somebody else a measure of control and a financial stake in the firm. Raisa Volkov does not share authority.

The most annoying part of all is that I still admire her. She built this firm from the ground up and made a name for herself, not only in New York, but around the country.

Yeah, I'm a pathetic fangirl.

"Elena!"

Oh great. Her Royal Highness is summoning me. I rotate my chair toward her office door and smile politely. "Good morning, Raisa. What can I do for you?"

"Why don't I have the Caldwell case file? Someone didn't put it on my desk this morning."

"Someone" hadn't gotten out the file because another someone hadn't said she needed it.

Raisa jabs a finger in the air in my general direction. "Go get it."

Naturally, the most obnoxious woman in New York looks like a supermodel. She has long legs and a slender body, with ebony hair that glistens beautifully and skin that glows even in lighting conditions that make me look sallow. According to the male interns, her dark eyes lend her an aura of mystery.

She storms up to me dressed in her Armani pantsuit, towering over me in a way that makes me feel like a munchkin, and taps one finger on my desk. "Why aren't you getting that file? Go. Now."

"Yes, Raisa. Right away."

I scurry off to the file room and retrieve the documents she wants. Everything is on the firm's servers, but lawyers seem to have a weird aversion to looking at files on their computers. They even take notes on pads of paper, instead of digital tablets. That leaves us paralegals and interns to brave the dusty, windowless file room to get whatever the attorneys need.

At least the maze of cubicles where we all work gets some sunlight, even if it's secondhand. The attorneys' offices rim the cubicle zone, and every office has large windows. The glass walls can be turned opaque by flipping a switch, but most of the time they're clear, giving the grunt workers a touch of natural light.

When I get back to my desk, I see Raisa's office door is shut. I swig my cold coffee, then approach her door. Just as I raise my hand to knock, the door swings inward.

"There you are," Raisa says, like she's been waiting hours for me to come back. It's been ten minutes. She snatches the file out of my hand. "Get in here. We need to talk."

A sour taste creeps into my mouth. She's about to fire me. On day three.

Cursed, for sure.

I dutifully walk into her office. When she shuts the door, I flinch. I feel like a peasant about to be guillotined, and the thump of the door was that giant blade lopping off someone else's head. Next up, me.

Raisa points at one of two chairs positioned in front of her desk. "Sit."

A man stands at the window, facing away from us. The sunshine burnishes his blond hair with streaks of molten gold.

I flump onto the chair.

Raisa settles onto her large executive chair behind the desk. "I've hired someone to replace Lucas Miller."

Though I've never met Lucas Miller, I've heard the office gossip about him. He handled corporate law before he quit suddenly a few days before I started my job here.

Raisa waves a hand negligently toward the man who still faces away from us. "Meet Lucas's replacement, Chance Dixon."

The man pivots on his heels to face me.

A tingle sweeps over my entire body, and I suddenly can't take in a whole breath. I stammer something resembling "hello," though what comes out of my mouth isn't actually a word.

The sexy Brit from the hotel stares at me, his face blank.

I stare right back at him, probably looking like a stupefied moron.

Raisa doesn't seem to notice our reactions to each other.

Damn, he looks even better than Friday night, dressed in a navy suit that brings out the color of his eyes and accentuates the panty-melting beauty of his body. It ought to be illegal to look so good.

His blank stare dissolves into a smile that curves his lips little by little, heating up with every millimeter his mouth moves. His gaze warms too, burning into me with the heat of the midday sun toasting my bare skin. One side of his mouth kinks upward more than the other in the sexiest lopsided smile I've ever seen.

My lips curl up at the corners, while my body rouses the way it had Friday night, readying for whatever this man wants to do to me.

We're in the office. With my boss. And I am getting more and more turned on just looking at Chance Dixon.

Still oblivious, Raisa motions for Chance to sit in the chair beside me.

I try not to stare anymore, but honestly, I only have so much willpower. When he passes by me, his ass is an arm's length from my face. I've never seen him naked, but I've had my leg strapped around him and felt those taut, powerful glutes.

He settles that perfect bottom onto the chair beside me, propping one ankle on the other knee.

Raisa smiles at him with all the flirtatiousness of a teenager, even batting her eyelashes. "I'm so pleased you've finally come home to our firm, where you belong." She aims her businesswoman smile at me. "Chance is my husband."

"Ex-husband," he corrects.

The lovely blush of desire that warmed my entire body snuffs out. Her ex-husband? She'd called him husband, no ex. Coupled with the way she batted her lashes at him, that implies she doesn't think of him as her former spouse, but as hers, period.

Fantastic. I had a quickie in an elevator with the ex-husband of my bitchy boss who hates me, and she wants him back. Does he want her back too? If he volunteered to work here, he must want to be close to her. Why did he seduce me the other night? A divorce lawyer who's a cheater. Doesn't that just figure.

Nope, my luck has not changed one bit.

Back in the hotel, I'd hoped his name, Chance, might be a good omen or something. Wrong. The dice got tossed, and I hit snake eyes.

Raisa waves her hand in the way I've already figured out means she's dismissing me. "Elena, you will work exclusively with Chance until I say otherwise. Do whatever he says. Chance, think of her as your slave."

I glance sideways at him.

He smirks at me while he tells my boss, "Thank you, Raisa. I've always wanted a slave of my own."

The boss lady is focused on the papers on her desk, ignoring us. Once she dismisses you, all that's left to do is walk out the door. I'd learned this about Raisa Volkov after two full days as her slave.

Now she's handing me over to Chance. As *his* slave. My body loves the idea, but my brain keeps warning me to watch out.

Chance opens the door for me as we exit Raisa's office. He lays a hand on the small of my back, guiding me toward the office that previously belonged to Lucas Miller. They must have changed the sign on the door early this morning, because it now says "Chance Dixon."

He holds the door open for me. "Slaves enter first."

I want to scowl at him, but I pull myself together and stay professional. "Thank you, Mr. Dixon."

"Call me Chance."

"Rather not. Sir." It's dumb, but I hope calling him mister and sir will put some kind of distance between us.

Yeah, I said it was dumb.

He shuts the door while I take a seat in front of his desk, then he sits down in the spiffy executive chair. The office is spacious, though not as big as Raisa's. This is her firm, after all. Still, Chance's office features large windows that catch the morning sun at the perfect angle to make his gorgeous face look even more beautiful. The rays of golden sunshine kiss his skin, spilling down his face, onto his throat.

"I had no idea you worked here," he says. "But I'm glad to see you. After the way you ran off—"

"No running. I walked. And you never called me, so you're the one who has explaining to do."

"You gave me the wrong number. I had a lovely conversation with the owner of an Italian deli, but he didn't know any Elena." Chance rocks his chair slowly, keeping his focus on me. "I wondered if you gave me the wrong number on purpose."

"I wouldn't do that. Sorry I got it wrong, but I was kind of, um, confused." I fidget in my chair, which seems to be made of pins and needles. Or maybe that sensation is a figment of my freaking-out mind. "After hearing you argue with somebody on the phone, I started to think I'd made a big mistake."

"Do you still feel that way? Because I don't. I wanted more time with you."

His voice is soothing and stimulating at the same time, an odd combination that compels me to relax. "I don't regret it."

"I'm glad." He sinks back in his chair, shoulders slumped, and rubs his eyes. "It was Raisa on the phone that night."

And she's still into him. That much is obvious.

Does he want to reconcile with her?

Chance drops his hand, fixing me with an earnest look. "I shouldn't have shagged you in an elevator. But you were the most enchanting, sexiest woman I'd ever seen, and I had to have you. I've never done anything of the sort before."

I shrug. "What's done is done. I'm your employee now, which means it's strictly business between us from this moment on. Agreed?"

He studies me, those sapphire eyes sparking in the sunlight. "I don't want only business with you, Elena."

I love the way he says my name in that delicious British accent, with that husky timbre in his voice. Though my body wants me to crawl across the desk and curl up on his lap, I straighten, clear my throat, and say, "Strictly business. Please. I need this job, and my boss is clearly still in love with you."

"But I'm not in love with her." He strokes the smooth desktop with his long fingers, caressing it like he's making love to the polished wood. "I want you, Elena, not her. If it weren't completely inappropriate, I'd have you on this desk right now."

My body reaffirms its desire to do anything he wants, making me feel warm all over. No way will I have sex with him at work. Never going to happen. Never, never, never.

I gaze into his eyes, and his lips slide into a soft smile.

Not today, at least.

"Please have dinner with me," he says. "Let me make up for my behavior the other night."

Holy heaven, I want to say yes. Dinner with a sexy, gorgeous, charming British man? Double yes, count me in. But I have to say no.

"That would be inappropriate," I say. "You're my boss."

"I agree, but I can't resist a woman who knows at least twelve German numbers and who makes me so hard I could pound nails into a wall with my cock."

A laugh splutters out of me. "That's the silliest thing I've ever heard."

He grins. "At least I made you laugh."

It's not fair for him to be so cute and so swoon-worthy at the same time.

"Our relationship has to be professional," I tell him. "Nothing more."

He sighs. "All right, I'll give it a go. But I can't stop myself from wanting you, and I can't swear I won't at least try to kiss you."

"I'm sure you can restrain yourself if you really work at it."

"For you, I'll try anything." He leans back in his chair, but his fingers still stroke the desktop. "Raisa has it wrong. I am *your* slave, Miss Linwood."

Having no clue what to say to that, I excuse myself and head back to my desk in the cubicle zone.

And I keep thinking about him.

Chapter Three

Chance

I show extraordinary willpower by keeping my hands off Elena for a full three hours. But honestly, it's her fault when my resolve slips. I call her to ask for a file, and she says she'll bring it to me. A few seconds later, she sashays past the open door of my office on her way to the file room, hips swaying, head held high. A slight smile tugs at her mouth, but she doesn't glance my way. The sight of her tight arse and those breasts, covered but not really concealed by her clothes, does me in. I grab a paperweight off my desk and fist my hand around it. Loosen my fist. Tighten it. Loosen. Tighten.

But in my mind, I'm closing my hand around one of those perfect breasts.

Maybe I haven't seen her naked yet and don't actually know what her breasts look like, but I'm positive they are perfect. Elena Linwood has curves in all my favorite places and a mouth that I loved kissing.

How can I work with her and never touch her again?

I should resign immediately, then drag Elena into the nearest closet and shag her until she screams.

But I can't. First of all, it would be very wrong. After the way I behaved on Friday night, I want to prove to Elena I'm not an arse who cares only about his own pleasure. Second, I promised Raisa I'd help her with her little problem. If she thinks she can use this situation to seduce me into taking her back, she will be severely disappointed. I don't love her anymore. I respect her legal skills and determination, and I know deep down she's not a rotten bitch. Still, I don't approve of the way she's been treating her employees lately. Maybe I can convince her to stop taking her frustrations out on them. I'm the reason she's acting this way, so it's my responsibility to set things right.

How the bloody hell will I pull that off?

Maybe I should've accepted Garth Leonard's offer. I'd be in New Hampshire now, far away from Raisa.

And Elena.

No, I don't want to be anywhere else.

Elena sashays into my office and sets the file on my desk. "Here's the information you need, sir. Do you require anything else?"

Yes, I require her spread across my desk naked.

Shaking off the sinful idea, even though I love it, I wave toward the chairs on her side of the desk. "Sit, Elena, please. I'd like to talk to you."

She eyes the chairs, the most endearing crinkle forming between her brows, but then sits down—on the edge of the chair, like she plans on fleeing any second.

"This is awkward, I know," I tell her. "But pretending we haven't met before, haven't known each other intimately before, isn't the answer."

"What we did wasn't intimate. It was a quickie with a stranger."

"I like you, Elena. Is that a crime?"

She gets that sweet little crinkle again, making me want to kiss it away. "No offense, Mr. Dixon, but you don't know me. I don't know you either."

"Oh, I know a few relevant facts about you." I retrieve a folder from a drawer and lay it open on the desk. "I know you're twenty-seven, single, and you share an apartment with your brother. You grew up in a small town in Wisconsin and graduated from Northwestern, summa cum laude. You were accepted to Columbia Law School but backed out. Since you had already moved to New York by that point, you stayed and worked as a secretary in a law office until you received your paralegal certification."

She stares at me for several seconds, not blinking, her hands clamped over her knees. "How do you know all that?"

"Raisa is very thorough. Before she hires anyone, she has a complete background check done on them." I tap the open folder. "This is yours. Raisa gave it to me."

"That's... kind of creepy."

"It's business. Raisa is, admittedly, rather paranoid." I close the file. "But I want to know more about you, all the things that don't show up in a background check."

"Do I get to run a background check on you?"

"No need." I lean back in my chair. "Ask me anything you like."

"How about all the same facts you have on me?"

"Of course." I keep my gaze on hers while I speak, entranced by the deep caramel color of her eyes. "I'm thirty-four, divorced, not seeing anyone at the moment." I smile and wink. "Unless you agree to have dinner with me."

She shakes her head, though a smile she's trying to prevent dimples her cheeks. "Continue with the facts, please."

"All right. I grew up in the English countryside, in a quaint little village. I attended Oxford but got my law degree from Yale. I live alone. Since this job is only temporary, I'm staying in the hotel across the street, the one where you and I met." I shrug one shoulder. "I didn't graduate with honors, like you, but I did well enough academically. I've been working for a medium-size firm in Chicago, but I've taken a sabbatical to lend a hand here."

"Until Raisa hires a permanent replacement for Lucas Miller." When I nod, she asks, "What exactly happened with him?"

I'm about to say I can't talk about that when I realize there's no good reason to be cagey. The animosity between Raisa and Lucas isn't a secret, though Elena might not have heard about it yet. She only started working here on Thursday, which I know because Raisa told me.

"Ten days ago, Lucas Miller resigned," I say. Miller had turned up at Raisa's apartment Saturday a week ago to deliver his resignation in person, resulting in an argument so loud that her neighbors called the police, but I shouldn't tell Elena that part. "Lucas never got on with Raisa, and her recent behavior pushed him over the edge. He quit without notice. That left Raisa in a desperate situation, since several of Lucas's clients have court dates coming up soon."

"That's why you're here."

"Yes. I'm the emergency reinforcements. I've done a fair bit of corporate law, so I was qualified to take over as lead counsel."

"I thought attorneys couldn't quit a case unless the client's doing something wrong."

"That's true," I say, and decide I ought to tell her the whole story after all. She'll be my right hand on these cases, and she'll probably find out anyway via the office grapevine. "Lucas Miller didn't just resign. He was arrested ten days ago, on a Saturday night, after he went to Raisa's apartment and started screaming at her. He also tried to hit her, but she slammed the door in his face before he could. Lucas had a severe mental breakdown and was taken to the hospital."

"Holy cow. I had no idea. I heard somebody say he 'went off the deep end,' but I figured it was an exaggeration."

I shake my head. "Unfortunately, it's not. Raisa contacted a judge she knows well to get permission for me to take over Miller's cases."

"Now I feel kind of bad for thinking Raisa drives me crazy. I meant it as a metaphor, not the actual truth." Elena slides back in her chair and crosses her legs. "Raisa is a lot older than you, isn't she?"

"Yes, she's forty-eight. I imagine you read the *New Yorker* piece on her last year."

Elena nods. "The article described her as a powerhouse player on the New York legal scene. I already knew about her, though, about how she built her own firm from the ground up and became the queen of divorce court. That's why I wanted to become a lawyer, and it's why I wanted to work here. She's amazing." Elena twists her mouth into the most disarming expression of frustration. "The journalist who wrote that piece neglected to mention Raisa is a raging bitch."

"She wasn't like that until recently." I hesitate, wondering how much I should reveal to Elena, but if I want to see more of her, outside of work, I suppose I ought to share more with her. "Our divorce was finalized two months ago. Raisa has always been tough, sometimes rude, but she didn't become a raging bitch until the final decree came through. It's my fault she's been terrorizing the staff."

"Uh-huh," Elena says with a touch of suspicion. "Freshly divorced sounds like big-time trouble to me. Maybe you shouldn't screw other women until you and Raisa get over each other."

"I *am* over her. Have been for a long time. Our divorce might've been finalized two months ago, but we were separated for more than a year before that."

"Still don't want to get in the middle of your marital problems."

And I can't blame her for not wanting to get in the middle of it, but I've never met a woman who intrigues me the way Elena does. Or one who gets me randy the way she does. I want to know her better, but she won't let me. Working with Elena every day might kill me. At the very least, it will leave me with blue balls.

We watch each other for a moment, Elena seeming to size me up while I catalog all the things I love about her body. Full breasts, the kind that make me dream about all the things I can do to them with my mouth, my hands, and even my cock. Creamy skin with the faintest freckles on her face. Strong legs. I know that because she'd gripped me with one of those legs while I drove into her like a maniac. Her elegant fingers had clutched my head while I devoured her nipple. Her face is more than lovely, it's like a masterpiece of beauty sculpted by Michelangelo himself.

My curiosity gets the better of me, not for the first time, and I ask, "Why didn't you go to law school?"

"None of your damn business." She stands up and squares her shoulders. "What can I do for you this morning, Mr. Dixon? I'm sure you need to get up to speed with Lucas Miller's active cases."

I do, but that's the last thing I want to think about right now. Still, I rub my neck and say, "Yes, please pull all the files and bring them to me. I'll get started on the five hundred and thirty-two emails clogging my inbox."

"That's my job. I sort through them, delete the spam and other useless stuff, and let you know when it's safe to open your inbox."

"I appreciate that, Elena. Thank you."

"You're welcome." She turns toward the door, then hesitates. "Would you like coffee? I get Raisa's every morning."

"No, thank you. But I'd love a cuppa."

"A cup of what? You said no to coffee."

"Tea. That's what cuppa means."

Elena almost smiles. "I'm guessing that's the British way to say it. Sorry, but you are the first British person I've ever met. I don't think watching Henry Cavill movies counts."

"Probably not." I relax, really relax, for the first time since I arrived in New York. "I would love that cuppa, though. If it's not too much trouble."

"Of course not." Her cheeks dimple again. "I'm your slave, after all."

And fuck, just like that I'm imagining every possible scenario for making her my slave.

"Should I close the door or leave it open?" she asks.

"Leave it open."

Elena walks out the door, giving me a clear view of her luscious arse.

My desk phone rings.

The second I pick up the receiver, before I can speak one syllable, Raisa says, "I want you, Chance. Come to my office and take me on the desk."

My thoughts rewind to a few minutes ago, when I'd fantasized about doing exactly that with Elena.

"No, Raisa," I say. "We've been through this before, ad nauseam. I don't want you anymore."

"Oh come on," she purrs, "we both know that's not true."

"It is."

And I'm not lying. Part of me will always care about Raisa, as a friend, but I stopped feeling any attraction to her a long time ago. Maybe I'd been so desperate to shag Elena on Friday night because I hadn't been with anyone since the last time Raisa and I had sex.

"I'm doing you a favor here," I tell Raisa. "Don't make me regret it."

"Please tell me you're not doing a barista or, heaven forbid, a call girl."

"None of the above." True, since Elena is neither of those things. Besides, I'm not technically doing her, not anymore. Maybe soon, I hope, but not yet. "This is strictly business, Raisa. Now, let me get to work on solving your unfortunate problem. Enjoy your black coffee."

I hang up on my ex-wife.

Earlier today, Elena had told me our relationship is strictly business, but the difference is that I meant it when I said those words to Raisa. Elena doesn't mean it. She can't. Not after what we did the other night. I scratch under my collar but can't eradicate the itch. How can I ever start something with Elena with Raisa down the hall, a few doors away? I need to get Elena alone, outside of the office, but she isn't having any of it.

As if on cue, Elena sashays into my office again, this time carrying a plastic tray. It holds a mug, packets of sugar, a small carton of milk, and a plastic spoon. While she comes closer, I notice the tray also holds a cookie lying on a white napkin.

Elena sets the tray on my desk, careful to keep that bloody piece of furniture between us. "Your tea, Mr. Dixon. I know this probably isn't how you Brits do teatime, but it's the best we've got here in the good old US of A."

"It's wonderful, thank you." I pick up the mug, reading the words painted on it. "The law is hot. Am I meant to read between the lines?"

"No, it's a novelty mug, nothing more. You're lucky I didn't give you the one that says 'you can bang my gavel anytime.' I think an intern left that one here."

I set down the mug and pick up the cookie.

"Brits like tea and biscuits, right?" she asks. "And biscuits are cookies, aren't they? If not, then I've been seriously misled by all those BBC shows I watched."

"This is perfect." I take a bite of the cookie. Uh, biscuit. Maybe I've been in America too long. The distinctive flavor fills my mouth, and I lift one brow. "Peanut butter?"

"Sorry, that's all I could find." She tilts forward a touch, peering down at my mug. "I hope the tea is okay, because all we have is Earl Grey or eggnog flavor. I'm sure that one's been lying around since Christmas. So I figured you'd prefer Earl Grey."

I pour milk into my tea and take a sip. "Just right. Thank you."

She wrinkles her nose, making her upper lip pucker. "No sugar?"

"No."

"Yech," she says, her nose twitching like the thought of unsweetened tea is about to make her sneeze.

I chuckle. "You really are the most adorable creature."

"Better get those files," she says, and marches out the door.

To hell with Raisa. I want Elena. Now.

But the phone rings, and I need to take the call. It's a client, after all.

Somehow, I will convince Elena to have dinner with me. I have to, or else I'll be the next attorney at Raisa Volkov & Associates who leaps off the deep end.

Chapter Four

Elena

When I take an armload of files to Chance's office, he's on the phone, so I drop them off and leave. Thank goodness he's busy. If I hear his voice anymore, I will go insane. The way he says my name gives me hot shivers. His accent makes my knees weak. When he smirks at me, I go instantly wet and hot between my thighs. But if he looks at me again, with that smoldering intensity, I will lose it. I might just hump him right there on his desk.

Shit. What is wrong with me?

I'm an adult. A strong, independent woman with career goals. I finally landed my dream job, and I won't screw that up by screwing the boss's ex-husband. Resistance would be easier if he weren't so nice, so charming, so… British.

He'd called me adorable. Twice.

And both times, hearing those words tumble from his nibble-worthy lips made me long to do anything he wanted. I had done that Friday night, but things are different today.

No nibbling on my boss's ex. Check.

Ten minutes before one—the time when Raisa and I both take our lunch breaks, separately—she calls me into her office. I take a seat on the peasant side of the desk, while Raisa sits regally upright on the queen side.

"You are very capable," she says. "I've been impressed with your work so far."

She paid me a compliment. Wow. "Thank you, Raisa."

"I feel I can trust you with a special assignment. It requires total confidentiality. I'm relying on you, Elena, so don't disappoint me."

No pressure there. None at all.

My stomach is twisting into knots, but so what?

"I appreciate that," I say. "I won't let you down."

Could she be about to let me in on the Hazelton case? It's the biggest divorce in New York in a decade, maybe longer.

"Here's what I need you to do," Raisa says. "Convince Chance to come back to me."

For a couple seconds that feels like an hour, I gape at her—on the inside. A good paralegal never shows her true horror. "I don't quite understand what you're asking."

I understand, but I can't believe it. Maybe I hallucinated it.

"Chance and I belong together," she says. "Letting him go was a terrible mistake, and I know I can get him back. With your help."

"Um, what exactly do you want me to do?"

"First, find out if he's dating or sleeping with anyone. If so, I need all the details you can wheedle out of him." She eyes me like I'm a cow being auctioned off for meat. "You're passably pretty. Use your feminine wiles to get him to open up to you. Honestly, I don't care what you do as long as you find out what I need to know. Then we can move on to step two."

As much as I really, really don't want to know, I ask, "What's step two?"

"You talk me up to Chance and convince him he belongs with me."

Fabulous. This is exactly the career move I need, becoming pimp and marriage counselor for my boss.

Who also happens to be the ex-wife of the guy I let bang my gavel Friday night.

Yep, I'm cursed.

"What do you think?" Raisa asks, looking at me expectantly, almost excited.

Jeez, what can I say? She's my boss, and getting fired after three days will not improve my resume. "Sure, I'll do it. Anything to help."

"Thank you, Elena." She leans forward, her tone and expression turning conspiratorial. "This is strictly between us. Confidential."

"Of course." I make a zipper motion across my mouth. "My lips are sealed."

While I push myself up out of the chair, Raisa rushes around her desk to where I stand.

And she throws her arms around me.

"I knew you were the kind of woman who would understand," she says while clinching me tighter. "I'm so grateful, Elena. You're an angel."

Yeah, I feel like total crap inside. Like I'm the scum that grows in a toilet that's been ripped out and tossed into a garbage dump in a swamp. That's me, Elena the green, slimy scum. What kind of "angel" agrees to help her boss win back her ex-husband, when that "angel" has done the deed with her ex-husband?

Cursed. Damned. Nauseous. I'm all those things.

I'm so getting fired.

Raisa lets go of me, and I swear her eyes are shimmering with almost-tears. She retreats behind her desk, swiveling her chair to face the window, to face away from me.

After about thirty seconds of silence, I decide she's dismissed me, and I leave.

Since I brown-bagged lunch today, I walk a few blocks to a little park where I can sit and eat in solitude. When I get back to the office, Raisa is eating Chinese takeout in her office. I almost go in there to ask if she needs anything, but Raisa reassigned me to be Chance's slave. I don't work for her, not for the time being. I belong to the sexy Brit.

Every time I think about that, my entire body tingles.

No sex with Chance. Get that out of your head, woman.

Right. No sex. No fondling. No kissing.

Ogling is allowed, though. Right? I mean, what harm can come from me drooling over him, as long as nobody sees me doing it? If a tree falls in the forest and no one hears it, the tree never fell, right? And yes, in this ridiculous metaphor, Chance Dixon is a tree. Well, his dick certainly gets stiff enough to pass for a tree. And it's thick like a big, hard oak, and—

Stop that this instant.

I tiptoe up to Chance's office door, hoping to see he's not back from lunch yet. At least then I'll have a brief reprieve from needing to fight my lustful urges. Jeez, it's barely been half a day. How am I going to survive weeks? Maybe months?

Just my luck, he's in his office—and he catches me peeking around the doorjamb at him.

Chance smiles, in that so-damn-sexy way. "There's my slave. Would you care to wash my feet?"

Yes, with my tongue. Not only his feet, but every inch of his body.

"Oh please," I say, rolling my eyes as I step into the office. "I just got back from lunch and wanted to see if you need anything."

"Actually, yes, I do." His gaze roves up and down my body, and his tongue slips out to wet his lips. He clears his throat, swerving his attention down to the papers on his desk. Gathering them up, he offers them to me. "Would you mind going through these depositions and drafting a summary?"

"Sure thing." Hallelujah, work to do that doesn't involve pimping or lying. I snatch the papers from him and make a beeline for the door.

"Elena."

My tummy flutters, and my knees wobble the teeniest bit. Oh God, I wish he'd never say my name again.

And I wish he'd say it every five seconds.

Yeah, I'm flip-flopping like a beached whale.

I paste on my professional smile and face him. "Yes, Mr. Dixon?"

He sighs, tapping his pen on the desktop. "Do I have to order you to call me Chance? I don't like being called mister."

"Sorry. I was trying to be professional and respectful."

"And I appreciate that, but it's not necessary."

I realize I've hurt his feelings, and I feel bad about that. My stupid idea to create distance between us by calling him Mr. Dixon is done. I rewind the conversation and start again. "What do you need, Chance?"

"For you to have dinner with me."

Damn, I want to say yes so badly. "I can't. The firm has a policy about coworkers dating."

"Yes, and it says all that's required is reporting the relationship to Raisa within thirty days. We have plenty of time to worry about that later, if things work out between us."

If things work out. I don't see how that can happen. He's my boss's ex, and she commanded me to help her get him back.

"No, I'm sorry, Chance. I can't get involved with you."

Spinning around, I hurry out of his office. How can I even think about having dinner with him? It was bad enough when he was my boss's ex-husband. Now, not only is he my boss's ex, but I've been tasked with convincing him to go back to her. I've got to stay away from Chance as much as possible.

Luckily, summarizing the depositions takes the rest of the afternoon.

Unfortunately, that means when I come to work the next morning, I have to venture into Chance's office again to ask what he needs me to do today. Since erotic dreams about him plagued my sleep, I'm in less than top form this morning, so frazzled in fact that I forgot to stop at Starbucks and buy a latte. How can I survive the morning without my coffee? The stuff in the break room is terrible.

Before I even attempt to see Chance, I need caffeine. With a choice between terrible coffee and a cup of tea, I go for the tea. I even brew Chance a cup, then drop my mug off at my desk while I take the other mug into his office.

He's sitting behind his desk, forehead crinkled, staring at a document.

I place his mug on the desk beside the document. "Good morning, Chance. I thought you might need it, so I brought you a cuppa."

And I'm so damn proud of myself for remembering the British word for a cup of tea.

He glances up at me and smiles a little, his forehead smoothing out. Taking a sip of tea, he studies me. "Thank you, Elena. You look incredible this morning. In my dreams last night, we had a very good time."

"You shouldn't say things like that at work. Someone might overhear."

"Yes, and then Raisa might fire me." He says that with a twinkle in his gorgeous blue eyes and an amused slant to his lips. "I'm sure you can console me when that happens. I've already fantasized about you doing that."

I really, really, really need to tell him to stop flirting.

Before I crawl onto his lap and unzip his pants.

Yeah, I know what I *should* tell him, but my mouth has other ideas. Or maybe it's my hormones talking when I hear myself say, "You look pretty damn incredible too. And in my dreams, we had more than a good time. We rocked."

Chance grins, and every part of me that can melt does. "Why would you say something like that? You keep telling me we shouldn't have sex or even go out to dinner. But you're flirting with me." He sets down his mug and slants toward me. "And I love it."

"I didn't mean to. What I said was inappropriate, and I apologize." I'm totally lying, but who cares? This is too much fun. "How can I make it up to you?"

He pushes his chair back and pats his lap. "Come here, Elena."

My name. Again. Flowing from his kissable lips.

I want to go over there, but I don't dare try it. The door is open, and he hasn't darkened the windows, but I'm not at all convinced that will stop me from behaving in a very unprofessional manner. With him, I have zero willpower. Not one itty-bitty scrap of it.

"Work, Chance," I force myself to say. "This is a law office, not a strip club. What work do you need me to do for you?"

He sighs like I've said the most boring, annoying thing imaginable. "If you insist on doing your job, I have research for you to dig into."

I walk out of Chance's office five minutes later with enough research on my plate to keep me busy all week. I could almost cry from relief.

No more faltering willpower. Instead, I can hide out in law libraries.

Coward? Me? Nah.

Chapter Five

Chance

I've been acting like a sleazy lawyer. People make jokes about those kinds of lawyers, the ones who have no morals and no ethics, no compunctions about doing anything and everything to get what they want. I've prided myself on being a decent bloke who happens to be an attorney, and my clients appreciate that. Raisa has always thought I was too rigid and ought to bend my ethics now and then. Not break them, but simply stretch the boundaries a little in the name of serving my clients' interests. I refuse to do that.

Yet here I am sexually harassing a paralegal.

Granted, I'd met Elena before I started working here. We had sex a few days ago, and I still can't wrap my head around the idea she works for my ex-wife and now for me, temporarily. How can I not flirt with Elena? I've kissed her, fondled her, fucked her. I know more about her body than any employer has a right to know, but I can't erase Friday night from history. I don't want to, anyway.

Sure, the firm's policy on dating gives me leeway. But I'm technically her boss, which pushes me into a gray area.

I have to stop my inappropriate behavior—at work.

How can I convince her to see me outside of the office? I can't figure out how to arrange that when I've resolved to behave like a professional, ethical attorney.

"Fuck," I hiss under my breath.

Elena disappears for the rest of the day, no doubt ensconced in a law library somewhere.

I try my damnedest not to think about her, but it's like trying not to breathe. Elena Linwood is temptation incarnate, not to mention being sweet and competent and thoughtful. She'd brought me tea this morning, voluntarily. I survive the entire day, managing to do my job despite fantasizing about the sexiest paralegal I've ever met.

At ten o'clock, I decide I've worked long enough today. Raisa is still in her office when I shut the door to mine. I can tell by the light leaking out around her office door, though she's turned the windows opaque so I can't see into the room. My hopes of skulking out of here without needing to speak to her are shattered when I'm halfway to the elevator and her office door opens, spilling light across the array of cubicles and all the way to the elevator.

"Chance," Raisa calls out. "I need to speak to you. Immediately."

I growl, too softly for Raisa to hear. Why hadn't I left five minutes earlier? She might not have noticed then.

"I'm knackered, Raisa," I say as I turn sideways to glance at her. "Whatever it is can wait until morning."

She disappears into her office for a few seconds, long enough that I almost believe she's given up. Then she emerges again, her purse slung over her shoulder, and shuts off the light. Only the ambient glow from outside the windows illuminates the space as she trots down the center aisle of the cubicle farm and straight to me.

"Let's have dinner in your hotel room," she says. "We can talk there."

"No. This is my relaxation time." And my time away from her. "I'm off the clock until morning."

She makes a noise that implies I'm an idiot. "Lawyers are never really off the clock."

"This one is."

"Don't be this way, Chance." She runs her hands up and down my lapels, inching closer and closer until her body almost touches mine. "After a long day of working, we both need to blow off some steam. And you have a nice big suite right across the street."

When I'd first met Raisa, she had been the sexiest woman on earth to me. These days, I can't look at her without remembering the things she did to drive me away. I don't want to speak to her, much less take her to my hotel room.

All I want is Elena.

"Forget it," I tell Raisa. "That ship sailed and sank a long time ago. The me who wanted you drowned in the wreck."

I might have stretched that metaphor a bit too far.

Raisa moves to kiss me.

"Leave off," I say, pushing her away. "Try to remember I'm doing you a favor by working here."

Her expression hardens, the way it always does when I deny her something she wants. "Who are you sleeping with, Chance? You must be doing someone."

"Even if I am, it's none of your concern." The fact that I frequently want to throw Elena over my desk and ravish her has no bearing on this conversation. "Good night, Raisa. I'll see you in the morning."

Thankfully, the elevator doors slide open.

I step into the car.

And thankfully, Raisa doesn't follow me.

Like a pathetic, divorced man, I spend the evening eating pizza and drinking beer, then drop onto the bed and fall asleep on top of the covers. I don't get drunk. That's not what a trustworthy lawyer does at night, not even when his ex-wife has tried to seduce him and the woman he wants in his bed has said no. Two beers is my maximum. I sleep on top of the covers strictly because I'm too exhausted to give a damn.

Naturally, I dream of Elena.

I wake up harder than usual in the morning and need a thirty-minute shower to get rid of my lust for the delectable paralegal. I rub one off three times before I feel ready to face the world.

And the woman whose voluptuous body caused the problem.

When I arrive at work, Raisa is the only one there. She's in her office with the door closed, and I do not bother saying good morning. After her actions last night, I have no desire to see or speak to her. I've just gotten my cuppa from the break room when Elena turns up. Some of the other employees got here a few minutes before her, though she's still early. The workday officially starts at nine, but she's here at eight.

Elena smiles brightly at her coworkers, laughing and talking with them while she makes her way to her cubicle while carrying a Starbucks cup in her hand. She's beautiful. Alive. Sexy. Elena Linwood burns like a brilliant flame, and I want to bask in the heat and light she gives off.

Apparently, I've turned into a bad poet as well as a smitten fool.

Locking myself in my office seems like the best course to avoid a sexual harassment charge. If I speak to Elena, I might not be able to stop myself from telling her how desirable she is.

Fuckable is a better description of her. Completely fuckable.

At lunchtime, I peek out of my office like the coward I've become.

Elena is still at her desk, poring over some sort of work. She lifts her head at the exact moment I look at her and smiles, waving her fingers at me.

I nod and retreat into my office.

She appears at my doorway a few seconds later. "I was going to order some lunch, Chinese delivery. Do you want some?"

Lunch with Elena. That sounds wonderful, but likely to get me disbarred.

"We're all having a working lunch," she says. "You can join the plebs in the conference room, if you want."

"Plebs? This isn't ancient Rome, and I'm not the emperor."

"No, that would be Raisa." Elena's cheeks dimple, which always makes me want to kiss her. "But I am your slave, remember?"

She speaks those words in a soft, sensual tone, clearly flirting with me.

I want to spend time in her presence, even if it's a group lunch. "All right. Count me in."

"Good." She smiles, the expression lighting up her face. "You'll like the gang. They're not uptight or anything."

Elena leaves me, and I wait a few minutes before heading to the conference room. I need those minutes to convince myself this isn't a rubbish idea. I should meet more of the staff and get to know them a bit, show them I'm not the empress's consort who does her bidding. I've always tried to be an approachable boss. Here's my chance to prove that to my new coworkers.

Yes, that's right. I'm being a good boss. This has nothing whatsoever to do with Elena and her perfect tits.

When I walk into the conference room, all heads swivel toward me. And the conversation stops dead.

Elena gets up and lays a hand on my arm. "You all know Chance Dixon. He's taking over Lucas Miller's cases. I invited Chance to our little working lunch, so let's make him feel welcome."

I feel oddly uncomfortable, what with a dozen people staring at me, so I pat my stomach and say, "Where's the food? I'm ready to pass out from hunger."

"It'll be here any minute," Elena says.

My attempt to seem like an average person, not an evil lawyer, seems to have crashed and burned. Everyone is still staring at me.

I try a different tack. "Who wants to play pin the tail on the lawyer's arse?"

"Me," says a young man at the other end of the table, raising his hand.

Several more hands shoot up, and I'm beginning to wonder what I've let myself in for.

"Instead of shoving pins in Chance," Elena says, "why don't we tell him what we've all been working on? Jared, you can start. You've got the McNulty case, right?"

"Yeah," says the young man who'd been first to volunteer to shove a pin in my arse.

Elena urges me to sit beside her, and somehow, I manage to keep myself from sneaking a hand onto her thigh. The food arrives a few minutes later. For the next forty-five minutes, I eat the best Chinese food I've ever had while discussing the firm's cases with the paralegals who do most of the real work. Elena is the brightest by far, but the others have impressive legal acumen too. Elena jumps in to help her coworkers hash out research problems, or to mediate disagreements between them.

I can't help watching her. Admiring her. Wishing I could fuck her right here on the conference room table in front of all these people. It's not simple lust, though, not anymore. I'm coming to appreciate the clever mind behind the beautiful face and body.

After lunch, we all go back to our assigned desks.

Work keeps me occupied for the rest of the day, and I don't see Elena until it's nearly lunchtime the next day. She's been at the law library again, doing all the research I commanded her to do for me. Now, I wish I'd commanded her to take dictation in my office instead. Not seeing her, not hearing her voice out there in the cubicle farm, it makes me feel…anxious. Which is ridiculous. But here I am, chewing on the end of my very expensive gold pen while I wonder what Elena is doing right now.

Finally, I give up and go to her. She has a Starbucks cup on her desk, with her name scrawled on it.

"What are you drinking?" I ask.

She glances up at me, smiling in a distracted way. "Morning. I always have a butterscotch latte."

"That's not coffee."

"Maybe not for people who don't put sugar in their tea, but for the rest of humanity, it is."

Leaning against the cubicle wall, I study her. "It's not morning, Elena. It's lunchtime. You need to take a break."

"Oh, I brought a bag lunch today." She picks up a depressingly brown paper sack that's slumped on her desk and shakes it. "See? I'm all set. Have a good lunch, Chance."

I grab the extra chair that's shoved into the far corner of her tiny cubicle and set it down an arm's length from where she sits. My arse barely fits on the flimsy plastic-and-metal contraption. "It's lunch, Elena, not an invitation to an orgy. I want to confer with my paralegal over a meal."

Her lips tighten in a sexy little smile even while she types on her keyboard. "Sure, you want to confer with me."

Her tone implies something very, very wrong and very, very filthy.

Can she read my mind?

"Just lunch," I say. "Think of it as a business meeting."

"Right, business." She throws me a sly sideways glance. "You're all business whenever we're alone, aren't you?"

"We won't be alone. I'll take you to my favorite bistro, where there will be plenty of other people and plenty of light. No dark corners, I swear. We can sit by the window, if you like."

I want dark corners and a smoky atmosphere, with sensual music playing in the background. I want to do filthy things to her anytime, anywhere. But I promised myself I would not make any advances.

Today. Tomorrow is another story.

She still seems reluctant, though I sense she might be wavering.

"Relax," I say. "I'm British, remember? We say cheerio, and we love tea and crumpets. How much trouble could I possibly get you into?"

"Playing on American stereotypes of Brits? That's cute, but not convincing." She folds her arms under her breasts, which makes me notice them even more. Leaning in, she whispers, "You are the man who seduced me in an elevator."

"Guilty as charged. Let me make it up to you."

She chews on her bottom lip while scrutinizing me.

I squirm in my horrid little chair while seconds tick by.

Elena sighs and dumps her brown bag into the trash bin under her desk. "All right. I'm yours for lunch."

My mind conjures up several different ways I could mold that statement into a come-on, but I resist the impulse. Instead, I remain calm and professional while we board the elevator.

As soon as the doors close, I say, "You really should take a chance more often."

She raises her delicate brows at me. "Is that a dopey pun about your name?"

"It was unintentional, I swear. I can't help that my name is also a commonly used word." I lean in so close I can see the darker rims around her caramel irises. "But for the record, this Chance loves to be taken."

Elena laughs and shakes her head.

Chapter Six

Elena

Chance takes me to a quaint little bistro ten blocks away from the office, one he swears nobody at the office knows about—except Raisa, and she only ever came here with him. She doesn't like the place, he says, so she'll never come back here. We sit by the picture windows, where we have a beautiful view of the skyline across the river, and he insists I sit beside him instead of across the table from him. When Chance examines the menu, he sighs and looks disappointed.

"What's wrong?" I ask. "Thought this was your favorite restaurant."

"It is, but I always lament their lack of British foods. I'd kill for some bangers and mash."

"Okay," I say like I have no idea what he's talking about, because I don't. "I'm guessing that's not some weird sex slang."

"No, it's weird food slang for sausage and mashed potatoes." He goes back to perusing the menu while he tells me, "I haven't had bangers and mash in ages."

"Why don't you cook that for yourself?"

He glances up at me, moving only his eyes. "My cooking skills begin and end with heating water for tea, and I do that in the microwave."

"Maybe I can figure out how to make bangers and mash for you." I say the words before I realize what I'm suggesting. I want to cook for him? Yeah, I kind of do. Huh. "Is it some special kind of thoroughly disgusting British sausage?"

"It can be any type of sausage." He fake-frowns at the menu. "What, no bubble and squeak? I may have to reconsider this as my favorite bistro."

"Bubble and squeak? You just made that up, didn't you?"

He smirks at me over the top of his menu. "No, I did not. My mother makes that the day after she cooks up a traditional roast dinner. She uses the leftovers to make bubble and squeak."

I give him a teasing smile. "Otherwise known as dumpster diving?"

"Very funny, but we don't dig through the rubbish bin for left-overs." He sneaks a hand under the table to grasp my knee. "Care-ful. If you keep harassing me, I might have to do something com-pletely inappropriate."

We order our food, and I pretend to be disappointed when he orders a hamburger with French onion soup. It's not British, as I point out, but he puts his hand on my knee again to let me know he's about ready to get inappropriate with the snarky American sit-ting next to him. I order the same thing, earning a sarcastic com-ment from him about what a copycat I am.

Throughout lunch, we talk. About anything, everything, what-ever pops into our heads. I learn that he comes from a middle-class family that owns a beautiful, historic home in the English country-side, but when he asks about my family, I avoid answering. It would spoil the mood, and I love this mood we've got going here in the cutest bistro I've never seen before. He lets me get away with not opening up, at least for a while. We make each other laugh, a lot, and commiserate about working with Raisa.

Five minutes before we have to go back to the office, Chance finally pushes me for an answer to a question he asked me the first day we worked together. "Why didn't you go to law school?"

"What?" I'm acting dumb to avoid answering, obviously.

"You heard the question." He turns his chair slightly toward me. "You're very clever, hard-working, and write the most perfect legal summaries I've ever read. If I asked you to write an argument, I'm sure that would be perfect too. You should be an attorney, not a paralegal. I know you were accepted to law school, so why didn't you go?"

I slump in my chair, absently stirring the teeny puddle in my soup bowl, all that's left of my lunch. I can't look at him when I explain, "My dad ran out on us when I was six. I barely remember him. Mom worked two jobs to support me and my brother, Kyle. Six years ago, she got sick. Cancer. For eleven months, she fought so hard to beat it, but she couldn't. She died a week before I found out I'd been accepted to law school."

Chance settles his hand on my knee again, but he's not copping a feel this time. "I'm so sorry, Elena."

I shrug one shoulder. "I'd already gone into debt to pay for my bachelor's degree. Mom had life insurance, but not a lot of it. Racking up even more debt to pay for law school seemed like a huge extravagance, and besides, I had to take care of Kyle. He was fifteen at the time. So, I gave up on law school, got a crappy job as a legal secretary, and signed up for a paralegal certification course. Took me eighteen months to finish it. Working for Raisa is the second paralegal position I've had." I laugh a little, with no humor whatsoever. "It was my dream job."

"You excel at your job. Don't let Raisa ruin it for you. She'll calm down once she gets over the divorce and accepts that I am never going to be with her again."

I wince, unable to disguise my discomfort. How can I not tell him what Raisa ordered me to do? He deserves to know, but I can't tell him. Raisa ordered me to keep it secret. I don't know how long she'll wait for me to bring him to her on a silver platter.

How on earth does she expect me to do that, anyway? Even if I wanted to, which I absolutely do not, I have no clue where to start.

"What's wrong?" Chance asks.

"Can't tell you. Raisa swore me to secrecy."

He drums his fingers on the tabletop. "Does this secret have something to do with me? Is that the real reason you've been reluctant to get involved with me?"

"I can't say."

Chance scoots his chair a little closer to mine. "Look at me."

"Please let this go. I could lose my job."

"If this involves me, then I have a right to know. Raisa won't fire you, because I won't tell her I know the secret. All right?"

Chewing my lip, I think about what I should do. Not telling him has been eating a hole in my stomach, but telling him might make things worse. I like Chance, a lot. He's such a nice man, and he's been so sweet to me. But he's my boss's ex-husband, and she wants him back.

I groan miserably. "Raisa ordered me to help her win you back."

"She what?" he says sharply, his gaze narrowing. "What exactly did she tell you to do?"

"Whatever it takes to find out if you're sleeping with someone, and if so, who it is. I'm also supposed to say stuff about how wonderful she is and how you two belong together."

He grunts with what sounds like disgust, leaning back in his chair. "The woman's gone off her rocker. I'm sorry, Elena, you should never have been put in the middle of this."

"Not your fault my dream job turned into pimping for my boss."

His lips flatten. "I'll have a talk with Raisa. Your pimping days are over."

"No, you can't," I say too quickly, with too much panic in my voice. "I mean, she'll fire me. I need this job."

I clasp my hands on my lap, my fingers twitching restlessly.

"All right," he says. "I won't let on that I know about her ridiculous plot, but I will make sure she understands I will never go back to her. I've told her before, but this time I will leave no doubts about my feelings for her." He lays a hand over mine, stilling my restless fingers. "At least now I understand why you've been so anxious about getting involved with me."

"You're my boss's ex-husband. Of course I'm anxious."

"But you might've gone to dinner with me in spite of that. Am I right?"

I consider my answer for a moment before I say, "Yes."

He gives my hand a quick squeeze. "Knowing Raisa thinks she can get her claws into me again makes you even more anxious, because you worry she'll fire you if she finds out you and I are seeing each other."

"That's right. Now will you give up on the idea of dating me?"

"No. I will not let Raisa bollocks up my life any more than she already has."

"Great." I tear my hands away from his. "I'm your revenge fuck."

"Elena, no." His gaze is so earnest it makes my throat go thick. "Being with you is not how I avenge myself on Raisa. I'm not vengeful at all. She cheated on me, repeatedly, and often with men who worked for her. I stopped loving Raisa a long time ago, because of what she'd done. When I found out about her infidelity, I walked out the door and never looked back."

"But you work for her now."

"As a favor. I may not love her anymore, but I don't want her to suffer either." He braces an elbow on the table and sets his forehead in his raised palm. "Meeting you is the best thing that's ever happened to me. I don't want to walk away from you, but I understand if you need to distance yourself from me."

Do I want that? Is being with Chance worth the risk of losing my job? Maybe I shouldn't want to keep my job, considering what Raisa has pressured me into doing for her. Not that I've enacted her plan yet. But still…

"I need to think about all of this," I say. "Maybe we should keep our distance for the time being."

He keeps his head in his palm while I slap money on the table to cover my part of lunch, grab my purse, and hurry out the door. I don't see any taxis, so I start walking and head for the subway station I'd seen down the street. I'm crossing in front of an alley when Chance catches up to me. He grasps my arm and tows me into the alley, backing me up to a building.

And he kisses me.

It's no sweet and tender kiss, either. He takes possession of my mouth like he's starved for the taste of me, his lips mashed to mine, his tongue hungry and unyielding while his teeth nip at my lower lip. I moan and give in, devouring him as completely as he's devouring me, dissolving into the kiss, reveling in the velvety heat of his tongue and the blustering of his breaths on my skin.

He cages me against the wall with his body, all those muscles crushed against me, flexing as he whisks a hand up and down my side. I thrust my fingers into his hair and wrap my leg around his, all but begging him to take me right here, right now.

A car horn honks, and still I want him.

Chance pulls his head back, breaking the kiss, but keeps his body plastered to mine. He's breathing as roughly as I am. "I want you, Elena. It's more than sex, but I swear I'll go insane if I can't have you again, soon. Why should Raisa drive a wedge between us? We can't let her have that kind of power."

"What can we do? She's my boss and—"

He silences me with his lips, peeling them away from mine so very slowly. "She's abusing her position by ordering you to help her with a personal situation. That means she has no bloody right to play the victim."

I can't speak. The look on his face, the tone of his voice, those things convince me he's not doing this for revenge. He genuinely wants to be with me.

And he feels so good pressed against me.

He feathers his lips over mine. "Have dinner with me, Elena. In my hotel suite."

"What will we do after dinner?"

One side of his mouth kicks up. "I'll leave that to your imagination."

I swallow, but my throat still feels tight. A forbidden affair with my boss's ex-husband? That's not like me at all, but I want this man. Want him like crazy. He's right about Raisa abusing her position, so maybe that gives me a great excuse to take what I want and not feel bad about it.

"Come on," he whispers, his voice so sexy it makes my tummy flutter. "Take a chance."

"You've already used that pun. Try coming up with a new one."

"How about this?" He backs up a step, depriving me of the sensation of his body against mine. "Roll the dice, because Chance will always be on your side."

I can't help smiling. "How can I say no to that?"

"Does that mean yes?"

"Mm-hm." I lunge forward to plant a firm but quick kiss on his lips. "Yes, Chance, I will have dinner with you."

He releases a gusty breath, his shoulders sagging. "Thank you."

It's so cute how relieved he is, but I'm forced to make him a little unhappy. "But we can't do it until Friday. We've got all those cases you need to catch up on, and you need to prepare for depositions and that injunction hearing and—"

Chance raises a hand, nodding and sort of frowning. "Yes, you're right. All of that takes precedence, which is damn irritating. Promise me we will have dinner Friday night."

"I might have to work over the weekend too."

"But we can take one night off." He leans in again, his lips ghosting over mine. "Say you'll be mine Friday night. Please, Elena."

Suddenly, I have trouble catching my breath. With him so close, smelling so good, I can manage only one word. "Yes."

He grins. And then he kisses me again, even hotter and longer than before, leaving me as warm and soft as a caramel candy in the sun. It feels wonderful.

We go back to work, and though I get my job done like I should, my mind keeps creating images of what Friday night might be like.

Chapter Seven

Chance

For the next two days, I have a hell of a time concentrating on work. I get to see Elena even more than I'd hoped, since she's helping me prepare for depositions and all those other things that sounded so important a few days ago but now seem inconsequential. But I'll take any excuse to spend time with her. We have lunch together on Thursday at Elena's favorite spot, where we have waffles, her favorite, and I tease her about eating breakfast for lunch.

I love teasing Elena. And I love that she teases me too.

When Friday finally arrives, I find myself checking the clock—any clock, wherever I am, from the one on my mobile to the one in Times Square—to see if it's time for my date with Elena yet. Tonight, I'll have her in my bed. Finally. I've had her in an elevator, but this will be our first real date and our first time making love in a soft bed with silk sheets.

I know she'll look stunning with her naked body stretched out on that bed.

We don't get to have lunch together. Elena is at the law library again, and she took a lunch with her, in another of those depressingly brown paper bags. I have pizzas delivered to the office for the paralegals and interns, and some of the other attorneys join me in eating with them. Raisa does not.

Twenty minutes after we finish lunch, Elena returns to the office. I hear her lovely voice, though I can't tell what she's saying to her coworkers. I wait a few minutes, to let her settle in at her desk, then I call Elena into my office. While I wait for her, I darken the glass wall between my office and the cubicle farm until it's opaque. No one will think that's odd, since I often darken the glass for privacy. And I need privacy for what I have in mind.

I'm leaning against the window frame when she walks in.

She lowers her sweet arse onto the chair across the desk from me. "What can I help you with? More research?"

"Yes. Very important research." I crook a finger at her. "Come here, Elena."

"Why?"

"Because I asked you to."

Her lips curve into a teasing little smile. "No, you ordered me to. Bossy much?"

"Yes." I wave my arm this time. "Get your edible little arse over here this instant. Is that bossy enough for you?"

Elena sets her notepad on the desk and stands.

"Shut the door," I say.

"Why?"

"I'm sure you can guess why."

She closes the door and comes up to me. "Not at work."

"Then why did you shut the door?" I loop an arm around her waist and pull her closer. "You know what I'm after."

"I have to say we shouldn't, even though I want what you want." She takes my tie between her thumb and forefinger, sliding them up until her fingers meet the knot. "But I thought you wanted to wait until tonight."

"For the main course, yes. But we can have an appetizer right now."

"Appetizer? Mm, I like the sound of that." She drops to her knees in front of me, her face inches from my cock. "I am famished."

This isn't quite what I'd had in mind, but who am I to deny a woman what she wants? "Go on, then."

She unbuttons my trousers and finds the pull on the zipper, takes it between her teeth, and drags the zipper down. Her gaze stays locked on mine, and I can't look away from the sight of her lips peeled back, the little metal pull trapped between her teeth while she tugs it down, down, down. By the time she's done, I'm breathing hard.

And she hasn't even touched me yet.

Elena slips her hand inside my trousers and eases my cock out. It's already hard for her, and the sensation of her soft hands on me steals any breath I might've been trying to suck into my lungs. While she glides her hands up and down my length, I force myself to take slow and steady breaths while I brush hair away from her face and cup her chin.

"You're wonderful, Elena."

"I haven't done anything yet."

"No, I don't mean you're wonderful for this. You are wonderful all the time."

"Thank you." She puckers her lips and gently blows air across the head of my erection. When I shudder, she smiles. "Let me show you how wonderful I can be."

She opens her mouth, as if she's about to take me inside, but instead shoves my trousers and boxer shorts down to my ankles and presses her lips to my inner thigh. With her mouth open, the liquid warmth of her tongue moistens my skin. I brace my hip on the window frame, watching her face while she glides her tongue up my leg, swirling it while she travels higher and higher. Her hair brushes my cock, and I suck in a sharp breath at the sensation of her silky locks on my skin. Just when her mouth comes within millimeters of where I want it, badly, she moves to the other thigh and starts again, lovingly kissing and licking her way up toward my groin.

The vixen darts her tongue out to within a hair's breadth of my cock, then curls it back into her mouth.

"Are you trying to drive me insane?" I ask.

She slides her tongue across her bottom lip, little by little, the movement so slow and sensuous it makes my entire groin tighten. "Wouldn't you just love to die from pleasure? After all, the French call it *la petite mort*, the little death."

Christ, I would love to die that way—but with Elena's body wrapped around me, her silken flesh gripping me over and over in the most decadent massage. The fantasy of it makes my cock jump, and a delicate laugh tumbles from her lips. I love the sound of her laughter. It makes me want to hold her in my arms forever.

She folds her hand around my length and slides it up and down. "Can't wait till I get to see the rest of you. Just seeing this"—She plants a firm, quick kiss on the head of my erection—"makes me want you like crazy. You have the most beautiful dick in the world."

I know it's bollocks, but I don't care. Maybe I don't have the most beautiful cock on earth, but she gave the compliment with total sincerity. And hunger. Lots of hunger. Hearing her speak those words in her hushed, sultry voice… I might die before she finishes and still be the happiest soul in the afterlife. "As much as I'd love to listen to you praise my cock, better get on with it before the phone rings or someone knocks on the door."

"Yes, sir," she purrs, while she reaches behind my balls to run her fingers along the skin there.

No woman has ever touched me in this way, and it feels incredible.

She keeps stroking my length while she laves the head with her tongue, then flicks it over the very center. And she does it again. And again.

I choke on the breath I'd been trying to inhale.

This time, her laughter is throaty and so erotic it makes me throb for her. "Maybe I should stop torturing you."

Her torture is heaven, but even bliss can be too much. I don't need to tell her that—good thing, since I can't speak—because somehow, she senses exactly how much I can take.

Elena opens her mouth and slides those luscious lips over my cock, taking it deep inside.

I groan at the slick heat of her mouth on my skin. But when she laps at my flesh, I sag against the window and let out a long, guttural noise somewhere between a groan and a growl. She makes soft little grunting sounds while she works me with her mouth and her hand, sounding for all the world like she can't get enough of doing this. I thrust a hand into her hair, gripping the windowsill with the other one, and I swear to God my eyes roll back in my head.

"Fuck, Elena," I say, while her ravenous noises grow louder. I can hardly breathe, my chest heavy with the weight of pleasure.

She closes her free hand around one of my balls and massages it with her fingers.

My every muscle goes rigid, the breath is trapped in my lungs, and I can't stop my body from giving in to Elena's demands. I come so hard and fast I swear I see stars and hear the angels singing to welcome me into heaven. I don't die, though. Elena keeps working me until I'm done, and somehow, I find the strength to breathe again. My heart is pounding, and I can't swear I didn't shout or make some sort of loud noise that's unmistakably the sound of a man coming inside the mouth of the most perfect woman on earth.

I stare at Elena, dumbstruck by her. Isn't she the woman who kept telling me not to flirt with her at the office? And now she's done something far more intimate, and she's done it with tenderness and enthusiasm.

She licks her lips so slowly, and with such satisfaction, that I know I'll go hard again any minute if she keeps that up.

I run my thumb over her lips. "You are… I can't think of a word that's good enough to describe you. Passionate, for sure. And surprisingly brazen. You, Elena, are amazing."

"Well, I did keep saying no to you, and you've been so patient. I figured you'd earned a little blow job."

"A *little* blow job?" I grasp her arms, urging her to stand. Then I cradle her face in my hands and kiss her softly. "That was the Mount Everest of blow jobs. The lovers you had before me must've been very happy blokes."

"Sure, they liked it. But they didn't enjoy it anywhere near as much as you do."

"What a crowd of idiots. Any man who doesn't feel like he's halfway to the stars when he's got your mouth on him must be barmy."

"I don't care what other guys think. But I love that you loved it."

"One good turn deserves another." I turn to face the window, with Elena in front of me. "Sit back, relax, and let me send you to the gates of heaven."

"Do you usually get all poetic after an orgasm? I didn't notice it in the elevator that night."

"We were interrupted then. I won't let that happen again."

"Better not, or I might have to throw your phone out the window." She leans her hips against the window frame. "I hope you're not fibbing about showing me heaven, because I'm so turned on I can hardly stand it."

"You won't be disappointed." I kneel before her, slipping my fingers under the hem of her skirt. "I guarantee it."

Someone knocks on the door.

The nasal voice of Marla, one of the paralegals, says, "Elena, are you in there? We need to leave for the law library if you want to get that research done today."

"Fuck," I snarl under my breath.

Elena throws her head back and whimpers, though not in the sexy way I'd planned to make her utter a noise like that. She calls out, "I'm coming."

But dammit, she *isn't*.

She bends down to kiss me. "Sorry, duty calls."

"Forget the law library. I planned to lure you into every dark corner on this floor so I can kiss you and tease you all afternoon."

"Believe me, I'd much rather sneak into dark corners with you." She straightens and smooths her skirt and blouse. "The law library is musty, and the pop in the vending machine is warm. You smell and taste so much better."

With that, she leaves me.

I sit on the floor for five minutes before I get back to work. My mind taunts me with visions of Elena naked, spread out on my bed, writhing and moaning and calling my cock the most beautiful in the world. She is the most beautiful woman I've ever seen or ever will see. She's more than that, though. She's clever, playful, passionate, determined...and all mine tonight.

The second I get to my hotel room, I'm turning off my damn mobile and telling the desk clerk to hold all calls. No one is going to interrupt us. Nothing will get in the way of my plans for Elena. I will worship her body all night.

Chapter Eight

Elena

The elevator rises toward the nineteenth floor, taking me to my secret assignation with the boss's ex-husband. Yep, this is the same elevator in which Chance ravished me a week ago. Why do I keep thinking of him as my boss's ex? He's my… What? Lover sounds kind of sleazy, for some reason. We have to sneak around so Raisa won't find out. Maybe sleazy is the word for it.

Being with Chance doesn't feel sordid. It makes me feel so good in so many ways, despite the fact I promised to help Raisa get him back.

I glance down at my dress to make sure it didn't get wrinkled on the cab ride to the hotel. I had to go home to change clothes. I'm wearing my red dress, the nicest thing I own, the one I bought for an office Christmas party two years ago. The firm I'd worked for then had rented a ballroom for the party and invited everyone to dress up. Chance texted me earlier to say "wear something special," so here I am in my red dress.

The elevator stops. I get out and, following Chance's instructions, turn left and walk to the door at the end of the hall. It has a sign on it that says "Presidential Suite."

I'm going to have sex in a suite at a luxury hotel. For a moment, I just stand there while I let that fact soak into my psyche. Until tonight, the fanciest place I've done the deed was at a Motel 6 in Pittsburgh.

Straightening, rolling my shoulders back, I knock on the door.

It swings open instantly, like he's been standing right on the other side waiting for me.

Warmth rushes through me at the sight of him, and I have the dumbest urge to fan myself with my hand.

Chance is wearing nothing but a towel.

I do raise my hand to fan myself but stop short of my face. Then I wave at him like an idiot to cover the fact I'd been about to fan myself. Honestly, can anyone blame me? He looks hotter than hot in a white towel that seems like it'll fall off at any second. I let my gaze wander over his naked chest, admiring the lines of all those muscles while I imagine running my tongue over every single one of them.

"Good evening, Elena."

When he smiles at me, the seductive slant of his lips makes me want to throw myself at him.

"Uh, hi," I say. *So lame, Elena.* "Guess I'm overdressed. I thought 'special' meant formal, but I guess I should've worn a towel."

"I'd thought to feed you first, but then I realized I can't wait one more second to make love to you." He offers me his hand, and when I take it, he guides me into the room. "You are stunning, Elena. Even more beautiful than when you wear a conservative business suit. I love that tight skirt you wore the other day, but this dress is even better."

"Thank you." I watch him shut the door, unable to tear my focus away from his chest. I know what his dick looks like—and feels like, and tastes like—but seeing all of him makes me so aroused I fight to keep from tearing that towel off. "I love you in a suit, but terrycloth is definitely the sexiest thing I've seen you in."

He whips off the towel, tossing it away.

We are standing in a living room. A large, curved sofa takes up most of the space, with various tables and some chairs arranged around it. I can see a doorway that leads into the bedroom. Floor-to-ceiling windows overlook the city, and the lights of countless buildings and streetlights twinkle like stars, overshadowing the sky. Sliding glass doors open onto a balcony where a table and chairs wait, but we're not going out there.

Chance takes my hand and leads me into the bedroom.

An enormous bed is the centerpiece of the room. A window offers a view of the city, but the semitransparent drapes obscure the vista. Chance turns a dial on the wall beside the door, and the lighting inside the room dims to a sensual glow that seems to burnish his skin, turning him into a golden statue of a sex god.

Damn, he's gorgeous.

I notice the covers are already pulled back on the bed.

He comes up behind me and unties the bow I'd carefully tied earlier, the one that keeps my halter dress from falling down to my waist. He lets the straps go. They slide down my body until all of me from the waist up is bared to him. He slips his fingers inside the fabric and pushes my dress over my hips. It flutters to the floor, a pool of silky scarlet at my feet.

I thank heaven I decided against wearing pantyhose, but I'm even more grateful I had the audacity to ditch the underwear. Waiting for Chance to strip those off might've killed me. His fingers grazing my skin, the soft murmur of his breaths, and the scent of him… All those things have me so turned on I'm not sure I can walk the five feet to the bed. Weak with lust? I've never experienced this before, but I like it.

He scoops me up and carries me to the bed, setting me down on the unbelievably soft sheets. They feel so good against my skin that I want to roll around on them, but I can't move. The vision of him entrances me. Sure, I've seen naked men before. But Chance is not like anyone else. He stands beside the bed, far enough away to grant me a full view of his nude body, and gives me time to absorb the sight.

I drink it all in, every muscle and every bit of flesh, from his strong thighs to his washboard abs and those biceps that are well-defined but not outrageously big. His smooth chest begs to be kissed and licked, but my gaze keeps drifting back to that mouth-watering cock, framed by his lean hips.

He saunters to the bed and climbs onto it, kneeling at my feet. While he explores my body with his gaze, he groans softly. "Elena, you are a work of art."

If anyone else told me that, I'd think it was bullshit. But Chance isn't the kind of man who lays on the phony compliments so thick you need a shovel to dig your way out of it. I know he means it.

I watch him while he keeps exploring me with his gaze, loving the way his lips part and his pupils grow larger. He skims his hands up and down his thighs like he's imagining doing that to me. I want him to touch me so badly the weight of it settles low in my belly and triggers a molten slickness between my thighs.

He lowers onto his hands and knees, his face poised over mine. The blue of his eyes mesmerizes me, and I feel like I'm spiraling down into their shimmering depths, lost in an ocean of desire. He touches his lips to mine, tenderly at first, then with more pressure. When his tongue flicks out to taste my skin, I can't stop myself from opening for him, all but begging him to claim my mouth. He slips inside, oh so slowly, and the sensation of his tongue on mine elicits a soft moan from me.

God, the flavor of him. It's indescribable, and it intoxicates me like no liquor on earth could. I give in to the feel of his tongue coiling around mine, teasing and tempting me with every leisurely swipe, until I'm clutching his arms and making sharp moans that verge on whimpering.

I haven't experienced his body on mine yet. He holds himself up on his arms, hovering over me without touching me.

He breaks the kiss and looks into my eyes.

The intensity of his gaze burns into me, setting my body on fire, a tingling wave of heat that stuns me. I want him so much it almost scares me. But I can't be afraid when I'm with Chance. He's the best combination of everything—safety and risk, lust and tenderness, dirtiness and sweetness.

"Elena," he murmurs, nuzzling my throat. His husky voice weaves my name into a seductive spell.

"Yes," I whisper, raking my fingers through his hair. "Yes, Chance."

We've said almost nothing, but it means everything.

He kisses the corner of my mouth. "I love the way you say my name."

"I love saying it."

A breath rushes out of me when he drags his mouth along my throat, then kisses his way down to my breast. His tongue slides around the nipple, moistening my skin but never touching the stiff, aching peak. I bury my hands in his hair, but still his body lingers above mine, not touching me. I arch my back, desperate to reach him, but I can't quite get there.

He flicks his tongue over my nipple, only once, so swiftly I wonder if I hallucinated the sensation. Then he blows a current of cool air across the peak.

I gasp and arch my back again.

"Elena," he says. "Beautiful, sweet, sexy Elena."

Wetter. Hotter. Hungrier. I need him inside me but can't find my voice to tell him.

He draws my nipple into his mouth and suckles it.

A sharp cry erupts out of me. Helpless to stop myself, I grip his arms and throw my legs around his hips. He grunts but keeps his mouth sealed around my nipple, consuming it like he can't survive without the taste of my flesh on his tongue. Though I buck my hips, struggling to find his erection and take it inside my body, that part of him is still out of my reach. My moans become whimpers that tacitly beg him to take me.

"Not yet," he growls, releasing my nipple.

"Please, Chance."

He crawls backward until his face is above my hips. Staring down at my mound, his eyes narrowed to slits, he utters a single syllable that he draws out into a throaty groan. "Fuck."

I spread my thighs.

Chance mutters something else, something I can't make out, and lowers himself onto his elbows. His face is directly above my sex, and I know I'm so aroused he must smell and see it. He gently separates my folds with two fingers, concentrating on the task like it's the most vital thing he's ever done. With my core exposed to him, he freezes.

The air teases my swollen flesh and the wetness that coats it. I moan for the millionth time, but I don't even care if I sound desperate and pathetic. A coil inside me tightens more and more with everything he does to me.

He shimmies backward a little more, and his head dives between my thighs. Groaning deeply, he glides his tongue up and down my cleft, first on one side, then the other.

I clench the sheets so hard my fingers ache, but other parts of me ache even more.

Up and down he strokes me, over and over until I'm gasping and writhing. He stops suddenly, his face between my legs but his tongue no longer touching me.

"Please," I beg.

He presses his mouth to my taut nub.

"Oh God," I moan as I thrash and lift my hips.

He pulls my clitoris into his mouth and suckles with the same strength and determination he'd applied to my nipple, only this time he's touching the most sensitive part of me. I cry out, my back flattening into the mattress, my entire body wrenching from the power of the climax that barrels through me. I want to scream, but I can't capture enough air to fill my lungs. So instead, I grip his head and ride out the pleasure, my heart pounding and my sex pulsating.

When my release finally subsides, I lay limp on the bed, my chest heaving. I manage to mumble two words. "Oh, Chance."

He raises up on his elbows to look at me. "You taste so good I could do that all night."

I regard him with what must be a dazed expression. Though he's given me the best orgasm ever, I want more. I want all of him.

Chance kisses my belly and rises to crouch over me again. He grabs something out of a drawer in the bedside table. I realize it's a condom when he rips the little packet open. Within seconds, he's rolled it on.

Anticipation sizzles through me, and I can barely breathe. Just two words spill from my lips, those syllables infused with all the longing and lust I've stored up inside me for days.

"Please, Chance."

Chapter Nine

Chance

Elena Linwood is perfect. The moment she shed her cloth-ing, she let go of all her inhibitions and gave in to the pleasure, every moan and every movement evidence of how she abandons herself to the moment. I couldn't watch her come, with my head between her legs, but now I have the chance to do just that. Witness her pleasure. Experience it. Feel it, see it, taste it, drown myself in the way she revels in sex. I got a glimpse of it that night in the eleva-tor. But tonight…

Elena gazes at me with a mesmerized expression, her lips parted and her every breath a whisper of unspoken desire. A faint blush col-ors her cheeks, but she's finally caught her breath. When she smiles, it's slightly crooked and entirely captivating. "Wow, Chance. That was… I mean, I don't know what else to say. You rock."

I chuckle. "Thank you, love. I appreciate the compliment."

"Oh no, that was not a compliment. It was unbridled adora-tion." She reaches out to stroke my cock with her hand. "I'm so ready for the rest."

With all of her laid out beneath me, I sit back on my heels and take a moment to absorb the sight of her nude, aroused body. Her taut nipples jut up, their color darkened to a dusky shade of rose. I skim my hands down her belly, past her perfect little navel, and spread them over her hips. She has the most intoxicating combination of curves and muscles I've ever seen, soft in all the best places but with enough strength to make sex with her an aerobic workout, if I want that. With her clever mind and sense of humor, I have no doubts we could have the most inventive, energizing sex imaginable. And I can imagine many, many creative ways to make her gasp and moan.

Right now, all I want is to touch her—with my hands, my mouth, everything—and then lose myself in the sweet release of making love to her.

I rest my fingertips over her mound and wriggle my fingers to tease the curly hairs. When Elena sucks in a breath, I ease my fingers between her folds. It's like wrapping pure silk around my hand, silk drenched with warm, sweet honey. I know what she tastes like, and I'm hungry for more of her, but I pull my hand away. Time for me to prove to her I can do better than shoving her against an elevator wall. It's only been a week since that first night, but it feels like a lifetime of waiting and wanting her.

"Chance," she murmurs. "Please, I want you so much."

The way she catches her bottom lip with her teeth, it's the sweetest thing I've ever seen, and the most arousing. I straddle her body again and push inside her gradually, letting myself experience every inch of her hot flesh. It closes around me like her mouth had earlier today, only better because now she's wrapping around me completely, her body a glove that encloses my cock. I remember the sensation of her mouth and tongue on my skin, but having all of her molding to my length… The pleasure is indescribable.

She grips my arms, lifting her hips into my thrusts.

I can't look away from her even if I wanted to. The lust in her eyes makes me crave her even more, but there's a tenderness behind the need, and it compels me to take all of her I can take. I lower my body onto hers little by little, waiting to see if my weight is too much. When her lips curve into a satisfied smile and she nods, I press all my weight down on her. God, the feel of her. All that smooth skin against mine, the rigidness of her nipples contrasting with the cushion of her breasts. I brace my arms at either side of her shoulders, my face above her head. The flowery scent of her hair makes me dip my head to draw in a lungful of it. She smells so good, from her hair to the musk of her sex.

I pull my hips back and plunge deep.

"Oh yes," she moans. "I love this."

Christ, I love it too. She's so wet and warm and willing, and I want this feeling of intimacy and desire to stretch on forever, so I can memorize every second of it. She bends her knees, framing my hips with them, and wraps her arms around me, her every breath transformed into a moan or a tender little sound of enjoyment. I bury my face in her hair while my thrusts become faster and more powerful. Her name spills from my lips again and again, the tone of my litany growing harsher the more I say her name. Her neck arches, and she whispers into my ear the words that shatter my self-control.

"Don't hold back. Please, I want all of you, all the way."

I lever up with my arms, pull my hips back until I've almost left her body, and drive into her. Though the pace and strength of my thrusts increases, I still can't tear my gaze away from hers. Even the bouncing of her breasts can't make me break the tether linking our gazes. Her eyes are half closed, her expression the embodiment of desire. I watch in awe as her climax comes over her gradually, first her face tightening and her eyes squeezing shut, then her fingers clenching my arms until the nails dig into my skin, and finally her entire body freezes and her mouth falls open on a frozen breath.

Her slick softness around my cock transforms into pulsing waves of muscle that grip and release me, over and over, while the breath she'd held rushes out of her as a strangled cry. She shouts my name even as her body relaxes for a moment only to tighten again with another wave of rippling spasms that push me over the edge with her. I thrust so hard and deep her body bounces, and I come apart inside her. It's like an electric jolt firing under my skin, making every muscle rigid while I throw my head back and shout.

I collapse on top of her.

She threads her fingers through my hair, peppering light kisses over my throat.

I haul in breath after breath until I've regained some of my wits. Then I withdraw from her body reluctantly—she feels so fucking good—then toss the condom in the bin beside the bed and roll onto my side next to her. Elena still seems dazed, her eyes closed and her breathing heavy.

"Have I done you in?" I ask.

"Mm-mm." She takes a deep breath, exhaling it slowly, and flips onto her stomach. Her elbows raise her head and shoulders as she throws me a sidelong look, her sexy lips curling into a smile of pure satisfaction. "That was fantastic. Elevator sex was hot, but this was beyond better."

"Glad you enjoyed yourself." I skate my palm along the curve of her spine. "You are the most sensual woman I've ever taken to bed."

"So, what now? Dinner? Or more sex?" She tosses her hair in a deliberately saucy way. "I vote for more sex, followed by room service."

"But you wore a sexy frock for me. Don't you want the elegant dinner I promised you?"

"Yeah, but I want more of you first. How late is the restaurant open?"

"Until ten, I think." I run my palm back up her spine and along her shoulder. "I need to tell Raisa I'm seeing someone."

Yes, don't I know exactly how to ruin a mood? As much as I'd rather make love to Elena for hours, we need to talk about how this will work once we get back to, well, work.

Elena springs up into a sitting position, her wide eyes on me. "You can't tell Raisa we're dating. She'll fire me so fast the whole building will spin. I'll never get another job if she tells everyone what a husband-stealing slut I am."

"I won't tell her who I'm dating. But she needs to know I am seeing someone, so she'll give up her ridiculous idea that she and I might reconcile."

"Oh, I'm sure that'll put her in a great mood."

"Relax, we can get through this together." I sit up and frisk my hands up and down her arms. "We're adults, and we don't need permission to have a relationship. Raisa will calm down, eventually."

Elena's head droops, her hair falling over her face. "I'm such a scummy liar. Raisa asked me to help her win you back, and instead I sleep with you."

"She had no right to order you to interfere in her personal life." I cradle Elena's face in my hands, lifting her head so she looks at me. "I want you, Elena, not my ex-wife. I like you, and I want us to get to know each other. That's what dating is, right? It's been a while since I tried it."

"I like you too, Chance. And I want the same thing, but…"

Raisa. My ex-wife is the "but" standing between me and Elena. I need to clear the air with Raisa and make sure she understands there is no chance of reconciliation. I've told her before, many times, but this time she will listen. She has to.

Because I will never give up Elena.

"Let me handle Raisa," I say. "Maybe it was a mistake for me to take the job at her firm. Quitting might be the best way to prove to her I mean it when I say it's over."

"Fabulous idea," Elena says with breezy sarcasm. "That'll put her in a terrific mood. I'll be fired ten seconds after you quit and blacklisted an hour later."

"Raisa isn't vindictive. She's still coming to terms with the divorce, but she will get over it."

"Maybe you should find her a boyfriend, so I don't have to play matchmaker for the two of you."

I cup her face again and kiss her gently. "Don't assume the worst. Let's see how this plays out when I tell Raisa I'm dating someone else."

Elena moans with so much misery that I can't help folding my arms around her. "Trust me. I know Raisa, and she listens to me. I will not let her do anything rash."

She snuggles into me, her cheek on my shoulder, the sweet warmth of her surrounding me. "Okay. I trust you. Do whatever you think is best."

"Thank you." I comb my fingers through her hair, loving the feel of the silky strands on my skin. "Everything will work out, you'll see."

And I pray I won't be making a liar of myself.

Chapter Ten

The next morning, everything starts out wonderful. I wake up with Chance's body molded to mine, his arm draped over my belly and his breaths fluttering my hair. We both lie on our sides, and his stiffening cock pushes against my backside. I lie there for a few minutes, enjoying the comfort of starting the morning this way and remembering all the pleasure we gave each other last night.

Eventually, Chance wakes up. Before I can even finish saying good morning, he's making love to me. It's the sweetest sleepy sex ever, and the best way to start the morning.

But afterward, I have to disappoint us both. "I need to work today, and tomorrow. Not only do I have stuff to do for you, but Raisa piled on more."

"I should work too, but I'd much rather stay in bed with you."

His sleepy-sexy voice makes me want to curl up with him under the covers and never leave. But we both know what we need to do, so we climb out of bed and take a shower together. Okay, maybe that "shower" involved orgasms. We did get clean too…eventually.

I freak out when I realize I'll be walking into the office wearing a red evening dress that's a rumpled advertisement for the fact I didn't sleep at home last night. My panic seems to amuse Chance.

He smiles and says, "The hotel has a boutique, and there's a clothing store down the street. I'll pay, obviously, since it's my fault your clothes are a mess. I'm the one who tossed your frock on the floor and never bothered to pick it up."

"Even if it wasn't wrinkled, I can't wear an evening dress to work."

"I said I'll buy you whatever you need."

Maybe I should say no to letting him buy me an outfit, but I can't think of any reason not to let him. I need work-appropriate clothes. Sure, I should've thought to bring an outfit for the morning, but I'd expected to leave after dinner and sex. We never made it to the hotel restaurant, though. Chance ordered room service, and we fed each other while naked on the bed. Which probably explains the crumbs stuck to my ass.

Last night was so good I half suspect I dreamed it.

Today might turn into a waking nightmare. Raisa will be at the office for sure.

Way to be positive, Elena.

I pull on my fancy dress and let Chance take me to the hotel boutique. Everything is so expensive I don't feel comfortable buying a new outfit there.

"Go on," Chance says in a tone so seductive I'm ready to do anything he asks. "Splash out this one time."

Yeah, I'll probably do that if I figure out what the heck it means. "I'm not planning to jump in a swimming pool."

He makes a sound that's halfway between a laugh and a sigh. "Splash out means to spend an obscene amount of money on something you don't need."

"But I do need clothes, something I can wear to work without making everybody think I've won the lottery. Please take me to the shop down the street." I raise my hands, palms pressed together in a pleading gesture. "Please, please, please."

"Have it your way."

We head down to the other boutique, which turns out to be middle-of-the-road expensive instead of I'm-married-to-royalty extravagant. I choose an elegant but reasonably priced pantsuit, ignoring Chance's flirtatious comments about how much he loves me in a skirt. I love his smile and his winks whenever he tells me something like that.

We agree to arrive at work separately. Chance goes first, since he always gets there earlier than anyone else except for Raisa. This morning, he's not as early as usual. I amble in twenty minutes later.

Only a handful of my coworkers are there. I briefly wonder if some of those lucky dogs got the weekend off, then realize they're probably off doing research somewhere or writing summaries in their PJs at home.

Chance is already in Raisa's office. I can't see them because the door is closed and the glass has been turned opaque, but I hear their voices. Even when I can't understand the words, I recognize Chance's voice. And I realize, based on their tones, that they're arguing.

Not loud enough to raise eyebrows. Luckily, everyone else is busy and not paying attention to the voices coming from Raisa's office.

I sit down at my desk and try to work, but my gaze keeps gravitating to the door to Raisa's office. How bad is it in there? Is Chance okay? I can't go in there to check without some legitimate excuse.

Grabbing a folder from my desk, I march up to Raisa's office door. Their voices are louder now, but I still can't make out the words. Chance sounds annoyed. Very annoyed.

I hesitate for a couple seconds, then knock.

Everything goes quiet inside the office.

The toe of my brand-new shoe taps furiously while I chew the inside of my lip.

At last, the door swings open.

Chance looks tired, but he moves aside and gestures for me to enter the room.

I can't make my feet budge. "I, um, need to talk to you about that pharmaceuticals case. I have the summaries you asked for, but I want to make sure it's everything you need."

He gives me a grateful look, one Raisa can't see since his back is turned to her. "I'll take a look later, but thank you for checking in with me."

Raisa rises from her chair, shoulders back, chin lifted, her cool gaze trained on me. "You should join us, Elena."

"No," Chance says. "This has nothing to do with her."

She ignores him and speaks to me. "Come in, Elena."

I shuffle into the office, my feet like big rocks attached to my legs with massive iron chains, and take a seat in one of the chairs on this side of Raisa's desk. Chance drops into the other chair. Only a couple feet separate us, but though I long to touch him, I don't do it.

Raisa can't know about us. Not unless Chance told her, and he wouldn't do that. She is one of the top legal minds in the country, a smart woman who can be very perceptive when she wants to be. So far, she's seemed oblivious of the chemistry between me and Chance, but maybe she's set her perceptive mind to the task of figuring out who he's dating.

I assume he's told her that much.

Raisa remains standing, like the teacher about to ream her wayward students. Or student. She's looking straight at me when she says, "I know about you and Chance."

Every ounce of blood in my body seems to evaporate, leaving me cold and stunned. I feel like I might pass out, but that's just crazy. I don't faint because my boss finds out I'm sleeping with her ex-husband. I sit up straighter instead, my hands flat on the folder on my lap.

Chance's gaze flicks to me. "She knows I sweet-talked you into telling me about her little scheme. I've made it clear to Raisa I don't appreciate or approve of the way she bullied you into helping her spy on me."

I can't think of a damn thing to say. Spy on him? I guess he's talking about Raisa's plan to win him back.

Chance aims a squinty-eyed look at Raisa. "I've set her straight on all of that."

Raisa waves a hand in my direction. "Forget about the plan, Elena. I shouldn't have asked you to do that."

"And?" Chance prompts.

She meets my gaze. "I'm sorry for what I did."

Wow, she apologized. Maybe I won't be fired after all.

"I appreciate that," I tell her.

"See?" Raisa says to Chance. "It's all settled."

"Yes, that's a good start." He gets up and nods to me, then to Raisa. "This matter is settled, and I'd better not hear anything more about you trying to win me back."

"Of course not," Raisa says.

Chance casts a furtive glance at me, smiling faintly, then walks out.

"Shut the door," Raisa calls out, and he does it.

I'm alone with my boss. Who just found out her ex is seeing someone else. So yeah, I grasp the arms of my chair while pretending to be relaxed.

Raisa sits down, clasps her hands on the desktop, and eyes me with her lips pinched. Though I've worked for her for barely more than a week, I've come to know that expression. It means she's figuring out whether I've kept something from her. Which I have. Big time. My conscience urges me to confess everything, but even if I wanted to, I can't do that without talking to Chance first.

"I know what you've been doing," Raisa says, leaning back in her chair, still staring at me in a way that makes my skin crawl.

Fighting the urge to scratch my arms, I try to look innocent. Jeez, I was dealing with one of the toughest lawyers in New York, and I thought I could fool her? Well, she hadn't figured out the truth yet. Maybe that snowball wouldn't melt in Hell after all.

"You had a fling last night, didn't you?" Raisa asks. "It's all right. After being at the law library most of the week, I imagine you needed to cut loose for a night. But I need you sharp, Elena, not tired and distracted."

I almost cry from relief. She clearly doesn't know I slept with Chance last night, though she's guessed I spent the night with someone. "I'm fine, really. Only had one martini last night, so no hangover."

"Good, but I'm not talking about hangovers." She waves a finger toward my face. "You have bags under your eyes, and that's a new suit from Sheri Ann's boutique. She's a friend, and I know what she keeps in stock. And the price tag is hanging from your armpit."

Is it? I lift my arm, and yes, the tag is hanging there. Damn. Isn't that just my luck? Raisa knows the woman who owns the boutique where Chance bought me a new outfit. I hope Sheri Ann didn't recognize Chance. I mean, if Raisa bought clothes there…

She's studying me again, like she knows I've done something but can't quite put her finger on it.

"If that's all," I say, "I should get these summaries to Chance."

"Not yet." She swivels her chair side to side. "You've let me down, Elena. I asked you to do one simple thing—find out who Chance is sleeping with—and you failed."

"I'm sorry."

She puckers her lips again, steepling her index fingers under her chin. "Never mind. I'll find out on my own. You're dismissed."

And of course, she waves her hand to indicate I should leave.

I've just shut the door behind me, intending to head for Chance's office, when a strange noise inside Raisa's office makes me stop. I tip my head to the side, listening. It almost sounds like crying. Sniffling, for sure.

Oh God, she's upset. About Chance dating someone else.

Which means her tears are my fault.

Feeling like the slimiest, wartiest toad on the planet, I go to Chance's office and shut the door behind me when I get there. I set the folder on his desk. "She's not giving up. I've been fired from being her little spy, but Raisa says she'll figure out on her own who you're sleeping with."

"She's bluffing. Lawyers are good at that."

"After I closed the door to her office, I heard Raisa crying."

He goes stiff, his unblinking gaze nailed to mine. "Crying?"

I nod.

"Shit." He runs a hand over his mouth. "I can't help that. What am I meant to do? Take her back so she won't feel bad?"

"No, of course not. But maybe we shouldn't—"

He surges up from his chair and slants over the desk to kiss me. His mouth lingers on mine for a moment, a long and blissful moment of feeling his warm lips and tasting a hint of the tea from the mug that sits on his desk. Though he peels his lips away, he doesn't move back. He stays there, an inch from my face, his sapphire eyes gazing into mine, and tucks a lock of hair behind my ear with one finger.

I try again to say something but manage to speak only one syllable. "Chance—"

Then he kisses me again, fervently, pulling back only enough to speak. His lips graze mine. "I'm sorry Raisa is upset, but she made a mess of things when we were married. She doesn't get to play the victim now. I want you in my life, Elena. We're not doing anything wrong."

"The firm's policy says coworkers who start dating have to report it to Raisa. I don't want to tell her, but my damn conscience kicked in this morning."

"We will tell her, once she calms down. The policy gives us thirty days, remember?"

"She seemed pretty damn calm when she told me I'd failed her and that she'll figure out on her own who you're sleeping with."

"And then she cried." He drags the backs of his fingers down my cheek. "I just told her I'm seeing someone. Let her digest that information before we tell her the rest."

It makes sense. But I have an annoying habit of being the good girl who follows the rules to the letter, sometimes going beyond what's required in my zeal to do the right thing. Maybe this once I can *not* be that girl. Waiting until we find out for sure if we really want to date seems like the smart thing to do. What if after a few more days we realize we're not right for each other?

Sorry excuses, I know.

But Chance is kissing me again, and all thoughts zip out of my brain, flying off into the sky.

He steps back and settles onto his chair. "I suppose we should discuss those summaries."

For a second, I can't remember what the hell he's talking about. Then the knowledge surfaces in my hormone-addled brain, and I hand him the folder and sit down.

For the next twenty minutes, we talk about legal summaries.

And I keep thinking about that boutique owner and what she might've seen.

Chapter Eleven

Chance

We survive the weekend, both of us working our arses off because we have a lot of work to do and because it keeps us away from Raisa. Overworking ourselves also stops us from sneaking into the file room to have sex, or sneaking into the restroom to have sex, or— Well, let's just say there are plenty of spots where we could enjoy each other.

But we don't. We behave like professionals.

It's bloody awful.

We survive Monday too, though barely.

Elena agrees to meet me in the hotel restaurant for dinner, claiming she won't get any food unless we eat first and go upstairs after. She might have a point. At lunch, I took her to a different boutique to buy a new dress for our date tonight. I hadn't known Raisa was friends with the owner of the boutique down the street from the hotel. But then, I hadn't been a part of Raisa's life for more than a year. Longer, really. We led separate lives even before the official separation.

I finish putting on my tie and head for the door while fantasizing about how delicious and entirely fuckable Elena will look in the emerald-green dress she'd let me buy for her. I got a glimpse of it when the clerk slipped the dress into a bag, but Elena had refused to let me watch her trying it on.

"You can't come into the fitting room with me," she'd said, smiling and shaking her head. "I have a feeling I won't get the dress on if you're there."

"Are you implying I'll strip it off you the second it touches your skin?"

"Not implying. Saying it." She tapped my chest with one finger. "You will strip me naked in five seconds, tops."

Since I couldn't deny I probably would—all right, definitely would—I had to give in and wander the aisles of women's clothing while I waited.

Now, hours after our shopping trip, I remember all the clothing items in that store and which ones would've looked best on Elena. Anything would look good on her. She has a beautiful body, yes, but also a heart-melting smile that makes her eyes sparkle. I'm hopelessly infatuated with her.

Thinking about seeing her, in a few minutes, I straighten my tie that doesn't need straightening and swing the door open.

Raisa is standing there, her hand raised to knock.

I stifle a curse.

She smiles, like we have a date and she's early. "Chance, darling, I was just coming to see you."

"You know I don't like it when you show up without calling first." I hadn't liked it during our separation, and that was part of the reason I'd taken a job in Chicago. I also don't like it when she calls me darling. "We're not married anymore. Call first next time. I have an appointment to keep."

She doesn't move. "Please, darling, let's talk this through."

"We have nothing to talk about." I push her hand away when she tries to touch my cheek. "We are divorced, Raisa, and I've moved on. You need to do the same."

"But I love you, Chance."

I sigh, my shoulders flagging, and rub my eyes. "It was a mistake to take this job with you. I thought I was helping, but I'm only making things worse. I'm sorry, but I think I should go home."

"No, please, stay."

I hear the elevator doors open and glance down the hall.

Elena steps out into the hallway. When she sees me and Raisa, her eyes widen.

She looks fantastic in that frock.

Before I realize her intention, Raisa throws her arms around my neck and kisses me.

Elena stumbles backward into the elevator, furiously punching a button so many times she might break it.

I grasp Raisa's arms and push her away from me. "Stop this. It's over. I'm sorry you can't accept that, but you need to."

Tears shimmer in Raisa's eyes, but I don't have time to feel bad for her. After what she's done to me in the past, and her idiotic plot to win me back, I feel no obligations to her. Not anymore. I race down the hall to the elevator, reaching it as the doors shut. I get a glimpse of Elena and her stricken expression, then she's gone.

I sprint toward the stairs but stop at the door. Even if I can run down nineteen flights, I'll never get there before the elevator, before Elena leaves.

Raisa finds me standing at the stairwell door, staring at it. "That was your new lover, wasn't it?"

She doesn't sound irritated. Instead, I sense compassion in her voice. I can't help looking at her.

"Whoever she is, you don't need her," Raisa tells me, taking my hand. "Give me another chance. I'll be different this time, better, more what you need."

I know she's not making a pun when she tells me she wants another chance. She honestly believes I might take her back.

"You lost me a long time ago," I say. "It's too late. Move on, Raisa, please."

Her eyes grow large, lending her face an innocence and pain I haven't witnessed since the day I told her I was moving out of our apartment.

Christ, I don't want to hurt her. But this can't go on, Raisa scheming to win me back while I try to romance Elena. Maybe Elena's right, and we should declare our relationship to Raisa. I need to talk to Elena first.

"I'm sorry," I tell her. "I have to go. It's for the best."

And I swear fate is on my side when I run for the elevator and get there at the instant the doors slide open. An older couple exits the car. I hurry inside and punch the button for the lobby.

Half an hour later, after enduring a long taxi ride amid a traffic jam, I finally stand outside the door to Elena's apartment. I pray she's here. Though I'd checked the hotel restaurant and the bar, I hadn't found her there. She must have come home.

I knock.

A moment later, the door opens—and Elena gapes at me.

She's still wearing that dress, the green number with a low neckline, the one that molds to every curve on her body.

"Hi," she says, still seeming surprised and confused.

"May I come in? I want to explain what you saw."

"Raisa was trying to seduce you, right? I figured that one out already." Elena motions for me to enter. "My apartment isn't swanky, like your hotel, but it's comfortable."

"I'm not a snob."

"Yeah, I know." She hunches her shoulders. "Sorry I ran away, but I kind of freaked when I saw Raisa."

"No worries. I finally got the chance to run after a woman."

I walk into the apartment, taking in the small but very puffy sofa and two puffy recliners. Multi-layered white curtains frame the windows, beyond which I catch a glimpse of the Manhattan skyline glittering with lights. This building is far enough away from that view to be relatively affordable. As affordable as anything gets in New York.

Elena is barefoot.

My attention stalls on her dainty toes and the lavender nail polish on them.

She wanders into the kitchen. A bar separates it from the living room.

I follow her while she opens the refrigerator and pulls out a bottle of beer. "Want one?"

"Love one. Thanks." I take the bottle she offers, watching while she grabs one for herself. "Could we sit down? I was on foot for the last two blocks. Traffic was terrible."

She leads me to the sofa and sits down, patting the cushion beside her. "Relax, I know Raisa surprised you with that kiss. It was obvious."

I drop onto the sofa a little too roughly, making it jump. "Sorry, I'm exhausted from the walk."

She sets her beer on the coffee table. "Two blocks wipes you out? How did you ever survive in New York the first time?"

"A talk with Raisa always leaves me exhausted. Besides, I had to give up on the taxi and run to get here."

"Run?" Elena's brows knit together over her adorable nose. "What was the rush?"

"To find you." I take a sip of my beer, then set the bottle on the table. I angle toward her and take her hand in both of mine. "I was afraid you jumped to the wrong conclusion and thought I was reconciling with Raisa. I'm not, by the way."

"Never thought that." She shuts her eyes for a moment, then looks at me again. "I feel horrible. Raisa is clearly still in love with you, and I promised to help her win you back, then I went and slept with you instead."

"She had no right to make you do that for her."

"I know, but she won't give up. This afternoon, I went to the break room to get some coffee, and I saw Raisa there. She didn't see me. She was crying again, Chance. Crying. Raisa."

What am I meant to do about that? I don't want to hurt Raisa, but I've clearly failed to hammer it into her brain that we will never be a couple again. "I don't love her anymore. I want to be with you, Elena, and that unfortunately means I have to hurt Raisa. No way around that."

"Yeah, I know." Elena lays her other hand over mine. "I guess we have to accept that Raisa will be upset. But I really think we need to tell her about us."

"I don't think that's a good idea, not yet. Let's wait and see if this thing between us is really going somewhere."

"No, please, we have to tell her. And if she fires me, oh well. I'm sure they need paralegals in Siberia."

"You don't need to run that far away. Come with me to Chicago."

Elena lays her palm on my cheek. "That's sweet, but we barely know each other."

"We can change that." I turn my face into her palm and kiss it. "Raisa can't fire you for following the firm's rules about co-workers dating. I'm an attorney, Elena. I'll help you sue her for wrongful termination if she does fire you. But first, I'll try again to talk sense into her. It might work."

"Maybe," Elena says, sounding as unconvinced as she looks. "We're taking a risk either way."

"We are. But you should've said you're taking a chance. I'd jump on that offer."

"Oh, but I knew you'd do that." She taps her finger on my lips. "Not giving you any ammunition to use in seducing me."

"Why not? That's why I came here."

She shakes her head. "No, it's not. You came here because Raisa upset you, and you need comforting."

"Do I get some, then?"

"Absolutely." She leans in, her breaths teasing my lips. "How do you like the dress?"

"I love it." I can't disguise the hunger in my voice, because I am starved for her. I feasted on that body two nights ago, but I need more. "Where's the bedroom?"

She hooks a thumb over her shoulder. "Down the hall."

"Too far." I consider the small sofa and calculate whether I can fit on it lying down. The answer is no. "It's either you on my lap here, or both of us on the floor."

Laughing softly, her face alight with joy and lust, she straddles my lap.

I slip my hands under her dress, skating them up her thighs to her arse. "You've got knickers on."

"Mm-hm." Her tongue peeks out between her lips while she focuses on undoing my tie. "Thought it might be fun to let you rip them off."

"It will be. Enormously." I hook my fingers inside her knickers and yank, but they don't rip. I try again, yanking harder, but still can't break the bloody things. "There's a slight problem with your plan. Your underwear seems to be woven from steel fibers."

She laughs again, tossing my tie halfway across the room. It lands on one of the recliners. "Oh come on, Chance. You don't give up that easily, do you?"

I love her this way, uninhibited, laughing, playing with me. She's adorable and beautiful and sweet and sexy. The fact she has a sharp mind behind all that feminine loveliness makes her even more enticing.

And she's right. I don't give up that easily.

Since I can't tear the blasted underwear off her, I pick her up by the waist and lay her down on the sofa beside me. I make quick work of getting rid of those knickers, flinging them across the room so they get caught in a ruffled layer of one of the curtains. The pale-blue lace panties stand out against the white curtains.

"There," I say, setting her on my lap again. "Please continue."

Elena flashes me a naughty smile while she begins unbuttoning my shirt. "It's like Christmas morning, unwrapping you."

The door bursts open.

We both swing our heads around to look at the man who's lugging a huge suitcase into the apartment. Head down, he grunts when he lifts the suitcase to get it over the threshold.

"Hey, Ellie," he says without glancing up. "I know I'm home early. Cancun was—"

The man lifts his head and spots us. His expression goes blank.

Elena leaps off my lap. "Kyle, what are you doing here? Your trip was supposed to be ten days."

"Yeah, but like I was about to say, Cancun was awesome until the hurricane hit." Elena's brother drags his suitcase to the bar. "We got out just in time. I dropped Amelia off at her place."

Elena fusses with her dress, which only makes her look more guilty.

Kyle wanders over to us, stopping at the end of the sofa. His gaze flicks to the blue knickers hanging from the curtain and then narrows on me. But he's squinting at Elena when he says, "Who's the dude making time with my sister on the sofa?"

I get up and offer him my hand. "Chance Dixon. Elena and I work together."

"Uh-huh." Kyle shakes my hand. "How come Ellie didn't mention you to me? We talked and texted since I left for Cancun."

Elena wraps her arm around mine. "Chance and I met after you left. I didn't tell you about him because this is so new, and we're not sure if it'll go anywhere."

"I get it." Kyle's mouth twists into a sarcastic smile. "I leave you alone for a few days, and you hook up with the first British guy you meet. It's cool."

"Are you being snotty, or are you really okay with this? I can't tell."

Kyle laughs. "Come on, Elena, we're all grown-ups here. Do the nasty with whoever you want, as long as it makes you happy."

I wish my ex-wife had the same mature attitude.

Elena hugs her brother. "Thank you, sweetie. I'm glad you're okay with this, because I really like Chance. A lot."

My lips tighten into a smile, and I make no effort to stop it. Elena likes me a lot. My smile broadens. She likes me.

So much for being a mature adult.

"Don't mind me," Kyle says. "I'm gonna drag my stuff into my room and crash. Unpacking can wait till tomorrow."

He does exactly that, hauling his suitcase down the hallway.

Elena and I watch, and I wonder what my odds are for seducing her tonight—with her brother in the apartment.

At the door to his room, Kyle pauses to smirk at us. "Make as much noise as you want. I'm so bushed I'll be dead to the world the second my head hits the pillow." He nods at me. "Nice to meet you, Chance."

"Pleasure meeting you too, Kyle."

He goes into his room and shuts the door.

I turn to Elena. "Where is your room?"

"Right across the hall from Kyle's."

"What are the odds you'll let me fuck you tonight?"

She grins. "One hundred percent, you lucky dog."

The woman I adore dashes down the hallway, waving for me to follow.

And I run after her.

Everything else can wait until tomorrow.

Chapter Twelve

This time, the morning after a night with Chance is a lot more fun. I don't worry about showing up to work wearing an inappropriately fancy and sexy dress, because we're in my apartment. When I ask Chance if he needs to rush home to change clothes, he says, "I don't give a toss what anyone thinks of my clothes, and besides, I'm living across the street from the office." Okay, fair point. He can rush up to his hotel room to change. And if he's late, I doubt Raisa will care. She wants him back and reaming him for being tardy won't win him over.

After a round of fun wake-up sex, Chance wants to take a shower with me, like we'd done the morning after our big date in his hotel suite. I'm all for repeating that experience, but there's a problem. The shower is only slightly bigger than I am. Kyle barely fits in it by himself, so I know Chance and I have no, um, chance of squeezing in there together. This apartment does not have a tub. Chance is disappointed but agrees that the two of us getting sardined in the shower will only result in a 911 call and an embarrassing use of the Jaws of Life.

We reach a compromise. He stands outside the shower watching me get clean, then I watch him do the same. He's even hotter when he's wet. The water rolls down his body, outlining every muscle and making his hair glisten. When he tips his head back to rinse his hair, running his fingers through it, I get tingly all over. But when he slathers sudsy body wash all over himself, I'm pretty sure he does it slowly on purpose to give me an incredible view of his soapy bod. I want to climb in there and bathe him with my tongue.

I won't fit. Damn.

But post-shower sex is awesome.

When we finally walk into the kitchen, Kyle is already there whipping up pancakes and bacon.

"Morning," he says. "You guys sure take a long time to get showered and dressed. Kinda noisy about it too."

He gives me a smug smile.

I roll my eyes.

Chance and I perch on stools on the other side of the bar from Kyle. I can't resist laying my hand on Chance's thigh and feeling him up. The bar hides what I'm doing from Kyle's view, not that I think he'll care if he sees it. Kyle has wanted me to get a new boyfriend for almost a year, ever since the last one dumped me for a dog groomer. Apparently, wiping poodles' asses is sexier than being a paralegal. Who knew?

I give Chance's thigh a squeeze.

He rests his hand on the back of my stool and leans in to kiss me. It's a sweet kiss, nothing naughty about it. I suppose he's being polite, holding back in front of my brother, but I like the kiss. Sometimes simplicity is the sexiest thing.

Kyle flips a pancake. It sails through the air only to smack down right where it started, only now its cooked side faces up. My brother is an expert pancake flipper, and I've always envied him that talent. I can't flip a burger without it sticking to the griddle.

"Very impressive," Chance tells Kyle. "You're quite the cook, aren't you?"

"Nah." Kyle flips another pancake, since he has four of them on the griddle. "I can do basic stuff like pancakes and fried eggs." He points his spatula at me. "Elena's the real master chef around here."

"Don't listen to a word my brother says," I tell Chance. "He's a massive liar. I'm no better at cooking than he is. Kyle's trying to make you think I'm amazing so you'll be horribly disappointed when I finally cook for you. Little brothers are obnoxious that way."

Chance kisses my cheek. "I doubt Kyle is exaggerating your skills, but I know what younger siblings can be like. I have two of them."

"What? How come you haven't mentioned them before?"

He shrugs. "Never came up in conversation."

"But I told you about Kyle over lunch the other day."

"True." He scratches his jaw, eying me sideways. "I suppose I should've said something then, but I love listening to you talk."

Kyle bursts out with the phoniest guffaw I've ever heard. "Damn, you've got it bad. Don't you, Brit boy?"

I aim an exaggerated scowl at him. "Be nice. Chance is my boyfriend, so don't be obnoxious."

"Boyfriend?" Kyle looks smug again, but his closed-mouth smile is aimed at Chance this time. "If you're dating my sister, that means I get to razz you big time. Know anything about NASCAR?"

"I've heard the term," Chance says, "but that's about all. It's car racing, isn't it?"

"Yep." Kyle grins with wicked glee. "Let me tell you all about it."

Kyle proceeds to recite every moment of the last NASCAR race while Chance pretends to listen when he's really massaging my thigh. I have no doubt he's not hearing a word of Kyle's monologue. My brother doesn't care if nobody's listening. He can babble away about stock car racing for hours.

After that, Chance and I head to the office via taxicab. During the drive, we discuss Raisa.

"I'm thinking we should wait," I say, "before telling her about us. I thought about it a lot while I was dreaming, and I realized you're right. We need to make sure this thing between us is going somewhere before we go public."

"You thought about it while you were dreaming?"

"Uh-huh." I glance at him sideways. "Don't you do that? Work out problems in your dreams?"

"Not really." He lets his head fall back against the seat. "I'm glad you've seen it my way. We only met twelve days ago, after all. It makes sense to get to know each other better before outing ourselves. That would also give Raisa more time to accept she can't win me back."

"So we're agreed? Keep it on the down low for now?"

"Yes."

I realize what he said and have to ask, "You've been keeping track of how many days we've known each other?"

"That's right. Every day with you is worth counting." He kisses me, long and slow and sexy as hell. "Sneaking around could be exciting."

The way he says those words, with his voice a smoky murmur, excites the hell out of me.

I nibble on his lower lip. "How long do you think we need to wait?"

"Two weeks. If I'm not head over heels in love with you by then, it'll never happen."

His statement sounds innocuous, his tone so casual, that I think it must mean something different in British. I stare at him, my pulse suddenly throbbing faster, and wonder if he means what it sounds like he means. Does he think he's falling for me? Or that he might very soon?

I like him a lot, more than I've liked anyone in a long time. But could I fall for him?

Deciding I might be reading too much into what he said, I change the subject. "Tell me about your siblings."

"I have two brothers, both younger. I'll be seeing them—" He shuts his eyes, groaning. "I forgot. I'm flying home next weekend, leaving Friday afternoon."

"Guess it pays to be the boss's ex. You started work last week, and Raisa's letting you take off early next Friday?" I shake my head. "She'd rip me a new one if I asked for ten more minutes on my lunch break."

"I'd planned this trip months ago. When Raisa asked me to work for her temporarily, I said yes with the condition that I don't have to give up my holiday."

"How long will you be gone?" I already feel a little queasy knowing he won't be here for a while.

"The weekend," he says. "Back at work on Monday morning."

I don't know what to say. Not seeing him for a weekend shouldn't upset me, but it does. I'll miss him. We'll have this coming weekend together, so it's dumb for me to wish he'd stay here instead of going home for a few days.

Chance kisses me again, tenderly this time, and only for a second. "Come with me."

"To England? I can't. Raisa won't give me the afternoon off."

"I'll rearrange my plans. We can leave right after work on Friday."

"But—I—" His suggestion has me so off-kilter I can't speak an entire sentence. We hardly know each other, and he wants me to go away with him for the weekend. When I manage to form a sentence, I ask, "Are you inviting me to meet your family?"

"I guess I am."

He sounds as surprised as I feel.

The thrill of knowing he wants to take me home to his family lasts about three seconds. Then I moan miserably. "I can't go. We lowly paralegals must slave away all weekend, you know. I'm sure next weekend will be no different."

He twists his mouth into an annoyed slant and rubs his eyes. "Forgot about that. Can't you get all your work done during the week? I'll help."

"You want to do grunt work? That's my job, not yours."

"Let me pitch in. Please."

"You want me to go with you that badly?"

I expect him to change his mind, but instead he says, "I know it's early in our relationship, but I absolutely do want you to meet my family. My parents and my brothers. If it's too much too soon, say so. I won't be offended if you'd rather not."

For several seconds, I hold perfectly still and consider the question. Do I want to meet his family? He's met mine, but then, my only family is Kyle. Chance has parents and siblings. I assume they all met Raisa, multiple times.

"Does your family like Raisa?" I ask.

He makes a pained face. "They tolerated her. She's brash and sometimes curt, and she never appreciated my family's way. We're not stuffy. We're…outgoing."

Okay, so I won't be compared to Raisa and found lacking. But they might still dislike me for other reasons.

Chance touches my cheek. "If you're worried my family won't like you, relax. They won't be able to keep from falling under your spell."

"That's sweet, but you're sleeping with me. Of course you think I'm awesome."

His mouth twists into a frown, but it smooths out quickly. "That's not why I'm with you, Elena. You're more than a lover to me. I feel more comfortable with you than I ever did with Raisa, or with any other woman." He smiles, almost shyly. "Will you come with me next weekend?"

I think about it for a nanosecond. "Yes, I'd love to."

This time when he kisses me, it's hot enough to steam up the windows of every vehicle on the street and the ones on the shops alongside it. I don't even care that the cabbie sees us.

When we get to the building that houses Raisa Volkov & Associates, Chance sprints across the street and up to his hotel room to change clothes. I head for the office, so it won't be obvious we've been together. I'd rather wait for him, but we need to keep up appearances for two more weeks.

I'm going home with him. To England. To meet his family.

Holy shit.

Chapter Thirteen

Chance

Two weeks with Elena, enjoying her company and getting to know her better. What can I say? I've never had a better two weeks in my life, despite the nagging worry about how Raisa will react when we tell her about our relationship. I try not to dwell on that. I meant it when I told Elena I will sue Raisa for wrongful termination if she fires her. My ex-wife has lost the plot, at least in her personal life. At work, she's as brilliant and determined as ever, the qualities I used to love about her.

Elena has erased all of that. I adore her, like I never did Raisa. Elena is open and sweet, as brilliant as Raisa but without the fierce need to always win. Maybe I shouldn't compare the two women, but I can't help it. Elena has a light inside her I've never seen in any other human being, an inner glow nothing could ever extinguish.

Her legal summaries are perfect. She gathers research and collates it in a way that makes my job easier. She ought to be an attorney, not a paralegal, which I told her only a few days after we met. When I tell her again, ten days into our two weeks, she leans back against the puffy sofa in her apartment and sighs.

"You assume that's what I want," she says.

"Isn't it? You gave up on law school because your mother had passed away and you needed to care for your brother."

"That might have been the reason I didn't go back at the time, but things have changed." She tucks her legs under her, angling her body partway toward me where I sit beside her. "At first, getting paralegal certification was a detour, and I still planned to go to law school someday. But after a while, I realized I like being a paralegal. Lawyers have to go to court and argue with other lawyers and with judges. After watching that stuff for six months, I decided I'll stick to research, writing summaries, interviewing clients, and all the no-courtroom stuff that I love doing."

"You love research? I've never heard a paralegal or a lawyer say that."

She hunches her shoulders. "What can I say? I love it. Using my brain to ferret out the right information is a lot more fun than playing the lawyer game. And it is a game, right? Like chess and poker mushed together."

I laugh, enchanted by her way of describing the legal profession. "Mushed together? Well, I can't deny there's a lot of bluffing and even outright lying involved. That's why I quit my job in Chicago."

"Thought you took a sabbatical."

"Yes, but this morning I submitted my resignation. I've had enough of the underhanded bollocks."

She studies me for a moment, seeming to weigh whether to say something. Finally, she asks, "Are you staying at Raisa's firm permanently?"

"No. I've had enough of her underhanded bollocks too."

"What will you do?"

I run a hand through my hair, not sure how to answer. "That's yet to be decided."

Elena inches closer to me. "I heard a rumor you're stinking rich. Is that true?"

"Who told you that?"

"Office gossip. I haven't asked you about it because gossip is, well, gossip and it wasn't any of my business." She fingers the top button on my shirt. "Now it is."

"The gossip is partly true." I slip my arm around her, tugging her closer. "I'm not filthy rich, but I have enough money to live comfortably without needing to work for quite a while."

"Would it be rude to ask how you got to be wealthy? Was it a big settlement for a client?"

"You're not being rude at all. I've gotten a few sizable settlements for clients, and I have a mate who's a financial adviser. He helped me invest wisely." I glance around the small apartment with its inexpensive furniture, and I suddenly wonder if my financial situation makes her uncomfortable. "My family are what you might call upper middle class, but they're not stinking rich and definitely not uptight snobs."

"I'm looking forward to meeting your parents."

The way she changed the subject makes me think she might be uncomfortable after all. "Does it bother you that I have money?"

She gives me a sweet, if small, smile. "I have money too, just not the gobs and gobs of it you have. My bank account balance is eight hundred and fifty-two dollars and nineteen cents. Does that bother you?"

"No. But that's different."

"Because I'm not rich and you are. I'm supposed to be jealous or disgusted or something. Sorry to disappoint, but I'm none of those things."

"You honestly don't care?"

"About your money? No. I care what kind of person you are." She kisses me, and her eyes are millimeters from mine when she says, "You are a good man, Chance Dixon. That's what matters."

"You are an exceptional woman, Elena Linwood."

"Are you trying to outdo me with your compliment? I said you're a good man, so you have to say I'm exceptional."

I know she's teasing me. Her tone of voice and the twinkle in her eyes tells me as much.

She tickles me under my chin. "You are pretty exceptional too."

How else can I respond to that? I fuck her on the sofa, since Kyle is out with his girlfriend, and marvel at what a lucky bastard I am.

Near the end of our two weeks, the morning of the day when we will leave on our holiday, I wake up with Elena's body half sprawled over me. The covers have slipped off her shoulders and one leg, exposing her creamy skin. I want to wake her with a kiss and make love to her slowly, but we both need to get to the office.

So I wake her with a kiss and stop there.

We've spent most of our nights for the past two weeks in her apartment. I like it here. It's comfortable and feels like a home. My hotel has all the posh amenities, but it lacks warmth. I'll sleep anywhere with Elena, even in a tent in the middle of the Arctic.

Elena and I say goodbye to Kyle, since we'll be heading for the airport directly after work. I've gotten to know Kyle a bit, and I like him. He has a wry sense of humor and clearly loves his sister. I appreciate loyalty. After being married to a woman who thought cheating was acceptable as long as she claimed to still love me, I'm grateful to have met two honest and forthright people like Elena and Kyle Linwood.

We arrive at the office to find Raisa isn't there. One of the other attorneys tells us she called in sick.

Raisa has never taken a sick day in her life.

Elena and I head into my office to discuss her latest research for one of my clients.

We've just sat down when she asks me, "What's going on with Raisa? That woman never takes a day off. I heard that when she had the flu, she wore a mask and came to work anyway. Do you think she's okay?"

"Ted Fan seems to think so. He's the one who talked to Raisa this morning."

"Should you check on her?"

"Raisa is not my responsibility anymore. Whatever's going on with her is not my concern." I realize that sounds insensitive, which isn't what I intended, so I add, "I only mean that it wouldn't be appropriate for me to check on her, considering that she believes I'll go back to her."

"I guess you're right." Elena chews on her lip for a moment, then grabs the phone off my desk. "I'll call her."

"Raisa has made your life hell. You're not obligated to check on her."

"Don't worry, I can handle it." She dials the number and gazes into space while she waits for Raisa to pick up. I can tell when she does, because Elena sits up straighter. "Hi, Raisa, it's Elena. I heard you're sick and wanted to see if there's anything I can do."

I can hear Raisa's sharp voice when she barks something at Elena. How sick can the woman be if she has the energy to be rude to her employee?

"Uh-huh," Elena says. "I'd love to help, but I have plans this evening that I can't cancel. Maybe Sadie can do that for you?"

More sharp words from Raisa. Her voice rattles the speaker.

Elena looks at me, biting her lip so hard it turns white. She shakes her head, hiking up her shoulders.

Like hell she's giving in to Raisa and giving up on our holiday. Maybe Raisa somehow found out about our trip and is pretending to be sick so she can command Elena to stay here. The idea sounds paranoid, but with Raisa you never can tell.

I snatch the phone away from Elena. "What urgent nonsense are you bullying Elena into doing for you? She's my paralegal. You gave her to me for the duration, until you find a replacement for Lucas Miller."

"Chance, darling, it's so good to hear your voice." She coughs, but it sounds fake. "I have a terrible cold, and I need Elena to do a favor for me. There's no need to get snippy about it. You'll have her all day, and after that, she'll help me. I know you're leaving for England straight after work, so this won't inconvenience you."

Oh, the clever, devious woman. She must have found out about me and Elena, somehow, and she's conniving to keep us from going away together.

I hope I'm being paranoid. Pray for it, actually.

Raisa shatters that hope when she says, "I'll be needing Elena's help all weekend. She's the best paralegal I have, you know. I lent her to you as a favor."

"This is bullshit, Raisa."

"Why do you care so much about a paralegal? You've never minded that I make them work evenings and weekends without paying them overtime."

Yes, I have minded. It may be common practice and legally acceptable to not pay paralegals overtime, but I've never agreed with that way of doing things. It's not the issue right now, though.

"Elena has a life," I say, "and you're abusing your position by forcing her to work overtime."

Raisa fakes a sneeze. "I need to take cold medicine and sleep. Tell Elena I'll see her this evening."

She hangs up on me.

I slam the phone into its cradle.

Elena sighs. "It's okay. I'll do what she wants. It's probably too soon for me to meet your parents, anyway. You go, and have fun."

"Fun?" I flop back in my chair so forcefully it slides across the floor. "I won't enjoy a holiday when I know you're wiping Raisa's nose all weekend."

"She's not really sick, you know. I won't need to wipe her nose."

"That's not the point. I won't go anywhere without you."

Elena smiles, but there's a touch of sadness to it. "That's sweet, but I want you to go. I know you've been looking forward to seeing your family, and they must be excited to see you too."

I spring up from my chair, and this time it sails backward to smack into the windowsill. "I am going to sort this Raisa nonsense right now."

"You can't." Elena waves a file folder at me. "We need to go over this research before your appointment with Arvid Klausen at eleven o'clock. After lunch, you're in court for two hearings. If there's time after that, we need to go over the depositions for the Cutler case."

Fuck. I forgot about all of that. The second I realized Raisa was interfering with my weekend with Elena, everything else fled my brain. I've never let work slide, for any reason.

"I'm not going anywhere," I say. "If you can't go, then I'm not going either."

"Weren't you listening a minute ago? I don't want you to give up visiting your family for me."

My parents are excited about my visit, but the thought of going without Elena, of leaving her here to be Raisa's slave... I feel a strange pressure in my chest when I think about it. She's right, though. I can't speak to Raisa today to sort this mess, and I don't want to let my family down either.

"All right," I say, feeling like a condemned man about to eat his final meal. "I'll go. But we will both confront Raisa Monday morning and tell her about us. It's time."

"I agree." Elena hands me the folder. "Now, let's get to work."

I manage to focus on work, but as the hours go by, that pressure gets heavier and heavier.

Chapter Fourteen

Elena

After a weekend of serving Raisa, like a Roman slave girl without the toga, I can't wait to see Chance again. Despite knowing Raisa has been faking her illness—she has a bottle of cold medicine on her living room table but never took the plastic seal off it—I still feel bad for her. Yeah, okay, I'm a sap. She cheated on her husband and ordered me to help her win him back, but she's also a human being. I get the feeling she honestly regrets ruining her marriage and losing Chance.

I also get the sneaking suspicion she knows I'm the one Chance is seeing.

Sunday evening, Raisa frees me from my servitude, at least until tomorrow.

Chance's flight arrives at eight o'clock, an hour from now, and I can't wait until tomorrow to see him. I run across the street to the hotel and sip a margarita at the bar while I wait. When I see him walk through the automatic doors, I jump up and run to him. Okay, I fling my entire body at him.

He catches me, chuckling, and says, "I'm happy to see you too."

"God, I missed you so much."

I kiss him like we haven't seen each other in months, not caring one bit who sees us making out in the lobby. Chance keeps one arm around me while we get in the elevator and head up to the nineteenth floor. He kisses me even more passionately in the elevator, since there's no one around, and I wish he'd take me like he did that first night. He doesn't—at least, not until we get inside his room.

We've barely spoken to each other, but I'm so happy to be with him again that I don't care. Who needs words? Our bodies say everything that matters.

After sex, we lie naked on the bed with no covers over us, entangled in each other's arms.

"How was your trip?" I ask.

"It was good to see my family." He nuzzles my hair. "But I missed you."

"Raisa kept me busy all weekend." I lift my head off his chest to look at him. "I think she knows about us."

"I think so too."

"That means tomorrow is doomsday."

He cups my chin, his blue eyes intent on mine. "Everything will be fine, you'll see."

"You're awfully confident about that. Did you talk to Raisa already?"

"No." He rolls over so I'm under him. "Let's not talk about my ex-wife anymore. There will be plenty of time for that tomorrow. Tonight, I want to make up for lost time, two days' worth of not shagging you."

We make up for lots of missed shagging, and I fall asleep in his arms.

The banging of a fist on the door wakes us both at six a.m.

Chance yanks on a pair of pants, the ones he ditched last night when we both rushed to get naked, and jogs out of the bedroom to answer the door.

I get dressed in a hurry and find Chance in the living room, an envelope crushed in his fist and a paper in his hand. He glances up from reading the paper.

"She's off her rocker," he says. "The bloody woman has completely lost her mind."

"What's happened?"

He looks at the paper again and shakes his head. "The law firm of Raisa Volkov & Associates is no longer paying for my suite, and

I'm to vacate the premises immediately. You and I are both to report to Raisa's office at eight o'clock."

"What? Shit." I spin around, searching for my purse. Where did I leave it? "I have to go home and change, which means I'll be late."

Chance crumples the paper and hurls it across the room. "Stop, Elena. She knows damn well you're here. Don't know how, but she knows. Go down to the hotel boutique and buy something, damn the price tag. I'll dress and pack and meet you there to pay for it."

I do what he says, because I have no frigging idea what else to do. The woman I'd been enslaved to all weekend, even felt sorry for, is sharpening her ax and taking practice swings with it.

By the time I find a skirt suit that fits and doesn't look as outrageously expensive as it is, Chance strides into the boutique and offers up his credit card to pay for it. I get dressed in the fitting room. We say nothing to each other, but his thunderous expression tells me he is not pleased with Raisa.

The hotel concierge, who seems to know Raisa and not like her very much, offers to have Chance's bags sent to my apartment.

We walk into the offices of Raisa Volkov & Associates together.

All eyes gravitate to us. Everyone comes out to watch us go into Raisa's office, even the attorneys who usually stay in their offices with their doors shut.

Chance shuts the door.

He and I take the chairs in front of Raisa's desk.

She sits in her leather executive chair, spine straight and shoulders back, gazing at us with regal assurance.

My mouth has gone dry. My eyes burn because I've stopped blinking.

Raisa folds her hands on the desktop. "You are both fired."

Chance makes a derisive noise. "Come off it, Raisa. You always overreact when you're angry. Once you've calmed down—"

"I am calm, Chance." She nails him with her frigid glare, the one everybody says she reserves for clients who've lied to her. "You've been screwing my paralegal and haven't informed me of your relationship. That's a violation of the firm's policy on dating."

"That's bollocks, and you know it," Chance says. "The policy states employees have thirty days to report their relationship to you."

Raisa rises from her chair, towering over us where we sit. "I said you are fired. And you can be certain"—she swerves her frigid glare to me—"that you won't receive a letter of recommendation from me. In fact, I'll make sure every firm in the city knows about the gold-digging paralegal who stole my husband."

Chance flies out of his chair. "Elena didn't steal me. You destroyed our marriage years ago, and I should've left you then. I tried to make it work, but you couldn't stop fucking other men, could you? I'm finally happy, and you can't stand it."

Raisa remains unruffled, gazing at him like he's one of the plebs and not her ex-husband. "Don't you want to know how I found out about your treachery?"

Chance looks about to explode, so I get up and place myself between the two of them.

"How did you find out?" I ask, though it hardly matters now.

She lifts her nose. "Sheri Ann at the boutique told me you two had been there and looked very cozy. I didn't want to believe it, but then Chance delayed his flight to England so he could leave after work. He hates to take evening flights, what with the five-hour time difference. Still, I wasn't sure until I asked you to deliver those papers to me after hours, and you claimed to have plans."

Chance comes up beside me, scowling at Raisa. "You wouldn't have evicted me from the hotel unless you had ironclad proof."

"I do." She picks up a manila envelope that was lying on her desk and hands it to him. "Did you really think I wouldn't have a contact at the hotel? Desk clerks are woefully underpaid and easy to tempt with a few hundred dollars."

Chance opens the envelope and slides out the contents. It's a single sheet of paper. When he flips it over, I see the paper is a photograph that was clearly produced on a desktop printer, like the one sitting on a table behind Raisa.

The photo is of us. Me and Chance. In the hotel lobby. Kissing passionately.

Raisa points at the door. "Get out. Both of you. Any personal effects you've left here will be sent to you."

Did her voice quiver the teeniest bit? I search her face and realize her lips are trembling too, barely enough to notice. When I glance at the trash can beside her desk, I see a bunch of balled-up tissues inside it.

Maybe her anger is an act, or a cover for the fact she finally understands Chance will never take her back. I hope that's the case, because if it is, she might get over the initial shock and decide not to ruin our lives after all.

Chance stares at her for a moment, then tosses the photo onto her desk, takes my hand, and leads me out of the building. I tell him he can stay at my apartment for as long as he needs, but he says he has "things to take care of" and leaves as soon as he's dropped me off at my place. His bags are waiting by the kitchen bar. The hotel must have sent them over right after we left the suite, and Kyle must've accepted the delivery.

My brother has gone to work, so I'm alone in the apartment.

In a numb haze, I change into sweats and eat ice cream straight from the container while watching soap operas. I've never watched a soap in my life, and I have no idea what's going on in the complicated stories. It doesn't matter. I'm not paying attention to the TV.

Am I really blacklisted?

The only thing I can do is wait for Chance and hope everything works out the way he swore it would last night.

Chapter Fifteen

Chance

When I get back to the office, the one I was fired from by my ex-wife, Raisa has already left for court. Security won't let me into the office, anyway. I walk back to where I parked the car I hired after leaving Elena and sit there trying to figure out what to do next. I need to talk to Raisa, but she might be in court for hours with her latest divorce case. As much as I want to go back to Elena, I'd planned to have everything sorted first.

Since I can't think of anything else, I decide to get started on my plans for the future. I hope my future includes Elena, but I can't be sure of anything today. Elena is kind and compassionate, the sort who never wants to hurt anyone, even the woman who made her work life miserable. I know Elena admires Raisa professionally, but I think on some level she feels sorry for my ex-wife.

It's all my fault. I should never have come back here.

But if I hadn't, I would never have met Elena.

Though I make a few calls, my plans aren't sorted quite yet, and I finally realize I should go back to Elena's apartment. All my things are there, and I need a place to relax—or try to—so I can figure out what the hell I can do to stop Raisa from ruining Elena's career.

The drive from the office seems to take forever.

I have to park two blocks away from Elena's apartment building, and by the time I knock on her door, I'm in need of a lie-down. Two blocks isn't far to walk, but this day has already taken its toll on me. I can't imagine how Elena feels, but at least I'll be here to support her.

She opens the door and throws her arms around me. "I'm so glad you're back."

A relief so intense it makes me feel weak rushes through me. How can I miss Elena so much after ninety minutes away from her? It seems ridiculous, but I did miss her very much. Maybe it's the stress of our confrontation with Raisa, or guilt over not doing what Elena had wanted and telling Raisa about our relationship sooner. Or maybe it's just Elena. Her smile. The way her hair smells. The feel of her body pressed to mine.

"Come on," she says, taking my hand and leading me into the apartment. "You look like you need booze and a comfy sofa."

"I do. But isn't it rather early for a drink?"

"Not today it isn't."

While I take a seat on the sofa, she gets two glasses and a bottle of brandy from the kitchen. Elena pours our drinks and leaves the bottle on the coffee table. I relax into the overstuffed cushions, rest my feet on the table, and lay my arm across the sofa's back. Elena snuggles up under my arm. The tension inside me disintegrates before I even take my first sip of brandy.

After my second sip, I say, "Don't worry about Raisa. I'll talk to her later and convince her not to blacklist you. She's angry. Once she calms down, she'll see reason. Arguing with a judge always makes her feel better, so I'm sure she'll be in a more reasonable mood after court today."

"I hope so." Elena swirls the liquor in her glass, staring down at it, but doesn't drink. "Otherwise, my career is toast. If the legendary Raisa Volkov wants you gone, you'll disappear from the New York legal scene for good."

"She's not the queen of New York law." I set my glass on the table beside the sofa. "If you want to stay in New York, I understand. But there is another option."

"Yeah, I can move to Greenland."

"That won't be necessary." I curl my finger under her chin and urge her to look at me. When her eyes roll up to focus on me, for a moment I can't speak. She's so beautiful, so sweet, so clever and brave and wonderful. "Come work with me, Elena."

She blinks several times, her eyes large. "I don't understand. You're unemployed too."

"I'm going to start my own practice. There's a lovely little town in New Hampshire where the only attorney within fifty miles is retiring. I met that attorney, Garth Leonard, at a conference a few months ago. We got to talking, and he asked if I'd like to take over his practice." I tuck a lock of hair behind her ear. "I spoke to him this morning. He's retiring in two weeks, and I'd like to accept his offer."

"You're moving to New Hampshire?"

I place a gentle kiss on her forehead. "Only if you come with me."

She sits up and gazes out the window, gnawing on her lip.

"This won't be a glamorous law office," I tell her. "It's a quiet little town full of good people who need legal advice but can't pay top dollar for it. Garth Leonard does have a few wealthy clients, but most are average people. If you want a high-powered career, you'll be better off staying in New York. But I'm hoping you might want what I want—a good life, regardless of prestige or social position."

I've known her for not quite a month, but I feel like I understand what she really wants deep down. If I'm wrong, I'll lose her. If I'm right…

"You don't like New York, do you?" she asks, still gazing out the window.

I swallow a mouthful of brandy before I answer. "I don't dislike it. But being with you has made me realize I want a quieter life, like I had with my family before I moved to America and got involved with Raisa."

"If I say no, you'll go to New Hampshire anyway."

"No, of course not. I'll stay with you either way."

She swerves her head to look at me. "You would give up what you want to be with me?"

"Yes, of course." I clasp her hands between mine. "I love you, Elena."

"How can you be sure after such a short time?"

"I trust what I feel." Lifting her hands, I kiss her fingertips. "I needed fourteen months to decide I loved Raisa. After a week with you, I knew what we have is real, more real than anything I found with her. I trust you, I want you, and I love you."

Her lips twitch upward at the corners twice, then she lets the smile take over, lighting her up from the inside out. "I love you too, Chance."

Something like euphoria sweeps through me, and I can't stop myself from dragging her in for a deep, passionate kiss. She tastes like brandy, but she feels like heaven.

When we separate our mouths, I ask, "So which is it, New York or New Hampshire?"

Elena smiles, and the sweetness of it stabs a wonderful pain into my chest. "I grew up in a small town, and I'd love to go to New Hampshire with you."

I grin, and then I carry her into the bedroom and make love to her. We don't leave her bed for two hours. That's when I receive a text message from Raisa asking me to meet her at her apartment. Elena tells me to go and get it over with.

After kissing Elena goodbye for five minutes, I head for Raisa's.

She answers the door still dressed for court, in her favorite black skirt and jacket. "Come in, Chance."

No "darling" this time. And her entire demeanor, from her facial expression to her posture, is somber.

We go into the living room. She sits in the armchair, while I take the sofa.

Raisa stares down at her hands, wringing them like she has something stuck on her skin and can't get it off. "You and Elena must hate me. I've been horrible to you both. I'm sorry."

I can't speak. Raisa Volkov never apologizes. When I open my mouth, about to try to speak, she holds up a hand to silence me.

"Let me talk first," she says, with no trace of her usual haughtiness. "Ever since you filed for divorce, I've convinced myself you would come back to me eventually, that the separation was a phase you needed to go through. When the final decree came through, it was like a sucker punch. I still refused to accept you didn't want me anymore."

"I know."

She rubs her neck, wincing. "When I introduced you to Elena, I knew you were attracted to her. How could you not be? She's very pretty and very intelligent. Still, I didn't think you would actually get involved with her. I've been in denial for weeks, until I couldn't ignore the truth anymore. Paying the hotel desk clerk to spy on you was unforgivable."

"What are you getting at, Raisa? I know all of this already."

She squeezes her eyes shut, sucks in a breath, and looks at me. "You can both have your jobs back, if you want them. I haven't blacklisted Elena, and I never will. In fact, I'll give her a glowing recommendation if she'd rather find a position at another firm."

I watch her for several seconds, unsure whether to trust her change in attitude. "Are you saying you've accepted that I don't love you anymore?"

"Yes. I know it's over between us, and I hope Elena will make you happy. I know I failed at that."

"The problem was that you never really wanted me back. You hate to lose, and for a divorce lawyer to get divorced was too big a loss for you to stand for."

She nods. "I have an appointment with a therapist. Maybe she can help me work out why I could never be satisfied even when I had a good man in my life."

"Your change in attitude is awfully sudden." I probably sound suspicious, and I am.

"I know it seems that way, but this has been coming for a while." She clasps her hands on her lap, swallows visibly, and says, "Everyone at the office heard our argument this morning. Now they look at me like I'm insane, and they've been literally tiptoeing around me. I took a good, hard look at myself today, and I didn't like what I saw."

A clock on a nearby table ticks softly, but the silence between us is deep, the distance vast. We don't really know each other anymore. After more than a year of denial, I believe Raisa has finally accepted the truth.

"I'm glad you've come to your senses," I tell her, "but I won't be coming back to work with you. Neither will Elena. We talked about it earlier and realized we want something else."

A sigh rushes out of Raisa, deflating her posture. "I understand. And I wish you well, Chance. Elena too. She really was the best paralegal I ever hired."

We say goodbye, for the last time, and I rush back to Elena's apartment.

She hugs me so hard I can't breathe, but I don't care. I bury my face in her hair and lift her off the ground. We kiss, then I drag her down onto the sofa and show her exactly how much she means to me, making her come three times right there in the living room. Watching her climaxes roll through her again and again is the most beautiful thing I've ever seen.

When Kyle comes home that evening, we tell him the news.

He grins, slaps me on the arm, and hugs Elena. "That's awesome, Ellie."

She eyes him like she isn't convinced he means that. "Are you sure you're okay with this? I'm moving to another state."

"New Hampshire isn't that far away. I can live in the dorms next semester. It might be fun."

"But you'll be all alone."

He laughs. "Come on, Elena, I'm an adult now. You don't have to take care of me all the time. Besides, I have a girlfriend and bros I'm real tight with. I won't be a poor little orphan boy all alone in the big city."

"Yeah, I know," she says, her eyes tearing up. "But I'll miss you."

"I'll visit you guys, don't worry." He hugs her again. "Go be happy."

Kyle lets go of Elena and pulls me into a quick, rough hug. "You better take care of my sister. If you make her unhappy, I'll have to do something about it."

"Understood."

He slaps my arm again. "Relax, that's the standard brother thing to say. You're cool, and I've never seen Elena smile as much as she does since you showed up."

I've been smiling a lot more too, since the night I first laid eyes on Elena and she recited German numbers to me. Our future is about to unfold, and I don't mind not knowing exactly what might happen. Whatever comes, we'll handle it together.

Once Kyle goes into his bedroom, I pull Elena into my arms. "Count to twelve in German for me."

She smiles and shakes her head. "Oh please, you couldn't have been serious when you said that was cute."

"I didn't say it was cute." I nibble on her earlobe. "I said I loved the way you pronounce the number twelve. Say it again, and I'll give you the sort of kiss that will make you come for me so hard you'll scream."

"A kiss can't do that."

"Sure it can." I flip her onto her back on the sofa, strip off her sweatpants and knickers, and squeeze between her thighs. I admire the rosy flesh in front of me, groaning with hunger when I see how wet she already is for me. "The lips I want to kiss aren't on your mouth."

"Oh, that kind of kiss." She links her hands above her head, shimmying her hips. "*Zwölf.*"

And I kiss her in the most intimate way imaginable.

I can do this every night for the rest of our lives. I can hold her, kiss her, shag her, love her, and so much more. None of this would've happened if I hadn't seen her drop her head onto the hotel bar, looking miserable and adorable at the same time.

When Elena comes, that light she always has inside her explodes like a star going supernova. I want to watch her do that over and over, all night, every night, forever.

"Let's go to bed," I say. "And you can tell me what sort of house you want us to live in."

Epilogue

Elena
Three months later

I lounge on a cushy chaise, on the patio of the beautiful house owned by Chance's family, and watch my brother playing football with three Brits. Chance and his brothers got a kick out of teasing Kyle when they asked if he'd like to join them for a football match. Being American, Kyle assumed they meant the game in which large men wear huge shoulder pads and helmets and they carry an oval ball.

"Do you know how to play?" Reese had asked. He's the youngest brother, and according to Chance, the one who loves to orchestrate practical jokes.

"Yeah," Kyle had said. "I love football. Played it in high school."

"Are you a good kicker?" Dane asked. He's the middle brother and the most reserved one, Chance had told me, though he'd also said Dane enjoys a good joke as much as anybody.

"Oh yeah," Kyle said. "I love a good kickoff."

Chance chimed in to say, "Now remember, there's no getting your kit off until after the final whistle, or you'll be severely penalized. We play by FIFA rules."

"Fee-what?"

"The Fédération Internationale de Football Association," the love of my life said as if my little brother ought to know that already. "How can you be an experienced footballer if you don't know about FIFA?"

"Well… uh…" Kyle shrugged. "I guess you Brits have your own football association and gave it a Frenchy name. In America, we've got the NFL."

Reese grinned. "Does that stand for Nutters and Fucking Losers?"

And that's when I stepped in. They'd had their fun, but my poor brother was looking more confounded every second. The Dixon boys can harass Kyle more later, when we eat lunch and he hears the bizarre British names for the dishes offered to us.

"They're talking about soccer," I said. "Brits call it football."

"Are you serious?" Kyle asked. "These uptight dickwads think soccer is football? That's beyond lame, guys. Pushing a ball around with your feet is a game for girls."

Now, twenty minutes later, the four of them are kicking a ball around like old friends. They all decided to go shirtless for the game, calling it "the British way," though I know they were teasing my brother again with that claim. Kyle has already tackled each of the Dixon boys at least once, twice for Chance. I think my brother enjoys ramming into my fiancé. Chance can handle it. He might be a lawyer, but he's no slouch at athletics. With a body like that, of course he's a fantastic athlete.

He certainly has all the moves in bed.

I watch the guys for a while longer, admiring my hunky soon-to-be-hubby's bod—and, okay, his brothers' bods too. The Dixons are one handsome bunch. Their parents are good-looking too, but not buff. I met them this morning when Chance and I first arrived at the Dixons' home in the countryside, not far from London. William and Claire Dixon had greeted me with enthusiastic hugs. Nobody mentioned Raisa, but Chance's mom had said how happy she was that her son had found such a sweet girl. I took that as an oblique reference to his ex-wife, the antithesis of me.

Claire and William had excused themselves after that so they could make lunch for everyone. The Dixons might live in a big, spiffy old house, but they still do their own cooking. They have a housekeeper to do everything else.

The boys wander back to the patio. They'd left their shirts in a pile on the grass, and each grabs his on the way back to me. All but Reese pull their shirts back on.

Kyle tugs on his shirt while he trots up to me. He winks, then stretches out on the patio on his back, hands linked under his head.

Reese drops onto a chair, holding the soccer ball in both hands and turning it around and around. His shirt is draped over his shoulder.

Dane sits in a chair beside Reese and takes off his glasses to wipe sweat from his forehead with his shirt.

Chance takes the other chaise, next to me, and leans in to kiss me, holding his lips against mine for a blessedly long moment.

"Lucky me," I say when he pulls away. "Surrounded by gorgeous, sweaty Brits."

"Having fun?" he asks.

"Oh yeah. I could get used to this." I glance at his brothers, then smirk at Chance. "I could have my own harem."

"No, you cannot." Chance lifts my left hand to kiss the diamond ring glittering on my third finger. "You're my slave, remember?"

"How could I forget?"

Kyle snorts. "Oh please. Will you two ever get over the slave thing? It was cute in the beginning, but I'm about ready to report Chance to the cops for running a sex trafficking ring."

Yeah, ever since Chance and I got engaged, Kyle has relished every opportunity to torment us with sarcasm.

Chance's brothers are no better.

"Where can I get my own slave?" Reese asks, still turning the ball in his hands. "I've asked for volunteers, but oddly, nobody wants to sign on for the job. How did you ever convince Elena to serve you?"

"She doesn't serve him," Dane says. "She services him, like an old car that needs constant maintenance."

"And plenty of lubrication," Reese adds with a sly grin and a wink.

"That's enough," Chance says. "You've harassed the Americans enough. Give them at least an hour to recover before you start in again."

Looking at Chance, who's sweaty and smeared with dirt, I can't resist. I have to say, "You need a shower, honey. Your personal mechanic insists on it."

"Give him a good wash and wax, Elena," Rees says, tossing the ball onto the lawn. "I need some maintenance too."

I lay my hand on Chance's thigh. "Sorry, I only service one vehicle."

"Enough car jokes," Chance says. He gets up and offers me his hand. "Let's go, love. I'm feeling filthy."

I let him lead me into the house and to the bathroom. Within thirty seconds, we're both naked. I thank heaven the Dixons have a large bathroom with a shower plenty big enough for me and my honey.

He grabs a bar of soap. "You first."

Chance and I have showered together many times, since we moved to a house in New Hampshire that has a generous-size shower. We've got our law practice there too. Sure, I'm the lowly paralegal in the eyes of most people. But Chance and I are partners in every way that counts—at work, at home, and in our hearts.

A few months ago, in a hotel bar, I'd been offered one hot Chance and taken it. I will never regret that. And yeah, that pun is intentional.

During lunch, we all talk about the wedding. It's in two weeks, and we're having it in America so Chance's family can see our home in New Hampshire. They've never been to America before, since Chance always flew to England to see them—because Raisa hadn't wanted to entertain guests. I'm looking forward to hosting the Dixons, and our house is plenty big enough to hold Chance's parents and brothers along with Kyle and his girlfriend, not to mention our friends.

When I explain about the guest rooms in our house, Reese says, "You used to live in New York City, didn't you? That's where you met Chance."

"Yes, I shared an apartment with the most annoying roommate ever," I reply, flashing Kyle a sarcastic grin. "That would be my darling brother."

Kyle points his fork at me. "Watch it, sister. I know what you and Chance used to do on the living room sofa."

I expect Reese to make an off-color joke, but instead he says, "I'd love to see New York."

The conversation moves on to other wedding-related topics.

Later, Reese corners me and Chance in the sitting room.

"About your apartment," he says to me. "Have you given it up? Or rented it to someone else?"

"No, I haven't sublet it or given it up. Kyle might want to live there over the summer, before he goes back to the dorm in the fall."

Reese studies both me and Chance for several seconds, then he asks, "Could I stay there?"

"At my apartment?" I glance at my fiancé, but Chance simply shrugs. He's leaving the decision up to me. I tell Reese, "Sure, I guess you can do that. We left all the furniture there, so it'll be kind of like a cozy hotel."

"You mean it?" Reese asks. "I can stay there?"

"It's all yours."

"Brilliant!" he says, grinning, his eyes alight with excitement. "Imagine all the girls I can meet there."

Oh boy, those New York ladies are in for it. When Reese Dixon lands in America, every unmarried woman better hold on to her panties. He'll melt them with one wicked smile.

Chance certainly had that effect on me. And he still does, every day.

Reese trots out of the room shouting, "Dane! Guess what? I'm going to shag a New York girl just like Chance did."

Chance arches one brow at me. "Do you have any idea what you've done?"

"Probably not."

Heaven help those New York girls.

Chance's Version

One Hot Chance
Chapter One

I've never believed in fate, so I can't blame the universe for the trouble I find myself knee-deep in tonight. Why did I ever agree to work for my ex-wife? Even temporarily? After meeting with her this evening to discuss my new role in her firm, Raisa Volkov & Associates, I don't feel excited about my new job or even interested in it. No, I feel like the blokes I see in the hotel restaurant who look like they've just had their balls strangled by my ex-wife. Her law firm is in the building across the street. And this is the closest place where those men can get drunk.

Rubbing the back of my neck, I stop halfway across the lobby to consider those blokes who are downing hard liquor like it's the first liquid they've had in months. Maybe I should join them.

Yes, wouldn't I feel so much better tossing back glass after glass of vodka in a bar filled with lonely, pathetic men whose testicles have shrunk to the size of peanuts.

I scan the restaurant, growing more depressed by the second—until I spot a woman sitting on a stool at the bar. She looks as miserable as I feel. Her hair glistens in the subdued lighting, and the way her skirt molds to her body shows off her beautiful figure.

She glances around the restaurant, and her expression becomes even more miserable.

That look. I must wear the same one. Seeing that woman, so alone and dispirited, makes me want to march over there and cheer her up.

How will I do that, exactly?

She drops her head onto the bar, facedown, and waves her hand when the bartender says something to her.

The impulse to go over there becomes too powerful to ignore. I force myself to walk at a normal pace instead of rushing like I want to do. When I reach the woman, she still has her face on the bar.

"Are you all right there?" I ask. She doesn't move or make a sound, so I lay a hand on her arm. Her creamy skin is soft as silk. "I said are you all right?"

"Mm-hm." She peels her face off the bar, blinking rapidly like she's struggling to make sense of what she sees.

The beauty of her face and of those caramel-colored eyes steals my breath and my ability to speak. All I manage to do is smile.

She smiles back. "I'm fine, but thanks for asking. I love polite British men."

I lift one brow and can't help smirking. Didn't she just say she loves me? Well, men *like* me. British men. "How do you know I'm polite? I've barely spoken five words to you."

"Seven, actually. Unless you count the ones you said twice, which would mean eleven words. Not including what you said a second ago."

A charming blush colors her cheeks. She shifts her gaze this way and that, then bites down on her bottom lip. She seems embarrassed by what she said, which only makes me want to drag her into my arms and kiss her. What on earth am I doing with this woman? I should be upstairs getting pissed in my suite, not flirting with an American woman who makes my cock get hard when she smiles. I should walk away.

But I lean against the bar because I've clearly lost my mind. "It's comforting to know you're intelligent enough to count to at least eleven."

"I can count to twelve in German."

"Can you?" I want to hear more of her lovely voice, and I don't give a toss if she babbles nonsense to me. "Let me hear it."

She slants toward me. "*Eins, zwei, drei, vier, fünf, sechs, sieben, acht, neun, zehn, elf, zwölf.*"

"Say *zwölf* again. I love the way you pronounce it." I lean in so close I can see the darker rims around her golden-brown irises, and I brush hair away from her face. My fingers graze her skin. "Say it again, please."

The sexy angel grins. "See, you are polite."

"For the moment." I trail my fingertips down her cheek to the corner of her mouth. "Say *zwölf* again, and I'll kiss you."

I *need* to kiss her. Those lips tempt me, and suddenly, I want to do much more than kiss her.

"What if I don't want to kiss you?" she asks, though her tone is sultry.

I drag one finger across her mouth, slowly, sensuously. "You do."

She licks my finger. "*Zwölf.*"

Fuck, the way she says that word, in that throaty tone… I can't stop myself. I slide a hand into her hair, pull her face closer, and kiss her.

Her lips, they're soft and warm and faintly slick. I explore those lips with my mouth and tongue, sampling her skin that tastes like mint. Maybe she uses flavored lip balm or lipstick or whatever they call it. I don't care, because all I want is to feel this woman's mouth on mine for days, weeks, maybe forever, until she melts in my arms. When I slip my tongue between her lips, she does just that. She melts into me, her breasts mounding against my chest, while I tease and devour her until my cock is so hard that the need to fuck her overpowers all my common sense.

I pull away, but only a little. "Come to my room with me."

"What?"

"Come with me, upstairs, to my room." I catch her bottom lip with my teeth, swipe my tongue over it, and release her flesh little by little. "You're the most adorable creature I've ever seen, and I want to make love to you all night long."

"Oh God, yes. Let's go to your room."

I glance at the margarita sitting on the bar. "Do you want to finish your drink first?"

"No, I'm done with it."

Thank heaven for that. I can't wait one more minute to have her, so I sling an arm around her waist as she slides off her stool and hooks a large purse over her shoulder. I guide her across the lobby to the elevator with her sensual body hugged to mine and my hand on her hip.

The elevator doors open. Three people hurry out, leaving the car empty.

We get in, and the doors glide shut.

I turn toward her, still hugging that luscious body. "Can't wait. I'm on the nineteenth floor, which means we have time."

"Time for what?"

Can't speak anymore. I back her up to the wall and possess her mouth, thrusting my tongue deep, until she moans and latches her arms around my neck. Christ, she tastes incredible, feels incredible, and the sensation of her body molded to mine drives me past the line that separates reason from madness. I swipe my tongue around hers like I can't survive without the flavor of her in my mouth, like her soft lips and her agile tongue are the only things keeping me alive.

She moans again, the sound rougher and needier.

Fuck, I want her. Need to be inside her. So I shove her skirt up, tear off her knickers, and unzip my trousers while I seal my mouth around her nipple. Her blouse and bra separate my mouth from her skin, but nothing can stop me now. I suckle her stiff peak, and she arches her back and clutches my head. I have just enough sense left to remember to get a condom out of my pocket. I always have one with me, though I've never needed it until tonight, and I give up her flesh only long enough to get the condom on.

Scraping my teeth across her nipple, I hoist one of her legs up and drive into her.

A cry bursts out of her.

I push inside her again and again, desperate to penetrate her so deeply that our bodies might become one. I love the feel of her hot, velvety flesh surrounding my cock and her hairs tickling my skin. Maybe I should hold back, take more time to make sure she comes, but I can't control my lust for this beautiful girl who recited German numbers to me. I consume her with a kind of unrelenting passion I've never experienced before, my movements growing wilder, greedier, almost rough. The need to come is nearly overpowering, but I want this to go on forever, with her body wrapped around me while the slapping of our flesh as we collide becomes a frantic rhythm. She bounces on my cock, and I grunt every time I slam her into the wall.

She cries out at the instant her body clinches me, over and over, like her climax will never end. It pushes me over the edge too, and I come so hard for so long that my ears start to ring because I've stopped breathing. I unleash everything I have inside her lush body, then we both go limp.

The beautiful woman in my arms sags against the wall.

I nuzzle her neck, with my cock still buried inside her, and pepper light kisses on her skin as I make my way up to her ear. I want more time with her, more than a quick shag in an elevator.

A phone rings.

Fuck, it's mine.

Digging my mobile out of my pocket, I answer it. "What do you want?"

"Chance, darling," my ex-wife says. "We need to get together and talk more about your new duties at my firm."

"I'm busy," I snap, sounding annoyed because I am. The last thing I want to do is see or speak to Raisa. "We can talk about this Monday."

The elevator stops. The doors open.

And the woman I want to spend the night with hurries into the hallway.

"Wait," I call out to her.

She turns toward me, her lips compressed even while they seem to quiver slightly.

I hold the phone to my chest and speak to her. "Please wait. I'm sorry about this." Raisa shouts something, though my chest muffles her words. I hiss into the phone, "Not now."

I look at the woman with the caramel eyes again, wanting to beg her to stay but unable to speak the words.

She shakes her head and rushes away.

"Goodbye, Raisa," I growl into the phone, then I disconnect the call and shove the mobile into my pocket.

Zipping up my trousers, I race after my mystery woman.

She's hurrying through the stairwell door. I get there a second after it closes, shove it open, and sprint down one flight. She's there, sitting on the last step, with her face cradled in her hands.

A sigh rushes out of me. I haven't lost her.

She peeks through her fingers at me.

I kneel beside her. "I'm sorry about that. I shouldn't have answered my phone."

The loveliest woman I've ever seen shrugs, still peeking at me through her fingers.

Gently, I pry her hands away and clasp them in mine. "Please come to my room. I'd love to spend all night with you. You're the most enchanting woman I've ever met."

Her mobile chimes, like she has a text message, but she seems hesitant to look at it.

"You can check that," I say. "It's all right."

"Sorry." She pulls out her mobile and reads the text.

Her expression turns pinched, and she glances up at me through her lashes, biting down on her lip.

"You need to go," I say.

She winces. "Yeah. It's, um, a family thing I forgot about."

"May I know your name?"

"Elena." She rummages in her purse, bringing out a slip of paper and a pen, then she scribbles something on the paper. Offering it to me, she says, "Here's my number."

"Thank you, Elena." I love the way her name rolls off my tongue, as sweet and enticing as the woman herself. "I'm Chance, by the way."

We both get up.

I kiss her cheek. "I'll ring you tomorrow, if that's all right."

"Yes, I'd like that."

She walks away from me, disappearing through the door at the bottom of the next flight of stairs.

The next day, when I ring the number she gave me, I wind up speaking to the gruff owner of an Italian deli. He's never heard of Elena.

Maybe fate does exist—and it doesn't like me at all.

One Hot Chance
Chapter Three

The shock of seeing Chance again has waned, a little bit, but I still want to crawl onto his lap like I imagined doing the other night. Luckily, I have lots of work to distract me from thinking about Chance for the next three hours. Well, maybe I think about him once or twice. Or…fifty times.

Then I have to see him because he calls me to ask for a file.

I walk into Chance's office and set the file on his desk. "Here's the information you need, sir. Do you require anything else?"

He waves toward the chairs on my side of the desk. "Sit, Elena, please. I'd like to talk to you."

Should I sit down? Is it safe for my libido? I eye the chairs, trying to decide whether I can control myself in his presence, since I'm not sure a desk is enough of a barrier. Finally, I settle onto the edge of a chair. At least this way I can run out the door if his silky British accent makes me too lustful.

"This is awkward, I know," he says. "But pretending we haven't met before, haven't known each other intimately before, isn't the answer."

"What we did wasn't intimate. It was a quickie with a stranger."

"I like you, Elena. Is that a crime?"

"No offense, Mr. Dixon, but you don't know me. I don't know you either."

"Oh, I know a few relevant facts about you." He retrieves a folder from a drawer and lays it open on the desk. "I know you're twenty-seven, single, and you share an apartment with your brother. You grew up in a small town in Wisconsin and graduated from Northwestern, summa cum laude. You were accepted to Columbia Law School but backed out. Since you had already moved to New York by that point, you stayed and worked as a secretary in a law office until you received your paralegal certification."

Holy shit, how does he know so much about me? I stare at him for several seconds, not blinking, my hands clamped over my knees, before I can manage to speak. "How do you know all that?"

"Raisa is very thorough. Before she hires anyone, she has a complete background check done on them." He taps the open folder. "This is yours. Raisa gave it to me."

"That's… kind of creepy."

"It's business. Raisa is, admittedly, rather paranoid." He closes the file. "But I want to know more about you, all the things that don't show up in a background check."

"Do I get to run a background check on you?"

"No need." He leans back in his chair. "Ask me anything you like."

"How about all the same facts you have on me?"

"Of course." He keeps his gaze on me while he speaks, which makes me start to heat up in ways that are so not professional. "I'm thirty-four, divorced, not seeing anyone at the moment." He hits me with that swoon-worthy smile and winks. "Unless you agree to have dinner with me."

Yes, yes, please yes. I want to say that, but instead I shake my head and struggle not to smile. "Continue with the facts, please."

"All right. I grew up in the English countryside, in a quaint little village. I attended Oxford but got my law degree from Yale. I live alone. Since this job is only temporary, I'm staying in the hotel across the street, the one where you and I met." He shrugs one shoulder. "I didn't graduate with honors, like you, but I did well enough academically. I've been working for a medium-size firm in Chicago, but I've taken a sabbatical to lend a hand here."

"Until Raisa hires a permanent replacement for Lucas Miller." When he nods, I ask, "What exactly happened with him?"

I've heard through the office grapevine that Raisa and Lucas Miller hated each other, but that's all the details I've gotten so far.

"Ten days ago, Lucas Miller resigned," Chance says. "Lucas never got on with Raisa, and her recent behavior pushed him over the edge. He quit without notice. That left Raisa in a desperate situation, since several of Lucas's clients have court dates coming up soon."

"That's why you're here."

"Yes. I'm the emergency reinforcements. I've done a fair bit of corporate law, so I was qualified to take over as lead counsel."

"I thought attorneys couldn't quit a case unless the client's doing something wrong."

"That's true," he says, swallowing hard. His features tighten, but then he seems to reach a decision and his whole demeanor relaxes. "Lucas Miller didn't just resign. He was arrested ten days ago, on a Saturday night, after he went to Raisa's apartment and started screaming at her. He also tried to hit her, but she slammed the door in his face before he could. Lucas had a severe mental breakdown and was taken to the hospital."

"Holy cow. I had no idea. I heard somebody say he 'went off the deep end,' but I figured it was an exaggeration."

Chance shakes his head. "Unfortunately, it's not. Raisa contacted a judge she knows well to get permission for me to take over Miller's cases."

"Now I feel kind of bad for thinking Raisa drives me crazy. I meant it as a metaphor, not the actual truth." I slide back in my chair and cross my legs. "Raisa is a lot older than you, isn't she?"

"Yes, she's forty-eight. I imagine you read the New Yorker piece on her last year."

I nod. "The article described her as a powerhouse player on the New York legal scene. I already knew about her, though, about how she built her own firm from the ground up and became the queen of divorce court. That's why I wanted to become a lawyer, and it's why I wanted to work here. She's amazing." I screw my mouth up when I think about that article. "The journalist who wrote that piece neglected to mention Raisa is a raging bitch."

"She wasn't like that until recently." Chance hesitates, seeming to consider whether to tell me something like he had a moment ago. "Our divorce was finalized two months ago. Raisa has always been tough, sometimes rude, but she didn't become a raging bitch until the final decree came through. It's my fault she's been terrorizing the staff."

"Uh-huh." I probably sound suspicious, because I am. "Freshly divorced sounds like big-time trouble to me. Maybe you shouldn't screw other women until you and Raisa get over each other."

"I am over her. Have been for a long time. Our divorce might've been finalized two months ago, but we were separated for more than a year before that."

"Still don't want to get in the middle of your marital problems."

As much as I want Chance—and heaven help me, I want this man like crazy—the worst thing I can do is to get between my new boss and her ex. Sounds like a sure way to get fired.

Chance and I watch each other for a moment, and his gaze roams over my entire body like he's taking an inventory of every part of me. The desire in his eyes and on his face is unmistakable, and when he roves that gaze over my breasts in slow motion, they tighten and tingle. I need his mouth on me again, his cock inside me, his hands all over me.

"Why didn't you go to law school?" he asks.

"None of your damn business." I stand up and square my shoulders. Since I can't get naked with him on his desk, I don't need to be in his office anymore. Plus, I don't like talking about the reasons why I skipped law school. "What can I do for you this morning, Mr. Dixon? I'm sure you need to get up to speed with Lucas Miller's active cases."

He rubs his neck. "Yes, please pull all the files and bring them to me. I'll get started on the five hundred and thirty-two emails clogging my inbox."

"That's my job. I sort through them, delete the spam and other useless stuff, and let you know when it's safe to open your inbox."

"I appreciate that, Elena. Thank you."

"You're welcome." I turn toward the door but pause on the threshold. "Would you like coffee? I get Raisa's every morning."

"No, thank you. But I'd love a cuppa."

"A cup of what? You said no to coffee."

"Tea. That's what cuppa means."

It's the cutest word I've ever heard for drinking tea, and he's the cutest man I've ever met. A smile tugs at my lips. "I'm guessing that's the British way to say it. Sorry, but you are the first British person I've ever met. I don't think watching Henry Cavill movies counts."

"Probably not. I would love that cuppa, though. If it's not too much trouble."

"Of course not." That smile tugs harder and tightens my cheeks. "I'm your slave, after all."

Why did I say that? Now I'm having visions of every possible way he could make me his slave.

"Should I close the door or leave it open?" I ask.

"Leave it open."

I get a mug of tea for Chance, plus a packet of sugar, a little container of milk, and a cookie. Isn't that how Brits like it? Then I put it all on a tray and carry it into his office, setting the tray on his desk right in front of him. "Your tea, Mr. Dixon. I know this probably isn't how you Brits do teatime, but it's the best we've got here in the good old US of A."

"It's wonderful, thank you." He picks up the mug, reading the words painted on it. "The law is hot. Am I meant to read between the lines?"

"No, it's a novelty mug, nothing more. You're lucky I didn't give you the one that says 'you can bang my gavel anytime.' I think an intern left that one here."

He sets down the mug and picks up the cookie.

"Brits like tea and biscuits, right?" I ask. "And biscuits are cookies, aren't they? If not, then I've been seriously misled by all those BBC shows I watched."

"This is perfect." He takes a bite of the cookie. "Peanut butter?"

"Sorry, that's all I could find." I tilt forward, peering down at his mug. "I hope the tea is okay, because all we have is Earl Grey or eggnog flavor. I'm sure that one's been lying around since Christmas. So I figured you'd prefer Earl Grey."

He pours milk into his tea and takes a sip. "Just right. Thank you."

I wrinkle my nose. "No sugar?"

"No."

"Yech." *Oh jeez, Elena, way to impress your hot new boss.*

He chuckles. "You really are the most adorable creature."

"Better get those files," I say and hurry out the door.

I swear if he smiles at me and chuckles that way again, I can't be held responsible for my actions. It's completely his fault.

Chance Dixon will ruin me for sure.

One Hot ROOMIE

Hot Brits, Book Two

Chapter One

Reese

I dig the key out of my pocket and unlock the door, pushing it open to walk into my new flat—temporary flat, loaned to me by my brother's fiancée, for the sole purpose of finding an American girl to shag. All right, maybe that isn't the reason I gave Chance and Elena. My brother and his almost wife wouldn't have lent me this flat otherwise. When I'd announced to Dane, my other brother, that I was going to shag an American girl, no one took me seriously. Everyone heard me shout it, but they know I love to make jokes.

This time, I'm not joking. That's my plan. Find, win over, and sleep with a New York woman.

Why not? It's a bit of fun, nothing more. A holiday from my life which has started to, as my almost sister-in-law might say, suck royally.

"Another hot British guy in the Big Apple," Elena had said when she and Chance saw me off at the airport, for my big holiday in the US. "Try not to leave a trail of broken hearts. You Dixon boys are impossible to resist."

My brother found a wife in America, but I'm not after that. Women never want to date me, much less marry me, because they know I'm good for one thing. All I need is a girl in my bed.

Well, the bed is optional.

I drop my bag on the floor beside the sofa and turn in a circle to get the full view of my new temporary home. Elena's flat, which she told me Americans call an apartment, has big windows with a view of the city. She says at night the view is spectacular, with all the skyscrapers glowing with lights. I suppose that view might help me win over an American girl. It can't hurt.

A bar separates the living room from the kitchen, where I see the refrigerator, the cooker—ah, the oven—and all the other items a kitchen is meant to have. Elena told me her brother Kyle, a college student, had left the refrigerator stocked with beer in case he wanted to stay here for a weekend now and then as a break from living on campus. Elena also said she left food in the fridge for me, so I won't have to live on beer. She gave me the numbers for all the best takeaway restaurants in the area too.

Elena called them takeout restaurants. I need to remember these American words if I'm going to impress the ladies instead of confusing them. Chance warned me about that problem.

He and Elena are getting married in fourteen days, in New Hampshire of all places. It's where they live now. That means I have two weeks to make my American dream come true. I jumped on a plane the day after Elena offered me her flat. Chance paid for my ticket because it was expensive to get a last-minute flight and because I'm, well, financially challenged at the moment.

Losing my job has that effect. Not my fault I'm unemployed. Sometimes it just happens, and yeah, it royally sucks.

I drop onto the sofa, stretching out lengthwise on the very puffy cushions. Elena and Kyle used to share this flat, and they've left all the furniture. That includes the sofa, two equally puffy chairs, and a table. I cross my ankles, link my hands behind my head, and sigh with contentment. Closing my eyes, I begin to formulate a plan for hunting down eligible women.

"Oh!"

A feminine voice bursts out with that exclamation.

I spring off the sofa, as surprised by the intruder as she seems to be by me. The girl has on nothing but a sleeveless white top and plaid knickers that barely cover her arse. Her honey-brown eyes are so wide with shock that I wonder if they'll pop out of their sockets.

She shakes her head furiously, making the ponytail she's gathered her blonde hair into flap like a dog's tail. "No, no, don't rape me. I'm a virgin."

"What? I—You're the intruder."

"Am not. I have a key."

"So do I." Raising the key, I wave it in the air. "Here it is."

This girl is pretty, and she's got a body I'd love to touch and kiss and lick all over. Maybe I've already found my American girl to shag.

If she'll stop accusing me of being a sexual predator.

"Kyle said I could have the place," she says. "So go. Scoot."

"Elena and Chance invited me to stay here. Alone." I inch closer but stop when her eyes get even wider. "Ring Elena and ask. She'll tell you."

The girl eyes me, her mouth contorting into the most endearing look of suspicion and curiosity. She hurries to the bar, leaning over it to grab something off the kitchen counter. The movement makes her tiny knickers slip down just enough to give me a glimpse of her arse cheeks.

She straightens, now holding a mobile phone, and taps its screen several times. Holding the phone to her ear, she keeps her suspicious gaze trained on me. "Your aura looks okay, but I better check with—Hey Elena, it's me. Did you invite some British guy to stay here? At your apartment. What? Kyle said I could."

I watch her lips pucker while she listens to whatever Elena is telling her.

"Ugh, that Kyle." The girl rolls her eyes. "He's a sweetie but such a dufus sometimes." She eyes me again. "Are you sure he's safe? Yeah, of course, but… Uh-huh. You're the one who told me I'm too trusting. How do I know this really is Reese Dixon?"

Though I'm missing half the conversation, I can guess most of what's going on. Elena is explaining to her friend that I'm not a psychotic sex offender who escaped from prison an hour ago and is desperate to get a leg over with the first female he sees.

I might be gagging for it, but not because I'm a predator. I've been experiencing a bit of a drought lately.

"Okay," the girl says. She holds her phone away from her face to peer at the screen. Her gaze flicks to me and then back to the screen. She sighs and tells Elena, "I guess he is who he claims to be. Thanks, hon."

She hangs up, sets her phone on the bar, and walks up to me. She tips her head back to meet my gaze.

The sexy little American offers me her hand. "I'm Arden Clover Pesti. It's nice to meet you, Reese Dixon."

I shake her hand, loving how soft and warm her skin is. She smells good too, like powder and cocoa butter. "It's nice to meet you too. Arden, is it? That's an unusual name, especially for a girl."

"Yeah, it's weird, I know. Blame my parents. They're big-time hippies, even though the hippie thing ended in, like, nineteen seventy-seven."

"Hippies?"

"Flower children, bohemians, beatniks, et cetera."

"I know what the word means." I love that she's keeping her hand in mine, even though the greetings are over. Her skin is like porcelain, with the faintest freckles on it. "Are you friends with Elena, then? Or just Kyle?"

"Elena is my BFF. We're like this." She pulls her palm away from mine so she can link the fingers of both hands in a locking gesture. "We're tight. Inseparable. I mean, except for the past nine months when I was in Ecuador with the Peace Corps."

"That's an admirable thing to do."

She shrugs. "I wanted to see the world, so I joined up. All I ever saw was Ecuador."

I scratch the back of my neck, wincing slightly. "Sorry I scared you. Elena said I'd have the place to myself."

"The Linwoods have definitely got some crossed wires going on."

Although Kyle Linwood had left beer in the apartment, it was Elena who'd told me that. I never actually spoke to Kyle. The Linwoods got their wires crossed for sure.

Arden smiles sweetly at me, swinging her hands at her sides. "Elena mentioned you've never been to America before."

"That's right. My brother has lived here for a long time, but I never got round to visiting him."

"Well then." She spreads her arms wide and grins. "Welcome to the United States of America and to New York City."

I can't help chuckling. She's so unbelievably adorable.

"Thank you," I say. "I feel at home already."

She comes closer, standing on her toes to look me in the eye, and her expression turns serious. "New York is awesome, but there are a few things to watch out for. Cabbies will be obnoxious. It's their way. Never buy a falafel from a street vendor who has facial hair. Never have a mixed drink, unless you want to get roofied." She leans in more, her nose almost brushing mine. "And watch out for the greys. They'll sneak up on you while you're sleeping, so keep a can of mace by your bed."

When she uses the term greys, I get the impression she's not talking about hair, which leaves me hopelessly confused.

"Oh," she says, popping upright and holding up a finger, "I almost forgot. Never flush the toilet on a Tuesday before eight a.m."

"I see." I don't, not even a little, but I'm enjoying listening to her lovely voice. She can tell me any barmy thing she wants, and I'll listen without saying a word. "I appreciate the advice."

She nods, seeming satisfied. Then she wanders off down the hall that Elena told me leads to a bathroom and two bedrooms.

Greys? What the bloody hell is that sexy, barmy girl on about?

I ring Elena to ask. "Arden told me to watch out for greys, but I have no idea what that means. I didn't want to offend her by asking."

Elena laughs. "She's a hoot, isn't she? You'll get used to her. Arden's the smartest person I've ever known, next to Chance, but she can be a little kooky."

"Are you going to tell me what greys are?"

"Maybe I should let you figure that out on your own. Or you could ask Arden. She's not easily offended."

In the background of the call, I hear my brother's voice, but I can't understand what he's saying.

"Gotta go," Elena says, "Chance needs me. He's completely hopeless when it comes to picking out place settings for the wedding, but we have to do that before we fly to England tomorrow."

"Isn't midnight an odd time to shop for place settings?" I have no idea what those are, but it sounds like a daytime shopping event.

"Yeah, but we tried shopping in the store this afternoon. Chance kept getting distracted by shiny objects like big-screen TVs. Online shopping is the only way to keep him focused."

Elena and I say goodbye, and I carry my bag down the hall.

Arden dashes out of one of the bedrooms, holding a length of aluminium foil in her hand.

"Here," she says, offering the foil to me. "You might want to sleep with that over your head to keep the microwaves from altering your brain chemistry. The waves are strongest at night."

What else can I do? Her earnest expression convinces me she's serious, so I take the foil. "Thank you. It's kind of you to look out for my brain chemistry."

I watch her perfect arse wiggle while she spins around and trots back into her room. She shuts the door, cutting off my view of her bum.

Oh yes, I'd love to shag that girl. So what if she's barking mad? I'm not going to date her, much less marry her.

Maybe my American adventure begins right now.

Chapter Two

Arden

I'm not totally insane, I swear it. Yes, I love weird things like auras and aliens, and sometimes I go a little overboard in telling people about them. It's become a kind of self-defense mechanism. I mean, after a dozen guys try to seduce you so they can try to get their grubby hands on your money, you tend to get a little paranoid. Babbling about my kooky interests turns out to be the quickest way to get rid of those losers. I don't believe everything I say, though I do believe in the possibilities of things that can never be proved. Sometimes I accidentally scare off a solid prospect with my weirdness. C'est la vie.

Yeah, those three words are the extent of my French expertise. And I got those from a Robbie Nevil song. Oh, that reminds me. I'm also obsessed with eighties pop music. So, I'm super popular on karaoke night but pretty much treated like a plague victim the rest of the time.

I flop backward onto my bed, making it bounce and creak.

Bright side? I have the most amazing best friend in the world. Elena Linwood, soon to be Elena Dixon, has always appreciated my loony side. I adore her to pieces. And her fiancé? Whew, break out the firehose. I haven't met Chance Dixon yet, but I've seen pictures of him. Not only is he smokin' hot, but according to Elena, he's also great at his job and a super nice and super fun person. She's so lucky, and I'm so happy for her.

As for Chance's brothers, I wasn't supposed to meet them until the wedding two weeks from now. Elena told me they're hot too, but that Dane is the cerebral type and Reese wants to "shag" an American girl. If I were going to walk into the living room in my undies and bump into one of them, I would've hoped for Dane. Instead, I got Reese. The hound. The one who finds women's numbers on restroom stalls and calls them. Seriously. Elena told me that.

But Reese has the most beautiful blue eyes, and I'd love to push my fingers into that thick, dark hair. Can't forget about his body either. Holy shit, he's hot. And while I was in Ecuador, I had lots of time to think about stuff and decide I don't want to be a virgin anymore. I want to have sex as soon as possible, preferably with a decent guy.

I sigh miserably, flinging my arms out like a snow angel without the snow. Reese is gorgeous, but in addition to what Elena told me about him, I'm getting a vibe from him that screams "player." How did Elena get so damn lucky with Chance?

Well, they did start out having a quickie in an elevator…

My tummy grumbles. I'd been on my way to the kitchen for a snack when Reese scared the holy living shit out of me. Maybe he's gone into his room by now. Maybe I can sneak out there and grab something to eat.

When did I become a coward? Me, the girl who bungee-jumped off a bridge. And participated in a midnight seance. And chased UFOs across the Mojave Desert. Of course, those lights in the sky had turned out to be drones operated by bored teenagers. C'est la vie, as my motto goes. Nothing ventured, no adventure gained.

I pull on my favorite T-shirt—the one that features a glow-in-the-dark alien face—and my favorite pair of shorts. They're pink, naturally, but they don't glow in the dark. I have panties that do that, though.

Appropriately dressed, I amble out into the living room.

Reese is sitting on the sofa, staring down at his phone. He smiles and types something, then notices me.

"There you are, Luscious," he says, like that adjective is my name. "Did you finally remember why you came into the living room the first time?"

"Yes. I'm hungry."

I sashay past him—honestly, sashaying is my normal way of walking, can't help it—and don't look at him. In the kitchen, I open the fridge to consider its contents. Beer. Lots of beer. *Jeez, Kyle, are you a lush or what?* Elena left some food, so I look past the four six-packs of Coors and a twelve-pack of Budweiser to decide what I want to eat. It's all healthy food, like hummus and yogurt. My tummy demands decadence, not diet stuff.

Reese comes up alongside me, peering into the fridge. "Don't you have any biscuits?"

"Do you see any cookies? I'm not hiding them in my undies."

He smiles at me, the expression full of sly humor. "You know what biscuits are. Damn that Chance. How can I confuse you the way he did with Elena if you already know all the British words? It's not fair at all."

"Trust me, I'm plenty confused."

"But I meant to charm you with my Britishisms." He glances at my skimpy shorts, his gaze traveling up to my slightly oversize T-shirt and its alien face—and to my breasts. "I want to charm the fuck out of you, Luscious."

Oh yeah, my player vibe is screaming again.

"My name is Arden." I hook a finger under his chin, lifting it until he has no choice but to look at my face. "Arden Clover Pesti. Not Luscious. Got it?"

"If you insist."

"Thank you."

He jams his hands in his jeans pockets and peers into the fridge again. "How can a girl who sleeps with aluminium foil on her head be so uptight?"

"Alu-what? I guess that's British for aluminum foil." I fold my arms over my chest. "I'm not uptight. But I don't know you, and nicknames are things friends or relatives give each other."

"Fair point." He shuts the fridge. "I'll hold off on calling you Luscious."

"I appreciate that. Now, do you like pizza?"

"Yes, I love it. Love a good takeaway, full stop."

"Takeaway's British for takeout, right?"

"Yes."

"Okeydokey," I say, turning toward the bar, where the landline phone is. "I'll order some pizza."

Reese excuses himself to go unpack and change into different clothes. The stuff he's wearing looks fine to me, but whatever. I make the pizza call and sit down on the sofa to wait for the delivery to arrive. Reese comes out of his room a few minutes later and takes a seat at the other end of the sofa from me. He's wearing pajama pants and a T-shirt that has a red rose on it with the words "England Rugby" underneath it.

Pointing at his shirt, I say, "Guess you're a rugby fan."

"Yes, but I also played rugby at school."

"Let me guess. You were the star player."

He shrugs, almost seeming shy about it. "Maybe I was, but it's a team sport. Couldn't have won games by myself."

"Is rugby like soccer?"

"Similar, but with differences. And we call that other sport football, not soccer." He glances down at his clothes. "I almost wore my Manchester United shirt."

I probably look confused. Manchester what? Honestly, why do British people assume Americans understand them?

Reese smiles. "Manchester United is a football team."

"And by football, you mean soccer."

He rolls his eyes, huffing. "No, I mean football. You Americans have a bloody stupid idea of what that word means."

"And you Brits are so damn arrogant about your sports. I mean, it's only a game."

"*Only* a game?" He gapes at me like I've suggested the sun is nothing more than a forty-watt light bulb. "Don't tell Kyle you said that. He worships American football and is obsessed with stock car racing."

"Yeah, I know. That's why I've never dated Kyle, besides the fact he's my best friend's brother."

I prop my feet on the coffee table, crossing my ankles.

Reese rakes his gaze all the way down my body to my feet and back up again. "Please tell me you were joking about being a virgin. You said that to stop me from attacking you, right?"

"Not completely. I am a virgin."

I've had orgasms, lots and lots of them, but only my hands have ever touched me down there. Sometimes I really want to pop that cherry, but men are such dicks. Most of them. The good ones are, of course, already taken.

"Does Elena know that?" Reese asks.

"That I'm a virgin? Yeah. My family knows too, since we talk about pretty much everything."

His lips curve into a wicked smirk. "Do you want to stay a virgin? Because I'm the best first time you'll ever have."

"Not exactly humble, though, are you?" I lean back and shake my head. "Sorry, I've taken a vow to stay untouched until I meet the man I'm going to marry."

That's baloney, since I've decided to get laid ASAP, but I'm trying to discourage Reese.

Uh, why am I doing that? He's hot, I'm horny, and we're both adults.

But he's also the brother of my best friend's fiancé. My brain keeps telling me that makes it wrong somehow, but my body thinks that's bullshit.

He sighs with immense sarcasm at my claim I'm waiting for marriage. "What a shame."

"The right guy is worth waiting for."

"Hmm." He braces his elbow on the sofa's back, raising his hand to rest his chin on it. "Who is your perfect man?"

"Don't know. Someone who"—doesn't care about my money or my pedigree—"treats me with respect and love. A man who adores me. You know, the kind who always considers my feelings and does whatever he can to make me feel appreciated and loved."

"You want a gay man, then?"

"No." I give him a fake scowl. "I want a good man."

"I'm very good. Ask any of the girls I've been with."

"Sex isn't part of the formula for a good man. I mean, I want to have sex with the guy I marry, but that's not the most important thing."

Reese studies me like he's trying to figure out what kind of alien species I belong to, his eyes faintly squinted and his lips faintly puckered. "You really are barking mad."

"Excuse me? I'm quirky, not crazy."

"Oh, don't get me wrong." He scoots a little closer, his voice lowering to the sexiest rumble I've ever heard. "I'd love to get a leg over with you. And I guarantee you'll be glad you gave up your innocence to become a sinner with me. I do sin better than anyone."

He is cute. A real hunk of man candy. And he smells soooo good. Is that cologne or aftershave? The spicy scent of it wafted over me when he leaned in, and now I can't stop smelling it. My nether regions love that aroma, and how close his lips are to mine. I'm getting slick and warm and deliciously achy.

"Thank you for the offer," I force myself to say. "But I'm good the way I am."

"Yes, I agree. You are perfect, lush—" He stops short of calling me Luscious again and frowns a little. "Is it all right if I call you darling? Or is that too close to the word I'm not allowed to use?"

Oh what the hell. It's not like I'll jump his bones if he calls me that word again.

"Go on," I say, waving my hand like I'm a queen granting my royal permission. "Call me Luscious."

He grins. "Thank you."

"Whatever."

The doorbell rings, and Reese springs off the sofa to get our food. He returns a minute later with a large pizza box and sets it on the coffee table, then flips the lid up.

His brows draw together over his nose. "They must've bollocksed up the order."

I shimmy closer to the sofa's edge, rubbing my hands together and humming with hungry delight as I lay eyes on our snack. "Mm, yummy. They got it exactly right."

"But this isn't pizza." Reese lifts a slice, eying it like teeth might erupt out of it to bite his nose off. "No cheese. No meat. It's some sort of pastry crust with what looks like applesauce all over it."

"Yep. It's an apple strudel pizza." I grab a slice and take a bite, moaning because it tastes sooooooo good. Cinnamon and sugar and apples, all mushed into one warm, gooey slice of food heaven. I close my eyes while I chew, moaning some more because, damn, I'm so hungry and this is like an orgasm in my mouth. After I swallow my large bite, I say, "Try some. It's the most delicious thing I've ever put in my mouth."

Reese says nothing. He sits there with a slice of gooey goodness in his hand, but he's not staring at the pizza. He's staring at me.

"What's wrong?" I ask. "Don't you like strudel?"

"I love it," he says, his voice huskier and deeper, the sound of it shivering heat through me. "But I'd rather devour you."

"No sex. Remember? I'm staying a virgin until—"

"Then you shouldn't consume dessert pizza like you're about to climax." He sets down his slice and inches closer to me. "A bloke only has so much willpower, you know."

I gaze into his hooded eyes for a long, long moment, struck by the intensity of his desire for me. No guy has ever looked at me that way. Suddenly, I want to toss the pizza and mount him right here on the sofa. Reese Dixon might prove to be the biggest temptation I've ever laid eyes on, and I'm having trouble remembering why I need to discourage him.

Twenty-eight years old and still untouched. Maybe a night of hot, meaningless sex with Reese Dixon is what I need to help me unwind after nine months of living with an Ecuadorian family.

Sleeping with Reese wouldn't be simple sex, though, would it? His family and my friend make it complicated as hell.

In my mind, I mutter a thousand nasty curses as I leap off the sofa and retrieve a plate and a can of beer from the kitchen. While Reese watches me with a curious expression, I slap three pieces of strudel pizza onto the plate and march back to my room. Okay, maybe I'm sashaying. Like I said, that's my normal way of moving, and I can't help it.

Though I might be exaggerating it a little to torture Reese.

Chapter Three

Reese

Arden is gone when I wake up in the morning. Her bedroom door is open, and her bed is neatly made, but she's not there. I wander into the kitchen and find a note taped to the refrigerator. It says, "Out getting breakfast. You're welcome." I can't decide if she's saying "you're welcome" because she's bringing breakfast home for me too or if she wrote that strictly because she's off her rocker.

I sort of like her insanity. It's adorable, in a very strange and slightly disturbing way.

While I wait for Arden to bring food—I assume that was the meaning of her note, not that she's out eating at a cafe while I'm starving to death here—I have a shower and then ring my brother Chance. Since his almost wife and almost brother-in-law got me into this mess, I decide he should be the one to fix it. *Find me another flat*, I plan to tell him.

But as I'm scrolling down my list of contacts to find Chance's number, I reflect on last night and the sexy little American dressed in nothing but her underwear. Maybe I don't want to move. Yet. Not until I see if I can get Arden naked and make that hot body sweat and writhe. She's a virgin and my almost sister-in-law's best friend. Does that make it wrong to seduce her?

Probably. But what if…

I growl at myself, because even I'm not that much of an arse, and tap my phone's screen to dial Chance's number.

"What's wrong?" Chance asks, his tone giving away the fact he's smirking from the safety of our parents' house in the English countryside, too far away for me to tackle him to the ground for being cheeky.

"Nothing's wrong," I say. "Didn't Elena tell you about the Linwood family blunder?"

"Yes, and I assumed you would be a gentleman and get yourself to a hotel."

"Why would you assume that? It's me you're talking to. Reese, not Dane the boring and uptight brother. It's me, the fun one in the family."

"Right. What was I thinking?" Chance sighs. "Please don't harass Arden. I haven't met her yet, but Elena loves the girl to bits. If you do your usual shag-and-run routine, my fiancée will not be pleased."

"What sort of dick do you think I am? I never run. I kiss them goodbye and walk out the door at a normal pace."

"Elena told me Arden is, ah, not like the other women you've been with."

I drop onto the sofa. "Do you mean because she's barmy, or because she's a virgin?"

"Both." Chance pauses. "Arden told you she's a virgin?"

"Yes." I relate last night's surprise to Chance and finish up by saying, "So you can see why I want to stay here. She's a charming nutter and the sexiest girl I've ever seen."

"Leave her alone, Reese."

I hate it when he uses his big brother voice. I feel like a schoolboy who got caught stealing girls' bras and shrinking them in the clothes dryer.

And yes, I've done that. Not in ages, though.

But if I shrink Arden's knickers, they'll be almost nonexistent. Hmm… That's not a half bad idea.

"Don't do it," Chance chastises.

"What?"

He huffs, part humor, part big brother bossiness. "Whatever it is you're thinking of doing. Keep your randy paws off Arden."

"Fine, I will. But don't blame me if the girl tears my clothes off."

"That happens to you all the time, doesn't it? Women going into a sexual frenzy the second they see you. I should call the New York Police Department and warn them of the danger."

"Ha-ha." I grumble, because I know Chance is right and I should keep my randy paws off Arden Clover Pesti. Christ, even her name is oddly arousing. "You trusted me enough to let Elena lend me her apartment, so trust me not to deflower her best friend."

"All right. I'm sure you can't get into too much trouble in two weeks. Then, you'll be in New Hampshire for the wedding, where I can see you."

"Yes, yes, you've done your bloody annoying big brother thing." I hear someone fiddling with the lock on the apartment door and sit forward, feeling bizarrely excited at the prospect of seeing Arden again. "Got to go. See you in New Hampshire, and kiss Elena for me."

"I will."

Though Chance can't see it, I smirk as I say, "Make it a good, deep kiss. From me."

"Bugger off, Reese."

He hangs up on me.

I still hear noises from the door, like Arden is having trouble getting it unlocked, so I rush over there and open the door.

She stumbles into me, her left arm laden with two eco-friendly reusable canvas sacks, while with her right hand she grips the door key. The sharp end of the key stabs me in the gut, but it doesn't really hurt. Not much, anyway. Her entire body careens into me, her breasts mashed against my chest and the top of her head nudging my chin. The shopping sacks seem about to fall out of her grasp, so I hug her to me tighter, strictly to stop her from dropping the sacks.

Yes, that's why I hold on to her luscious little body. For the safety of her groceries.

But she feels so good, so warm and soft but with ample muscle tone. And she smells incredible too. Not like perfume or some other scented whatever, but like it's just the way this woman smells. And it makes my cock wake up.

I ease her away from me and take the sacks. "Are you all right?"

"Me?" she says, staring at me with a vaguely dazed expression. "I stabbed you. Are you okay?"

"You stabbed me with a key, and I don't think those are usually fatal." I smile, and because I'm holding her sacks in one arm, I can pat my belly when I add, "See? Right as rain."

"I've never understood that saying. What's so perfectly right about rain?"

"Don't know." I nod toward the kitchen. "Am I taking your groceries there?"

"Yes, please. Thank you for carrying them."

"I might be a louse, but I'm not rude."

She shuts the door and follows me into the kitchen, where I set the sacks on the counter. Arden starts taking items out and lining them up on the counter in neat little rows.

Leaning against the counter, I can't help watching her and smiling. "Are you obsessive-compulsive?"

"No. I like neatness, that's all. Why be messy? There's no purpose to it."

"You won't like living with me, then. I toss my clothes everywhere and never touch a feather duster."

"Uh-huh. I can see that about you." She flashes me a playful smile, but then turns serious. "Why did you call yourself a louse?"

"It was a joke. But I do love women, and I usually leave as soon as we've both come."

"You mean you screw them, pat them on the head, and walk out the door."

That's almost exactly what I said to Chance, but without the head-patting. How does this girl I've known for five minutes understand that about me? Maybe she receives microwave thought transmissions.

She raises her brows, like she's expecting a response to her assessment of me.

And I suddenly feel itchy all over. "Yes. I kiss them, then I walk out."

"Why?"

I start to scratch my arm but stop myself. Trying not to look at her, I pretend ignorance. "Why what?"

Evasion is always a good choice when a woman pokes her charming little nose into your affairs. Not that I've had any affairs. It's strictly been come-and-go for me. And I don't mean "come" as in walking into the bedroom. Once we've both gotten off, what else is there to do but leave?

Arden stops unpacking her groceries and turns to face me, crossing her arms over her chest. "Why are you afraid of relationships?"

"I am not afraid. Relationships aren't for everyone, you know."

Her lips pucker while she roves her assessing gaze over all of me. "That's what people who are afraid of falling in love say. They usually have some kind of trauma in the past that makes them terrified to try again."

"Sorry to disappoint you, but I'm not traumatized," I say, sounding annoyed because, bloody hell, she is annoying me. And I'm getting itchier. Could I be allergic to interrogation? "Can we please stop talking about my sex life?"

"Sure, whatever." She resumes unloading her sacks. "I'm making banana oatmeal pancakes with your choice of Greek yogurt or syrup on top. Oh!" She pulls out what looks like a tiny milk carton, grinning. "Whipped cream too. If you're into that sort of thing."

Of course I am. I love decadence in all its countless varieties, but her grin and her sensual body are making me picture all the ways I can use whipped cream to make her squirm and gasp and finally scream my name.

No, you arse, you can't. She's off limits, remember?

Yes, yes, yes, I know that. Honestly, I do. I know I cannot touch her.

But fantasies are completely allowed. So tonight, I'll be locked in my bedroom fucking my own hand while I imagine I'm fucking her.

I stifle a groan. Being an upstanding adult is awful.

Arden has emptied her grocery sacks and proceeds to fold them, stacking them next to the refrigerator before she starts gathering the ingredients for our breakfast. I offer to help out as her cooking slave, and she cheerfully bosses me around. I love it when she smiles at me over her shoulder and says, "Mash the bananas with the potato masher, not your fingers."

"But if I use my fingers, you can lick them clean for me." Yes, flirting is also allowed. Chance didn't order me not to do that. He said to keep my hands off Arden, that's all.

Her lips twitch upward. "You have a one-track mind, don't you?"

"No, I have two tracks available at all times, running parallel." I wink. "One of them is reserved for dirty thoughts."

"Yeah, I can tell."

We go back to cooking, and soon we've got two plates loaded with banana oatmeal pancakes. A glass of milk sits next to each plate, which we've placed on the bar. Arden and I take our seats on the stools and dig in. I pour enough syrup over my pancakes to start a flash flood of stickiness, but Arden is judicious in her use of syrup. She does, however, spoon a mountain of whipped cream onto her stack.

I watch her shove four layered pieces of pancake into her mouth. "Do you believe all those barmy things you said last night?"

She swallows her huge mouthful of food. "Some of it. The part about not flushing the toilet before eight on Tuesday is pure baloney. Most of that stuff is my way of testing guys to make sure they're not schmucks."

"Did I pass the test?"

"I'd give you a B plus."

"Should I be flattered or offended by that?"

Arden pretends to consider me, her head tilted to the side. "Too early to say."

We go back to enjoying our breakfast, and once I've finished eating, I turn to Arden. "Let me wash the dishes. I insist."

"I won't argue with that." She consumes her last bite of pancake, leaving a smear of whipped cream right next to her mouth. "I like having a hot British guy as my kitchen helper."

Though I hear her words, all I can think about is licking that cream off her skin. Sweet, decadent cream. The word makes me picture her naked with my head between her legs while I taste the best kind of cream there is.

Arden lunges forward, pressing her mouth to mine.

I freeze, trying so damn hard not to kiss her back. Chance said not to touch her, but she started this. Doesn't that absolve me of any wrongdoing? She kissed me. And her mouth is silky and warm, her lips sweet from the cream clinging to her skin. I burn to taste her, to flick my tongue out and lick the cream off, then plunge my tongue into her mouth.

But I can't.

Her tongue slips out, gently probing between my lips, all but pleading for me to ravish her—or maybe for my mouth to open so she can ravish me.

I want that. Want it so badly that holding back is like a physical pain.

She pulls away just enough to speak, our mouths a hair's breadth apart. "I thought you wanted to kiss me. Was I wrong?"

"No, you're not wrong. I do want that. But…"

Damn my brother. But it's not his fault. I should've gone to a hotel.

"But what?" Arden asks.

"I can't."

"Why not?" She brushes her lips over mine, and her voice lowers to a tantalizing whisper. "I might be a virgin, but I can still kiss. I enjoy it a lot."

Now my cock is not only awake, it's clamoring for me to take her up on that offer and ravish her mouth, then her body.

I jump off my stool and trip over my own feet, grabbing the bar for support. "I promised I wouldn't."

Arden studies me, her lips caught between her teeth. "Who did you promise that to? Not me."

"Chance. He made me swear I wouldn't touch you. You're a virgin, for heaven's sake."

I spin around, meaning to run for my bedroom, but Arden grabs my arm and stops me.

"All I want is a kiss," she says, her voice hushed and sultry. "I'm not planning to have sex with you, Reese. Isn't it my choice who I kiss or don't kiss?" She moves in front of me, looping her arms around my neck and raising onto her tiptoes, her mouth so close I can almost taste her. "And I want to kiss you."

What am I meant to do? My willpower has never been that strong.

So I groan and kiss her.

Chapter Four

Arden

Reese is an incredible kisser. And I know what I'm talking about. I mean, I've been kissed a lot. His lips stay firm for a brief moment, then they soften and slide over mine, damp and with a touch of sweetness on them from our breakfast. I lick at his lips, and he teases mine right back. I sag into him, abandoning myself to the kiss, to the moment, to this virtual stranger who makes me want to taste him in every way imaginable.

I open for him, desperate for a deep kiss, and he thrusts inside to explore my mouth like he wants to spend hours doing only this, curling his tongue around mine, plowing deeper only to withdraw almost all the way. I wrap my tongue around his, loving the way he responds with a hungry groan and an equally hungry swipe of his own tongue. We dance a sensual tango with our mouths for several minutes, so long that I lose track of the time, lost to the sensations and flavors.

Reese wraps an arm around me, tugging me closer.

He feels so incredibly good, with my body mashed to him, his muscles flexing and tightening against me. He smells incredible too and tastes so delicious I never want to stop kissing him. Last night, I'd kind of thought he was one of those jerks who loves to say suggestive things to embarrass me, but this morning I've decided he's not like that. He helped me make breakfast. How many guys would do that? He makes me laugh, like when he smeared whipped cream across his upper lip and called it his "old man mustache" and invited me to "give it a lick." He grinned when he said that, so I knew he was teasing.

But I'd wanted to do that.

Reese Dixon is gorgeous and hotter than hot, sexier than any guy I've ever dated.

He shifts a hand to my ass, massaging it while he groans into my mouth.

I'm so ready for more, aroused by his kiss and his body and his… everything, to the point that I want to rip his clothes off, drag him to the floor, and screw his brains out.

He did pass my first test by not getting annoyed with my kooky antics.

Reese lets go of me and staggers backward a couple steps. His eyes are wide. His mouth gapes open while he shakes his head at me. "I can't do this. Chance… Elena… I promised…" He shakes his head harder, almost frenetically. "This is too wrong even for me. I'm sorry."

"Elena's my best friend, but she doesn't decide who I kiss." I hesitate for only a second before I say, "Or who I sleep with."

Though he still gapes at me, his brows squish together in the cutest expression of total confusion. "You want to sleep with me?"

And his voice jacks up so high on the last word that he almost squeaks it. Which is even cuter.

I giggle, because he's so darn lovable like this, not the cocky Brit who can't believe I'm a virgin, but simply a guy who's baffled by the fact I want him.

His eyes narrow, and his mouth slants into a smirk. "You dare to laugh at me? If we slept together, you'd never snicker at me again. I'm fantastic."

Yeah, I laugh some more, a little louder now. "You're just the cutest."

"Cute?" His smirk kicks up into a sly smile, and there's humor shimmering in his blue eyes. "You do realize I'll have to prove to you how not cute I am. And we will be naked while I'm providing that proof."

"I'd love that." I move closer, stopping a few inches from him, gazing up into his eyes. "I want you, Reese."

His playful cockiness fades away, replaced by a softer, surprised expression. "We met last night. Why would you want to have sex with me?"

"Do you have any idea how long I've been resisting the urge to get naked with a guy? It wasn't super hard, until now." I inch even closer, resting my palms on his chest. "Until you showed up and scared the shit out of me."

He sets his hands on my hips. "I'm not the relationship sort. If we do this, I won't stick around to cuddle with you or meet your family or any of that bollocks."

I smile. "You have to stick around. We're living in the same apartment."

"Well…" He steps back, drawing out a distance between us so my hands fall away from his chest. "I've been thinking I ought to get a room in a hotel."

"You mean Chance told you to move to a hotel."

I love Elena, so if she thinks Chance is amazing, then he must be. Elena wouldn't be marrying him otherwise. But Chance Dixon has no right to decide with whom I share an apartment or whether I screw that someone or not. So what if Reese is Chance's brother? It's still none of his beeswax.

From the moment I saw Reese, I wanted him. He's beyond sexy. And I'd decided before I left Ecuador that I want to get rid of this pesky virginity. I've waited a super long time to pop that cherry, and I don't want to wait one day longer.

Maybe nine months in a faraway country has made me a touch boy crazy.

"Please don't leave," I say. "I got back from Ecuador two days ago, and I haven't really had anyone to talk to in months. The family I lived with down there was nice, but it's not the same as having a real friend. You're fun. Sometimes full of yourself, but yeah, fun. I'd love for you to stay."

He regards me for a minute, his lips twisting this way and that, his fingers curling and uncurling.

When I think he's about to say he's leaving, he sighs and throws his hands up. "Fine. I'll stay. But I cannot have sex with you, Arden. My brother will have my hide if I do."

"Nobody needs to know. It can be our secret."

"Chance will know. Trust me." Reese ambles to the sofa and collapses onto it, then pats the cushion beside him. "Sit. Let's... talk or whatever. You should find out who I am before you toss your virginity in my lap."

I laugh while I pad over to the sofa and sit down near him. "Toss my virginity? Not sure how that works. It's not like I have an actual cherry in there that I can whip out and hand to you."

His upper lip curls. "That's the most revolting image I've ever been forced to picture."

"Yeah, I realized how gross it was while the words were spewing out of me. Sorry. I have a tendency to say inappropriate things."

"Do you?" His lips curve into a sexily teasing smile. "I think I'm going to like you, Arden Clover Pesti."

"Most people think I'm nuts."

"Well, you are slightly barmy. But it's endearing, in a strange way."

"Thank you. I love being strange."

He cocks his head like he's analyzing me. "How old are you?"

"Didn't anyone ever tell you women don't want to be asked that question? I'm surprised a player like you doesn't know that."

"I'll have you know I've never asked a woman her age before." He angles his body toward me a little. "But I'm curious to know how long you've been holding on to your virginity, and why. So, how old are you?"

"Guess that's a fair question, considering I told you I want to have sex." Get naked and crazy with him, actually, but I don't want to scare him off. "I'm twenty-eight."

"You don't act twenty-eight."

My lips twitch, but I stop myself from smiling. He seems sincere in his belief that I don't act the way someone my age should. "How do you think twenty-eight-year-olds usually behave?"

"I don't know. Less demented."

This time *his* lips twitch, and I realize he's kidding.

Crossing my arms, I lift my chin. "Okay, Mr. I'm So Hot You'll Forgive Me for Being a Smart-Ass, how old are *you*? I mean, since I answered—"

"It's all right. I'm not shy about anything." He sets one ankle on the other knee. "I'm twenty-four."

"A younger man. Wow, that's even hotter."

"Older women definitely are hotter." He winks. "Even if they're still innocent."

"Who said I'm innocent? I've had orgasms, you know. Loads of them."

His brows shoot up. "You have?"

I give him a fake chastising look and wag my finger at him. "Don't make assumptions about me. You'll almost always be wrong."

"Lesson learned." He slants forward, resting his arm on the sofa's back. In a hushed voice I'm sure is pure sarcasm, he asks, "Are you sure they're orgasms? Since you've never had sex, how would you know?"

A laugh snorts out of me. "Yeah, like there's any doubt about it when I'm writhing on my bed and can't breathe because I'm coming so hard."

He stares at me for a few seconds, without blinking, then clears his throat and sinks back into his corner of the sofa. He grabs a throw pillow and puts it on his lap. "So you, uh, self-pleasure."

Oh holy cuteness, it's so absolutely adorable that he can't seem to make himself say the word masturbate. Which makes me want to torture him a little. He deserves it after being so shocked that I'm a virgin, and so shocked that I want to have sex with him.

"I don't do it all by myself," I say. "I have Rod."

"You—" His eyes bulge like they might explode or something. "Who the bloody hell is Rod? I thought you didn't have a boyfriend. And you said you're a virgin, so how in the world could some bloke called Rod give you orgasms?"

No, I'm not lying. I do have Rod. But I might be allowing Reese to get the slightly wrong impression about my little friend.

Rod is my favorite vibrator. Yeah, I named it. I'm kooky, remember?

The human sex machine sitting on the sofa with me has stopped gawking, but he still looks flummoxed. "Does he give you oral sex?"

"No, it's more hands-on." I sigh and gaze into space, smiling a touch, like I'm remembering all the fantastic O's Rod has given me. "Rod gets me off faster than any of my other fuck buddies."

"You're what?"

And now Reese's eyes are bulging again.

Maybe I should have mercy and stop torturing him, but I'm having too much fun.

Reese scrubs a hand over his face, twice, until the shock softens into total confusion. "I think you have a very different definition of virginity than anyone else on the planet. How many fuck buddies do you have? Do you take your kit off for them?"

"What's a kit?"

"Your clothes."

"No, I keep my nightie on. But a good, hard come always leaves me zonked out, so I go to sleep right after." I act like I'm sentimental about it when I say, "As for how many fuck buddies I have… Well, there's Rod, obviously. And Big Jim, who gets the job done slower but with more intensity. And oh, I can't forget Jack. He's like a bunny rabbit, all energy and super-quick climaxes."

Reese's confusion has morphed into a suspicious expression. He eyes me like he's almost figured out what I'm talking about. "Jack is like a rabbit. Why do I feel like you're having me on in the worst way?"

"Okay, I admit it. I'm talking about my vibrators."

He blinks quickly several times before a naughty smile spreads across his face. "You have three vibrators? Quite a randy little thing, aren't you?"

"Staying a virgin doesn't mean I have no sexual urges." I tilt my head, eying him kind of the way he'd eyed me a minute ago. "How many women have you slept with?"

"Oh no, I have more sense than that. I never tell a woman the answer because no girl really wants to hear it."

"That many, huh? You're a real hound, I guess."

"I'm a ladies' man."

"Which is code for man-whore."

He scoots closer and speaks in a deeper, softer voice. "I'm experienced, which means I can guarantee you won't want Rod or Jack anymore after you've been with me."

"Awesome. Let's do it now."

"I can't perform on command like a ruddy vibrator." He shoves a hand into his hair. "I feel like we should get to know each other a little first."

"Are you always so shy about getting it on? I mean, from the way you talk, I assumed you'd be raring to go."

"This is different for me." He scrunches up his whole face and groans. "I can't do it, anyway. I promised Chance, and I don't break my word."

"Wow, you are the sweetest, most honorable man-whore I've ever met."

"Thanks. I think." He relaxes, a big breath gusting out of him. "Tell me one thing. What in the bloody hell is a grey?"

Chapter Five

Reese

I'm trying to resist Arden, honestly I am. Resistance isn't in my nature, though, not when it comes to women. And this woman is so… irresistible. I paused there because I tried to think of a different word to describe her, but nothing else came to mind. She's curvy and sensual and bizarre and barmy. Whenever she smiles, her cheeks get these sweet little dimples in them, right at the corners of her mouth, and it makes me want to kiss her again. I also love the dimple at the top of her arse, where those delectable cheeks meet. I glimpsed that dimple last night when Arden was traipsing around in her knickers.

A scrap of plaid, that's all it had been. A scrap that barely covered her bottom.

This morning, she's wearing jeans and a short-sleeve jumper, both of which cling to her alluring shape.

Sweater, not jumper. I'm in America now, so I need to remember the differences.

"Reese, are you awake?"

She's waving her hand in my face, and I realize she's been talking while I've been fantasizing about her.

"Ah, sorry," I say. "My mind wandered. What were you saying?"

"You asked me what a grey is. I explained, you missed it, and I'm not super inclined to tell you again."

"I'll listen this time. You have my word." Assuming she doesn't smile again, making that dimple reappear. All bets are off then.

All her clothes might be off too.

Except I promised Chance I wouldn't do that. Damn him. Chance has no right to tell two adults what they can and can't do. Or maybe I'm making excuses because I lust for Arden's body.

She taps my nose with her fingertip. "You're not listening again."

I realize she's right and smack my forehead. "Sorry. Don't know what's wrong with me today."

"Maybe it's jet lag."

"Could be." It's not, but at least that sounds like a good excuse for my behavior. "Let's try that again. What is a grey?"

"An alien."

I blink a few times while I watch her, because I can't believe she means what it sounds like she means. Maybe she's referring to immigrants from another country. That would make a lot more sense. Though I'm not aware of another country that has grey people in it.

She must mean grey hairs. Right? But how would that be an alien…

"What do you mean by 'an alien'?" I ask.

"An extraterrestrial being, as in a living creature from a planet other than Earth. They have grey skin, spindly arms and legs, and big black eyes."

She's looking at me like I'm the one who's a little crazy.

"Extraterrestrials," I say, still trying to come to terms with that one. "You actually believe grey aliens are visiting your bedroom in the middle of the night."

"No," she says with a faint laugh, like that's the dumbest thing she's ever heard. "Of course not. I'm not sure they abduct people either, but I completely believe alien life exists and that it's possible they've visited Earth."

"Do you really sleep with aluminium foil on your head?"

"That would make me insane, so no, I don't do that. It was part of the test, which you passed." She wiggles her bum like she's trying to get more comfortable. "Don't you believe in anything unusual? Things you haven't seen or touched yourself?"

"I believe your tits are beautiful and soft, even though I haven't touched them."

Her lips crimp like she's trying not to smile. "I offered to have sex with you, and you turned me down."

"No, I delayed making a decision." I fidget but can't get rid of what feels like a rock under my arse. I suppose it's a figment of my imagination, which is warning me to steer clear of Arden and her edible body. "I promised my brother I wouldn't touch you. He swears Elena will be devastated if I corrupt you."

"Corrupt me?" She laughs outright this time, and it lights up her expression. "You're so cute. I told you about Rod and Jack. How can you think I'm innocent and incorruptible? I have a filthy, filthy mind, and you'd probably blush if I told you the things I've imagined doing with you—and to you."

Her gaze flicks down to my cock.

And of course, that makes blood rush into it.

What has she been imagining doing to me? Since she looked down there, I'm guessing—hoping, maybe praying—she wants to get her mouth on me.

More blood rushes south.

"Let's go outside," I suggest. "For a walk. We can keep talking while we do that, and fresh air will be good for both of us."

"Sure, that sounds fab. I know a park we can go to."

"Brilliant. Let's do that."

It's a beautiful, warm morning, so we don't need coats. I try to talk Arden into wearing one, claiming I'm worried she'll catch cold when I'm actually afraid I'll snap and fuck her on the sidewalk if I have to look at her breasts cradled in whatever bra she's wearing. The fabric of her sweater stretches tight over those mounds. She won't wear a coat, so I'm probably doomed.

"Into the lift," I say when the doors open for us.

"The what?"

"Oh. Sorry. I meant elevator. I forget the American words for things."

"Don't worry about it." She walks into the elevator, and I follow. Once the doors slide shut, she asks, "Are you sleeping with anybody right now?"

I roll my eyes at her. "No, Arden, and I won't be sleeping with you either."

"But you want to." She stuffs her hands into her jeans pockets, cocking one hip. "I still don't get why you're anti-relationships. What are you afraid of?"

I make a noise that even I think sounds vaguely like a growl. "I told you earlier, I'm not afraid. Relationships aren't for everyone, you know. I remember reading somewhere that monogamy is a construct of modern civilization, but it's not natural for human beings. We need to shag lots of people in order to propagate the species."

And aren't I so fucking proud of myself for using all those big words. Won't she be so fucking impressed.

She snorts and shakes her head at me. "That's what players say to excuse their sleazy behavior. But you don't strike me as a sleazoid, so I'm guessing you have another, deep-seated reason for being afraid of commitment."

Oh yes, she's so fucking impressed. I really am an idiot, aren't I? Maybe I shouldn't have used the word shag in my little diatribe meant to convince her my lifestyle is noble.

I hope I'm not trying to convince myself of that.

Maybe there's a reason for my behavior, and I don't know what it is. Maybe I should figure that out.

Another time.

"What is a sleazoid?" I ask. "Can't tell if I should be offended until I know what on earth you're talking about. Is that another kind of alien being? Sleazoids must have red skin and forked tails to match their giant, forked dicks."

"Do you have a forked dick?" She raises up on her toes, angling her head down and peering at my crotch. "Maybe you should show me, strictly so I can decide if you really are a sleazoid."

When she moves only her eyes to peek up at me through those thick lashes, her lips kink up at the corners. It's the sexiest thing I've ever seen, and of course, my dick loves it.

Is she trying to seduce me? Little Arden Clover Pesti, the virgin who believes in aliens? I've had women seduce me before—I've always loved when that happens—but none of those other women called me a sleazoid and asked to see my forked penis as part of the seduction. It shouldn't be working on me, but it is. I want to whip out my cock and show her the proof I'm not a sleazoid from the planet Arsehole.

Arden sighs and faces the elevator doors.

Everything she does and says makes me want to call my brother. I know exactly what I'll tell him. "Bugger off, Chance, I'm shagging Arden today. Tell Elena it's not my fault her friend is the world's first nymphomaniac virgin. Cheers. See you at the wedding."

Instead, I glare at the elevator doors until they slide open. Then I shake off my irritation and follow Arden out of the building, listening while she tells me about every building and object we pass on our trip to the park. I learn all about the street vendors too, and I buy us both ice cream cones along the way. I love watching her lick that ice cream. Her pink tongue snakes out, curls around the ice cream, and glides back into her mouth with the tip rolled over. With every sensuous lick, she closes her eyes and moans.

All I can do to stave off a flaming hard-on is to cough into my fist and focus on the most disgusting image I can think of—the rotting corpse of a dead hedgehog I'd once seen in the woods near my parents' house.

The image doesn't cure my problem, but it helps a little.

When we get to the park, Arden leads me down a wide, paved path that takes us past flowering trees and park benches. We see children flying kites and older men playing some sort of game inside a court that has a glass roof over it. Arden informs me they're playing bocce. I've heard of the game, but I have no idea what's involved.

"I don't really understand the game myself," she admits when I ask her about it. "But some people really like it. I once dated a guy who was totally into bocce, and he told me it's related to a British game called bowls. No idea what that is."

"It's a very boring game where you roll little balls around and try to get them close to another little ball." I groan, remembering the times I've sat through games to be polite. "My brother Dane loves bowls. But I didn't realize bocce was the same thing."

We pass a couple of brick buildings, then Arden sits her lovely arse down on a bench and waves for me to join her. I do, but I keep an arm's length between us. Like I said, resisting temptation is not in my nature. Chance has ordered me to go against my every impulse and act as uptight as he is. Or was. He seems to have loosened up a lot since he met Elena. She must be a bloody fantastic lay.

She's also very sweet and very clever. Arden is starting to remind me of Elena, but without the business suits or the inexplicable adoration of my uptight brother. No, Arden is not stuffy. She's like a breath of fresh air that's been imbued with the essence of sunshine.

She's a free spirit. Turns out I like that.

And I keep liking that about her until she scoots across the bench, coming dangerously close to me. "Don't sit so far away. I like smelling you."

"Smelling me? Did I forget to use deodorant this morning?"

The enchanting girl laughs.

Every time Arden does that, the sound is sweet and almost musical, and it tickles my senses in the strangest way. And every time she does that, I want to kiss her until she melts in my arms.

I can't do that, though. Chance has forced me to dig out the willpower I never knew I had, so I can resist this free-spirited angel who claims to have a filthy mind.

Willpower is awful. Why does anyone want to have it? Why do people brag about theirs? It's the worst invention in the history of the universe.

Our bench sits right under a tree covered with white flowers that give off a sweet, delicate perfume. When a breeze shivers the flowers, a few petals come loose and float down to light on Arden's hair and shoulders. She looks like an angel, smiling at me with those white petals clinging to her blonde hair.

I want to strip her naked right here, lay her across the length of the bench, and push inside her supple body. No, that won't work. I can't fit on the bench that way. But I could lift her onto my lap and let her ride me.

Tossing that fantasy into the mental rubbish bin, because I've developed a terrible case of willpower, I focus on the grassy area across from us. "It's nearly lunch. Where should we eat?"

The sexy angel leans in, her nose brushing my cheek, and inhales deeply. "Mm, you really do smell yummy."

I never use cologne, so I have no idea what she thinks she smells. Maybe the body wash I used? No, not that. What then? I don't want to know, because I'm sure the answer will cure me of this willpower disease I've contracted.

And that would be a bad thing... why?

Her nose grazes my cheek again. "I could just eat you up."

All the air in my lungs splutters out of me, and I'm fairly certain I spray saliva all over the sexy woman who's sitting much too close to me.

"Why are you fighting it?" she asks. "You want me. I want you. And you did swear you'd be the best first time I could ever have."

I swallow a groan. Why did I say that last night? What kind of moron am I? Chance hadn't issued his directive yet when I told Arden I would be the best first time she could have. Now the sneaky girl is using my own words against me.

"Forget what your brother said," Arden tells me. "He has no right to interfere in my life."

"What about Elena? She'll hate me if I—you know." Now I can't even say the words. *Take your virginity.* What's hard about saying that? Nothing. But I can't make the words leave my mouth. They seem to be stuck somewhere between my brain and my throat.

Arden settles a hand on my thigh and skates it up and down, her longest finger grazing my cock.

I'm not sure she even knows she's almost touching that part of me. My dick knows, and it loves the tickling sensation. My willpower thinks it's torture. I'm on the fence. Teetering. Tipping more and more in the direction of Arden.

Straighten up, Reese, or you're a dead man.

Arden slides her hand up my thigh, over my hip, and all the way up to my chest. Her lips flutter over my earlobe when she whispers, "For nine months, I slept in a strange house with somebody else's kids down the hall, and I didn't even have my vibrators. I had nothing to do at night except listen to the parents getting it on in their room. The noises they made, all those little grunts and gasps and moans, it made me wonder why the hell I'm still a virgin. I had to give myself a happy ending every night, manually. My right hand developed a permanent cramp."

Naturally, my mind shows me a fantasy of her doing that.

"Why are you telling me this?" I ask. And why does my voice sound rough, like I've swallowed a mouthful of sandpaper? I'm having trouble breathing, and my cock is straining to get out of my trousers.

"I'm telling you," she says, in the sexiest whisper I've ever heard, "because I had decided to lose my virginity before I ever met you. But now that I have met you, I can't think of anyone else I'd rather let pop my cherry."

Though I've always hated that term, when she says it the words ignite a searing, irresistible need in me. I grip the bench so hard my fingers hurt, but even the pain can't douse my lust for Arden.

"Please, Reese," she purrs into my ear. "I want it to be you."

I want that too. More than want it. I hunger for her like a starved man who's been offered a sumptuous, succulent meal for the first time in months. And yes, I want to devour her.

But I seem to have this annoying, wriggling thing in my brain that makes me do the last thing on earth I want to do right now. I think that wriggling thing is called a conscience.

Which explains why I jump up, force a smile I'm sure looks slightly manic, and tell Arden, "I have to go. Time for me to get a hotel room. Thank you for showing me some of the city, but it's really not appropriate for me to, uh, share an apartment with you."

And I run off.

Well, I don't literally run. I walk away very, very quickly from the sensual woman on the bench who all but begged me to fuck her. I, Reese Dixon, walk away from a girl who wants sex.

Only as I'm crossing the lobby of the first hotel I find do I realize I'll have to go back to that bloody apartment to get my things. If I have any luck at all, Arden won't be there.

I'm not feeling that lucky today.

Chapter Six

Arden

When I get back to the apartment, suffering from intense sexual frustration, I grab my phone and call Elena. She's not answering her cell, so I leave a message telling her we need to talk pronto. I can't believe my best friend would tell her fiancé to order his brother not to sleep with me. I mean, it's my body. It's my choice. And if Reese is such an awful guy, why would Elena lend him her apartment? Chance must have come up with the boneheaded idea of treating me like I'm an idiot who can't make a decision for herself.

To be fair, Chance and I haven't met. He doesn't know me, but his fiancée does. What did Elena tell him? What could she say that would make him think I need protecting from his brother?

The word virgin. That makes most guys think I'm fragile.

I fume for a while, then decide to get started on the work project I don't actually need to start for a couple weeks. I'd planned on using this time before Elena and Chance's wedding to relax. She insisted I didn't need to help her with the wedding arrangements, and she wants me to take it easy since I'm freshly home from Ecuador.

New York isn't my home, but I thought I'd have more opportunities to get laid in a megacity, instead of back home in Stockbridge. My hometown in Massachusetts doesn't have a broad selection of man candy.

Work takes my mind off things for a couple hours.

Then the phone rings, and I see it's Elena calling.

"Hey, hon," I say when I pick up. "How's England today?"

"Beautiful. How are things at your end?"

"Fab. How's your British stud today? Is he plotting more ways to interfere in my life?"

Elena is silent for a few seconds. "What are you talking about?"

"Didn't Chance tell you? He ordered his brother to keep his hands off me."

"Chance did what?" Elena pauses again, but she doesn't sound confused or surprised when she speaks again. Instead, she sounds like my best friend who wants to hear all the details. "Do you want Reese's hands on you?"

"Yes, dammit, I do. And your honey is seriously messing with my plans."

"What plans do you have for Reese?"

"I want him to take my virginity. That's the plan."

Silence. For such a long time I think I've shocked my best friend so horribly that she's passed out.

Finally, Elena laughs. "Oh, those Dixon boys really do have the magic touch with the ladies, don't they? I mean, I had sex with Chance in an elevator five minutes after we met. Can't blame you for wanting to get it on with Reese. He's as hot as Chance, maybe hotter." She lowers her voice to a whisper. "Don't tell Chance I said that."

"My lips are sealed."

"You always did have a soft spot for the bad boys."

"That's because they're so much fun." I twirl a lock of my hair around my finger while I remember Reese's naughty smile when he told me he'd be the best first time I could ever have. "I like Reese. He's more fun than any guy I've met before, and I really, really want my first time to be with him. I had a sexual epiphany in Ecuador, and I don't want to wait any longer. Look, I'm not after a relationship. I know Reese isn't that kind of guy, but I'm also pretty sure sex with him will be incredible. Don't I deserve a rockin' first time?"

"Of course you do."

"Then you'll tell Chance to back off?"

She makes a noise that's like a groany hum. "I don't know, Arden. Maybe you should wait until you get to know Reese better. I mean, he's a sweetie, but… Chance knows him better than I do. I trust his judgment, and if he thinks it's a bad idea, then it probably is."

"You just said Reese is a sweetie."

"But he has a reputation for being the bang-and-run type. I don't want you to get hurt."

Now it's my turn to groan, though mine is more moany groan than groany hum. "It's my life, Elena. Being a virgin doesn't make me mentally incompetent."

"I know. You're wicked smart, but you're inexperienced when it comes to men. We both know why that is, but like I've told you for years, you can't avoid taking risks forever."

"Which is exactly why I want to sleep with Reese."

"That's not the kind of risk I mean, and you know it." She hesitates yet again, and I can hear her fingernails drumming on some kind of hard surface. "Get to know him. Take these two weeks to become friends with Reese, then decide. You need to try dating, really dating, before you take the next step."

"Says the woman who screwed her fiancé on the night they met."

"I don't want you to regret this, that's all. Besides, you just came back from nine months in South America. At least decompress before you jump in the sack with Reese or anybody."

Decompress? Maybe I do need some downtime, but I'm tired of everyone telling me what to do. My parents never told me what to do, though they offered me advice. My grandmother is another story. Date this guy, don't date that guy. Take this job, don't take that one. Grams is kind of bossy. It's a side effect of her job.

"Have you even told Reese who you are yet?" Elena asks.

"No. I was hoping I wouldn't have to."

"Bite the bullet, Arden."

"Fine," I say with a sigh. "I'll tell him."

I hear a man's voice in the background and know it must be Chance. Elena announces she has to go. We say goodbye, with my promise I won't sleep with Reese until I've at least told him who I am. Where I come from. Why I've stayed a virgin. Elena gave me his cell number, but it takes me an hour to work up the courage to call. When I do, I get his voice mail. I leave a message asking him to please, please, please stop by the apartment so we can talk. I say it's urgent, to make sure he'll show up.

And if he can handle my pedigree, maybe we can get it on tonight.

Problem is, ever since my talk with Elena, I've been starting to think she might be right. Maybe I ought to spend more time with Reese before we hook up. I don't want to wait. Thinking about him makes me ache and burn in all those secret places where no one has ever touched me before. No one but me and my harem of vibrators.

How long do I have to wait? A week? A month? I have no idea what length of time is sufficient before I can hump Reese, the hottie who makes me tingle all over every time he smiles.

Maybe I have gone sex crazy. Elena might be right that I have other reasons for wanting to cross that line with Reese.

So I decide to deal with my lust the way I always have. I change into a billowy nightie, get Rod, and sit on the sofa tucked into the corner with my legs stretched out. Leaning my head back, I picture Reese. His mouth. His eyes. His hot body. I remember how it felt to have my hand on his thigh, so close to his dick. Maybe I won't sleep with him for a while, if ever, but I can use a fantasy of him to help me get some relief.

I picture him naked. All those muscles. His hips undulating while he thrusts into me again and again.

With one hand, I cup my breast through the nightie and pinch the already stiff peak. Oh yes. Reese. Doing that. With his mouth and his teeth. I bend one knee, letting it fall to the side, and slip my hand under my nightie to glide the vibrator up and down my slick cleft. I've watched enough late-night cable to know how it might go if I ever do sleep with my new roommate.

Oh yes, Reese. His expression tense with the need to come. His ragged breaths. His cock filling me with every thrust.

I switch on the vibrator and thrust it inside me the way I imagine Reese doing with his dick. I keep rolling my fingers around my nipple while I work the vibrator, throwing my head back and moaning. I let go of my breast and grip the sofa's back, writhing and gasping while I drive myself closer and closer to climax.

My fantasy keeps going. Reese flipping us over so I'm on top, riding him while he grasps my hips and says dirty things to me.

"Oh yes," I moan. "Yes, Reese, do it like that. Oh God, please, harder, deeper."

I'm almost there. Almost. So close.

Rod needs a little help, so I rub my clit with my other hand while I buck my hips into the thrusts of the vibrator and crank it up so it's buzzing like a giant, crazy bee.

"Oh Reese! Make me come!" My release rocks me like an earthquake, starting with a jolt as my entire body clenches. When the first spasm hits, I shout, "Reese! Yes!"

"Bloody hell."

Though I hear Reese's voice, I think it's in my head, part of the fantasy. With my eyes closed, I keep going while the orgasm pulses through me, keep going until the very last spasm fades. Breathing hard, I open my eyes.

And see Reese standing at the other end of the sofa.

His mouth is gaping. His eyes are wide and kind of wild. He has one hand in his hair, the other at his side where it keeps fisting and loosening. He's staring at me, at the vibrator lodged between my thighs.

I realize I should probably be embarrassed, but all I can think about is how much I want him to take over for Rod. Screw what Elena said. I deserve hot sex with a hot Brit.

"What are you doing?" he says, sounding breathless.

"Giving myself a big O." I turn the vibrator off and grab a tissue to wipe it down. "If you won't do me, I'll do myself."

"But you—" He scrubs that hand in his hair, looking at my face now. "Did you do that because you knew I was on my way over here?"

"How could I know that? I had to leave a message for you."

"Yes, and your message said I should let myself in."

Oh yeah, I had said that. Well, to be fair, at the time when I left the message, I wasn't planning on having a round of solo sex. I also hadn't expected Reese to rush over here so fast.

I stand up. "Are you okay?"

The bulge in his pants is way bigger than usual.

He shoves both hands into his hair, the movement raising his shirt enough that I can see the waistband of his pants.

And the tip of his erection poking out.

Not long ago, maybe an hour before Reese barged into the apartment, I'd been totally on board with Elena's idea that I should wait awhile before getting naked with Reese. Somewhere between getting off on my own and him catching me in the act, I'd jumped overboard. Maybe it's hormones talking. Maybe I should go to my bedroom and shut the door.

But I don't want to.

I love the way Reese is breathing hard, his cheeks are slightly pink, and his cock looks hard enough to crack eggs on it. Not that I'm going to do that. I would love to get my hands on that beefstick, though. And my mouth on it. Suddenly, I forget all the reasons why I should deny myself the thrill of getting it on with the hottest guy I've ever seen who also has the hottest British accent I've ever heard and who makes me hotter than I've ever felt before.

All that wetness dribbling down my inner thighs is because of him.

His chest is still heaving when he lowers his hands and asks, "What did you want to talk about?"

Oh God, I love the rough tone of his voice. Add in his accent, and wow, he could give me a multi-O experience just by reading the phone book to me.

"I was planning to tell you," I say, "that I've changed my mind and we shouldn't have sex."

His face blanks. "Oh."

"But I changed my mind again. I want you inside me, Reese, right now."

"What the—You can't keep changing your mind." He grips the back of his neck, averting his gaze. "I still can't do it, Arden. You're still my almost sister-in-law's best friend, and my brother will still murder me if I touch you."

"Oh please. Why are we letting other people decide what we can and can't do? We're adults. We make up our own minds."

I walk up to him and rub my finger over the red tip of his erection, where it pokes up out of his pants. "I want you, Reese."

"Bloody hell." He grabs my hand before I can run my finger over him again. "This is wrong."

"No, it's not." I guide his hand to my breast, molding it to my body with only the thin nightie separating my skin from his. "It felt so right when I was making myself come while imagining you were inside me. The fantasy of you rocked my world. Now I want the real thing."

He stares at me, mouth open, his tongue sliding across his bottom lip.

I press his hand more firmly to my breast. "Be my first time, Reese. Tonight."

Chapter Seven

Reese

This beautiful, sexy girl is standing in front of me, holding my hand to her tit, asking me to fuck her. I've been propositioned before, several times, but never like this. *Be my first time*, she says. Only once was I a girl's first time, and that was my first time too. I want Arden. Want her like mad. But I keep hearing Chance's voice in my head telling me to be a good little boy and not ruin his fiancée's best friend, the sweet and sort of barmy girl who joined the Peace Corps and who believes in aliens.

But her eyes are pleading with me, and her luscious body is tempting me with all those curves and those breasts, one of which I'm currently fondling. Because she shoved my hand onto it.

Even a monk couldn't stop from getting hard if a woman did that to him. Particularly this woman. And particularly after what I saw her doing a few minutes ago. Honestly, I was hard the second I walked into the flat and found her enjoying one of her sex toys on the sofa.

My mind decides to give me a vivid replay of that moment, of Arden writhing on the sofa while she fucks herself with a vibrator. Was that Rod? Maybe it had been Jack. Christ, I hope it wasn't Big Jim, because I have a feeling a real dick might have a hard time living up to a device that has a name like that.

I'm still having trouble catching my breath. Her tit feels so good, supple and warm with the nipple stiff and pushing against my palm. She smells like sex, because she was giving herself a jolly good time a few minutes ago. The scent of it, musky and sweet, is eroding my willpower much too fast.

"Arden," I say, trying to be mature and levelheaded about it, "I'm not sure we should do this. Chance and Elena—"

"They don't run my life, or yours." She massages the back of my hand, the one wrapped around her breast. "I've waited long enough. You're nice, even if you are British, and you're so damn sexy. I want you, but if you don't want me…"

"Of course I want you." I realize what she said a moment ago and ask, "Why did you say 'even if you are British'?"

"Well, to be honest, when I think of British people, I picture the queen. She's, like, a thousand years old."

"Do I look like the queen?"

Her gaze slides up and down my body, then settles on my cock. She bites her lip. "No, you don't look anything like that."

If she doesn't stop staring at my erection, I can't be held responsible for what I do.

Leave her alone, Reese. It's Chance's voice again, repeating the words he said to me this morning. *Don't do it. Keep your randy paws off Arden.*

Right. The same way Chance kept his randy paws off Elena on the night they met. He told me about that, but he probably wishes he hadn't. I can use it as an excuse to strip Arden naked.

I shouldn't, but I want to. The need pounds inside me, like an alien creature has crawled into my body and demands I feed it Arden's pleasure.

Maybe I've spent too much time around her. An alien? *Get a grip, man.*

Lusting after Arden Clover Pesti might be wrong, but suddenly, I can't think of a single reason why I shouldn't take her up on that offer. After all, I'm the Dixon brother who does the wrong thing the right way.

One more time, for the last time, I ask, "Are you sure you want to do this?"

"Yes, Reese, I'm sure."

"And you haven't been drinking or smoking anything?"

"None of the above. Clean and sober and on fire for you."

I pick her up and carry her into a bedroom, not really noticing or caring whose bedroom it is. It turns out to be Arden's. I set her down on her feet near the bed. The pink bed. Since I know this used to be Kyle Linwood's room, I'm sure he didn't put the pink sheets and fuzzy pink blanket on the bed. Stuffed animals are lined up along the headboard, on top of the pillows.

"Does my girlie room bother you?" Arden asks. "I had my parents mail me some of my stuff, from my apartment back home."

"It doesn't bother me. I've been in worse girlie rooms."

Arden marches up to the headboard, stretches her arm halfway across the bed, which is as far as she can reach, and sweeps the stuffed animals off it. I watch as she crawls across the bed and shoves the rest of them onto the floor. When she climbs off the bed, her nightie rides up and reveals the round cheeks of her arse.

She sashays up to me, tipping her head back to meet my gaze. "How do we start?"

"By getting naked, Luscious."

"Duh. Right." She whips her nightie off over her head and flings it away. "How's that?"

I choke on whatever I'd been about to say, the words having flown straight out of my head. Arden is gorgeous, from her deliciously round tits to her deliciously round arse and those delicious little nipples that poke out at me like they're begging to be tasted. I pore my gaze over her, following her breasts down to her flat belly, and lower to the curly hairs that mark the spot where I want to have my head—between those creamy thighs, with my face buried in those hairs while I feast on her.

"Why aren't you naked yet?" she asks, not sounding bossy, just seeming confused by the fact I'm standing here like a bloody moron.

"Sorry, Luscious. Your beautiful body had me distracted."

I tear my clothes off and ditch them on the floor. My dick is flying at full staff now, waving at Arden like it can't wait to get inside her. I can't wait. It's been years since I got this excited about being with a girl, but something about Arden makes me want her so badly I swear I can already taste her on my tongue.

She bites her lip again.

And that does me in.

I grasp a handful of the covers and yank them off, leaving only the bottom sheet and the pillows on the bed.

Arden giggles.

Her breasts jiggle.

I pick her up and drop her onto the bed. She bounces a little, which makes her tits jiggle again.

"You are so gorgeous," I say while I crawl across the bed to straddle her. "Hands down the sexiest woman I've ever seen."

She smiles shyly.

Now she's shy? Not when she'd shoved my hand on her breast. Not when she'd asked me to be her first time. Definitely not when she stripped off her nightie. But now, when I'm about to take her body, suddenly she's acting shy.

And I love it. She's so thoroughly… disarming.

"You can still change your mind," I hear myself saying, though I can't believe I'm saying it.

She shakes her head. "Not changing my mind."

Crouched on all fours over her body, I dip my head to kiss her. She slips her tongue between my lips, a tentative exploration, and when I curl my tongue around hers, she dives deep. I kiss her slowly, taking my time to heighten her desire and get her ready for me. Of course, she's made herself ready with her little friend on the sofa. Mine won't be the first rod she's taken into her body, but I will be the first actual human to feel her wrapped around me.

Just thinking about that makes me so hungry for her I can hardly breathe.

Well, I might also have trouble breathing because she's devouring me like she wants to taste the back of my throat. I love her enthusiasm, but I have better plans for her.

I give up her mouth and bend my arms so I can reach her tits. Her nipples stick straight up like tiny signposts guiding me to where I want to be, and I tease one of those peaks with my tongue, flicking it side to side, then up and down, until she starts to breathe more heavily. Her mouth opens and closes, over and over, while I tug her rigid peak into my mouth and suckle it.

"Oh that's good," she moans.

The sultry tone of her voice fires a bolt of lust straight into my cock. I need to hurry if I'm going to last until I've got her melting for me, so I kiss and lick a path down her belly, crawling backward at the same time. I can smell her cream even more now, the scent of it intoxicating me and overpowering my senses—and my good sense. I want to thrust inside her right now. But I won't. This is her first time, and a vibrator isn't the same as a real man.

When I reach her mound, I bury my face in all those curly hairs and suck in a deep draft of her feminine scent. Fuck, it's incredible. She moans, and I comb my fingers through those hairs, all the way down to her opening.

"Reese," she breathes, "please hurry. I've waited so long…"

She's already wet—drenched, actually—so maybe I don't need to take as much time as usual. But I never, never skimp on the foreplay. What kind of first time would that be? She deserves everything.

I part her folds with two fingers, intending to get down to it, but I can't resist taking a moment to admire her body. All that beautiful, rosy flesh glistening with the proof of her desire for me. Or maybe that's for Rod.

Why I ask, I can't say for sure. But I glance up at her and say, "What were you thinking about when you had that vibrator inside you?"

She reaches down to ruffle my hair with her fingertips. "You, Reese. I was thinking about you the entire time. You're the reason I got so turned on that I needed to relieve the pressure."

"You do realize an actual man is different from a mechanical device. For one thing, I don't vibrate." I smirk. "Usually."

"Ha-ha. I know a man is different. I might be kooky, but I'm not stupid."

"I know. Just wanted to make sure you don't have… impossible expectations."

She raises her brows and gives me a teasing smile. "Are you going to do me sometime this year? Or do I need to break out Big Jim to get the job done?"

"Is that a challenge?"

"Totally."

"Well, in that case…"

I suck her clit into my mouth and keep sucking hard until a sharp cry erupts out of her and she half whimpers, half shouts, "Yes, Reese, yes!" I take her taut nub between my teeth and tug, then swirl my tongue around it until her breathing turns into staccato panting.

"Oh God," she moans. "I'm about to—"

That's when I stop. I pull my mouth away and lick the flavor of her off my lips. "That's good enough, right? You can suck me off, and we're done."

She gapes at me, her cheeks speckled with pink and her breasts heaving. "What? I—What?"

"Relax, I'm joking."

Her eyes roll upward. She shuts her lids and shakes her head. "You are such a dick."

"No, I have a dick. There's a difference, Luscious." I move her thighs further apart, giving myself another moment to appreciate her rosy flesh that's swollen and slick, the perfect cradle for my cock. Then I realize something. "Shit. I forgot the condom."

Arden makes a sound I can best describe as complete frustration mixed with sheer lust. "You didn't bring one? What kind of man-whore are you? I would've thought you'd always have one on you."

"I do." Patting her thigh, I slide off the bed to find my trousers. Once I've retrieved the condom from the hip pocket, I climb back onto the bed to straddle her again. I wave the condom packet at her. "See? I'm a respectable man-whore after all."

"Oh thank God," she whimpers. "I want you, not Big Jim."

"Glad to hear I rank higher than your sex toy." I get the condom on and kneel between her thighs, encouraging her to bend her knees. "Are you ready?"

"Yes, you asshole, I've been ready forever and ever."

Though I try not to, I can't stop the chuckle that spills out of me. "You're even sexier when you're frustrated. But I hope you'll have something nicer to say than 'asshole' when I'm done."

Before she can say anything else, I push inside her.

Chapter Eight

Oh. My. God. This feels so incredibly, unbelievably, mind-blowingly amazing. Reese slides into me inch by inch, taking time to let me adjust every step of the way. He looked big, but now that I'm feeling all of him, the only thing I can say is wow. His cock is thick and firm and hot. He glides inside me, lubricated by my body and how outrageously wet I am for him.

Partway in, he pauses. "Is this all right? Does it hurt?"

"No, it feels good. Really good."

"What about now?" He pushes a little harder, but only goes in a tiny bit deeper. "Does that hurt?"

I suddenly realize what he must be worried about. "Don't worry. I broke that silly hymen a long time ago."

His brows shoot up. "You did? With what, Big Jim?"

"No, that was before I had a vibrator. I used the handle of a hairbrush."

"Why would you do that?"

"To get off." I tighten my muscles around him, making him suck in a breath. "Don't stop, please. I'm fine, and I need more of you. So shove that big, gorgeous dick in there harder."

He splutters, like he's about to either laugh or choke, or maybe both.

But he does it. He pulls out until only the head of his cock grazes my entrance, then he thrusts into me with one long, firm, powerful stroke. It's so good, so perfect, so much better than I even imagined. He fills me, consumes me, touches part of me no one and nothing, not even Big Jim, has touched before. Yeah, it's a little uncomfortable at first. I'm not used to having something so big inside me, but I get used to it quickly. And I love it.

"You feel so awesome," I say, desperate to touch him, but I can't. He's kneeling between my legs, holding my thighs while he thrusts in and out, in and out. "That's it, just like that. I love the way you fill me up. Don't stop. I want to feel you come inside me."

He groans deeply, his eyes sliding shut, the look on his face evincing pure pleasure, like I'm the best thing he's ever felt. "Ah, Arden. You're so tight and hot and slick." His whole face scrunches up. "I want to feel you come all over my cock."

"I will. I'm going to. I—" A cry disrupts my words as I clutch the pillow under my head and lift my hips in my desperate need to take him as far inside as humanly possible. A climax builds within me, like a tsunami rolling across the ocean, getting higher and higher the closer it barrels toward the shore. I know I'll come soon, any second, and I can't wait to feel that happen while he's driving into me. "Yes, Reese, more. Harder. Faster. Please, I need you to—"

He growls—swear to God he does, like a ravenous animal—then plants his hands on the bed at either side of me and lunges into me so hard and so deep and so fast that I can't hold back anymore. That tsunami crashes through me while I scream his name and lash all my limbs around him, my body milking him so fiercely I wonder if I'm hurting him. Oh shit, this is better than I imagined, better than I could ever have hoped.

Reese lets out a deep, throaty roar and plows into me with the hardest thrust ever. Then he freezes and shouts. I feel him pulsing, then he backs out and plows into me again, harder, his face wrenched with pleasure-pain. I feel him pulse again as he calls out my name in a strangled shout.

We're both gasping for breath.

He drops onto the bed beside me, landing on his back.

Neither of us speaks for a minute. I can't speak for sure, and I'm betting he feels the same way. Breathless. Awestruck. So completely satisfied that there's no word for it in any language on earth.

"Wow," I say when I can finally speak. "Wow. I mean… wow, Reese, wow."

He laughs softly. "Would you like to say 'wow' a few more times? To make sure I heard you. I may have gone blind and deaf from what we did."

"If you know I said 'wow,' you're not deaf." I wave a hand in his face. "Can you see that?"

"Yes, I see it." He grabs my hand and thrusts my middle finger into his mouth, releasing it little by little. "And I taste it."

His voice gets lower and sexier when he says that, and it makes my clit throb.

I don't know if I can survive another orgasm right now, so I tell him, "Please stop sounding all hot and hungry like that. It's making me horny again."

"And that's a bad thing?" He rolls onto his side to face me and feathers his lips over mine. "You are not only the sexiest woman I've ever seen. You're also hands down the best shag I've ever had."

"But I'm a virgin."

"Not anymore." He lays a hand over my mound, those long fingers curving over it, down between my thighs. "This belongs to me now. Finders keepers and all that bollocks."

"My vagina is not your property." I flip onto my side, gazing into his eyes. "But you can have a lease with option to buy."

He screws up his mouth, averting his gaze. "I'm not the sort who buys anything, not even a car."

"I wasn't begging you to marry me, Reese. It was a joke, that's all."

He lays back on the bed and rubs a hand over his eyes. "Maybe I've made a big mistake by taking your virginity. Naturally, you'll think of me as… someone special, or something."

"No, I won't. Promise." But I do feel kind of connected to him, which is dumb since I've known him for a smidge more than twenty-four hours. Still, that soft, glowy feeling in my chest is spreading into my tummy, and I think I might be in trouble. But I tell him, "Don't worry. I won't get all attached to you and cyber-stalk your fine ass after you go home to England."

"Hmm." Reese lifts his arm, a clear invitation to cuddle up, so I do. He folds his arm around me, his fingers caressing my skin.

"I like you, Arden, and this was bloody fantastic. But nobody can know what we've done. Chance and Elena wouldn't like it."

"Yeah, I guess you're right. Hurting them would suck, and it's not worth it since neither of us wants more than sex. And we're done with that."

I say the words—and intellectually, I mean them—but that glowy sensation won't leave me alone. Maybe it's the afterglow of a monumental orgasm. Maybe in a few hours, it'll go away. I don't want a relationship. All I wanted was to cross that finish line, and I've done it. Reese did it, actually. And holy wow, did he ever do a spectacular job.

"Good, we're agreed," he says, still holding me close. "One amazing night, and it's over."

"Yes. It's over." I paint tiny patterns on his chest with my finger. "Unless we do it one more time. Which, you know, would really be part of the same night."

"Right. I haven't fully inducted you into the world of earth-shattering sex yet, have I?"

"Mm-mm. Better get back to it."

He rolls me over so he's on top of my body and grins. "Are you ready to come even harder?"

I grin too. "Oh yes, please."

Chapter Nine

Reese

I wake up in the morning and realize I'm lying in Arden's bed. I'd meant to sneak out after she fell asleep. First, I'd meant to kiss her good night and casually walk out and go to my room. But she was so sweet and warm tucked under my arm, with her head on my chest, that I couldn't make myself tell her to move. Once she fell asleep, I kept lying there listening to her breathing and inhaling the scent of her, while she still had her head on my chest.

Eventually, I fell asleep.

Which explains why I'm in her bed, but not why I couldn't bring myself to leave her last night. I never spend the night with a woman, not anymore. The few times I did, the girl would get clingy and needy the next morning, and I had to be an arse and sneak out when she wasn't looking. Trust me, telling a woman you don't really want to date her, that having sex doesn't mean you're signing on for a lifetime commitment, never works. So yes, I skulked out.

But not last night. And not this morning.

I'm lying here in Arden's pink bed, but she isn't in it.

Have I been sneaked out on like I'd done to women in the past? Maybe it's my punishment for behaving like a "sleazoid." I'd only done that three times, and not in at least four years. Chance had given me a dressing-down for that behavior when he found out what I'd done, and believe me, there's nothing like a big-brother lecture to make a bloke never want to go through it again.

Besides, I never liked letting my family down.

Which sounds odd, I know. I'm the brother who screws around and doesn't stay for breakfast, but I also don't run off without saying goodbye. Not anymore. Not after seeing the disappointed look on Chance's face. He hadn't told our parents what I'd done, but his disappointment was more than enough.

I turn on my side in Arden's bed and get an exhilarating dose of her scent. Not only the aroma of sex from the three times we'd done it. The scent of her. I crush her pillow to my face and haul in an even bigger dose of her. The aroma fills my nostrils and overpowers my senses, making me feel strangely... relaxed.

Ah, the scent of Arden.

What am I doing? I spring up, sitting there with her pillow in my hands, and try to answer my own question. I can't be... enjoying this. Being in her bed. Waking up here. Spending the night with her.

No. I'm still sleepy, that's all.

I drop her pillow and get out of the bed, gathering my clothes and pulling them on while employing every fragment of my tattered willpower to keep from thinking about how fantastic her pillow smells.

Other aromas waft into the bedroom now. Is that bacon? Pancakes? I sniff the air, and my stomach grumbles.

Maybe Arden hasn't skulked away from me while I slept. In her bed. The pink one.

I tiptoe out into the hallway and down to the living room, like I'm a prowler about to get caught. Arden is in the kitchen, cooking something that sizzles on a skillet and humming softly to the music playing through her earbuds. I can't hear the music, but I recognize the tune as one of those power ballads from the eighties. The bar blocks my view of the lower half of her body, but I can see her shirt. The pastel plaid fabric looks so good on her, and she's left the shirt half unbuttoned so I can see the center of her chest and get a tempting glimpse of the sides of her breasts.

Why couldn't she have worn a turtleneck? Is that too much to ask for?

She looks up, sees me, and smiles as she takes her earbuds out. "Good morning, Reese. Hungry?"

That smile. It's the single most beautiful thing I've ever seen, full of bright, sunshiny joy.

Christ, I've turned into one of those lovey-dovey idiots.

"Good morning, Arden," I say. "I'm starved. Is that pancakes I smell?"

"Mm-hm. Blueberry this morning. I hope you like that."

"I'll eat anything. Just ask my family. Dane once dared me to eat a handful of grasshoppers, and I did it."

"Ew." She wrinkles her nose. "I don't cook insects for breakfast. Only for Thanksgiving dinner."

"Is that an American tradition?" I ask, taking a seat at the bar. "I thought it was turkey and pumpkin pie, but insects sounds a lot more interesting."

She aims her spatula at me. "You do realize I was kidding, right? I never touch insects, much less eat them. They're icky."

"Afraid of grasshoppers? Don't worry, I'll protect you from them." I pat my chest with both hands. "I'm your personal insect repellent."

Her snort transforms into a sputtering laugh. "That's even ickier. You're a walking bottle of chemical spray? Not sexy."

"Sorry. No more talk of creepy-crawlies, I promise."

"Good. Because I saw bugs the size of buses down in Ecuador." She flips a pancake, and only half of it lands on the griddle. She scoops up the half that's hanging off the side and tries to get it all on the cooking surface, but it winds up wrinkled. "Ugh. I'll eat that one."

"You're still doing better than I would. My mum won't let me near uncooked food anymore, not since I tried to poach an egg in the microwave and it exploded."

"How do you make an egg explode?"

"By cooking it with the shell on."

Arden smiles with her lips sealed, and it's the sweetest expression I've ever seen. "Guess you win the worst chef award."

"Don't I also win the wow award for most incredible taking of virginity?"

Her sweet little smile broadens into a grin. "Yep, you win that one for sure."

For some reason, I feel the need to add, "We can't do that again."

Her grin fades, but only for a few seconds, then that lips-sealed smile returns. This time, it carves out divots in her cheeks, like she has a brilliant secret that she's not going to share.

"What are you plotting, Arden?"

"Oh, nothing." She flips another pancake, this time getting all of it on the griddle, her head down but her eyes turned up to look at me. "Just imagining how I can seduce you."

"No, Arden." I try to sound stern, but I'm bloody awful at it. Resistance is not my strong suit, remember? "We can't do that anymore."

Even I don't believe me.

But dammit, I will try to not fuck her. Honestly, I'll try.

No, I won't try. I absolutely will *not* have sex with Arden. Never again. End of story.

She laughs, and her eyes sparkle.

"You think my resolve is funny?" I say.

"No, I think it's cute that you think you, a total player, can keep saying no when a woman wants you so bad she'll do anything to get you naked again."

Luckily, she finishes making the pancakes before I can think of anything to say in response. She wants to eat on the sofa, but I insist we have our breakfast at the bar.

Arden leans across the bar to set our plates there, making her half-unbuttoned shirt fall away from her body. I can see even more of her breasts.

My mouth waters, and not from the savory food she's placed in front of me.

She ambles around the bar to where the stools and I are waiting for her. The barmy girl whose shirt is half open is wearing nothing else but those plaid knickers I'd seen on the night we met.

"Why aren't you dressed?" I ask, and I almost cringe at the humiliating, panicked tone of my voice.

"I am dressed," she tells me. "Not ready for public viewing yet, but dressed."

And I can't think of anything to say to that.

Of course, she perches on the stool right next to mine. When I move to the next one over, she moves over too. The girl is relentless. I can't possibly be *that* good in bed. I mean, I'm good. But not so fantastic that women can't bear to not fuck me. Her insistence must be strictly because she was a virgin. I'm all she knows, about sex, so naturally she thinks I'm the most incredible lover on the planet.

Being around her might give me an ego the size of Australia.

I have no choice but to sit there with her inches away, the intoxicating scent of her more powerful than the smell of the pancakes and bacon. My willpower, which I'd thought—or maybe prayed—had reassembled itself, is getting new cracks. I'm only a man, not a robot with no feelings and no dick. Mine, by the way, is awake and ready for action. I really hope Arden doesn't peek under the bar and see that. The woman does not need more ammunition for blowing holes in my self-control.

She wriggles her bum on her stool while humming with pleasure as she chews a bite of bacon.

Never in my life have I needed my willpower so much, and it's failing me at every turn. Am I a complete and total arsehole? I'm starting to think the answer is yes.

"Let's go for a walk," I say. I'm done eating, since unfulfilled lust apparently makes me as ravenous as a starved lion who's caught a tasty gazelle. "It looks like a beautiful day out there."

"It is." She slips a forkful of pancake between her lips, and syrup dribbles down those lips and onto her chin, a single drop of it threatening to fall off. "But I was thinking we should go to the zoo."

"The zoo?" I say the words, but I'm not actually listening to her. That drop of syrup has captured all of my attention, because if it drips off her chin, it will land on one of those gorgeous tits.

While I stare at her chin and half pray for, half curse at the possibility of the syrup splashing onto her breast, she launches into a description of everything that's "awesome and so ridiculously fun" about the zoo. When she starts rambling on about museums, even that doesn't catch my attention. That drop of syrup is still hanging there, like it's frozen in place.

I'm five seconds away from licking it off.

Arden grabs a napkin and wipes her mouth and chin.

Something like disappointment ripples through me. Maybe later, I'll get the syrup and drizzle it over her naked body so I can lick off every last molecule of it.

No, you will not do that, you raging arsehole.

I volunteer to wash the dishes while Arden gets dressed. Actually dressed this time. She comes out of her bedroom wearing jeans, a loose-fitting shirt that falls below her hips, and sandals that show off her adorable toes and the neon-green nail polish on them.

"Let's go," she says. "You're a New York virgin, and I'm going to show you all the most fabulous places in the city."

"Sounds like fun." The zoo and museums don't appeal to me that much, but I love listening to her talk about… anything. "But as a reminder, there will be no sex."

I can't say for sure which of us I'm reminding.

Arden smiles, sexily, and takes my hand. "Don't you trust me, Reese?"

Not with my willpower. Absolutely not.

But I let her lead me out of the apartment, with my hand wrapped around her smaller one, and try not to think about how good she looks in her oversize shirt.

Christ, every last thing about her turns me on.

I'm absolutely doomed.

Chapter Ten

Arden

Reese hadn't been thrilled about going to the zoo or museums, but he gets really into it once we're there. I haven't done anything this fun in a long time, since way before I went to Ecuador. I love to have a good time, but my family history can make that difficult. When I mumble something like that to Reese, thinking he won't hear me, he does hear it.

"Don't you get along with your family?" he asks.

"Of course I do. They're amazing, I love them."

"What's the problem? Why does your family keep you from having a good time?"

Reese and I are in the butterfly garden, so I focus on the beautiful critters flitting around in here when I say, "It's nothing they do. It's the fact of who we are."

"I don't understand."

How could he? Everyone in New York knows my family, or at least my grandmother, but Reese isn't from here. I don't know how to start, so I go with the blunt approach.

"My grandmother is Celeste Arnaud."

Once I announce that, most people get it right away. Reese doesn't. He stares at me like I've babbled in another language.

"She's the founder of Bonsoir Beauty Inc.," I tell him. "The second-largest cosmetics company in the world."

"Oh." His brows crinkle with the cutest confusion. "I'm a man. Why would I know what you're talking about?"

"Because my grandmother is famous. Bonsoir is huge, and she's an icon."

He glances at a big orange butterfly, shoves his hands in his pants pockets, and sighs. "Afraid I've never heard of her. She's your mother's mother, right? Her last name is different, so I assume—"

"Nope. Grams kept her maiden name when she married Granddad because her company was already making a name for itself. She's also very proud of her French heritage. She's American, though. No accent."

"She's your father's mother, then."

"That's right. My dad is Marcel Pesti. My mom's name is Tally."

He watches me with a strange expression for a few seconds, then asks the question he's obviously been working up the nerve to ask. "I know it's a cheeky question, but how rich is your grandmother?"

"She's the number three female billionaire in the world. There are over two hundred of them, you know."

"No, I didn't know that." He scrunches his lips and hunches his shoulders. "Your grandmother is a billionaire?"

"Yeah, but she's not super stuffy or anything. Grams is pretty cool, when she's not butting into my life."

His mouth opens, but he seems incapable of speaking.

Yeah, talking about my grandmother often has that effect on people.

Desperate for something to say to break the tension, I announce out of absolutely nowhere, "I don't have any brothers or sisters."

At least his blank expression has disappeared.

He seems genuinely interested when he asks, "None at all? I can't imagine not having brothers."

"You guys are close, aren't you?"

"Always have been. Chance, as the oldest, thinks it's his job to keep the rest of us in line. Dane is the intellectual, the one who invents things. I'm the youngest, and the biggest disappointment."

"You are not a disappointment."

"If you knew me, you wouldn't say that."

"Does your family say that?"

"No. They're always supportive." He scrunches his mouth up again. "Well, except for one time. When Chance found out I'd shagged a girl and run away while she was asleep, he gave me a lecture about respecting women. The girl in question was best friends with Chance's girlfriend, so that's how he found out."

"You don't run out on women anymore."

"No. I did that three times, but never again after my brother's lecture." Reese glances at me, his mouth twisted into a wryly crooked smile. "Chance will call me an arsehole and a complete fuck-up when he finds out what I've done to you."

"You haven't done anything to me. We did it together." I move closer, leaning into him. "From what Elena says about Chance, he would never call you anything nasty."

Reese leans into me. "You're right. I'm feeling sorry for myself, that's all."

"Because you slept with me after promising not to."

"Not only that. I also lost my job."

I slip my hand into his big palm, threading my fingers through his, and rest my cheek on his arm. "What happened?"

"Does it matter?"

"Maybe it's not my business, but I'd like to know."

He closes his fingers around my hand. "I was a copywriter at an advertising agency, but I was made redundant three weeks ago."

"Redundant?"

"It means I was let go. 'Laid off' I think is what Americans call it."

"That's awful. What will you do now?"

He shrugs. "I'm getting redundancy pay, but I need to find a new job. I probably shouldn't have come here for a holiday instead of searching for a new position, but I needed… I don't know. A break."

"That's understandable. I'm sure your family gets it."

Reese squirms, his face pinching into a tight expression. "I haven't told them yet. They think I took time off from work."

"Why haven't you told them about getting laid off?"

"It's humiliating. Chance is a successful lawyer, even has his own firm now with Elena. Dane is successful too, has his own company, which leaves me as the unemployed loser in the family."

"No one would say that." I turn toward him, still holding his hand. "Getting made redundant doesn't mean you're a loser. It happens to a lot of people."

He angles toward me and studies me for a moment. "What about you? What's your profession? If you're from a wealthy family, do you even need to work?"

Though I would completely understand it if he were envious of my family and my life, he doesn't sound like that at all. He seems curious, not irritated.

Starting with the less shocking truth seems like the best plan. "I'm a freelance fact checker."

"Fact checker? What does that mean?"

"Authors and publishers hire me to make sure they got the facts straight in the stuff they publish, which means I do a lot of research. I specialize in science topics."

"I guess that shouldn't surprise me, since you're very clever." He gives me a playful smile. "Even if you are barmy."

"You should know by now that I'm not sensitive about how weird I am. I like being kooky."

"And you should be proud of your barmy nature. It's endearing." He pauses, glancing down at the ground, then looks at me again. "You didn't answer the other question. Do you need to work, or do you just like to?"

I want to tell him the truth, but that's never worked out well for me. Over the years, I've used the truth as a means of testing guys to find out if they're really interested in me or if they like the prestige of dating Celeste Arnaud's granddaughter. Ninety-nine percent of them fail the first test—my kooky behavior. Their eyes light up when I tell them the part hardly anyone knows about. And ninety-nine percent of the one percent who pass the first test will fail the second one.

Reese is different. I feel it. He passed my kookiness test, and after a couple days with him, I get the sense he might pass the other test. Do I want him to? He lives in another country, and we're such opposites.

What have I got to lose? I gave this man my virginity, so maybe I should go ahead and tell him everything.

"Did I push too far?" he asks.

"No, not at all." I take a deep breath and dive in. "Grams set up a trust fund for me when I was born. On my eighteenth birthday, I started receiving a monthly stipend that more than covers anything I might need or want. I can request more if I have an emergency or something. When my grandmother dies, I'll get the whole enchilada. I hope that doesn't happen for a long, long time."

Reese seems to be waiting for me to go on.

I suck in a breath and blurt out the rest. "My trust fund is five hundred million dollars."

His jaw drops. He keeps hold of my hand, but he doesn't move or speak for several seconds. "Five hundred million?"

I nod, biting my lip. "Grams is very generous."

"Well, that's bloody fantastic for you."

He's smiling, like he means that.

"You're not, like, disgusted?" I ask. "Or seeing dollar signs floating in front of your eyes? You don't feel the urge to ask me to marry you?"

"No," he says, laughing. "I don't do relationships, Arden, I told you that. But I'm glad you don't need to worry about money. It's awful having to think about that all the time."

"Chance has a lot of money, right?"

"He does, and I'm happy for him too."

"Not being well off doesn't make you a loser or a disappointment."

He lets go of my hand to scratch his chin. "I know that, but knowing it and feeling it are different things."

"You can have half my money if you want."

He chuckles at my offer. "That's generous, but no thank you. I don't know you well enough to accept a gift like that, and I wouldn't accept it even if we did know each other well. It's too much."

"You mean that, don't you?"

"I do."

I clasp his hand again and lead him away from the butterfly garden. "Tell me about your brother Dane. You said he invents things."

"Let's not talk about Dane right now."

"Why not? Does he make nuclear weapons for terrorists?"

Reese chuckles. "No, love, he doesn't work for terrorists. He started his own company a few years ago, to sell the devices he designs."

We pass the gorilla exhibit, but I keep us headed down the path because I have a destination in mind. And an activity in mind. He'll say no, but I'm determined to have my way. Reese doesn't seem like he can say no for long, which means I'll get what I want.

Him. His body. His incredible dick.

Maybe I'm going a little crazy with the "shagging," as Reese calls it, because I was a virgin until last night. But no, I'm sure it's more than that. It's him. Reese Dixon is so… lovable. Getting to know him a little better makes me want him even more.

"What kind of devices?" I ask.

"Devices? Oh, you mean the bits and bobs Dane makes." Reese grumbles, and if he's saying words, I can't understand them. Finally, he says, "My brother designs, manufactures, and sells sexual wellness devices."

I stop, bringing Reese to a halt with me. "Sexual wellness?"

Reese bows his head. "Dane makes sex toys. Vibrators. Dildos. Anything that helps women satisfy their needs."

"Only for women? He doesn't make things for men?"

"No. Only women." Reese's mouth jacks up at one corner. "As you can imagine, Dane is very, very popular with the ladies."

"Making sex toys doesn't mean he's great in bed." I seize a handful of Reese's shirt and drag him closer. "Nobody does it better than you."

"I appreciate the compliment, but I'm the only man you've been with."

"Maybe I should do your brothers, so I have something to compare you to."

"That's not funny." He slides an arm around my waist. "I'd love to do you right here in the zoo, on the main path, but we'd both get arrested for that."

I put my arms around him and raise onto my tippy toes, intending to kiss him.

He pushes me away and stumbles backward a few steps. "No, Arden, we're not doing that anymore."

"Who knew hot sex would make you so uptight?"

"I am not uptight. I'm trying to do the right thing, which I admit is a bit of a stretch for me. But I'm giving it a go, and your constant attempts to break my willpower aren't helping."

Am I being a total slut? If I am, it's kind of his fault for being so great at sex. Still, I don't want to scare him away. "I'm sorry. You're being so nice, and I'm acting like a crazy person. I promise to stop trying to seduce you."

"That would be helpful."

Guess I have to nix my plan to drag him into a secluded, shady spot and beg him to corrupt me some more. Well, let's say I'm pressing pause on that plan.

I turn and wave for him to follow me. "Come on. We've got plenty more places to see."

Chapter Eleven

Arden tows me down various paths until we exit the zoo. She stops us outside the entrance and smiles so brightly it gives me a different sort of warm feeling, the kind that makes me want to hug her instead of doing dirty things to her.

"Should we go to the aquarium or museums first?" she asks.

Her excitement about zoos and museums makes me like her even more. I know she loves science—she told me she specializes in that subject in her fact-checking job—and I want to see how excited she'll get about it. "Museums first."

"Awesome. I love museums even more than the zoo. Should we start with history or science?"

"Your choice."

She grabs my hand again and leads me away. "Science it is."

A taxi takes us to our destination, and now we're inside the New York Hall of Science surrounded by children and their parents. I don't see any other adults without children, only me and Arden.

"Is this a children's museum?" I ask.

"Technically, I guess. But the exhibits are fantastic." She eyes me sideways, her hand clamped around mine and her lips curling up in a teasing way. "I know you're a naughty boy, but surely you know how to have innocent fun too."

Christ, I wish she wouldn't say things like that. Or look at me that way. Or... exist. Nothing short of annihilating her from history seems likely to keep my cock at bay.

I let her guide me through the museum and can't help smiling every time she gets excited about something, anything, everything. I've never met anyone as happy as Arden. She takes pleasure in the simplest things, from a display of orange pink flagging tape that hangs above our heads to an exhibit about health and human evolution. Arden insists I pose next to the articulated human skeleton on display there so she can take a picture. Then she asks me to take a picture of her posing with the skeleton. Finally, she has us both pose with it while she takes a selfie of us.

Strangely, it's the most fun I've had in ages.

Next, she takes me to the American Museum of Natural History. I love watching her enjoy these places. She's so alive and engaged, excited by every little thing even though she tells me she's visited these museums many times. I've gone to museums with my parents when I was younger, but I never had such a good time doing it. My parents are plenty of fun, but no one on earth relishes life the way Arden does.

She insists we buy tickets for the Hayden Planetarium, which has some sort of show about alien planets. I let her decide where we sit once we're inside, and she chooses seats in the third row because, she assures me, "it's the absolute best place to see everything and feel like you're right in the middle of it all." We're very close to the giant black ball that she tells me is the projector for the movie-like show.

"Will your grey alien friends pop out of the projector?" I ask.

"No, they're way too covert to do something like that."

Lately, I've gotten to know her playful looks, and she's giving me one of them right now.

I smirk and say, "I'm sure you've been to these alien worlds we're about to see."

"Oh yeah, loads of times. I'm a frequent flyer on the ET Express."

The room goes dark as the show begins. Arden holds my hand throughout it, and we both lean our heads back to take in the experience. I find myself ignoring the film projected above our heads and instead watching Arden. The delight and wonder on her face captivates me, and rather than thinking about sex, I imagine walking through the park with her again, or having dinner with her, or… doing all sorts of normal, boring things that I know won't seem normal or boring if I'm with her. I realize with a mental jolt what it is I really want.

I want to date her.

We've known each other for a few days, but I want—no, I need more time with her. Time to see more of the world through her eyes. Time to hold her hand like I'm doing right now, and time to hold her in my arms while we talk or watch the telly or… anything.

Chance and Dane will never believe this if I tell them.

After the natural history museum, we go back to the apartment, having had our fill of fun for the day. Arden collapses onto the sofa, pretending to be so exhausted she can't stay awake. She has one leg hooked over the sofa's arm, the other on the coffee table, her arms flung out to the sides, and her eyes closed. She's also fake snoring.

"I'll make dinner," I say. "What are you in the mood for? Grasshoppers on a bed of wild rice?"

She cracks one lid open. "Ha-ha, you're hilarious. Do you even know how to cook rice?"

"I told you about the exploded egg incident."

"Right." She starts to heave herself off the sofa. "I'll make dinner."

"No, you won't." I grasp her shoulders and push her back down. "Relax. I'll figure something out."

And by figuring something out, I mean I'll ring a pizza place and have our dinner delivered right to our door. I even order one of those apple pizzas for dessert. Don't I know how to impress a woman?

We eat on the sofa and talk more in between mouthfuls of cheese-laden food.

"Tell me more about your parents," I say. "You mentioned they're hippies."

"Yep. They own a really cool shop in Stockbridge. That's in Massachusetts, which is right next to New York. The state, not the city. Anyway, Mom and Dad have a New Agey store called the Emerald Eye. Don't ask me why, but that's what my parents decided to call it."

"I thought you were from New York."

"No, I'm from Stockbridge. My grandparents are from New York, and Grams's company is here." Arden consumes a bite of pizza before continuing. "My parents aren't into the whole corporate lifestyle, even though Grams tried to get Dad to take a job at her company. More than once she's tried. Dad always says no. When he married my mom, they moved to Stockbridge. It's a cool, artsy town. That's where Mom's from, and where I was born and raised."

"How did you meet Elena?"

"In college. We both went to Northwestern. That's a university in Illinois." She studies her half-eaten slice of pizza for several seconds, then sets it down on the paper plate on her lap. "I wanted to see a new place, so I decided going away to college was the right option for me."

Eating a couple mouthfuls of pizza gives me a chance to think about what to say next. I want to ask her a million questions, but I don't want to seem like an annoying prick who's poking his nose into her life.

Finally, I settle on a question. "If you're not from New York, how do you know all the museums so well? And the zoo? And all the restaurants?"

"Because I've visited Elena lots. She lived here for years and years."

"Chance has lived in America for a long time, but I never visited him."

"You said once you never 'got round' to it. Why is that?"

I shrug. "Never thought about it. I grew up in the country, just outside one of those chocolate-box villages. I went to uni in London, but that's the extent of my travels, until now."

"What's uni?"

"University."

She sets her plate on the table. "What did you study in college?"

"Business." I give her a wry smile. "I know that sounds odd coming from someone like me, but I always wanted to have a business of my own. Hasn't worked out that way, though."

"What do you mean 'coming from someone like' you?"

"I'm not the serious type, like my brothers. Shagging and playing sports are my favorite pastimes."

"Seems like shagging is Chance's favorite pastime too. Elena says he's completely obsessed with getting her naked and—"

"You stop right there." I hold up a hand to emphasize how much I want her to not talk about my brother's sex life. Chance told me he screwed Elena five minutes after they met, but he didn't give me the graphic details of their elevator encounter. "I don't need or want to know anything about what Chance and Elena do in bed."

"Point taken." She tears off another bite of pizza and speaks with her mouth full. "When are you going to tell me why you're afraid of relationships?"

I open my mouth to deny it, again, but freeze. Ever since Arden first suggested I'm scared of relationships, I've kept thinking about that. Whether she's right. Whether there is a reason behind my behavior. I can't believe I want to talk to her about this, but I suddenly realize I do want that. "Let me start by saying I'm not afraid. But I might be... reluctant."

"Okay. I'll accept 'reluctant' for the moment."

Setting down my paper plate, I rub my hands up and down my thighs. "When I was at school, girls didn't pay much attention to me until I joined the rugby team. I was sort of shy back then. Sports helped me get over that. And when I started scoring the winning goals, girls started propositioning me. I guess I learned that sports and sex go hand in hand, and that women only want me for one thing."

"Hmm. Did your parents know what was going on?"

"Do you think I'm an idiot?" I say. "I learned how to hide things from them. They caught me with a girl in my bedroom once, and I got a stern talking-to. But by then, I liked sex too much to give it up. I got better at hiding what I was up to."

She chews her last mouthful of pizza and swallows before she asks, "Do you still think sex is all you're good for?"

"No. At uni, I realized I'm pretty good at business too, especially marketing and advertising."

"But you still think you don't want a relationship with any woman."

Here, tonight, with Arden... I'm beginning to reevaluate what I want. My realization from earlier today comes back to me, and

I know without any doubts that I want more than sex with this woman.

"Never mind, I'm being too nosy," Arden says. She grabs a fresh paper plate and puts two slices of apple pizza on it. She holds the plate between us. "Time for dessert."

After we eat the apple strudel pizza, we watch two movies on television, then it's time for bed. Arden asks if I want to sleep with her—just sleep, no sex—but I say I'd rather sleep in my own room. It's a lie. I'd much rather crawl into bed with her for the night, but I don't trust my willpower.

I walk her to her bedroom door.

She kisses my cheek.

"There's something I need to tell you," I say.

"Go on."

"I want to date you, Arden."

She stares at me, her gaze nailed to mine. "Date? As in… date?"

"Yes."

"Isn't that kind of what we've been doing all day?"

"Sure, but I want to make it official." I hold out my hand like I want to shake hers, realize that's a stupid thing to do, and clasp her hands instead. "Let's get to know each other for the rest of the two weeks until the wedding. No sex, just dating. Are you interested in that? With me?"

"Of course I am." She smiles shyly, the way she did right before we had sex for the first time. "I'd love to date you, Reese."

"Brilliant." I kiss her forehead. "Good night, Arden."

"Good night."

She goes into her room and shuts the door.

I'm dating. Me. Dating. It's a precursor to a relationship, and I'm volunteering for it.

And it feels bloody fantastic.

Chapter Twelve

Arden

This morning seems brighter and more beautiful than ever before. Reese and I are dating. For the first time ever, I feel like I'm with a guy who doesn't want my trust fund or my body. Well, not only my body. Reese asks about my family and the things I like to do. He lets me drag him through museum after museum and even seems to enjoy it.

I love being with him.

Okay, I've known him for barely more than two days, three counting today which has just begun. I don't love him. But I can love being with him and love the way he makes me feel. Reese is surprisingly sweet, given his reputation as a player. And his determination to not have sex with me only makes me like him even more.

Despite the fact I want to climb all over his naked body.

I've decided to give him the rest of the week for just dating. After that, I want him. If I have to prance around in my undies all day and all night to get his attention, I will do it. Maybe I'll try walking around buck naked in the apartment. He can't resist that, can he?

I climb out of bed, stretch, and yawn, while I think about what Reese and I can do together today. I haven't shown him the art museums yet. Or Central Park. Or Coney Island. Ooooh, so many wonderfully fun places to take him.

Today, we are going to make out. No sex does not mean no kissing, and I'm in desperate need of his lips on mine and his tongue in my mouth.

But I'd really love his tongue somewhere else...

I put on panties and a bra, then by habit I open the bedroom door. I don't like being shut in all the time, and I'm used to living alone. Reese's bedroom door is shut, so I assume he's still sleeping. I start doing tai chi, relaxing into the sequence of gentle, easy movements. The peacefulness of the routine sends all thoughts drifting away, so for once, I'm free of lustful fantasies about the sexy Brit sleeping across the hall.

Out the corner of my eye, I see the door to Reese's bedroom swing open.

And there he is. The reason for my insanely intense lust. Standing there with nothing on but a pair of black briefs. Sure, I've seen him naked and explored every inch of that body, but something about Reese in those tight briefs makes me start to tingle all over in the best way. It feels decadent and naughty.

He saunters across the hall to my room and leans against the doorjamb, tipping his head to the side while he regards me with nonsexual interest. "What are you doing? I don't know much about yoga, but that doesn't look like what you're about right now."

Looking at him makes me lose my concentration, so I give up on finishing my routine. "It's tai chi, which is very relaxing and steadying. Some people call it meditation in motion."

"You meditate?"

I sit down on the bed. "Yeah. Why are you so surprised? Aren't crazy people allowed to seek a higher state of consciousness?"

"Well, yes, of course." He ambles over to the bed and sits down beside me. "I've never seen anyone actually doing meditation or tai chi or anything like it. My family isn't into that sort of thing. Elena has Chance doing yoga, but I think he only goes along with that so he can use it to seduce her. I wouldn't mind watching a sexy girl twist her body into all those yoga poses."

He winks at me.

"Down, boy," I say. "Afraid I don't do yoga."

"We can invent our own version."

He's got that look in his eye, the one that makes me shiver in the most enticing way. But I agreed to celibacy, which was his idea, so he has no call to be looking at me like he wants to tickle my tummy and rip my clothes off.

And he really has no right to be so hot and British.

"You'd better stop talking," I tell him. "Your accent makes me horny, and I'm trying to stick to your no-sex plan. Better put on some baggy pants and a big old sweater too."

His sizzling bod in those black briefs is making my mouth water.

"I didn't bring any clothes like that," he says. "The weather's too warm, love."

"Yeah, but I'm still obsessed with screwing you. Can't help it. You look so damn good in… everything. So it's really your fault I'm obsessed with sex."

"I see." He slants toward me until his shoulder bumps into mine, and his voice goes all deep and sexy. "I can grow a thick beard if that will help."

"That will take too long, and besides, I doubt it would alleviate the problem." I slide my fingers along his jaw, loving the scratchy feel of it. "You're way hotter with morning stubble. A beard would probably turn me into a wild animal."

"But I might like that."

I smack his thigh. "Cut that out. No more flirting until you're ready to get naked with me again. Capisce?"

"All right, have it your way." He gets up and stretches, giving me a fantastic view of his body and the lump in his briefs. "What should we do today?"

"Let's play it by ear." I stand and shoo him away. "Go get dressed, you steamy hunk of man candy."

Reese grabs me, hauls me into that mouthwatering body, and plants a firm but brief kiss on my lips. "Anything you want, Luscious."

Then he saunters back into his room and shuts the door.

We make breakfast together—which, with this guy, means we spend more time laughing and kissing than actually cooking—and afterward we head out to my favorite art museums. It's the start of a week-long adventure consisting of visits to everywhere we can think of that sounds like fun. On day four, we visit Coney Island and have a total blast there. Bumper cars with Reese makes me laugh so hard my eyes water. On the roller coaster, I shriek and cling to Reese. He grins the entire time, keeping his arm around me.

After that, we play games like Whac-A-Mole and Water Racer—and I win a stuffed giraffe, which I give to Reese. He does a formal, courtly bow when he accepts my gift. And of course, he kisses me—though he keeps it PG rated.

I've never had such a good time. Ever.

We go shopping too, and Reese buys me a Cyclone T-shirt to commemorate the day we rode that roller coaster together. I buy him a shirt with a mermaid on it. He promptly whips off the shirt he's been wearing and pulls on the new one, spreading his arms and grinning. I get that glowy sensation in my chest again, like I had the night we did the deed, the one that feels good and weird at the same time. At the aquarium, we watch the sea lions and the fish and all that stuff, but then Reese pulls me into a dark corner and kisses me. It's slow and sensual and not at all in line with his plan for celibate dating. At least, it seems that way to me. I love it anyway. Not only does he have a magic dick, but he's also got a magic mouth.

Reese insists on buying me dinner at a pizza restaurant, which is delish, then we walk along the boardwalk hand in hand while we watch the sun dip lower and lower in the sky. Once it's dark, we head for the Wonder Wheel. I haven't been on a Ferris wheel in ages and ages. When I told Reese that earlier, he insisted we must ride one today. After we climb into a car, he slips his arm around me, and I rest my head on his shoulder. It feels nice and comfortable, like we've known each other for months instead of days.

As soon as the wheel starts moving, Reese nuzzles my cheek and whispers, "I'm not afraid of having a relationship with you."

My breath catches. Dating is one thing, but a relationship would take us to the next level. Is he really prepared for that?

I turn my face toward him, and our eyes meet. "Are you saying what I think you're saying?"

"Depends what you think I'm saying." He drags his fingertips down my cheek. "I want to get involved with you, Arden. Seriously involved."

My voice refuses to work. Stunned speechless? Me? Wow, it's hard to believe.

Reese brushes his thumb over my lips. "Do you want that?"

"A relationship? With you?" I smile. "Yes, I'd love that."

He smiles too, but it's no exuberant grin. It's sweet and tender.

"Don't relationships involve sex?" I ask.

"I, uh, guess so." He bows his head, scratches the back of it, then looks at me again. "But we shouldn't. Not yet."

"Okay, fine, we'll stick to celibacy." I slump on the seat and throw him a sideways glance. "It's not fair to be so irresistible when you refuse to have sex with me."

"I'll make it worth the wait, I promise."

Our car reaches the ground, and we climb out of it.

Reese slings an arm around me. "How about ice cream?"

Yeah, that's what I'm hungry for right now. Ice cream. Sheesh. Maybe if I get to lick it off him…

But we stay platonic for the rest of the evening and go to sleep in our separate rooms.

Damn.

Chapter Thirteen

Spending this much time with Arden has proved a hard test for my willpower. She's so sexy, even when she's shoving huge bites of pizza into her mouth. To survive a week with her, I've had to put up some walls between us. Real walls. The kind that separate my bedroom from hers.

Why can't I shag her again? I know there was a reason, but it's fading from my memory.

Did I actually tell her I want a relationship? Yeah, I did. And I meant it. Dating seemed like a huge step, but a relationship feels like jumping off the Empire State Building. I love that feeling. It's the best high in the world, next to making love to Arden. Which I can't do. Because I said we shouldn't.

Why did I do that?

I get a reminder the next morning when Chance rings me—to check up on me, naturally. I can't be trusted not to deflower every virgin in New York City.

When I answer my mobile, I speak before Chance can. "No, I'm not having sex with Arden."

"Good day to you too, Reese."

"Don't pretend you aren't ringing me to make sure I've kept my randy paws off your fiancée's best friend."

"Maybe I am, but that's not the only reason I rang you."

I sigh, leaning my head back against the sofa. I've been sitting here while I wait for Arden to wake up and emerge from her room. "What else do you want, Chance?"

"Elena needs Arden in New Hampshire on Wednesday instead of Friday. She needs help with some sort of wedding dress crisis. It sounds like nothing to me, but Elena's having an anxiety attack."

"Aren't you loving all the feminine bollocks that comes with a wedding?"

"What would you know about it? You've never proposed to a woman in your life—and proposing a one-night stand doesn't count."

I scratch my neck and my cheek, because I've suddenly developed itches all over my body. "You make me sound like a right bastard. If you think I'm such a dick, why haven't you flown over here to drag me away from Elena's best friend?"

"Relax, Reese, it was a joke. You're not a dick." He hesitates before asking, "Do you like Arden? Really like her?"

"What, are we children now? Do I like her. What an asinine thing to ask." I have no idea why the question makes me uneasy, or why I get snarky with Chance because he asked it. I also have no bloody clue why I say, "Do you think Elena would mind if I wanted to, um, date Arden?"

Since we're already in a relationship, why do I need to ask permission? If Elena vetoes the idea, I won't stop dating Arden.

But I want to know what my brother thinks of it.

Yes, I'm an idiot.

"Date? You?" Chance laughs, but it doesn't sound like sarcasm. "Never thought I'd see the day. I'll ask Elena."

I hear a noise like he's holding the phone away from his face, then he shouts his fiancée's name.

"Chance, I didn't mean you should actually ask her—"

But it's too late. He's not listening to me anymore, and I hear Elena's lovely laughter when he asks her, "Would you mind if Reese dates Arden?"

"Of course not," she says. "As long as he behaves."

"I'm afraid that's not at all likely."

"That's not funny," I say so loudly I'm almost shouting. "You two are off my Christmas list. And forget birthday presents too."

Elena laughs again, and Chance joins her this time.

The bloody pair of them. I'm seriously concerned about whether Elena and Chance mind if I date Arden, and they're laughing at me.

"It's okay," Elena says. "But Arden's the one you need to ask for permission."

Maybe I should admit to them I've already done that, she's already said yes, and we're already dating and in a relationship. No, that would be too much honesty.

Some sort of movement catches my attention out the corner of my eye, and I glance toward the hallway.

Arden has come out of her room wearing nothing but those damn plaid knickers and a bra so thin I can almost see through it.

"Got to go," I tell Chance and Elena. "See you in New Hampshire."

I hang up and jump off the sofa. "Good morning, Arden."

"Morning." She yawns, holding a hand over her mouth. "What were you yelling about?"

"Nothing. I was on the phone with Chance and Elena."

"You should've let me say hi too."

"Sorry. They were in a sarcastic mood, anyway."

Arden strolls over to the sofa but sits on the coffee table instead. She yawns again. "How's the happy couple?"

"Irritating and nosy."

She tilts forward to touch my knee. "Did you tell them anything about us?"

"If you mean did I tell them we slept together and it was the best sex ever, no." Now I'm squirming, because her hand on my knee has suddenly become the biggest turn-on in history. Her lack of substantial clothing doesn't help either. "But if you mean did I tell them we're dating, the answer is yes. I asked if Elena would mind that."

"What did she say?"

"That I need to ask your permission, not hers."

Arden smiles in *that* way, the one that dimples her cheeks and makes me want to drag her into my arms for a kiss so deep it'll be almost like sex. "You already have my permission, Reese, for dating and a relationship. Date me like crazy, date me like you really mean it, like you—"

"I understand." And I'm positive whatever she'd wanted to say next would've diverted all the blood in my body to one particular region. "Let's go out for breakfast this morning."

"Ooooh, I'd love that."

"You should pick the restaurant, love. I don't know what's good around here."

She rubs her palms together, her tongue poking out between her teeth while she considers the options.

And I want to fuck her. On the coffee table.

Instead, I tell her, "Why don't you think about where you'd like to eat while you get dressed?"

"Okay." She hops off the table and heads for the hallway, but she stops halfway there to glance back at me. "I really like you, Reese. You're lots of fun and so sweet. Not at all what I thought a player would be like."

She goes into her bedroom and shuts the door.

Arden likes me.

Chance had teased me about whether I like her, and I'd gotten snarky about it. How do I feel about Arden Clover Pesti?

I like her too. A lot.

For some reason, I feel the need to change into nicer clothes, so I hurry down the hall. My old jeans and T-shirt don't seem good enough for a formal breakfast with Arden. Unless she plans to take me to a fast-food restaurant. Then I'll be overdressed.

I freeze halfway down the hall. What am I going to wear?

Oh no. I've turned into a woman.

The door to Arden's bedroom flies open.

She's standing there wearing denim cut-offs that barely cover her arse and—what do they call those things?—a tube top with the tiniest sweater I've ever seen. It covers her shoulders, though barely, and stops a few inches past her underarms. The thing looks like it shrank in the wash, or maybe it's a doll's clothing.

But it's her feet that make me choke on my own tongue.

She wears heels so slender I can't imagine how she stays upright, and so high that I think she might be taller than I am while she's wearing those shoes. They have thin straps to hold them on her feet, and to show off her lavender-painted toenails. Those high heels are the sexiest thing I've ever seen.

And I want to lay her down on the floor, toss her legs over my shoulders, and take her right here. I want that even more than I did a few minutes ago. So badly that I'm fisting my hands and gritting my teeth.

"Ready to go?" she asks. When she looks down at my feet, she says, "You might want shoes."

"I know." The words come out as a growl. "I was going to change into something… else."

"Don't bother." She scans me up and down, her lips curving into a sensual smile. "You look plenty hot already. I can feel my panties melting as we speak."

I cough into my fist, mumble something even I can't understand, and rush into my room to get my shoes. When I return to Arden, she's leaning back against the wall beside her bedroom door, swinging a tiny lavender purse in one hand.

Somehow, I prevent myself from mauling her and offer her my arm like a gentleman would, though my feelings toward her at this moment are the exact opposite of gentlemanly.

Chance and Elena are fine with me dating Arden, so maybe they won't mind if I…

No, no, no, and absolutely fucking no, you flaming arsehole.

I ignore my carnal urges and escort Arden to the cafe she's chosen for us. It's a casual place, so I fit right in. Arden couldn't fit in if she tried, and I don't want her to. It's not because she's "kooky," as she calls it. She's a stunning woman, and whenever she smiles, the entire world lights up. Her laughter should be patented as a cure for depression. It makes me feel good every single time.

While I listen to Arden ordering our breakfast, I can't help smiling. She's thoroughly adorable. And yes, I let her order for me, because I'm that sort of modern man. You know, the type who lets women do everything for him, not because he's lazy but because he knows that's what women like. I respect female power and all that bollocks. I'm an evolved man.

All right, the real reason I let her order for me is because I love the sound of her voice.

But I do respect her, which feels strange. I like her, I respect her, and I want to shag her. Maybe I have evolved.

We eat crepes filled with sliced bananas and served with caramel sauce on top. I'm not sure about this meal, but I give it a go—and end up liking it. Arden makes me want to try new things. I gave her a new experience too, but I'm not sure sex is as important as trying new foods or going to new places I never would have visited on my own. Like the science museum. Or Coney Island.

The thought stops me. I'm holding a forkful of banana-filled crepe to my lips but can't move another millimeter to eat it. Going to a museum is better than sex? Did I just think that?

"Are you okay?" Arden asks. "You look kind of pale all of a sudden."

I shake off my disturbing thought and look at her. She's so bloody beautiful. And sweet. And clever. She's the most perfect woman I've ever met.

"Reese?"

"Sorry, fine, yes." I shove the forkful of crepe into my mouth and chew it while I try to figure out what's happening to me. Once I've swallowed my mouthful of food, I attempt to speak without sounding like an idiot. "There's nothing wrong with me. I had a strange thought, that's all."

"What were you thinking about?"

You. But I don't say that. I can't. My vocal cords refuse to produce any sound. I shrug and eat the rest of my breakfast, consuming bite after bite without any space between bites so I can't be tempted to blurt out stupid things.

Arden watches me for a moment, seeming a bit suspicious, but soon she goes back to eating her crepe. She doesn't ask me about my strange thought anymore.

I let her take me wherever she wants to go. We visit every tiny, off-the-map tourist spot in the city, and some in New Jersey too, and I love every second of it. Arden can turn anything into a wildly entertaining experience. I even agree to pose for a selfie with her, like we did at the science museum, because she seems to love those. I slip an arm around her waist and smile while she takes the picture.

And I haven't even thought about shagging her in at least two hours.

Chapter Fourteen

Arden

When we get home, after a day of sightseeing and eating and laughing and kissing, I text Elena the selfie of me and Reese that I took today. She responds a few minutes later with a series of emojis that all include hearts or kissing lips. I'm not kissing Reese in the photo, so I have no idea why she's doing that.

I reply with an emoji of a face with its tongue sticking out.

Yeah, maybe we're both reverting to junior high behavior.

But it's not funny at all when Elena calls me a few minutes later and says, "You're sleeping with Reese, aren't you?"

"What?" I can play dumb, even though I'm not.

"Come on, Arden. You took a selfie with him, and I've never seen you do that with any of those other guys."

"Reese is fun. I really like him. Is that a crime?"

"No, but hearing you say that only convinces me even more that you're sleeping with him."

"As if that's any of your business." Though she can't see it, I sit up straighter in my puffy armchair and lift my chin. "For your information, I am not currently having sex with Reese Dixon."

"Not currently?" Elena's tone changes, becoming softer and throatier, the way she always talks when she's discovered a juicy secret. "Does that mean you've done it already? Or you're about to do it?"

I sit there with my mouth open while I try to figure out how to avoid answering without Elena realizing that's what I'm doing. I suck at subterfuge, though. Always have.

My silence speaks all the words I didn't want to say.

"Okay," Elena says, "it's none of my business. But at least tell me one thing. Was it good?"

"If the question of whether I'm sleeping with Reese is none of your business, how is it okay to butt your snoopy little nose into the question of whether he's good in bed?"

"You're right. I'm sorry." She sighs with phony disappointment. "I guess I'll have to infer the answer. Chance is such an incredible lover that I'm betting Reese is fantastic too."

"Elena, honestly." I relax into my chair, twirling a lock of hair around my finger while I remember exactly how fantastic Reese was on the night we slept together. "I'm betting Reese is way better than Chance."

"Let's agree to disagree on that one."

We chat a little more, then say goodbye.

I hear the shower running in the bathroom, and my mind decides now is the right time to give me a high-definition, 3D, surround sound mental movie of Reese in the shower. Naked. Wet. The water drizzling down his body. Steam billowing around him while he runs his hands all over himself, spreading soapiness on all those muscles...

Lucky suds.

The doorbell chimes, and I drag my butt out of the chair to shuffle over to the door. I'd rather sneak into the bathroom and join Reese in the shower. But I behave like a good girl and open the door to greet whoever's there.

"Arden, darling," my grandmother says, opening her arms in an invitation to hug her.

I give in and accept the embrace. "Hey Grams, what are you doing here?"

She keeps her hands on my upper arms, though we're an arm's length apart now. "You look tired."

"Gee, thanks. You look old."

Her laughter is big and uninhibited, like always. She knows I'm joking because my lips turn up at the corners, and besides, she knows me too well to think I'd insult her. Ever since I hit puberty, Grams and I have enjoyed ribbing each other, affectionately.

Celeste Arnaud keeps her blonde hair cut short, but since she has lots of curls, it doesn't look severe. And yeah, she dyes her hair. Though she's in her seventies, she has zero wrinkles—thanks to a fantastic plastic surgeon. Her designer dress cost more than my first car. Grams stays slim too, and her perfect figure makes me look chunky.

I'm not jealous. I like my body, and I love Grams to pieces.

She cocks one hip and sets her hand on it. "Well, may I come in? I'm not used to hanging around in dank hallways."

I wave for her to enter and shut the door behind her. "It's not dank. This building is perfectly nice."

"Nice?" She stops between the bar and the sofa, swiveling her gaze this way and that. "I don't understand why you won't stay at my townhouse. This apartment is a hovel."

Yeah, I love her despite the fact she's an enormous snob.

"This is Elena's old place," I tell her, "and I like it here. It's cozy."

Grams closes her eyes and shakes her head. "Dear lord, how did I end up with a heathen for a granddaughter?"

"Watch it, Grams. I'll tell you all about the greys again."

She smiles and puts an arm around my shoulders. "All right. If you're happy, I'm happy."

"Thank you."

"But honestly, I don't see the appeal." She waves her other arm toward the windows in a grand gesture. "You don't even have a proper view."

The bathroom door opens, and Reese moseys into the living room. He stops at the other end of the sofa from us, and his gaze switches back and forth between me and Grams.

He's wearing nothing but a towel, slung so low on his hips that it seems like it'll fall off if he coughs.

Grams notices him—how could she not—and her brows lift. She rakes her gaze over him from head to toe, taking special notice of his towel and the bulge that's hiding underneath it. When she gets to his face, her lips kick up at one corner.

She looks at me. "Well, I believe I'm starting to see the appeal of this apartment."

Reese is looking at me like he wants to know what's going on.

"Um," I say, fumbling to get my brain in gear and stepping away from my grandmother. I point toward the half-naked elephant in the room and say, "Grams, this is Reese Dixon. Remember Chance, Elena's fiancé? Well, he's Reese's brother. Reese, this is my grandmother, Celeste Arnaud."

He strides across the room to shake my grandmother's hand. "It's a pleasure to meet you, Ms. Arnaud. Arden has told me all about you."

"Call me Celeste." She holds on to his hand even when he tries to pull it away. "Arden has told me nothing at all about you, but I think I can guess why. Gorgeous and British. I bet my granddaughter isn't a virgin anymore."

"Grams!" I almost shout it, and the syllable ends on a squeak.

She waves a hand like she's dismissing my freak-out. "It's about time you crossed that bridge, darling. But I'm dying to know more about your new… friend."

Grams slides her gaze up and down his body again, and I swear to God she licks her lips.

I'm helpless to squelch my indignant tone. "Grams, for heaven's sake. A senior citizen shouldn't be ogling a hot young man. What would Granddad think?"

"Your grandfather knows I only want him. Why should he care if I window shop?"

Reese is grinning.

And my cheeks are on fire.

"I have a fabulous idea," Grams says. "Let's all go out to dinner at my favorite restaurant. I have a standing reservation with a table on hold for me anytime."

"Your favorite place is super swanky," I say, "and I don't have fancy clothes. I doubt Reese does either."

"We'll stop off at Armani on our way to the restaurant." She ogles Reese again. "I'm sure he'll look scrumptious in a designer suit."

Once Grams makes up her mind, there's no stopping her. I let her take us out for shopping and dinner. Reese puts on jeans and a T-shirt for the trip to Armani, but nobody in the ultra-chic store cares about what he's wearing. All the female employees vie for the chance to get Reese fitted for a suit.

Maybe I get a teensy bit jealous of those pretty, stylish babes fawning over him. Maybe. Just a smidge.

And damn, he really does look scrumptious in an Armani suit.

Over dinner, Grams and Reese talk. A lot. I sit there like a lump in a designer dress, not saying a word. Normally, I have no problem with jumping right into a conversation, but tonight I've become a mute. Grams can't resist teasing me and Reese with sarcastic and often suggestive comments throughout dinner. This is her way of being friendly with my new boyfriend. She keeps telling him how amazing I am too, which is kind of embarrassing.

When Grams drops me and Reese off at the apartment, she whispers in my ear, "I approve."

"Um… thank you?" I honestly have no clue what I'm supposed to say to that, and dumb words are all I can come up with.

"He's gorgeous, yes," she continues, "but he's also whip-smart. Just like you. It's a perfect pairing, like chardonnay and escargot."

"I hate escargot. Slimy little dead snails in my mouth? Ew."

"Fine, forget the snails. I'm trying to say you and Reese are perfect for each other."

She kisses my cheek, says "adieu" to Reese, and leaves.

I'm alone with Reese. Sure, I've sort of lived with him for a week and a half, but tonight being alone with him feels different. He charmed the socks off Grams, or rather, charmed the silk stockings off her. She has never liked any guy I've ever dated, but she fell for Reese at first sight.

Kind of like I did.

He stands there across the sofa from me, in his Armani suit, looking so outrageously yummy. I want to eat him up, but something has changed between us. Something I can't yet identify. I know how to hunt down facts, no matter how obscure, but understanding this thing between me and Reese has me stumped.

Because I've never felt anything like it.

We're dating. We're in a relationship. But I don't know where this is all leading.

He sweeps his gaze over me while he unbuttons his jacket. "You are so beautiful, Arden."

"It's the dress. Armani makes any girl look fabulous."

"You've got it the wrong way round. *You* make the *dress* look fabulous."

"Thanks." My cheeks warm, but not with embarrassment. The heat of his gaze penetrates me, sizzling on my skin and deeper into the most intimate places. "You make that suit look so damn hot."

He crooks a finger, beckoning me to come to him.

I cross the distance between us, my gaze never leaving his, and stop right in front of him. Inches separate us, and I swear I can feel the heat of his body radiating into me.

Reese settles his hands on my arms, gliding them up and down so slowly and with such decadent tenderness that his touch sets off a tingling sensation in its wake.

"Mm," I hum, laying my hands on his chest. "I want you. Tonight. Please, Reese, don't say no again."

He kisses my forehead, my nose, my lips.

I slide my hands inside his jacket and push it off his shoulders. He takes his hands off me only long enough to shed the jacket. I grasp the knot in his tie and work on freeing it, while he showers light little kisses on my temple, down my cheek to my jaw, and on the sensitive spot just under my chin. The thought of being with him again, of feeling and touching his body again, excites me so much that I moan even while I undo his tie and toss it away.

When I grasp the top button on his shirt, he lays his hand over mine to stop me.

"Maybe we shouldn't," he says. "I want you so much it's killing me, but Chance and Elena—"

"Will get over it. They're cool with us dating, so they'll be fine with us getting it on once they realize it's none of their damn business."

"You're probably right." He slides his hands up to my shoulders and down my back to the top of the zipper on my dress. "Can't care anymore. I need you, all of you, naked, underneath me, on top of me, everywhere."

"Oh yes." I unhook the buttons on his shirt one by one, my fingers grazing his skin as I go, loving the way his breath catches. "Let's stop thinking and just do it."

He drags the zipper down, inch by inch, nibbling my earlobe while I shiver from the feel of cool air on my back and from knowing I'm about to have what I've craved for days. Him. Inside me.

I push the shirt off his shoulders.

Reese shrugs out of it, then plucks the straps of my dress off my shoulders. The dress drops to the floor, leaving me in only my flimsy lace panties and bra. I've worn the semitransparent one he liked this morning, or I assume he liked it. When he saw me in it, his eyes had glazed over, and his mouth had fallen open.

He takes in the sight of me, running a hand over his mouth.

Then he sweeps me into his arms and rushes me into the bedroom.

Chapter Fifteen

Reese

I sprint into Arden's bedroom and lay her down on the bed. The covers are over it, but I'm so excited about making love to her that I don't care. I pull her knickers off, then reach under her body to undo her bra and get rid of it too. She lies there naked, with the sweetest smile on her face, and bites her lip in the way that always makes me want her.

All right, I want her every second of every day. She doesn't need to bite her lip to get me worked up. But watching her release that lip little by little makes me even harder for her.

The thought I had a minute ago comes back to me. I want to make love to her, that's what I'd thought. Make love. Have I ever used that phrase to describe sex before? Maybe once before, and I think it was earlier today. Arden has done more than drive me to break my promise to Chance, or to break my habit of never staying in a woman's bed all night. Because of her, I want more than sex. Only with her.

A strange sensation hits me, like a hard thump to the chest. No one has struck me, though. This feeling is inside me. When I look into Arden's eyes, the thump turns into pressure, but it doesn't feel bad. I like the sensation.

"What's wrong?" she asks.

"Nothing. I'm fine."

I kiss her, softly at first, savoring the taste of her lips and the slickness of them. She tastes like strawberries, but I know from kissing her *a lot* that she likes to use flavored lip balm. Yesterday, it was peach. I take her bottom lip between my teeth and lick it, then slip my tongue between her lips in quick, light strokes until she moans and grasps my head, mashing her mouth to mine.

When I pull my head away, she makes the sweetest frustrated noise.

"Only a minute," I say, standing up, "and then I'll give you what you deserve."

She trails her fingers over her body, from her breasts all the way down to the hairs that mark the part of her I know will be slick and hot and ready for me. Arden gets aroused faster than any woman I've ever known, and I love that about her. I love her body. I love her smile too, and her laugh, her energy, her enthusiasm for everything, and—

I stop in the middle of taking my trousers off and stare at her. The things I've been thinking...

"You look anxious again," she says. "Like you did a few minutes ago. What's wrong, Reese?"

"Nothing."

"Bullshit." She pushes up on her elbows. "Tell me. Please. Have I done something wrong? Something that makes you not want me anymore?"

Christ, she thinks I don't want her? She'd have to be blind not to see exactly how much I crave her, because my cock is stiff and bobbing, all but waving at her to come and get it.

I finish undressing and crawl up the bed to straddle her body, gazing down at the face of the most beautiful woman in the world, the one who thinks I don't want her anymore. I sweep hair away from her eyes and kiss the tip of her nose. "I will always want you, Arden. Always. But I've been having these thoughts that I'm not used to having, and it's... confusing."

"What kind of thoughts?"

How do I explain this without sounding like a moron?

Maybe it doesn't matter if I sound stupid. Maybe she needs to know, even if the thought of telling her makes me slightly nauseous and more anxious than I've ever been. Don't I owe her that much? She gave me her virginity.

I take a deep breath and tell her the truth, though I have no idea what's about to come out of my mouth until it happens. "I love you, Arden."

Her face goes blank. She doesn't blink.

Why did I say that? We've known each other for less than two weeks. She must think I'm insane.

"I know it's awfully soon," I say, "but I—well, I feel—it, uh, well…"

Her lips curve upward millimeter by millimeter, easing into a smile that broadens into a grin so bright it lights me up too. "Relax, baby. I love you too. So you can stop stammering, even though seeing you flustered is completely adorable."

Only five of the words she spoke reach my brain—"baby" and "I love you too." She called me baby. And she *loves* me.

"Are you sure it's not too soon to say that?" I ask.

"No, baby, it's not too soon. I believe in love at first sight, so a week is actually kind of slow."

I kiss her and gaze into her eyes like a lovesick fool. And I don't even care. I'm a fool, and it feels good. I keep kissing her while I glide a hand down her body, slipping it between her thighs to caress her, stroking her folds and rubbing her clit with my thumb. Her back arches, and her mouth is torn from mine. I draw her earlobe into my mouth, still rubbing and stroking her, loving the way her breaths shorten and she grips my shoulders.

Her mouth falls open. She closes her eyes, lost to the pleasure that's building inside her.

"Arden," I murmur, then I claim her mouth in a deep kiss, thrusting my tongue in time with the movements of my fingers.

When she whimpers into my mouth, I know she's on the edge.

I am too, ready to explode and I'm not even inside her.

Her entire body goes rigid.

"Let go," I say. "Come for me, Arden. Don't hold back. I want to see and hear and feel all of it."

The climax seizes her hard and fast, and her knees bend toward her body like strings inside her legs have been cinched up tight. She squeezes her eyes shut, her nails digging into my shoulders, and she cries out.

I keep stroking her until she's done, mesmerized by the way her expression changes from shock to blissful pain to sheer pleasure, and finally, the most exquisite look of satisfaction. Her hair is a mess, her cheeks are pink, and she's still breathing hard. But I've never seen anything so perfect in my life.

She reaches down to close her hand around my cock. "I want my mouth on you."

"Have you ever done that before?" Since she was a virgin until I showed up, I doubt she's ever done what she's suggesting. Not that I don't want that. I do, of course. I'm a man, and we always love a good blow job. "You don't have to do that to make me happy. All I need is you."

"But I'd like to give you the same kind of thing you give me. I want to try." She lets go of my cock, her shoulders hunching. "But you're right, I've never done it before."

"Let's hold off on that until another time. I want to teach you all about sex. But for tonight, let me take the lead."

"Okay. You're in charge, baby."

My pulse speeds up, like it does every time she calls me that. "I love the way you keep calling me baby."

"You've called me 'love' several times."

"Have I? Maybe I fell for you at first sight after all."

She slides a hand into my hair and pulls me closer. We kiss more, kiss like we mean it, like nothing else matters except this night, in this room. The rest of the world might as well have evaporated, because all that exists for me right now is Arden.

I lay my body on top of hers.

She whispers against my lips, "Condom."

"Fuck."

I jump off the bed, find my trousers, and dig a condom out of the pocket. When I try to open the packet, I fumble it. The condom flies out of my fingers and lands on Arden's belly.

Laughing, she sits up and shimmies across the bed to sit on the edge. "Let me help. I've practiced putting condoms on a zucchini."

"A zucchini?"

"Mm-hm." She rips open the packet and begins rolling the condom onto me. "I knew eventually all that practice would come in handy."

The feel of her delicate fingers on my dick is making me breathe harder. She's got a look of intense concentration on her face, but it gradually gives way to a hunger that makes my balls tighten. By the time she gets the condom on, I've lost my breath completely. She's stolen it, and I don't mind at all.

Arden crawls across the bed on her hands and knees, giving me a perfect view of her arse—and her tits that hang down and sway with every movement of her body. She pulls the covers off the bed and lies down on her back.

"I'm ready," she says, almost purring those words. "Are you?"

"Ready, randy, and raring to go." I make my way up the bed to her, hovering over that luscious body, drinking in the sight of Arden for a moment before I lower myself onto her. "Am I too heavy?"

"No, I like it. Make love to me, Reese. Please."

She opens her thighs for me.

Braced on my elbows, I ease inside her. She feels so damn good, the way her body fits me like a glove. I take my time, letting us both experience every sensation, watching her face while I push in and pull out. The scent of her desire fills the air and intoxicates me, so much that I want to go faster, go harder, make her bounce and scream. But I need this to last. I need to feel her around me for as long as possible so I can memorize every second of it. This time feels different, more meaningful, and I never want it to end.

She wraps her legs around me, wraps her arms around me, and gasps every time I push inside her sweet, willing body.

"Arden," I whisper.

"Oh Reese, baby, I love you."

Those words rush through me like the most addictive drug on earth. I accelerate the pace, taking her harder, pulling out further before I plunge into her again. She clutches me tighter, not only with her legs and arms, but with her inner muscles too. God, she's close. I could push her over the edge so easily, but I want this to go on and on.

I rest my forehead on hers and force myself to slow down.

Her eyes are half closed and glossy. Her breaths tickle my skin every time she gasps. And that's all she does now. Gasp. Moan. Gasp again. My name spills from her lips a few times, and the wet sound of our joining echoes through the room.

Arden peaks in slow motion, her body clinching me tighter and tighter while her mouth falls open and her eyes flutter shut. When the full force of her release takes hold, she cries out and holds on to me with her entire body. I lift my head enough to see her face, so I can witness the intensity of her pleasure.

"Reese," she says, and it's a strangled cry.

I can't hold back any longer. I straighten my arms to get more leverage and thrust into her. Once is all it takes. I let go and lose myself inside her, pouring out everything I have while I shout her name.

Then I fall on top of her. Not the most romantic ending, but I seem to have lost all control over my muscles.

Arden combs her fingers through my hair, sighing with contentment. "You're the best lover in the world."

I chuckle. "You've never been with anyone else. How do you know I'm the best?"

"Because I do." She molds her lips to mine, but only for a moment. "I don't need to screw every man on earth to know that nobody else can compare to you."

"All right, have it your way." I slide off her body to lie on my back beside her, then link my hands under my head and smirk. "I'm the best ever."

"Don't get cocky about it."

"Why not? I'm always cocky, and you love it." I glance at her, still smirking. "Your grandmother thinks I'm amazing too."

Arden rolls onto her stomach, propped up on her elbows. "I love everything about you, Reese. You're more than amazing in bed. You're amazing, period. That's why I love you, because you're so sweet and kind and smart and funny."

"I love you for the sex."

She elbows me in the side. "You're supposed to tell me all the things you love about me, not go all sarcastic Brit on me."

"Maybe I should keep fucking you until you give up and admit that being British is what you love most about me." I palm her arse. "My accent is the reason you've never been able to keep your hands off me."

"Never denied that." She tips her head down and looks up at me through her lashes. "Keep talking. Your accent drives me wild."

I pull her on top of me. "Why don't I recite dirty limericks?"
"Yes, please."
I do that, and more.

Chapter Sixteen

Arden

The day after the night when Reese and I said the L word to each other, we fly to New Hampshire. On my grandmother's jet. She's coming to the wedding too, and no self-respecting billionaire travels commercial. Grams has the jet decked out with shades of pink and sunny yellow, including the seats. Reese doesn't seem to care about the girlie interior. He plops right down on the pink sofa, gesturing for me to join him.

I do. Duh. He's gorgeous, sexy, and British. Of course I do whatever he wants me to do and love every second of it. Unfortunately, all we can do on the plane is sit there and talk. Grams and Reese trade racy jokes, and I laugh. I don't know any dirty jokes or limericks or anything like that, so I let them have their fun.

Chance and Elena pick us up at the airport in a limo. We'll be staying at a bed-and-breakfast, since Chance and Elena's house isn't big enough to accommodate everyone. The rooms they do have are spoken for—by Elena's brother and his girlfriend, and by Dane Dixon.

"Why did Dane get first choice?" Reese asks, pretending to be offended.

At least, I think he's pretending.

"He's older than you," Chance says, "and he's much less irritating. Besides, I don't need to listen to you and Arden getting stuffed every night."

I raise my hand like a kid in school. "What does eating too much have to do with anything?"

Chance bursts out laughing. So does Reese.

Elena smacks her fiancé's arm. "It's not Arden's fault Reese never told her getting stuffed means having sex. You Brits have a responsibility to educate Americans in your bizarre language."

Okay, at least I now understand what Chance meant. And yes, Reese and I agreed to act like mature adults and tell Chance and Elena we're sleeping together. We broke the news as soon as we saw them. They've been much cooler about it than I expected, but I guess they finally realized Reese and I are old enough to make our own decisions.

The limo has two bench seats, so Reese and I sit on one side while Chance, Elena, and Grams sit on the other. Granddad went to Stockbridge to collect my parents, and the three of them are already here in New Hampshire.

"Whatever you want to call it," Chance says, "I don't want to hear my brother and his girlfriend doing it."

"Jealous, are you?" Reese says. "I've been declared to be the best lover on earth, so you're right to feel inferior."

"Who declared you're the best? That sounds like a rigged contest."

I raise my hand again. "Me. I told him that."

Elena rolls her gaze toward the roof and shakes her head, though it's sarcasm rather than annoyance. "Oh please, like you're an expert."

"Tell you what," I say, leaning forward to give her my best look of mock seriousness, "I'll let you have sex with Reese so you can find out for yourself."

Reese grins.

Chance throws an arm around Elena and pulls her against him. "My fiancée is not having sex with anyone else. But I'll get a leg over with Arden to prove her wrong about my brother."

Reese scowls, and I don't think it's sarcasm. "No, you will not."

"Not grinning anymore, are you?" Chance says to his brother—with a smug smile on his face. "Calm down, Reese. I don't want to steal your girlfriend. Elena's all I need."

Chance kisses Elena's cheek.

Reese hugs me to him for the rest of the car ride.

We get to relax for about an hour, lying in bed watching true crime shows because, apparently, that's the only channel our TV will let us watch. After that, I go with Elena to the dress shop where she bought her wedding gown so she can have the final fitting. She wants my advice about the veil—to wear one or not to wear one, how long should it be, et cetera—and I offer my opinions. Honestly, I think she wanted me here only because she's nervous. She adores Chance, but getting married is a big deal.

And she misses her mom. I know she does. Elena's mom passed away years ago, but not having her around for the wedding is hard. Maybe a best friend isn't a substitute for a mother, but I do my best to make this special for my best friend and to fill in for what Elena's lost. Her dad left when she was little, so her only family is Kyle. My dad will give Elena away during the ceremony because my parents love her like she's their daughter.

While I'm with Elena, Reese is with his brothers. Chance doesn't want a bachelor party, and Elena doesn't want a bachelorette party, so the groom is hanging out with his brothers and Kyle Linwood. They have a good time, based on how much those guys are smiling when Elena and I meet up with them.

That night, Reese and I have our own kind of fun. He teaches me more about sex, and every lesson ends with me shouting his name. He hasn't taught me what I really want to know. In fact, he seems embarrassed every time I ask him about oral sex. He's not at all shy about that when he's giving it to me, but he doesn't want to talk about how I could do the same for him. Guys are so weird.

The next day, we head to the wedding rehearsal. Dane is Chance's best man, and I get the feeling Reese is a little hurt by that. Reese will stand at the altar with his brothers, but he wasn't chosen to be best man. I'm Elena's maid of honor, but she doesn't have any other bridesmaids, so nobody's jealous of me.

Later, we all head to a restaurant for the rehearsal dinner.

I manage to get a few seconds alone with Chance and Elena, so I tell them I think Reese feels spurned. Maybe I shouldn't tell them that, but I can't imagine Chance wants his little brother to feel left out. It turns out I'm right about that, and Chance has a private conversation with Reese that makes him much happier. I don't know what Chance said, but I'm starting to see why Elena loves him. He's one of the nicest people I've ever met. He loves his family, especially his brothers.

Chance might be on my top ten list of nicest people, but Reese is *the* nicest. He'll always be number one on my roster.

When we get back to the bed-and-breakfast, we're both so exhausted we strip off our clothes, crawl under the covers, and pass out.

In the morning, I get to share a steamy shower with Reese. And I don't mean only that the water is hot enough to make real steam. We generate plenty of that on our own.

Today is the wedding. My best friend, the woman who's like a sister to me, is marrying the love of her life. And I'm in love with her brother-in-law. Or rather, the guy who will become her brother-in-law later today. It all seems kind of like a strange dream, but one that's also so wonderfully perfect.

I watch from the altar in the quaint little church while Elena walks up the aisle. Everyone in attendance is watching her because she's the most beautiful bride anyone could imagine. Her dress is lacy and swishy and makes her look like a princess—not that I've ever met a princess. I glance over at Chance and see him wiping at his eyes like he might cry at the sight of his bride coming toward him, about to vow to love, honor, and cherish him. He'll promise the same thing to Elena, and I know he'll mean it.

Reese is wiping at his eyes too.

Though I never would've pegged him as the sentimental type, I like knowing that he can get emotional when it's appropriate. It makes me love him even more.

And yeah, I'm crying. It's no discreet tearing up, either. Uh-uh, I'm full-on crying with tears running down my cheeks by the time Elena reaches the altar.

My gaze swerves to Reese right when he looks at me. He smiles and mouths, "You are beautiful." He's so full of it, because my eyes must be red and puffy, but I know he honestly thinks I'm beautiful, no matter what.

We keep looking at each other throughout the ceremony. I hear the wedding spiel, but I don't really pay attention to it. I keep thinking about the past couple weeks and how my life has changed so much. I'm in love with a British guy. He lives in England. I live in America. Will he ask me to move over there to be with him? What will I say if he does? Do I want to leave my home country? It wouldn't be fair to demand he leave his country to be with me. I have no idea how we'll work this out, and honestly, it's too soon to be worrying about that. But I can't stop the thoughts, the worries, that ricochet through my mind.

I glance at Chance and Elena right as he puts the ring on her finger. He's already wearing his wedding band, so they kiss. It's the sweetest, most romantic thing I've ever seen. And I cry. Again.

Then it's over.

Reese and I ride in the limo with Chance, Elena, and Dane. My parents and Grams are in another car, so I don't see them until an hour later, what with all the guests at the reception and the food and the dancing and—Jeez, weddings are such a production. I dance with both Chance and Dane, as well as my dad and their dad and a few guys I've never seen before. Apparently, they're friends of the Dixon brothers. I don't get to dance with Reese until another half hour later, when he tracks me down at the buffet table, claims my hand, and leads me out onto the floor.

It's magical, dancing with Reese. He keeps one hand on the small of my back, his other hand holding mine in the usual dancing posture. We spin around and around, floating across the floor inside our own little bubble, in time with the romantic music provided by a string quartet. He looks so dashing in his tux, like a prince or a duke or whatever they call those royal people over there in England.

But the song ends, and Elena waves at me. It's more like flapping her hand wildly. She wants me to go over there.

"The bride is summoning you," Reese says.

"Yeah, I haven't gotten to talk to her since we left the limo."

"Well, go on." He gives me a gentle push. "Don't leave the bride waiting."

I kiss him and hustle over to Elena. "What's up?"

"We haven't had time to talk about anything except the wedding since you got here. I wanted to catch up with you before Chance and I leave on our honeymoon."

"You know I haven't been up to much. Decompressing after Ecuador, mostly."

She gives me a funny look, like she's not sure if I'm full of shit. "What about you and Reese? How serious is it?"

I'd guessed she would ask this question sometime, but I didn't think she'd do it tonight. I have to answer honestly, even if she thinks I've gone insane. "I love him, Elena."

"Chance said Reese told him the same thing. He's completely in love with you and will do whatever it takes to make your relationship work."

Whatever it takes? Reese said those words? My heart does a strange pitter-patter thing when I hear that.

Then I remember something I've been meaning to ask her but haven't had a chance until now. I sidle up to her, hooking my arm under hers, and ask away. "Can I get your advice on a sex issue?"

Elena laughs, though it's almost a whisper-laugh. "You know, I've been waiting for the day you'd ask me that, but now that you have, I feel a little weird about it."

"If you'd rather not—"

"Ask me, Arden."

"Have you ever given a guy a blow job?"

She's just taken a sip of her champagne and splutters, like a cartoon character. "What? Well, yeah, I have."

My best friend is flustered by my question, but I charge ahead anyway. Desperate times or whatever. If Reese won't share the deets with me, I have to get them from Elena.

"Does Chance like it when you do that for him?" I ask.

Her smile is knowing, and she glances at her hubby who's across the room from us. "Oh yes, he likes it."

"Good. Can you give me some pointers?"

Her attention veers back to me, and her brows crinkle. "Pointers? We can talk about that another time, okay?"

"Can't wait. I need to know how to give Reese a blow job tonight."

"What's the rush? From what I hear, you two have plenty of fun already."

Yeah, my parents and Grams have made sly comments about the noise coming from the room Reese and I are sharing. They're happy for us, but they can't resist teasing us about it.

"Please," I say to Elena, "I need your help. A few pointers, that's all I'm asking for."

"Okay." Elena leans in and whispers in a conspiratorial tone, "Here's how you make a man's eyes roll back in his head…"

Chapter Seventeen

Reese

I'm talking to Celeste Arnaud and her husband when her granddaughter waltzes up to me and says, "Come with me, please. Grams, you don't mind, do you? I need to have a private moment with my honey."

Her honey? It sounds silly, but I like it. "Baby" is still my favorite thing Arden calls me, but I like any word she wants to apply to me.

"Go on," Celeste says. "I've been wanting to chat with Dane, anyway. Oh, there he is at the buffet table. I'll go grab him before someone else does."

All the women who aren't here with a significant other want to dance with my brother. I don't get it. He wears glasses, doesn't like to talk about himself or his work, and doesn't have the stellar sense of humor I have. Then again, I'm taken. So the ladies here have to settle for Dane.

I'm joking. You know that, right? Well, mostly joking.

My sexy little American leads me away to… a coat closet. No joke. She drags me in there, shuts the door, and pushes me back against the wall.

"What are you about?" I ask. "If Dane told you I was flirting with other women, he's a bloody liar."

"Oh, I know you'd never do that." She kneels in front of me. "I'm not going to yell at you. I have something else in mind."

"What are you—" My voice dies when she unzips my trousers. "Arden?"

"You wouldn't tell me how to do this, so I had to ask Elena." She pulls my dick out of my trousers and takes it in both her hands. "I want to do this for you, Reese."

"Uh, not here. Let's wait until we get back to the bed-and-breakfast."

"No more waiting." She licks the head of my blossoming erection. "You're coming for me whether you like it or not."

My laugh comes out choked and a bit panicked. "Arden, you don't have to—"

She kisses my cock and pumps it with one hand. "Why do you keep saying no? I thought guys *loved* getting blow jobs."

"Normally, yes, but not at my brother's wedding." My head falls back against the wall, and I groan when she takes me in her mouth. "Arden, please. Let's do this later."

Does that stop her? Of course not. She's determined, and when Arden wants something, I have no willpower to make me say no. This is even hotter than when she prances around in her virtually invisible underwear. Her mouth, her silky tongue on my skin, it's more than any normal human male could possibly resist. Not that I'm normal. Not that she's an average girl. And the way she slides her tongue over me while she sucks and pumps with her hand…

I grasp the back of her head and stop trying to resist.

The door flies open. Someone gasps. Another someone yelps.

Arden jerks away from me, falling backward and landing flat on her arse.

I stare at the man and woman who have stumbled onto our liaison in the coat closet, but I can't speak. Arden made sure of that.

The two people look familiar. My brain is thoroughly muddled by what Arden just did to me, so it takes me a moment of gawping to realize who these people are.

Arden's parents.

"Mom, Dad," she says, scrambling to her feet. "Why are you in the coat room? Are you leaving already?"

"No, flower girl," Arden's mother says. "We saw you and Reese come in here, and it seemed like you were taking a long time. We thought we should check on you, just in case."

"In case of what?" Arden says with a smirk. "In case we got trapped in coat cocoons spun by invisible aliens?"

Mr. Pesti glances at me—not my face, but down much lower where I'm still swinging free. He coughs and swerves his attention away. "Sorry we interrupted. Let's get back out on the dance floor, hey Tally?"

Arden's mother nods to her husband. "Oh yes, I'd love another dance with that hunky Dane."

For bizarre reasons I'm certain even she doesn't understand, Arden announces, "Reese is way hunkier than Dane and a better dancer."

"I'm sure he is," Tally Pesti says, winking at me.

Arden's parents leave the coat room.

She kneels in front of me again, stubbornly determined to finish what she started. The interruption from her parents has left me much limper than before they threw the door open.

I cup Arden's face in one hand. "Let's get back to this later, when we're alone in our room. I want to teach you more of my favorite things."

"And then you'll tell me how you like to be given a blow job?"

She looks so earnestly concerned about understanding what I like that I can't help dropping to my knees and kissing her, with only my lips. Anything deeper and I'll give in to her request right here in the coat room.

I rest my forehead against hers. "Yes, I'll tell you everything you want to know. Later."

Her smile, so bright and excited, makes my heart swell.

When I lead her back out into the reception hall, I glance around and spot Arden's parents dancing, smiling and laughing while they glide across the floor. Next, I see Chance and Elena dancing. She has her head on his shoulder, and he leans his head against hers while his eyes drift shut. His smile is the picture of contentment, and I wonder if I ever look that way when I'm with Arden.

I notice Dane and Celeste having a lively conversation at the periphery of the dance floor. They're not dancing, so I get curious about what they're discussing and decide to drag Arden over there. Is Celeste flirting shamelessly with my brother? I know her flirtations are only that, nothing more. Her husband is doing something that vaguely resembles the moonwalk with the girlfriend of one of Chance's mates. Celeste keeps glancing at her husband, her smile broadening every time she sees his strange dance moves.

Arden's family is full of nutters, I decide, but they're the friendliest, most lovable bunch of nutters I've ever met. They're clever too, a fact that most people probably overlook. Celeste is a billionaire, after all, and her husband serves as her chief operating officer.

We reach Celeste and Dane in the middle of their conversation.

"It's intriguing," Dane says, "but I'm used to running the business all on my own."

"And I don't want to change that. Think of me as your mentor and silent partner."

"What are you guys talking about?" Arden asks, her gaze flitting between her grandmother and my brother.

Celeste touches Arden's arm. "I'm propositioning Dane."

My brother opens his mouth two seconds before he manages to speak. "She means a business proposition. I've been telling Celeste about my company."

"Grams," Arden says, "you own a cosmetics company. Dane makes vibrators."

My brother clears his throat. "Sexual wellness devices."

Celeste makes a dismissive hand gesture aimed at Arden. "I know all about that. What do you think we've been chatting about? I've already expanded into perfume and jewelry. This is the next step in the evolution of Bonsoir. Our corporate motto is 'be your best after dark,' which ties in nicely with what Dane's company does."

Arden still seems confused. I'm right there with her. Cosmetics and vibrators? I have a sudden vision of women putting on makeup, spritzing on perfume, and grabbing their sex toys. Yes, it's important to look and smell your best when you're having a wank.

"You seem dubious," Celeste says to me. "Don't you want your brother to succeed? I can make him an instant billionaire."

I laugh, assuming she's not serious.

No one else is laughing.

"Wasn't that a joke?" I say. "Nobody becomes a billionaire overnight."

"Dane will," Celeste says. "With my help and the power of the Bonsoir brand behind him."

Christ, she means it. My brother, an instant billionaire? I can't decide whether to be happy for him or terrified of what Celeste will do to launch his company into the stratosphere.

She moves behind me and Arden to come up alongside me, clapping a hand on my shoulder. "I have a proposition for you too, Reese darling. How would you like to be my new vice president of advertising? My president of advertising will be retiring in a year or two, and I need to groom his replacement."

"Vice president? I've been a copywriter. And I'm twenty-four."

"So what? You're whip-smart, and I trust you. Trust is the scarcest commodity in business." She leans in to whisper in my ear. "If you're worried your coworkers will be jealous, let me handle that. I'm a genius at calming down internal strife."

That statement might've sounded arrogant coming from anyone else, but Celeste makes it sound reasonable. I believe she must be a genius at that, exactly as she claims.

"She really does rock the employee relations," Arden tells me. "Grams is great with people."

Celeste pats my shoulder. "Who knows? By the time you and Arden have your first baby, you might be the president of advertising at one of the world's largest corporations."

"Baby?" I splutter. "We're dating, Celeste. Only dating."

And I'm head-over-heels in love with Arden, but that doesn't change the fact we're still dating. It's been two weeks since we first met.

My girlfriend reaches across my body to smack her grandmother's arm. "Stop that, Grams. You're scaring Reese."

"I'm not scared," I announce.

Celeste kisses my cheek. "I'm looking forward to having you as a grandson-in-law."

"Grams!" Arden chastises.

"Still not scared," I declare, rather enjoying being sandwiched between beautiful women.

Dane, who's smirking, pushes up his glasses. "Arden, maybe you'd like to test drive some of my latest devices before they hit the market. I'm sure you'd have insightful feedback."

Arden tries to speak, but I jump in before she can get one word out. "No, she does not want to test your ruddy devices, Dane."

"What's wrong, Reese? Afraid she'll like my toys better than yours?"

I know he's having me on and trying his best to annoy me. Normally I wouldn't care. But whenever one of my brothers makes a slyly suggestive joke about my girl, I get... irritable.

This time, Arden beats me to the punch. "Oh, trust me, Dane. There's zero chance of your devices outdoing Reese. No offense. I'm sure your doohickeys are fantastic, but nothing compares to a real man."

I puff up like a turkey spreading his feathers for his mate. Yes, I'm a ridiculous arse. I don't care, because Arden announced to my smug brother that I'm a real man.

Dane chuckles. "Glad to hear it, Arden. Reese deserves a woman like you."

"What kind of woman am I?" she asks, and she's serious about the question.

Only Arden could try to give me a blow job in the coat room, then turn around and innocently ask my brother what sort of woman he thinks she is.

"The best sort," Dane says. "I've never seen my brother this happy before. You and Reese are perfect for each other."

Chance and Elena approach us then and announce they're leaving to start their honeymoon night. Tomorrow, they'll fly to the south of France for the first leg of their international holiday.

Arden and I go back to the bed-and-breakfast and get on with our lessons.

She is perfect for me. I think I've known that since the first time I saw her.

But it takes me three more weeks to summon the nerve to ask her the inevitable question. We're in my old bedroom in my parents' house, since the cottage we bought a few miles away isn't ready for us to move into yet. We're planning to alternate between America and England, so we can see both our families as often as possible. Arden has always worked from home, and Celeste loved the idea of her new vice president of advertising trading off stints in the New York and London offices.

Chance, Elena, and Dane are here for the weekend too. The newlyweds are just back from their honeymoon, and strangely, I want to hear all about it.

But right now, I'm sitting on the edge of the bed with Arden kneeling between my legs. She licks her lips and hums with pleasure.

"Mm, Reese," she says, "you always taste so damn good."

That's right. She now loves to get my cock in her mouth, and I love the way she does it. I'm a man, of course I love a blow job—especially from a stunning, passionate woman whom I just happen to worship.

I rub my thumb over her lips and kiss her forehead. "I love you, Arden. You really are the right woman for me."

"And you're the right man for me." She sits back on her heels and skims her hands along my thighs. "I love you too, baby."

"Will you marry me?"

Bollocks. I'd planned this whole speech, even practiced it in front of a mirror, but the words burst out of my mouth like my tongue has a mind of its own.

Her eyes bulge.

"Sorry," I say, covering my face with my hands. "That's the worst proposal ever, isn't it? I swear I had a romantic version ready to go, but—Gah, it flew out of my head."

Her soft, gentle hands peel mine away from my face. She smiles with such sweetness and tenderness that I get a strangely pleasant ache in my chest, the sort only she can give me. "I don't care how you propose, Reese. It's what you have in your heart that matters. And yes, I absolutely, positively want to marry you."

"Really?"

"Yes, really," she tells me with a laugh while she takes my face in her hands. "You're so cute when you're flustered. It makes me want to get it on with you."

"That would be my choice for how to celebrate our engagement."

She scuttles backward on her knees and flaps her fingers, telling me to move back.

I scramble backward up the bed until I bump into the pillows.

Arden hops up and takes a running leap at the bed. She lands straddling my calves, then crawls up my body until her face hovers above mine. "Ready to get hot and sweaty?"

"For you, always."

We decide to announce our engagement over dinner and even get Arden's parents and grandparents, along with Elena's brother, to join in via video call on three phones. Elena and Arden both shriek and jump up and down. Chance and I exchange amused looks, like we can't believe our women are so barmy. Who are we kidding? We love their enthusiasm.

Dane watches it all with one brow raised, acting like he thinks we're all barking mad.

I walk over to his chair and whisper in his ear, "Watch out, Dane, you'll be next."

He snorts. "Like hell I will."

"Famous last words, mate. Famous last words."

Arden's Version

One Hot Roomie
Chapter One

I'm lying on my bed in the apartment owned by my best friend, Elena, staring up at the ceiling while listening to my fave music through my earbuds. Elena's brother, Kyle, offered to let me stay here for a while so I can rest up after my stint in the Peace Corps, but I don't want to rest. I want to get laid, immediately. Since I don't know anyone in New York, my plan has some flaws. How will I meet a nice guy who's ready to get it on with no strings attached? Maybe I should ask Elena. I mean, she met her fiancé here and had a fling with him five minutes after they said hello.

My tummy rumbles. What I need right now is food.

So I ditch my earbuds, heave myself off the bed, and wander out into the hall, heading for the living room.

I stop dead at the end of the hall.

A man is sitting on the sofa.

"Oh!" The exclamation explodes out of me. My heart is racing, and my brain is plotting the quickest way to get to a phone or anything that I can use as a weapon.

The man vaults off the sofa, as surprised by me as I am by him.

And I suddenly realize I've got nothing on except my plaid undies and a tank top.

I shake my head wildly. "No, no, don't rape me. I'm a virgin."

"What? I—You're the intruder."

"Am not," I inform him. "I have a key."

"So do I." Raising a key, he waves it in the air. "Here it is."

My pulse is calming down a bit, though I really think it ought to keep pounding in my ears. I mean, who is this guy? He's gorgeous, but that does not mean he's safe. Why does he have a key?

If that's the actual key to this apartment…

"Kyle said I could have the place," I tell him. "So go. Scoot."

"Elena and Chance invited me to stay here. Alone." He creeps closer but stops before he gets near me. "Ring Elena and ask. She'll tell you."

I scrutinize him while I try to figure out what to do. He does have a British accent, like Chance Dixon. Elena can confirm or deny what this guy says, so I rush to the bar and lean over it to grab my cell phone off the counter. Straightening, I face the intruder again and dial Elena's number, holding the phone to my ear while I keep an eye on the British stranger. "Your aura looks okay, but I better check with—"

"What's up, Arden?" Elena says cheerfully.

"Hey Elena, it's me. Did you invite some British guy to stay here?"

"Invite who to do what? Where are you, sweetie?"

"At your apartment."

"I thought you were back in Stockbridge. My apartment? Why would you go there?"

"What? Kyle said I could."

Elena sighs. "Oh honey, I'm sorry if you got scared. I had no idea Kyle said that. Chance and I told his brother Reese that he could stay there. I tried to call Kyle last night to tell him, but I had to leave a voice mail. Sent a text too. Sometimes he forgets to check for messages. "

"Ugh, that Kyle." I roll my eyes. "He's a sweetie but such a du-fus sometimes." I look at the stranger who's watching me with a puzzled expression. "Are you sure he's safe?"

"Who?" Elena asks. "Oh, you mean Reese. Yes, I can vouch for Reese Dixon. Have you actually talked to him yet?"

"Yeah, of course." Well, sort of. "But…"

"He's a sweetheart, Arden. It's okay."

"Uh-huh. You're the one who told me I'm too trusting. How do I know this really is Reese Dixon?"

"I'll text you a picture of him."

"Okay." I hold the phone away from my face to peer at the picture she's just sent. I glance at Reese, and yes, he matches the photo. Sighing, I tell Elena, "I guess he is who he claims to be. Thanks, hon."

I hang up, set my phone on the bar, and walk up to the hot British guy standing by the sofa. I have to tip my head back to meet his gaze.

Then I offer him my hand. "I'm Arden Clover Pesti. It's nice to meet you, Reese Dixon."

He shakes my hand and I love how strong but gentle his grip is and how warm his palm feels on mine. "It's nice to meet you too. Arden, is it? That's an unusual name, especially for a girl."

"Yeah, it's weird, I know. Blame my parents. They're big-time hippies, even though the hippie thing ended in, like, nineteen seventy-seven."

"Hippies?"

"Flower children, bohemians, beatniks, et cetera."

"I know what the word means. Are you friends with Elena, then? Or just Kyle?"

"Elena is my BFF. We're like this." Why haven't I let go of his hand yet? I pull my palm away from his so I can link the fingers of both hands in a locking gesture. "We're tight. Inseparable. I mean, except for the past nine months when I was in Ecuador with the Peace Corps."

"That's an admirable thing to do."

I shrug. "I wanted to see the world, so I joined up. All I ever saw was Ecuador."

He scratches the back of his neck, wincing slightly. "Sorry I scared you. Elena said I'd have the place to myself."

"The Linwoods have definitely got some crossed wires going on."

Damn, Reese is hot. And sexy. I love his blue eyes and his muscular body and that panty-melting accent.

I smile, swinging my hands at my sides. "Elena mentioned you've never been to America before."

"That's right. My brother has lived here for a long time, but I never got round to visiting him."

"Well then." I spread my arms wide and grin. "Welcome to the United States of America and to New York City."

He chuckles, and his smile is so unbelievably sexy and cute. "Thank you. I feel at home already."

I move closer, standing on my toes to look him in the eye and give him my best deadpan expression. Time to test this guy to make sure he's not an asshat or a total player. "New York is awesome, but there are a few things to watch out for. Cabbies will be obnoxious. It's their way. Never buy a falafel from a street vendor who has facial hair. Never have a mixed drink, unless you want to get roofied." I lean in more, my nose almost brushing his. "And watch out for the greys. They'll sneak up on you while you're sleeping, so keep a can of mace by your bed."

Reese looks confused.

Good. That's an essential part of the test.

"Oh," I say, popping upright and holding up a finger, "I almost forgot. Never flush the toilet on a Tuesday before eight a.m."

"I see. I appreciate the advice."

He's still adorably confused.

I nod, satisfied that I've set the test in motion. Reese seems like the perfect candidate for popping my cherry, but I need confirmation that he really is a decent guy like Elena says. I wander off to my bedroom to give him time to wonder about all the kooky things I said.

Ten minutes later, I move on to stage two of the test.

I grab a piece of aluminum foil that I found in the closet earlier—why Elena left that there, I have no idea—and dash out into the hall.

Reese halts, his eyes flying wide. He's carrying a suitcase, obviously headed for the other bedroom.

"Here," I say, offering him the aluminum foil. "You might want to sleep with that over your head to keep the microwaves from altering your brain chemistry. The waves are strongest at night."

Reese Dixon eyes me like I've grown a pair of spiky purple horns. "Thank you. It's kind of you to look out for my brain chemistry."

I ogle his body for two seconds, my mouth watering when I notice how big that bulge in his pants is, then I spin around and trot back into my room. Shutting the door, I lean back against it and sigh. Wow, he's hot. He hasn't run away yet, despite my wacky behavior. And I need to get laid and lose my virginity. Like, now.

Lucky me, I've got a hunky Brit sleeping right across the hall.

Maybe my sexual adventure begins right now.

Reese's Version

One Hot Roomie
Chapter Two

I stand in the hallway for a minute, maybe longer, after Arden sashays into her room and shuts the door. I'm still holding the length of aluminium foil she gave me. Microwaves? Brain chemistry? Earlier, she talked about "greys," whatever the bloody hell those are, and urged me to avoid buying falafels from anyone with facial hair.

She's clearly insane. But she's also the sexiest girl I have ever laid eyes on. Those plaid knickers… Christ, I want to rip them off. First, I'll need to knock on her bedroom door and ask if I can please fuck her mindless.

Instead, I behave like a mature adult and fantasize about Arden's body while I stow my suitcase in the other bedroom. When I go back into the living room, my mobile chimes to let me know I have a text. I drop onto the sofa and read the message. It's from Elena.

How are you getting along with Arden? she asks.

Brilliantly. She's barmy, but I plan to shag her anyway.

What I actually tell Elena is *Arden seems very nice.*

She is. We're on the plane, talk to you later.

I think she's saying goodbye, but then I get another text: *Promise you're giving up your shag-an-American idea.*

The word shag clues me in to the fact Chance has commandeered Elena's mobile. Naturally, I have to get snarky about his statement. *Don't worry, Elena, I'm saving myself for you.*

Very funny, you sodding arsehole.

A smiley face appears on a new line, and I'm sure Elena added that.

Goodbye, Chance, I type with a smile on my face but not in my text message.

Movement catches my eye, and I glance at the hallway.

Arden is walking toward me wearing pink shorts and a T-shirt with an alien face on it.

"There you are, Luscious," I say, because she is luscious in every way. "Did you finally remember why you came into the living room the first time?"

"Yes. I'm hungry."

She sashays past me without glancing my way. I watch as she goes into the kitchen and opens the refrigerator to examine its contents. Her sweet arse looks incredible in those shorts.

I follow her into the kitchen, coming up alongside her, and peer into the fridge. "Don't you have any biscuits?"

"Do you see any cookies? I'm not hiding them in my undies."

Her mention of undies makes me glance at her arse, though she's too busy perusing the items in the fridge to notice.

I smile. "You know what biscuits are. Damn that Chance. How can I confuse you the way he did with Elena if you already know all the British words? It's not fair at all."

"Trust me, I'm plenty confused."

"But I meant to charm you with my Britishisms." I examine her skimpy shorts, letting my gaze travel up her sexy body to her slightly oversize T-shirt and its alien face. But it's her lovely, round tits that command all my attention. "I want to charm the fuck out of you, Luscious."

And fuck the fuck out of her too.

"My name is Arden." She hooks a finger under my chin, lifting it to drag my attention away from her tits. "Arden Clover Pesti. Not Luscious. Got it?"

"If you insist."

"Thank you."

Luscious seems much more appropriate to me, although Arden is close to ardent, a word that means passionate. I bet she's a fantastic shag.

I jam my hands in my jeans pockets and peer into the fridge again. All I see is beer and hummus. Oh, there's some yogurt. Christ, don't they have any real food here? "How can a girl who sleeps with aluminium foil on her head be so uptight?"

"Alu-what? I guess that's British for aluminum foil. I'm not uptight. But I don't know you, and nicknames are things friends or relatives give each other."

"Fair point." I shut the fridge. "I'll hold off on calling you Luscious."

"I appreciate that. Now, do you like pizza?"

"Yes, I love it. Love a good takeaway, full stop."

"Takeaway's British for takeout, right?"

"Yes."

"Okeydokey." She turns toward the bar, where I see a landline phone. "I'll order some pizza."

I excuse myself to go unpack and change into different clothes. Why, I have no bloody idea. Maybe I just feel dirty, and not in the way I like to feel dirty, after my long plane ride to America. I put on my England Rugby shirt and a pair of pajama trousers, then I return to the living room. Arden and her sexy little body are sitting at one end of the sofa, so I settle onto the opposite end.

She points at my shirt. "Guess you're a rugby fan."

"Yes, but I also played rugby at school."

"Let me guess. You were the star player."

I shrug. Star player? Girls used to call me something like that, but only so they could climb inside my shorts. "Maybe I was, but it's a team sport. Couldn't have won games by myself."

"Is rugby like soccer?"

"Similar, but with differences. And we call that other sport football, not soccer." I glance down at my clothes. "I almost wore my Manchester United shirt."

Arden looks so adorably confused that I want to kiss her. Everywhere. Starting with that luscious mouth.

"Manchester United," I tell her, "is a football team."

"And by football, you mean soccer."

Huffing, I roll my eyes. "No, I mean football. You Americans have a bloody stupid idea of what that word means."

"And you Brits are so damn arrogant about your sports. I mean, it's only a game."

"Only a game? Don't tell Kyle you said that. He worships American football and is obsessed with stock car racing."

"Yeah, I know. That's why I've never dated Kyle, besides the fact he's my best friend's brother."

She props her feet on the coffee table, crossing her ankles.

I rake my gaze all the way down her body to her shapely little feet with their bright-red nails and then back up again. "Please tell me you were joking about being a virgin. You said that to stop me from attacking you, right?"

"Not completely. I am a virgin."

Bollocks. I can't sleep with a virgin. Can I? Some part of my brain insists it must be wrong, but I ignore that advice. "Does Elena know that?"

"That I'm a virgin? Yeah. My family knows too, since we talk about pretty much everything."

I can't resist giving her a wicked smirk. "Do you want to stay a virgin? Because I'm the best first time you'll ever have."

"Not exactly humble, though, are you?" She leans back and shakes her head. "Sorry, I've taken a vow to stay untouched until I meet the man I'm going to marry."

I sigh like I'm severely disappointed, and it's only part sarcasm. "What a shame."

"The right guy is worth waiting for."

"Hmm." I brace my elbow on the sofa's back, raising my hand to rest my chin on it. "Who is your perfect man?"

"Don't know. Someone who treats me with respect and love. A man who adores me. You know, the kind who always considers my feelings and does whatever he can to make me feel appreciated and loved."

"You want a gay man, then?"

"No." She scowls, but even that turns me on. "I want a good man."

"I'm very good. Ask any of the girls I've been with."

"Sex isn't part of the formula for a good man. I mean, I want to have sex with the guy I marry, but that's not the most important thing."

"You really are barking mad."

"Excuse me? I'm quirky, not crazy."

"Oh, don't get me wrong." I scoot a little closer, lowering my voice. "I'd love to get a leg over with you. And I guarantee you'll be glad you gave up your innocence to become a sinner with me. I do sin better than anyone."

"Thank you for the offer, but I'm good the way I am."

"Yes, I agree. You are perfect, lush—" I cut myself off and frown. "Is it all right if I call you darling? Or is that too close to the word I'm not allowed to use?"

She stares at me for a moment, then waves her hand. "Go on. Call me Luscious."

I grin. "Thank you."

"Whatever."

The doorbell rings, and I jump off the sofa to get our food. I carry the large pizza box back to the sofa and sit down while I set the box on the table. I flip the lid up. "They must've bollocksed up the order."

Arden shimmies closer to the sofa's edge, rubbing her hands together and humming with hungry delight. "Mm, yummy. They got it exactly right."

"But this isn't pizza." I lift a slice of the…whatever this is. Not pizza, that's for sure. "No cheese. No meat. It's some sort of pastry crust with what looks like applesauce all over it."

"Yep. It's an apple strudel pizza." She grabs a slice and takes a bite, moaning like she's having an orgasm from the taste of it. Swallowing, she says, "Try some. It's the most delicious thing I've ever put in my mouth."

I stare at the barmy girl sitting beside me. Her moans and the sensual tone of her voice have flipped a switch inside me that diverts all the blood in my body to my cock.

"What's wrong?" she asks. "Don't you like strudel?"

"I love it." My voice has gotten huskier thanks to her erotic enjoyment of strudel pizza. "But I'd rather devour you."

"No sex. Remember? I'm staying a virgin until—"

"Then you shouldn't consume dessert pizza like you're about to climax." I drop my slice and inch closer to her. "A bloke only has so much willpower, you know."

Arden stares at me for a second, then leaps off the sofa and rushes into the kitchen to get a can of beer. As she passes the sofa, she snags three pieces of pizza and slaps them onto her plate. Then she races into her bedroom.

I need to get her naked. Tonight.

But she's a virgin, so I eat the rest of the apple strudel pizza and go into my bedroom like a good little boy.

One Hot CRUSH

Hot Brits, Book Three

Chapter One

Rika

How can a man who designs sex toys for a living be so awkward around women? I work for the hottest guy on the planet, who has the hottest British accent on the planet, but I might as well be a robot sitting behind this desk for all the attention he gives me. Dane Dixon can barely look me in the eye, and as for conversation… Jeez, it's like watching a blind biker roaring down a curvy road on his Harley. You just know he's about to careen off the edge and go splat.

But damn, he's one sexy wreck.

This morning is no different. I'm waiting patiently at my desk for my boss to arrive—as his personal assistant, I make it a point to get here before him—when Dane walks out of the elevator and straight to my desk. Head down, he seems focused on the issue of *Forbes* magazine he's holding in one hand.

"Good morning, Miss Solberg," he says. When he glances at me for half a second, he swallows hard and resorts to staring at his magazine again. "Do I have any pointers—uh, I mean, appointments today?"

"Yes, Mr. Dixon. Today's agenda is already on your desk." Like it has been every day for the past twelve business days since I started working for him.

"Oh. Of course." He swallows again, his Adam's apple jumping. "Let me know when—if I, uh, have…calls or whatnot."

"I will." Rising from my chair, I tug my jacket down. "May I get you a cup of coffee, Mr. Dixon?"

"Yes. Thank you, Miss Solberg. One sugar, no cream."

He always tells me that, like I don't know how he likes his coffee after twelve business days with him.

Not once has he ever called me Rika. I told him he could, but he said it wasn't "professional." He also never smiles at me. I long to see his smile because I'm pretty sure it will be devastating. I'd love to hear him laugh too, but no, he never does that either.

Is he always like this with women?

Dane rakes a hand through his dirty-blond hair. The light glints on his glasses, so I can't see his eyes. But I know they're gorgeous. I got a good look at them on my first day here, when he'd taken his glasses off to clean them. He has deep-blue eyes that I'd love to gaze into for hours while his body is above mine and his hips are thrusting into me.

I haven't had sex in months. Working for a hot guy who ignores me is sure to drive me bonkers.

"Do I have a meeting with Celeste today?" Dane asks.

Wow, he got out a complete sentence with no "uhs" or "ums." I feel like I should mark this momentous day on my calendar.

He does seem kind of sweet, in an uptight way.

"Yes, sir," I tell him. "Ms. Arnaud is coming at ten."

He nods, head bowed. "Thank you."

Then he hurries into his office and shuts the door.

And I wonder again if he's like this with all women or just me. I've only seen him talking to men, so it will be interesting to find out how he interacts with Celeste Arnaud, the CEO of Bonsoir Beauty Inc., which owns Dane's company. He signed a deal with Bonsoir six months back, and now he's spending some time in New York at the company headquarters to prepare for the relaunch of his brand of sexual wellness devices.

That's about all I know. And I found that out from Celeste Arnaud's PA, who gave me the grand tour of the headquarters and dished about all the good gossip. Not that I like to gossip. But it's the only way I could find out anything about my new boss. My friends Elena and Arden know Dane, but they haven't said much about him. He has two brothers, but I didn't learn that fact from office gossip. I've met Dane's brothers, because they're married to Elena and Arden, though I hadn't met Dane himself until I started working here.

I trot down the hall to the break room and get two cups of coffee, one with cream and sugar for me and one with just sugar for him. After that, I hurry back to my desk, dropping my coffee off there. When I knock on the door to Dane's office, he invites me in, so I swing the door open and waltz up to his desk. As I set his cup down in front of him, he glances up at me.

For about a nanosecond.

"Thank you, Miss Solberg," he mutters.

And then he goes back to staring at the papers on his desk.

I've just sat down at my desk again when the phone rings. I answer with my standard professional greeting. "Dane Dixon's office. This is Rika Solberg speaking. How may I help you?"

"Hey, girlfriend, how's the new job going?"

I feel better already after hearing my friend's voice. Elena Linwood, now Elena Dixon, married my boss's older brother. Elena and I met a month before she hooked up with Chance Dixon, but we hadn't become good friends until after that. I'd missed their wedding because my appendix decided the day before the big day was a good time for it to explode. Elena had introduced me to Arden, who married Reese Dixon, but I missed that event too. A hurricane grounded all flights that time.

"Elena," I say, relaxing in my chair. "How's your hot husband? Are you wearing him out?"

"This is me you're talking to, not Arden. I give my hubby time to recover in between sex marathons. Poor Reese never gets a break."

Yeah, Arden is very…ardent. But Reese never seems exhausted to me.

"How's your hot boss?" Elena asks.

"Ignoring me. Does he always stammer?"

"Dane? No, he's well-spoken. You should've heard the pitch he gave Celeste when she was considering merging his company with Bonsoir. Chance and I listened to him rehearsing it, and Dane rocked his speech."

Which is the exact opposite of what I've experienced with him. God, it must be me. He thinks I'm repulsive or stupid or something.

"I'll take your word for that," I tell Elena. "Did you just call to chat? Because I am at work, you know."

"Yeah, I know. I called to ask if you want to have lunch with me and Arden on Thursday. She's flying in from England with Reese the evening before, so we're going on a shopping spree."

These ladies can out-shop anyone—including me, but that's not much of an accomplishment. I don't like shopping. Yeah, that makes me a freak of nature.

"Sure," I say, "I'd love to see you guys."

"Great. We girls really need to catch up." She hesitates, then asks, "Does Dane really stammer when he talks to you?"

"Oh yes. He stammers, he blushes, he avoids looking at me… You get the picture."

"Wow. He must like you a lot."

I hold the phone away from my face to stare at it for half a second, then I return it to my ear. "Are you nuts? He acts like he can't stand being around me."

Elena laughs. "Oh sweetie, that's not how Dane acts when he doesn't like someone. If he can't untie his tongue around you, then he definitely has a giant crush on you."

A crush? Oh please. A giant crush? Double oh please.

No one has ever had a crush on me, as far as I know, so I can't say for sure how men act when they feel that way. Men like me, sure, but there's been no crushing. And come on, Dane Dixon cannot like me that way.

What, am I twelve years old again? A crush. That's just plain silly.

I tell Elena that, and she laughs again.

"Time will tell," she says in a knowing tone. "This is Monday. When I see you on Thursday, I predict you will have changed your opinion about Dane Dixon."

"After more than two weeks with him, I rather doubt he's suddenly going to start acting smitten."

"We'll see." She switches to a whisper when she adds, "I'll get Chance to talk to Dane."

"About me? No way, Elena. Don't you dare do that."

"To be honest, Chance will probably do that anyway. He likes to keep tabs on his brothers."

"Does 'keeping tabs' mean meddling?"

"Um…probably."

I stifle a pathetic moan. "I have to get back to work. See you Thursday."

"Looking forward to it."

Elena and I hang up, and I go back to sorting through emails. Dane likes everything to be organized in subfolders so he can tell at a glance which messages are the most urgent. I'm in the middle of doing that when Celeste Arnaud walks out of the elevator into my little domain.

She stops at my desk. "Good morning, Rika darling. You look lovely today. Has Dane told you that?"

"No." I squirm a little, uncomfortable with her question after what Elena suggested concerning my boss. "It wouldn't be professional."

"Nonsense. Complimenting someone is not unethical."

I hike up my shoulders. "Mr. Dixon thinks a lot of things are un-professional, unethical, un-whatever. Honestly, Ms. Arnaud, I don't think he likes me. Maybe you should get him a different PA."

She waves a hand to dismiss my claim. "He's anxious, that's all. Not used to the corporate lifestyle yet. And please, call me Celeste. I've told you before I don't stand on formality."

"Yes, I remember. Sorry, Celeste."

"That's all right." She glances at the closed door to Dane's office, then smirks at me. "Should I wait for you to announce me, like we're at King Henry's court?"

"No, but I will let him know you're here." I grab the phone off my desk and punch in the extension for Dane's office phone. When he picks up, I say, "Celeste Arnaud is here, Mr. Dixon."

"Please send her in. Thank you, Miss Solberg."

I hang up and motion toward the door. "He's ready for you."

Celeste leans in to pat my hand. "Don't worry, dear, I'll take care of Dane."

She strides into his office and shuts the door.

Take care of him? What on earth does that mean?

I have a feeling whatever she does will not put my boss in a good mood.

Chapter Two

Dane

Celeste Arnaud walks into my office like she owns it. Technically, she does. The woman is the billionaire CEO of Bonsoir Beauty Inc., and I am sitting in an office in the corporate headquarters. The chair I'm sitting in belongs to her. All my devices, my factory in England, and all my employees now belong to her ever since I signed a contract with Bonsoir. My arse probably belongs to her too.

Still, I like Celeste. It's hard not to like her. She may be in her seventies, but she loves to make racy jokes, and she loves to admire young men. Sometimes she licks her lips when she's looking at me, which makes me feel like a side of beef sizzling on a grill. Celeste is also the grandmother of my newest sister-in-law, Arden. That makes her family, in a way.

Celeste takes a seat on one of the chairs opposite my desk. She crosses her legs and leans back. "Dane darling, how are you? Looking scrumptious as ever, I see."

She calls everyone "darling." I've gotten used to it. I've also gotten used to being called "scrumptious" and "delicious" and "one hot beefcake."

"You're looking well too," I say.

Her blonde hair has grown a bit longer than when we'd first met, but it looks good on her. Despite her age, she stays trim and has no wrinkles—but Arden has informed everyone, in front of Celeste, that her grandmother keeps the best plastic surgeon in the world on retainer, in case she needs any touch-ups. Celeste doesn't care if her granddaughter says things like that. They are a strange family.

"Thank you," Celeste says. "Now, tell me why you're treating Rika so horribly that she thinks you hate her. Are you lusting after her? Is that the problem? I wouldn't blame you. She is beautiful and intelligent, so I'm sure you'd love to spend the night with Rika. Why don't you just do it?"

"What?" I stammer for a moment before I can give her a response that sounds anything like words. "Miss Solberg works for me. I can't do anything of the sort. Not that I want to."

"Aren't we friends, Dane?"

"Yes." What that has to do with anything, I have no idea.

"Then don't act so shocked when I bring up a sensitive subject. You know that's the way I am."

Oh yes, I know that. But she's never suggested anything like what she said a minute ago. It's insane. I cannot fuck Rika, even if I want to. Which I don't. I have no time for sex, much less romance, and Rika Solberg seems like the sort who needs more from a man.

Yes, I know that after speaking a grand total of thirty words to her.

"I don't have room in my life for a relationship," I say. "The re-launch is taking up all of my time."

"That's horse shit, and you know it." She slides forward in her chair until only her bottom rests on it. "Dane darling, your celibacy will ruin our re-launch. You need a girlfriend. If you want to date Rika, all you need to do is ask her and then report the relationship to HR if you decide to pursue one. Though it might be best if I reassigned her to someone else, to avoid any perception of an ethical dilemma."

I grab my coffee cup and down the last of its contents in one gulp. I drink too fast, which makes me cough. "What the bloody hell does my love life have to do with anything?"

"You sell sex," Celeste tells me in a tone that suggests I'm profoundly dense.

"No, I design sexual wellness devices."

She laughs softly, smiling at me with affection. "Women use your devices to give themselves orgasms. Do you think they want to know the man who designs the vibrators they use is holed up inside a tool shed in the woods, alone, like the Unabomber?" She tsks. "No, dear, they want to see a vibrant, sexy hunk of a man who has a bombshell on his arm."

"What are you talking about? No one is going to see me."

"Oh yes they are." She points a finger at me. "You are the face of the company. That's why we're re-branding it as Dane's Delights." She waves a hand like she's shooing away a fly. "The name you had for it was too boring."

"What's wrong with Bedroom Buddies?"

She snorts, clearly trying not to laugh at me. "It sounds like you're selling alarm clocks. Like it or not, Dane, we—*you* are selling sex. That means you need to embody the concept. A recluse who works twenty-four hours a day and lives on frozen dinners is not sexy."

I start to complain but shut my mouth before one syllable emerges. Maybe she's right. Maybe I do have a responsibility to seem less…reclusive. Celeste had told me from the beginning our partnership would require I make some changes, in my company and myself. I assumed she meant I would need to attend board meetings, not that she would instruct me to find a girlfriend.

But I signed the contract. I knew what I was getting into. Mostly.

"Fine," I say. "You pick someone, and I'll go out with her."

"I don't run a dating service." She tilts her head to the left. "Though maybe that should be the next addition to the Bonsoir ensemble. Well, at any rate, I cannot find you a girl. You need to do that yourself."

"How am I meant to meet a woman? You've got me scheduled for so many meetings I barely have time to drink my coffee."

"I know, darling, but you're a smart, capable man. You'll figure something out. And do it fast."

"How fast?"

"This week would be best. Honestly, it shouldn't be that hard for a gorgeous, charming man like you to meet a woman. She doesn't need to be the love of your life." Celeste stands up. "I have another meeting to get to."

"What?" I stand up too. "Was this meeting strictly a chance for you to order me to get a girlfriend?"

"Yes." She leans across the desk to pat my cheek. "See? I knew you were a smart boy. Oh, by the way, how are those two new devices coming along?"

"Very well." It's bollocks, but I can't tell her the truth. I haven't come up with a single good idea for a new device since the day Bonsoir swallowed up my company, and I've had no ideas at all since the day Celeste commanded me to design something new.

Celeste pats my cheek and leaves.

And I drop onto my chair again. Find a girlfriend? How the fuck am I meant to do that? I'm living in a strange city, for two months, and I don't know anyone here. My brother Chance lives in New Hampshire. My brother Reese alternates between New York and England, but he's over there until later this week. Besides, I can't ask my brothers for recommendations.

Chance, could you ask around for me? I need a woman, immediately. Doesn't matter if she likes me, just that she's pretty and willing to hang on my arm like a bloody ornament.

No, I'm not saying that.

Reese, you used to shag every woman in the UK. Could you loan me one of your ex-lovers?

That's even worse.

I have a week to find a girlfriend. Though I'm not as popular with women as my brothers used to be, I'm not completely incompetent. Even Celeste called me charming. Yet lately, I feel like I have no idea how to speak to a woman, much less convince one to date me. Working too much has left me…out of practice. It doesn't help that the last woman I took out on a date had wanted to go home with me only because she hoped I'd use my devices on her. She wasn't the first to want that, but she also seemed disappointed that I'm not "kinky."

In my mind, I hear the last words she said to me. *Why can't you be as exciting as your toys?*

A knock at the door alerts me to the fact Rika is about to enter my office. She's very polite, always knocking before entering and saying "please" and "thank you." Her politeness makes me want to bend her over my desk and do things an employer should not do.

I sit up taller, straighten my tie, and clear my throat. "Come in, Miss Solberg."

Rika sashays into my office.

Christ, she's beautiful. Long, chestnut hair that glistens in the sunlight coming through the windows. A perfect mouth, made scarlet red by the lipstick she wears. Those breasts, that arse, the way her hips sway when she walks. And the high heels she has on...

She walks up to my desk and offers me a folder. "Celeste wanted me to give you the latest projections for sales in the first month after the re-launch of Dane's Delights."

My name will be on every package that's sold. My name. Fuck, it's embarrassing. Do I really want women thinking of me and the word delight while they're using my devices?

I'd love to hear Rika Solberg whisper my name and the word delight in my ear. I'd love to watch her availing herself of my devices too. An image of that explodes in my mind, and blood rushes to my loins.

Rika always has that effect on me. She is the sexiest woman I've ever seen. For some reason, I can do nothing but stammer and splutter in her presence. I can't make myself look her in the eye either. She has the most beautiful eyes, pale brown with flecks of brilliant green. As soon as I think about her eyes, I can't stop myself from gazing into them.

I really should know better by now. Meeting her gaze makes my cock ache and my mouth spew nonsense.

"M-Miss Solberg," I say, sounding like a ruddy moron, "please— I mean, thank you. It—yes, I needed this."

I snatch the folder from her and pretend to be obsessed with its contents, though I have no idea what the papers inside it say. I expect her to leave.

She doesn't. Instead, she says, "Can I get you more coffee?"

"No. No, I—" *Shut up, you idiot.* But my mouth has other ideas. "I'm fine, thank you."

At least I managed a complete, if brief, sentence that made sense.

She still doesn't leave.

The woman smells like…I don't know. Something delicious. It reminds me of the sweets my mother used to make for us, but it smells even better wafting off Rika Solberg's body. Why does she smell that way? I've never heard of perfume scented like baked goods and candies. Is Rika trying to drive me insane? Maybe I should order her to wear loose-fitting clothes and some of those horrible sensible shoes. And I should tell her to stop brushing her hair. No more makeup either. Definitely no lipstick. And stop smelling so good too, please.

"Celeste told me to stay until you've gone over those numbers," Rika tells me. "Then I'm supposed to get you to sign off on it and send all of it back to her."

"Oh." I flip through the pages, not seeing a single number or letter that's printed on them, then I sign the last page and hand the folder back to Rika. "Here it is."

Her lips pucker just a little, and her brows tighten. "You looked at the numbers so fast. Are you sure you don't want to take more time?"

Not with her in the room. Watching me. Smelling so fucking good.

I wave her away, though she doesn't move. "It's fine. Thank you."

"Okay, if you're sure." She bites her lip, which makes me want to sink my teeth into every part of her body. "Is there anything else I can do for you?"

Those innocent words trigger something in me, like the switch that keeps me from saying insane things has been flipped, and my mouth wants me to sound like a lunatic. Celeste's command that I find a girlfriend replays in my mind.

And I have the worst idea. But it sounds like the best idea, like my only option, like the sort of thing I shouldn't do but want to do, badly—for reasons I can't explain. Rika is beautiful. And sexy. And clever. She would make the perfect ornament for my arm, when I'm forced to attend public events related to the re-launch. But I can't. She works for me.

I could fire her.

Yes, then she'll be thrilled to become my trophy girlfriend. *What a bloody moron you are.* If I phrase it differently, as if it's a business arrangement, then maybe it won't sound like such an insane idea.

"Are you okay?" Rika asks.

For once, my brain and my cock are in complete agreement. I meet her gaze. "Actually, there is one more thing you could do for me."

"What is it?"

The words "be my trophy girlfriend" get lodged in my throat. I open my mouth, but the only sound that comes out of it is a faint croaking noise.

Rika leans over my desk, peering into my eyes. "Are you sure you're okay? Should I call a doctor?"

"I'm all right. No need for a doctor."

"Okay." She keeps leaning over the desk, which makes her blouse fall away from her chest, giving me the barest glimpse of her cleavage. "What did you want to ask me?"

"Uh…" I tug at the collar of my shirt. "Would you have lunch with me? I need to discuss some business matters with you."

"Lunch?"

Why does she look so shocked? It's not that barmy for an employer to take his employee out for a working lunch. Maybe sharing a meal with her will calm this lust and help me decide whether Rika might be amenable to the trophy girlfriend idea.

Yes, that sounds like a reasonable plan.

"A business lunch," I say. "Nothing untoward about it. I'd like us to get to know each other a bit, strictly to improve our working relationship."

She straightens. "Okay, sure."

I stand up. "You should choose the restaurant. I don't know the area."

"Um, it's nine thirty," she says. "I guess you're still on UK time?"

"Oh. Yes, I suppose I am." No, I'm not, but at least that gives me an excuse for not realizing it's still morning. "You settle on a restaurant, and we'll take our lunch at one o'clock. All right?"

"Sounds good."

Rika sashays out of my office.

I admire her arse until she shuts the door behind her.

Christ, I'm in trouble.

Chapter Three

Rika

At precisely one o'clock, Dane walks out of his office and waves for me to follow him. We ride the elevator in silence, ride in a cab in silence, and enter the restaurant in silence. He settles a hand on my lower back as we walk inside and while the maître d' leads us to a table at the back of the restaurant. The curved booth is smokily lit and secluded.

Dane had asked the maître d' for a "private" table.

I don't think he meant this.

We slide into the booth, but Dane keeps an arm's length between us. The maître d' gives us menus and then leaves us here—alone, in our secluded, sexy booth.

No, it's not the booth that's sexy. It's the man sitting beside me.

A waitress arrives before we have a chance to say anything to each other. She sets down two glasses of water, then takes our orders and hurries away.

We're alone. Again. In a romantic little corner booth.

Dane fiddles with his shirt cuffs. "Well, I, ah—We should—" He clears his throat. "Tell me about yourself."

"What do you want to know?"

"Anything you'd care to tell me. For instance, do you have brothers or sisters?"

"I have a sister. She's a doctor, currently working in Lebanon with Doctors Without Borders." Yeah, she's amazing. My piddly job as a PA sounds shallow and worthless in comparison. Not that I'm jealous of her. I love my sister. "Maddie is two years older than me. She's an epidemiologist, out there saving lives every day."

"Do you get along?"

"Sure. We always have, though we're not as close as I am with my two best friends."

"You have best friends?"

"Yeah. Don't you?" Oh jeez, that sounded rude. "Sorry, I wasn't trying to be mean. It just came out that way. But since we're getting to know each other, maybe you'll tell me more about you too."

"Of course. And no, I don't have best friends. I have brothers, and we are close, but I don't know if we're best mate close."

"Chance and Reese think you are."

His brows hike up. "You know my brothers?"

"Sure. Elena and Arden are my best friends."

Dane stares at me, his face blank, for several seconds. Then he guzzles water from his glass. "You're friends with Elena and Arden. I did—Ah, I didn't know that."

Why does he seem disturbed by the idea? "If you're worried I'll gossip to them about what you say to me, I assure you I won't. A good PA respects her employer's privacy and the confidentiality of work-related information."

"I'm not worried about that. I was surprised, that's all." He takes another, more measured drink of water and studies me for a moment. "Do you know Celeste Arnaud, then?"

"Yes. She's the one who asked me to be your PA."

"Why would she do that?"

"Because I needed a job, and she thought you and I would be a perfect fit." I realize how that might sound and add, "In terms of work. A perfect fit as employer and employee."

"I see." He's still holding his water glass, but now he's gazing down into it like water is the most fascinating thing he's ever seen. "How long have you been a personal assistant?"

"Ever since I graduated from college. I have a degree in liberal arts, which means I studied lots of different things." I wait a couple seconds to see if he looks unimpressed, but Dane watches me with interest. "Snooty people think liberal arts is a nothing degree, but it's served me well. My education included everything from math and science to ancient history. Whatever my boss wants, no matter what their career is, I have some kind of knowledge that can be useful to them."

"You must be bored working with me. I haven't asked you to do anything except answer the phone and schedule my appointments."

"I'm not bored." Because lusting after him keeps me occupied during lulls in my work duties. The thought of a gorgeous man like Dane designing sex toys… That makes me even hotter for him. And it reminds me of something I've wanted to ask him since day one. "May I ask you a personal question?"

"Go on."

"Why sex toys?"

He jerks his head up. "What?"

"I mean, why did you decide to design sex toys? It's not a common career choice."

Dane taps his glass with one finger, his focus on the water inside it. "I, uh, couldn't decide what to do after university. My degree is in mechanical engineering, but the job I got after graduation was unbelievably dull. I couldn't imagine doing that for the rest of my life. I got a different job but still didn't feel inspired by my career. After trying two more positions, I thought I could do better if I started my own business. But I had no idea what that business should be."

I inch a little closer to him.

He sets his glass down but still avoids looking at me. "The girl I was dating at the time complained to me that none of the vibrators she bought gave her exactly what she wanted. I asked what she did want and, ah, she, um, told me in graphite—graphic detail."

Is he blushing? No, it must be the lighting.

Dane squirms, his mouth pinched. "Then she asked if I could make a vibrator for her, since I'm a mechanical engineer."

"And did you make one for her?"

He squirms again, and this time I'm sure he's blushing. "Yes. She… liked it. Things sort of mushroomed from there. Within three years, I had my own small factory near the chocolate-box village where I grew up. Online sales took off, especially after Chance's girlfriend started raving about my products on her website. She had a blog geared toward single women, and she often wrote about sex. I hadn't realized how popular her blog was until she recommended my devices to her fans."

"What made you decide to merge your company with Bonsoir?"

"Celeste convinced me it would be a smashing partnership. She also promised to make me an instant billionaire once the product line re-launches." He scratches the back of his neck, grimacing. "Not sure I want to be a billionaire. What would I do with all that money?"

"Buy a small country?"

He almost smiles, finally meeting my gaze. "Thank you for the suggestion, but I think I'll pass on that."

"Just think, you could be King Dane of Dixonlandia." It should Hotlandia, but saying so would be unprofessional. "Doesn't every man want his own harem of adoring concubines?"

Dane stares at me for several seconds, then his lips slide into a sexy grin and he chuckles.

Holy cow, he smiled at me. And I was right. He is devastating when he smiles. And that throaty laugh… It makes me tingle all over.

"I'll take your suggestion under advisement," he says. "I'm curious what your last PA job was."

"For two years, I worked for a city councilman in Rhode Island. It was a tiny town, but we still had a city council."

"Why did you leave that position?" He winces. "Sorry. Not my business, is it?"

I shrug. "Doesn't bother me. I quit because the jerk sexually harassed me. He asked me to go to a conference with him, but it turned out he only took me along so he could come to my room late at night and try to get his grubby hands all over me."

"That's awful. Did you call the police?"

"No, he didn't do anything criminal. He got handsy, and I slugged him."

Dane smiles again. "You can take care of yourself, can't you?"

"Yep. I took self-defense classes and karate lessons." I cross my arms under my breasts and give him a teasing smile. "So you better not mess with me."

"I wouldn't dare." He glances at my breasts, which I've inadvertently pushed up with my arms. "I hope you sued that bastard."

"No, I didn't."

"But Chance is a lawyer. Did you leave your job before Elena met him? I'm sure he would be happy to help."

"I quit way before I ever met Elena or Chance. But I don't want to sue anybody. I just wanted a better job with a nicer boss." I tap a finger on his chest. "And I got one."

He bows his head, clearing his throat. "I'm glad I'm better than a handsy councilman."

"You definitely are."

Dane lifts his head. "I don't remember seeing you at Chance and Elena's wedding, or at Reese and Arden's."

"My appendix ruptured on the day before Elena and Chance's wedding. I spent the weekend in the hospital." I cross my legs, which draws Dane's attention. I swear I'm not trying to lure him into looking at my legs. It was a total accident. "As for Arden and Reese's wedding, my flight to England got canceled at the last minute because of a hurricane. I'd been visiting my parents in Sweden, and I couldn't get another flight until the next day, which meant I arrived just in time for the last half hour of the reception. So yeah, I missed the weddings of both my best friends."

"I'm sorry."

"Not your fault." I shrug. "They showed me the videos, so it was almost like I was there. We weren't really close yet at that point, anyway. I hadn't known them very long. These days we're three peas in a pod."

Our food arrives, and we chat some more while we eat. Dane loosens up some and has an easier time talking to me. He tells me funny things his brothers have done—especially Reese, who seems to get into a lot of trouble. Since marrying Arden, he's settled down somewhat. Dane also tells me about the people who work in his factory back in England, how they're like family to him. I tell him the story of how Elena and I met. After the debacle with the handsy councilman, I'd taken a receptionist job at a dentist's office while I looked for another PA position. I wound up working one floor below Raisa Volkov & Associates, the law firm where Elena was a paralegal.

Dane stops stammering during our lunch together. He smiles when he talks about his family, and when I talk about mine.

He asks if I want dessert, but I say no.

"I'm too stuffed," I say, laying a hand over my belly.

"Elena and Arden didn't tell you, did they?"

"Tell me what?"

He almost smirks. "That to us Brits, getting stuffed means having sex."

"Really? Huh. I'll have to watch what I say to you, won't I? Might get myself fired for sexual harassment when I'm just telling you I'm too full to eat anymore."

He studies me, his blue eyes obscured by his glasses. "Rika is a lovely name, but I've never heard it before."

"It's short for Fredrika, which is Swedish. My dad is from Sweden. He moved to America for college and wound up staying because he fell in love with my mom, who's American."

"You said once they live in Sweden now. Where exactly?"

"Gothenburg, or Göteborg in Swedish. It's on the west coast. My dad got a job there five years ago."

Dane pays the bill with cash, leaving a very generous tip, and we head for the front of the restaurant. When I see the dimly lit hallway that leads to the restrooms, I tell Dane I need to make a pit stop, then I go to the ladies' room.

When I come out, Dane is standing in the hallway, leaning against the wall. When he sees me, he pushes away from the wall.

I stop in front of him. "Ready to go?"

"Not quite."

He grasps my arms and backs me up to the wall, pressing his body into me, bending his head to get closer to my face. "One thing first."

Dane's lips brush across mine, tempting me with the featherlight sensation, and his breaths tickle my skin. My lids flutter closed. The touch of his lips, the feel of his body, it all leaves me paralyzed in the best way. I flatten my palms on the wall while my fingers curl, scraping my nails over the surface. My breasts rub against his chest with every breath I struggle to take in, and my head grows light, my thoughts spiraling away from me. His entire body cages me to the wall while the bulge in his pants grows and stiffens, and an electrifying tingle of excitement shivers over my skin, raising goosebumps on my arms.

A breathy moan rushes out of me. My body softens, and I part my lips for him.

Dane pushes his tongue inside my mouth, sliding it around my tongue, the movements slow and sensual like he wants to taste every millimeter of my mouth. He grasps my hips, rocking his into me while he tugs my hips forward, making sure I feel every inch of his cock and the way it's hardening against me. He keeps kissing me in that intensely erotic way, so gentle and yet so powerful in his ability to set me on fire.

I'm burning inside, ablaze with the need for him to love my whole body the way he's loving my mouth.

This is wrong, isn't it? He's my boss. We shouldn't be doing this. But I don't care, because his lips feel so damn good, his tongue feels so damn good, and the hardness of his body and his erection pressing against me feels like heaven. I revel in the way he teases the roof of my mouth right before he wraps his tongue around mine. Oh God, he knows how to kiss.

My nipples go stiff, aching for his mouth on them.

Tunneling my fingers into his hair, I try to spread my legs for him, but my skirt prevents it. I whimper, partly from the way he's kissing me and partly because I want him inside me more than I've ever wanted a man before.

He pulls away so suddenly I stand there frozen, with my eyes shut, for a few seconds before I realize he's not kissing me anymore.

I blink several times.

"We should get back to the office," he says, sounding unaffected and looking at me like I'm his PA and we didn't just enjoy a steamy kiss in the hallway of a restaurant.

And we go back to the office.

Chapter Four

Dane

For the rest of the day, and for two days after that, I avoid Rika as much as possible. What did I do? Nothing. Yes, I'm deluding myself in the worst way, but I can't work with the woman unless I convince myself nothing happened. I didn't kiss her. I certainly didn't thrust my tongue into her mouth and paste my entire body to hers. That never happened.

Christ, she felt good, especially when her breasts were crushed against me.

No, she didn't feel good because I never did that.

I groan at my own stupidity. Do I actually believe I can erase what I did by pretending I'd never done it? Maybe not, but I can avoid Rika, thereby avoiding temptation too.

Except I can't avoid her. Whenever she buzzes my phone, and I pick up so she can tell me about whatever call or meeting I need to deal with, I hear her lovely voice. She always sounds cheerful—sexily cheerful. And I wind up stammering and mumbling stupid things to her. I also wind up with a throbbing cock.

Every time she knocks politely on my door, and I tell her to come in, she sashays up to my desk to give me whatever papers she's holding. It's usually something I need to review and sign. With her standing an arm's length away, I can't think well enough to read anything, so I pretend to consider the document even though I'm not seeing any of the words printed on the paper. Then I scrawl my signature and hand the document back to Rika, trying my damnedest not to glance at her.

I do it anyway, every time. My eyes have a mind of their own.

And of course, I'm left with an aching cock long after she leaves.

On the third day, Rika brings me a large brown envelope and sets it down on my desk right in front of me. Naturally, she knocked before entering my office. And naturally, she looks exquisite this morning, in a pale-blue business suit that has a form-fitting skirt. Her shapely figure leaves me speechless, again.

"Here you go," she says, her tone as bright as her smile. "Celeste sent over the mock-up of the new packaging. She wants your feed-back on it."

"Oh." I pry open the metal brads that hold the envelope closed. "Think—Thank you, Miss Saltzburg. Ah, Solberg. Sorry. Thank you, Miss Solberg."

Every time I look at her, even obliquely, I get tongue-tied. It's ridiculous, but I seem to have no power to stop it. And every time I look at her, I remember my idea, the one that sounded brilliant a few days ago but now sounds like pure insanity. Still, the longer I gaze at her, the longer I admire her figure, the less insane that idea sounds.

We have the chemistry to pull off a fake relationship. My outra-geous impulse to kiss her in the restaurant proved that.

No, I can't do it. She'll report me for sexual harassment, and I'll plead guilty.

Rika pivots on her high heels and walks out the door.

When she turns to close it, I hold up a hand. "Leave it open, please. I don't like being shut up in here by myself. At least with the door open, I sort of see you out there."

I freeze, realizing what I've said. Why the fuck did I tell her that? Now she'll think I'm a pathetic fool who can't handle being on my own.

She smiles—with sweetness, not pity. "Sure, I'll leave the door open. That'll make it easier for you to let me know when you need something. Just give me a holler."

Rika returns to her desk.

I can sort of see her there if I lean to the side and squint. But I do hear her voice when she answers the ringing phone. She has the loveliest voice I've ever heard.

And the softest lips I've ever kissed.

Focus, you idiot. Celeste Arnaud isn't paying you an enormous salary to daydream about Rika Solberg.

Right. Back to work.

I tip the large brown envelope up, letting the contents slide out onto my desk. It's a rectangle of red cardboard with the words Dane's Delights printed on it in gold lettering. But it's the picture in the upper left corner that shoots icy cold through my veins.

A picture of me. My face. Below that, I see my name, and apparently, my new title—"Dane Dixon, the man behind the O's."

"What the bloody hell?" I shout.

Rika sprints into my office. "What's wrong? Are you okay?"

"No, I am not bloody okay." I raise the cardboard mock-up so she can see it. "Why is my face on the ruddy box?"

She shrugs. "I'm guessing Celeste thought it needed a personal touch. Besides, you are the face of the company."

Yes, I am technically the CEO of my little corner of Celeste's corporate empire. She left me in charge, but clearly, it's in name only. I would never have approved packaging that has my face plastered all over it—and that declares I'm the man behind the O's. What the fuck is that?

Rika bites down on her upper lip, waiting for me to say something.

All I can manage is a string of spluttering nonsense that never quite manages to become words.

"What should I tell Celeste?" Rika asks. "She's waiting for your comments."

I take a deep breath and summon all the wits I can still find. The rest seem to have flown away. "Please tell her I don't want my face on the box, and I definitely do not want to be called 'the man behind the O's.' I am not an adult film star."

"Okay, I'll tell her."

"And please take…this away." I shove the mock-up at her. "One viewing was enough."

"Sure thing."

Rika takes the cardboard monstrosity and hurries out the door.

I try to focus on work. I'm meant to design two new devices, but after months of trying, I still can't come up with anything. Women have always been my inspiration, but I haven't had a date, much less a shag, in so long I can barely remember what a woman's naked body looks like.

Though I have fantasized about what Rika's naked body looks like.

After an hour of racking my brain, all I have to show for the effort is a pile of crumpled-up papers in the trash bin beside my desk. If I can't invent new sex toys, maybe I can at least meet another of Celeste's requirements.

I shouldn't do it. But I want to do it.

No, I don't *want* it. I *need* to do it. For the business. Not for my aching cock, but for my company.

Clearing my throat, I call out to Rika, "Miss Solberg, would you mind coming in here, please?"

She hustles into my office, halting in front of my desk. "What can I do for you, Mr. Dixon?"

"Please sit down." I gesture toward the chairs just behind her. "I need to discuss something with you."

Rika settles onto one of the chairs, shimmying her bum like she's finding the perfect position for it on the seat. Her arse looks fantastic in that skirt, and when she's sitting down, the fabric rides up enough to let me glimpse her knees. They're bloody fantastic too, and so are her smooth, sexy calves.

I stare at her legs like a brainless moron for so long that she finally speaks up.

"What did you need to discuss?" she asks.

"Oh. Yes. That." I pull my chair closer to the desk and spread my palms on it, then realize that must look odd, so I clasp my hands instead. And I clear my throat again. Twice. "The answer— the question, I mean—it, uh—"

Fuck. Why can't I speak when I'm in her presence?

In the restaurant the other day, we had a normal conversation. I need to channel the calmness I'd somehow marshaled on that day. Slow breaths. *Don't look at her legs.* Inhale calmly, exhale slowly. *Look her in the eye, idiot.*

After taking a few calming breaths, I meet her gaze. "Be my girlfriend."

She blinks once, in slow motion. Her mouth falls open. "Are you asking me out on a date?"

Wouldn't that be the worst attempt at asking a woman out? But I don't want a girlfriend, especially not one who makes me crave her so badly I can't think straight. Why did I tell her to be my girlfriend instead of asking if she'd mind doing me the favor?

"No, not a date," I tell her. "This would be a business arrangement. Celeste insists I must have a woman on my arm at public events. So it doesn't look like I'm a recluse living in a garden shed in the woods, or something to that effect."

"Yeah, that would be kind of creepy."

Does she think I'm creepy? I don't care. Maybe I do a little. No, I *don't* care.

She wiggles her bum again, then leans back in the chair. "You're not creepy at all, but the idea of some loner loser designing sex toys... That is kind of icky. I can see how it might not be good for sales."

I still don't understand why anyone needs to see my face or know my name, but Celeste is the expert. I've done reasonably well with my little company, but now she's about to launch it into the stratosphere like a rocket headed for Mars.

Do I want that? It seemed like a good idea when she suggested it. Today, I wish I'd never signed that contract.

"So, ah..." I fidget in my chair, though I'm positive the discomfort I feel has nothing to do with the seat. "Will you do it? Will you, um, serve as my, ah..."

"Pretend girlfriend?"

"Yes. That."

She studies me like she's considering the offer.

I fidget more. Or maybe I'm squirming. Or maybe there really is a nail poking through my seat straight into my arse.

Rika nods once and slaps her hands on her thighs. "Yes, I'll do it. What the heck? I don't have a boyfriend right now. Hanging out with a soon-to-be-billionaire could be fun."

How much fun will I be? I can barely speak a full sentence in her presence.

Before she can change her mind, I say, "Thank you, Miss Solberg. I will, of course, pay you for your time."

An entire sentence. No stammering. Miracles do happen.

"Pay me?" Her brows lift. "I already work for you."

A nervous laugh bursts out of me. "Oh, yes. Of course you do."

Rika crosses her legs, resting one hand on her raised knee. "Come to think of it, you're my boss. Isn't this a conflict of interest or an ethics violation or something?"

Bollocks. I don't want anyone to think she slept her way into this or any job. Though Celeste said she could reassign Rika if I decided to date her, there aren't any comparable positions available at Bonsoir. I checked yesterday. But I've gone too far to back out of it now, and I have no hope of finding anyone else who will take on the task of hanging on my arm, not in the timeframe Celeste gave me.

Another bloody brilliant idea occurs to me.

"I'll have to let you go," I say. "But I can find you another PA job. My brother Chance knows a lot of people in New York, so I'm sure he can help with that."

Her mouth opens, her eyes widen, and she makes a soft huffing sound. "Oh great. I get fired from the best-paying job I've ever had. How is that fair? I'd basically be doing you a favor while I get shafted."

"I'll make sure your new position pays the same or more than your current job. Chance and I will find you the perfect position." I haven't asked Chance if he'll help, and I may need to beg for it since I can't tell him why my PA needs a new job. Well, maybe I can tell him—just not the whole truth. "Since everyone will believe we're dating, they'll also understand why I need to find you a different position."

"Okay," she says slowly, like she's not quite sure about my plan. "I'm not an actress, you know. What if I can't pretend to adore you?"

"I'm sure you can." I adjust my tie, though it doesn't need adjusting, and squirm again. "We have, um, kissed. That should be all you might ever need to do in public."

Her lips tighten into a smirk. "You want me to shove my tongue in your mouth at publicity events? While you glue yourself to my body?"

I cough, splutter, and finally choke on my own saliva. Once I've stopped coughing, I tell her, "No, we won't need to do that. Simple kisses at the appropriate times will be the extent of it."

"And hanging on your arm. Looking pretty and gazing at you adoringly."

"You don't have to—I mean, it's not—" I take a breath and start over. "You don't need to adore me. Just behave like a normal woman who likes the man she's dating. That's all."

She nods. "I can pull that off, I guess."

"I'm sure you can."

Has she actually agreed to my plan? Why would she do that? It's an outrageous thing to ask of a woman.

"Are you sure," I ask, "that you really want to do this? I'll understand if it's too barmy for you to handle."

"Nope, I'm fine with it. Could be fun, going out to swanky places, eating outrageously expensive food." She twists her lips into a lopsided expression. "Except all I own is work clothes and casual stuff. Will I need to buy expensive dresses or whatever?"

"I will buy anything you need."

"Wow, thanks." She taps her chin, seeming like she's analyzing something. "So, I get free fancy clothes, free fancy food, and the company of a hot guy. Yeah, it might be taxing, but I can handle it." She hops up and offers me her hand. "It's a deal."

I slip my hand into hers for a brief handshake. Her palm is soft and warm. "Yes, it's a deal."

"Great."

We're actually doing this.

I drum my fingers on my chair's arms. What do I say now? Should I arrange our first "date"? Maybe I need to wait until Celeste has an event she wants me to attend. Celeste didn't spell out the details, but it seems to me that Rika and I should be seen in public before the re-launch. Otherwise, it might seem like a got a girlfriend strictly for that purpose.

Rika is smiling, and it seems almost playful. "Since I'm your fake girlfriend, do you want me to fake sleep with you? I can fake orgasms, no problem."

I choke on my own tongue this time. When I regain the ability to speak, I say, "That won't be necessary. We need to put on the pretense of a relationship only in public."

"Shouldn't people see me coming and going from your apartment? I mean, that's what a girlfriend would do. Right?"

Oh bollocks. She's right. I hadn't thought of that before.

"Uh, yes," I say. "I suppose you should do that. I'm staying at a hotel, though, not living in a flat. You don't need to stay the night. We can, ah, work out the demon—the details. Later. We can work it out later."

"Whatever you say."

"Thank you, Miss Solberg. I appreciate your cooperation."

She smiles and laughs, though it's soft and not derisive. "Don't you think you should start calling me Rika?"

Of course I should. Bollocks, bollocks, bollocks. Why couldn't I think of that either?

"Absolutely, I should. Thank you, Rika." Speaking her first name makes my cock twitch. Or maybe that happens because her hips and thighs are at my eye level, and I can't help staring at her body. "And you should call me Dane."

"Starting when?"

"Right now. We should have lunch together too, at a romantic restaurant."

"Ooh, sorry, I can't." She makes a pinched face. "I'm having lunch with Elena and Arden. Would you mind making our first fake date for dinner instead?"

"Yes, of course, dinner it is. I'll pick you up at eight. Uh, you'll need to give me the address."

"Sure thing." She rattles off her address while I write it down. "See you at eight, Dane."

Then she ambles out of my office.

Hearing her speak my name… Christ, I've got an erection now. Her swaying hips in that skirt, her sexy voice, that smile— and she said my name.

Can I survive fake dating her?

Chapter Five

Rika

Have I lost my mind? The evidence suggests that yes, I have. Why else would I agree to fake date my boss? I've lusted for Dane Dixon since the day I met him, despite the fact he gets tongue-tied around me. That's kind of cute, actually. When Dane gets flustered, I want to climb onto his lap and kiss his cheek. Then kiss other parts of him, starting with his lips. Since I've wanted him to pay more attention to me, our new arrangement feels like a dream come true.

So naturally, my reaction was to say, "Yes, please, sign me up! Woo-hoo!"

Maybe I didn't speak those precise words, but what I did say amounted to the same thing. I got so excited I wanted to fist-pump right in front of my uptight boss.

Until I realized he doesn't really want to date me. He wants to show me off in public, so everyone will think he has a girlfriend and he's not a creepy loner who beats off while watching internet porn in his tool shed. Okay, sure, I get that. It's an image thing. But why can't we legitimately date?

I should've asked him that. Shouldn't I? But no, I was distracted by my tummy fluttering and my heart fluttering because Dane Dixon was speaking to me. In complete sentences. Mostly.

How stupid am I?

Maybe it's not such a bad thing. I haven't had sex in months, and my last date ended with the guy suggesting I should stop being a "whore" for anyone who paid me to be their work slave. I don't see how working as a PA makes me a whore, but whatever. Even before that incident, I'd been having an insane amount of trouble finding a guy who's not a complete jerk or so wimpy that I have to order his meal for him.

Aren't there any real men out there anymore?

When I had lunch with Dane the other day, he hadn't needed me to order for him or tell him where to sit. He hadn't asked me to sign a legal waiver before he kissed me either. Yeah, one guy suggested that. Dane didn't. He backed me up to the wall and *kissed* me, like he meant it.

Oh, I loved that kiss.

Maybe that explains why I agreed to Dane's fake dating plan. One amazing kiss and I melted for him.

Now I'm sitting at my desk trying to figure out how I'll survive making like I'm his girlfriend for almost two months when I'm not his girlfriend. I'll have to pretend to be hot for him, pretend to adore him, pretend to love making out with him. Wait... I'm pretty sure we're not supposed to make out. Simple kisses for public consumption only, that's what he told me. Why hadn't I pointed out that we kissed way more than that when he took me out to lunch? No simple peck on the lips that time. He had made love to my mouth, and wow, I want more of that.

Sorry, you can't have that. Dane isn't your boyfriend.

Right. Not my boyfriend. I need to remember that. No thrusting my tongue into his mouth. No sucking on his earlobe. No fondling his hot body. Absolutely no unzipping his slacks so I can close my hand around his cock.

Oh God, I'm in so much trouble.

I manage to focus on work until noon, when I have to pick up the phone and tell Dane I'm leaving for my lunch break. Yeah, I could walk into his office and tell him. Bad idea. Considering the fantasies about him that I've endured ever since our little meeting earlier, I know I should not set foot in his office for a while. A long while. Like, days. Maybe months.

When he picks up his phone, I say, "Just wanted to let you know I'm off to lunch."

"Thank you for letting me know. Enjoy your lunch, Rika."

I love hearing him say my name. Love his voice, period. And his accent. I'd thought Elena and Arden were full of it when they told me a Dixon man's British accent will drive any red-blooded woman wild. Nope, they weren't lying. Dane's voice makes me so horny.

"Enjoy your lunch too," I say. "See you in an hour, Dane."

And I love saying his name almost as much as I love hearing him say mine. Dane. That one syllable makes me so horny too. Dane, Dane, Dane. Even thinking his name gets me hot.

Snap out of it, girl. He's not your boyfriend.

I stand up, roll my shoulders back, and head for the elevator.

Then I realize I forgot my purse. Jeez, I'm hopeless.

By the time I get to the bistro where Elena suggested we meet for lunch, I've gotten over the initial shock of what I agreed to do for Dane. Yes, I'm fine now. Away from his sexy presence, I feel much better. No lustful thoughts. I've kept my mind focused on the tasks I need to take care of after lunch. Now, as my two best friends and I sit down by the picture windows and browse our menus, all I think about is whether I want a club sandwich or an avocado chicken wrap.

"How are your hunky hubbies?" I ask absently while mulling my food choices. Do I want potato chips or salad as a side?

"Chance is great," Elena says. "He sends his love, and he asked me to tell you he's glad you're working with Dane now and he hopes your energy and enthusiasm will rub off on his brother."

Just like that, my thoughts swerve back to Dane. That kiss. His lips, his mouth, his voice, his—

"Reese says kind of the same thing," Arden tells me. "But he used the word uptight too."

Maybe Dane is kind of uptight, but he's also shown me his sensual side. Kissing me in the hallway of a restaurant? That doesn't seem uptight at all. I get the impression I make him nervous, though I can't figure out why. But when he pinned me to the wall with his entire body...

"Are you listening?" Arden asks.

"Uh, what?" Great. Now I sound like Dane whenever he speaks to me.

"She's not listening," Elena says. "Rika, why are you so distracted? The menu isn't that fascinating. Is something wrong?"

Dane Dixon is the reason I can't concentrate. I've had a giant crush on the man since the day we met, and now I'll be dating him. Kind of. Sort of. Not really. But there will be kissing, and I can't wait for that.

I groan, but only in my mind. Nobody needs to hear how sexually frustrated I am.

My two best friends are staring at me, waiting for me to explain my distracted state.

"Nothing's wrong," I say. "Lots to do at work, that's all. I have to help Dane get ready for the re-launch."

"Dane?" Elena says, lifting her brows. "I thought he insisted you call him Mr. Dixon."

Oh shit. How am I going to explain the fact that Dane now insists I call him by his first name? For that matter, how am I going to explain it when my friends see me going out on the town with Dane, like we're dating? I know one thing for certain. I cannot tell anyone I'm fake dating Dane. My friends will think I've lost my mind, which I probably have. Sure, they'd love it if I dated their brother-in-law for real, but that's not what he wants.

What choice do I have? None. So I tell them sort of the truth but leave out the part where it's all for show, not a real relationship.

"Dane and I are dating."

My friends grin.

"That's wonderful," Elena says. "I knew you'd like Dane. He's so sweet and sexy, smart too. You'll be perfect together."

"How fab is this?" Arden declares. "Soon you'll be our sister for real."

"I would be your sister-in-law, not your actual sister. But it's way too soon to talk about that. Honestly, we just started dating today. Dane's taking me to dinner tonight."

"Your first date?" Arden does some golf claps while grinning again. "This is amazing. Ooh, we have to help you pick out your dress for tonight."

"The emerald one," Elena suggests. "It brings out the green in her eyes."

Arden nods, her expression serious while she ponders what I

should wear for my fake date with my fake boyfriend. "That's a good choice. But which shoes? I say the strappy ones."

"Yes, definitely. Those black stilettos would go great with the dress."

I groan out loud this time. "Are you two done arranging my personal life? Maybe you want to tell me what to order at dinner or whether I should have dessert."

"No," Arden says, "that's up to you. But there is one super important decision you need to make before your date."

"What's that?" I instantly regret asking, because I have a squirmy feeling in my gut that warns me what she's about to say.

"Before you go out with Dane," she tells me, "you need to decide if you're going to sleep with him on the first date or wait awhile."

I have never gotten horizontal with a guy on the first date. My friends know this.

"That's right," Elena says. "Decide before you see him. I'm sure he'll be wearing a suit and he'll look good enough to eat. He is a Dixon after all. Hotness is in their DNA. I think they have a special gene that makes women go wild just from seeing them in a suit."

"I went wild for Reese when he was wearing jeans," Arden says.

Elena rolls her eyes. "You were a virgin when you met him, so we can't use your experience as a guide."

"You had sex with Chance five seconds after you met, so we can't use your experience as a guide either."

I've known Dane for a smidge more than two weeks, and though I've wanted to rip his clothes off, I haven't done it. Not yet.

"Can we talk about something else?" I ask. "I haven't even had my first date with Dane yet."

Arden leans forward, pinning her gaze to mine. "Maybe you should wait to sleep with him. Kiss him first to make sure you have chemistry."

Elena huffs. "Why wouldn't they have chemistry? They've worked together for a while now, which means they'd know if they aren't attracted to each other."

This conversation is making me crazy. Will they ever stop talking about my fake boyfriend? I'd hoped dropping that bombshell would be easy and we could go back to worrying about what to order. But no, I'm not that lucky.

"I've already kissed him," I blurt out. Why on earth did I say that? "Well, he kissed me. It was fine, so you don't need to argue about whether Dane and I have chemistry. Okay?"

"Just fine?" Arden says. "Ohhh, that's not good."

Elena nods. "Yeah, your first kiss should rock."

"Did he use too much tongue?" Arden asks me. "Or not enough? There's a delicate balance between—"

"Enough," I say. Maybe I bark that word. I've never gotten so annoyed by my friends before, but I need to change the subject pronto, before I really do go insane. "Dane is a fantastic kisser. End of discussion. There must be something else we can talk about."

"Sure, hon," Arden says.

"Well…" Elena fidgets, biting her lip. "I do have an announcement. Chance and I agreed I should tell you guys, and I've been dying to do that."

Thank goodness. A change of topic.

She smiles with her lips sealed, but it swiftly broadens into a brilliant expression of joy. "I'm pregnant."

Arden and I squeal.

The other customers in the bistro stare at us, but we don't care. One of us was bound to get knocked up sooner or later, and we love that it's Elena who reached that milestone first. She waited so long to find a good man who adores her. Now she's going to be a mom. I can't believe it, but I'm beyond happy for her and Chance.

Once we've calmed down, Elena glances at me and Arden. "I wonder who will be next to go the mom route."

"Not me," I announce a little too quickly. "I don't even have a boyfriend."

Two pairs of eyes veer to me.

Oh shit. I forgot I have a fake boyfriend.

"Well, uh," I stammer like Dane might. Maybe it's contagious. "I meant that Dane and I haven't even had our first date yet. He's not technically my boyfriend until after that, right?"

Oh yeah, I suck at lying.

But my friends seem to accept my explanation.

Elena smirks at Arden. "Guess that means you're next."

"Probably," Arden says in a thoughtful tone. "I mean, we have soooo much sex that it's bound to happen sooner rather than later."

For the rest of lunch, I manage to avoid talking about Dane Dixon.

But I think about him. A lot. Way more than a fake girlfriend should.

Yep. I am in so much trouble.

Chapter Six

Dane

I'm standing outside Rika's flat, fussing with my cuffs and my tie and the bouquet of roses I bought for her. Is that too much? We're not really dating. This is for show, but I felt like I should bring her something. Maybe chocolates would've been the safer choice. Are roses too romantic? Then again, we want everyone to believe we're a couple, so maybe I should've brought two dozen roses instead of one dozen.

After standing there for a minute or two, I realize I forgot to ring the doorbell.

"Bollocks," I mutter, and I punch the button.

I can't believe I actually suggested Rika should pretend to date me. The words came out of my mouth. She agreed, which left me thunderstruck. I hadn't needed to do much convincing either. Rika said yes almost immediately.

Why?

The door opens, revealing Rika.

I almost choke on my tongue again, because she looks stunning. Her green dress brings out the green flecks in her golden irises, and the way it hugs her torso and her hips accentuates her curves. Her shoes have very high, very slender heels and delicate straps that crisscross her feet, leaving her toes and most of her skin exposed. She's painted her toenails a pale shade of pink.

And her hair. She must have curled it or whatever women do to make their hair look sexy. Rika's long chestnut locks bounce around her face in loose waves and fall over her shoulders, mostly bared by her dress thanks to its thin straps. I want to bury my face in that hair and suck in a lungful of its scent. I know her hair is silky, because I felt it grazing my skin when I kissed her.

Her red lipstick makes me want to nibble on those lips, and her eye makeup has that sultry, smoky look.

Everything about her makes me want to fuck her right here in the hall.

Or we could go into her flat and have sex up against the door.

No, we can't. She's only pretending to want me.

"You look ravishing," I say, before I realize that sounds like a come-on. *Fake dating, remember?* Well, someone might overhear us, so I need to play the part. I thrust out the bouquet. "These are for you."

She accepts my gift and smiles, sniffing the roses. "Thank you, Dane. The flowers are beautiful, and they smell wonderful. Just let me put them in water."

Rika rushes off but returns a moment later without the flowers.

I offer her my arm. "Shall we go?"

"Yes." She slips her arm under mine. "Where are we going?"

"The Grand Salon at the Baccarat Hotel."

Her eyes widen. "Wow. I've heard that place is incredible."

"So have I, but I've never eaten there. So far, I've only ordered room service at the hotel where Celeste arranged for me to stay."

We start to walk down the hall, toward the elevator.

Rika curls her hand around my arm, leaning into me. "Where are you staying?"

"The Four Seasons."

She stops walking, swiveling her head to stare at me, her eyes wide again. "That's got to be the most expensive hotel in the city. Are you in one of those ultra-swanky suites? I bet you are. Celeste loves to go all out. She's a billionaire, so she can afford it."

I scratch my cheek, wincing. "I'm in the penthouse suite."

"Must be the biggest one they've got, right?"

"Uh, I don't know. It's something like forty-three hundred square feet." I glance around, trying to come up with a way to lessen the shock my accommodations have given her. "Your flat is very nice."

"You haven't seen it. So I guess you're telling me the door is very nice?"

She smiles teasingly and nudges me with her elbow.

"I, well—" No, I will not stammer through the whole bloody evening. Absolutely not. I take a breath to calm myself. "I meant the building is lovely."

"Celeste pays me very well, so I could afford to upgrade to a nicer apartment."

"Sorry, I'll make sure your new position pays the same amount or more."

"It's okay." She starts walking again, taking me along with her. "I agreed to be your fake girlfriend, so I can't complain about switching jobs. Besides, being your PA was only a temporary thing. You're here for two months, then we both move on."

The idea of moving on doesn't sound as appealing as it used to. I wonder why, but I decide to focus on our first date tonight and worry about everything else later.

Our first pretend date. I really need to keep that straight in my mind. She's hanging on my arm and smiling at me because I talked her into playing the role of my adoring girlfriend. That's all.

We make our way downstairs and outside, where I hail a taxi for us. Once we're in the vehicle, Rika hooks her arm under mine again, snuggling up to me, and rests her cheek on my shoulder.

She's playing the part, nothing more.

I know this, but I can't help feeling more…relaxed, with her warm body nestled against me this way. I want to nuzzle her hair, but that would be an idiotic thing to do. Then again, I'm supposed to be dating her—I want everyone else to believe that—so maybe I should shove my nose into her hair strictly to convince the driver that Rika and I are a couple. Never know, he might snap a picture of us with his mobile, and if we look like strangers sharing a taxi, that might ruin the sexy image Celeste insists I must have.

So I slip my arm around Rika.

But I stop short of burying my face in that silky, glistening hair.

"Have you been to this restaurant before?" I ask.

Rika lifts her head to give me a sardonic little smile. "Sure, I've been to one of the most expensive restaurants in New York. I date billionaires, you know."

She's teasing me, but I like it.

"Ah, sorry," I say. "That was a stupid question. I'm sure Celeste pays you very well, but not well enough to afford a place like the Grand Salon."

"Even if she did, I would've had to go there alone. My love life hasn't exactly been teeming with possibilities."

"No boyfriends?"

She shakes her head. "Not until you begged me to fake it with you."

"I didn't beg." I want to ask her why she said yes to my proposition, but her reasons aren't my business. "We'll share a new experience together, then, at the Grand Salon."

She lays her cheek on my shoulder again.

After our cab ride, we walk into the Baccarat Hotel arm in arm, with Rika smiling up at me like she honestly adores me. Has she taken acting lessons? I can't see any other way she could pull off a performance like this.

I had no idea what to expect from the Grand Salon, but I would never have expected this. The entire decor consists of platinum and off-white shades, but it's the proliferation of crystal that makes the interior jaw-dropping. It's everywhere, from the chandeliers to the glasses in which cocktails are served.

"Holy cow," Rika says as we're led to our table. "I heard this place was amazing, but this is just unbelievable."

I pull out her chair for her. "There's so much crystal."

"Of course there is." Rika says as if I shouldn't be surprised at all. "It's the Baccarat Hotel."

And now she sounds like she can't believe I don't know what that's supposed to mean.

"I remember the hotel's name," I say, and I might sound a touch snippy.

Once we've sat down at our table by the windows, she studies me for a moment. "You really don't know about Baccarat, do you?"

"Isn't that a card game?"

"Sure, but it's also the name of a famous French company that makes amazing crystal." She glances around the room, gesturing at the decor. "That's why this place is full of crystal. Baccarat owns the hotel."

"Oh. I see."

Why hadn't I known that? I asked Chance for a restaurant recommendation, and he told me he brought Elena here a week after he proposed to her, to celebrate in style. I hadn't researched the restaurant, but maybe I should have looked at the pictures on their website. Now I've made a fool of myself in front of Rika.

I clasp my hands on the table, trying not to act the way I feel—like I'm doing the exact opposite of impressing my date.

She reaches across the table to lay her hand over mine. "It's okay. I know about this place only because Elena told me. Chance brought her here after they got engaged."

"But I should have, uh, found out more before—Well, I should've known."

"Relax, Dane." She squeezes my hands. "I'm not judging you for your lack of knowledge about this restaurant."

Strangely, I do relax. The warmth and softness of her hands makes my muscles slacken, and the gentle tone of her voice soothes me.

"Let's see what's on the menu," Rika says, picking up hers. She opens the menu and raises her brows. "Oh. I knew this place was expensive, but I really had no idea. Chance must be richer than I realized." She glances up at me. "And you must be too."

"I'm not a millionaire. But yes, Celeste gave me a very generous salary and a signing bonus."

Rika's lips curve into a gentle smile. "Signing bonus, huh? I didn't get one of those. I thought Celeste was going to make you an instant billionaire, anyway."

"That's what she promised, once the brand re-launches. Still not sure I want that."

She considers me for a moment, but then goes back to perusing the menu.

A waiter arrives a few minutes later to take our order. He has a French accent, and I've never been good at understanding that. I stumble through ordering, though I have to ask the waiter to repeat things several times before I'm sure he got my order right. It's humiliating, especially since Rika places her order in French. I studied Italian at university, but I barely remember any of it.

I can't tell if the waiter is flirting with Rika, since I have no idea what they're saying to each other. He does smile at her, and they both laugh about something.

And I develop a sudden urge to tell that French wanker to sod off.

Rika asks me if I mind if she orders caviar as our appetizer. I shrug, and she speaks to the waiter in French again.

He takes our menus. "It's wonderful to see an elegant young couple who are so much in love."

The waiter leaves us.

So much in love? Where did he get that idea? I wonder again what Rika and the waiter discussed.

"You speak French," I announce. "Sorry. I didn't know you speak another language, so I'm surprised, that's all."

"I guess you don't speak anything other than English?"

"No. I've forgotten nearly all the Italian I learned at school."

She leans forward, lowering her voice to almost a whisper. "I told the waiter you're my hot British sugar daddy and you're trying to seduce me with a fancy dinner."

I've just taken a sip of water from the intricately carved glass, and I splutter. "What?"

Rika grins. "I'm kidding. I couldn't resist. You're so darn cute when you're flustered."

My mouth gapes, but I can't come up with a response to that. According to Reese's wife, Arden, being called "cute" is a compliment. It means a woman likes you. But Rika can't like me in the way Arden meant. Not when I behave like a cartoon character.

Our appetizer arrives, and while the waiter sets it down on the table, Rika rubs her hands together like she can't wait to devour it. "I've never had caviar before."

"Never?" I tap my fingernail on my crystal water glass. "I have. Caviar is…not my favorite food."

"Why didn't you tell me? We could've ordered something else."

"You seemed excited about trying it."

Her lips curl up at the corners, not quite a smile but definitely an expression of…what? Affection? I can't decide if I want her to feel affectionate toward me.

"You really are adorable," she says. "And such a sweetheart."

"Uh… Thank you."

I watch while Rika samples the caviar. First, her nose wrinkles. Then, as she chews and swallows it, her face lights up. "You know, that's not as gross as I thought it might be. Not my favorite food either, but it's not half bad. My family goes for simpler stuff, like T-bone steaks and twice-baked potatoes."

"That's much better than caviar. Do you get along with your parents?"

"Sure. We get together for the holidays, birthdays, whatever, and we always have a good time." She consumes another mouthful of caviar before she asks me, "What about your parents? Elena and Arden make it sound like the Dixons are the perfect family. I know Chance and Reese, but I've never met your mom and dad."

"We all get on well and rarely argue. Not much to say, really. We're boring."

"You're not boring at all."

I freeze with my glass a millimeter from my lips. She doesn't think I'm boring.

The waiter brings our entrees, and we stick to discussing the food and the decor while we eat. Afterward, I try to pay the bill.

Rika stops me with a hand on my arm. She leans in to whisper in my ear. "I should pay half. This is a fake date, after all. I'll give you my part once we're back at my apartment, so nobody sees us splitting the bill. I mean, I know it's common these days for couples to go dutch, but I figured that might embarrass you."

She cares if I'm embarrassed. She said I'm not boring, I'm cute, and I'm a sweetheart. Maybe I shouldn't read too much into her behavior or her words. If she were attracted to me, she would've told me. Wouldn't she? Or am I meant to take the first step?

Not that I want to or plan to.

I pat her arm and whisper to her, "Don't worry about the bill. Our phony relationship was my idea, so I will pay."

"Okay. Thank you, Dane."

"You're welcome, Rika." I love saying her name. It rolls off my tongue in the most satisfying way. "I am about to be a billionaire, after all. I can afford to spoil my not-girlfriend."

"You are such a gentleman. It's refreshing."

After I pay the bill, we take a taxi back to her apartment building. I walk her to her door, the way a gentleman would. Not because she called me that, but because I want to do it. I always walk a woman to her door. It's the polite thing to do.

Rika unlocks the door, swinging it open, but lingers on the threshold. "Thank you for a lovely evening, Dane."

I kiss her cheek.

She raises her brows. "That's all I get? I mean, we want everyone to believe we're hot for each other. Don't you think you should give me a real kiss?"

"Well—It's—" I want to do that, but considering how our first kiss affected me, I don't think it's a good idea. "I never kiss a woman on the mouth on the first date."

"Make an exception. For the sake of appearances."

"There's no one else around."

"But this building has security cameras on every floor. What if someone leaks a video of you not kissing me?" Her smile is teasing and sexy as hell. "Don't want potential customers to think you don't know how to please a woman."

"Ah..." I can't stop staring at her red lips. She might have a point about appearances. Or maybe I'm so desperate to kiss her again that I'll take any excuse. "Yes, you may be right."

I move closer, bending my head to seal my lips over hers. The first touch fires an electric jolt of lust through me, from my mouth straight down to cock. The scent of her overpowers my senses, and I thrust a hand into her hair, spreading my palm up from her nape so I can tip her head back. A breath rushes out of her. For this one moment, I let myself forget she's only pretending, that this isn't real, and I lose myself in the kiss. Her lips feel soft and slick and warm, and when I push my tongue between them, she opens her mouth more.

I can't hold back, not when she moans and grasps my arms like she wants to do so much more than kiss. Thrusting deep, I devour her mouth and gorge myself on the flavor of her, on the sensation of our tongues twining and our lips colliding while we both cling to each other like we need our bodies melded but the air between us has become an impenetrable barrier. Any thoughts I might've had left in my brain fly away, leaving nothing except the blind, overpowering hunger to consume this woman like I've never done with anyone else.

She grasps my lapels and drags me into her body.

All of her, crashing into all of me… It feels incredible. I back her up to the doorjamb and grind myself against her, heedless of the fact I have a raging erection that's now jammed into her belly. She moans again, the sound so erotic it's fraying my last thread of willpower. I grip her arse with both hands, kneading her cheeks, then whisk one hand up to her breast and close my fingers around it, loving the way her flesh yields to me—except for the stiff peak. I want my mouth on that nipple. Now.

But I don't do it. I massage her breast and her arse, knowing that's as far as I should go, as far as I can go. I shouldn't even be doing that. How long we kiss, I have no idea. It feels like an eternity of pleasure. I don't want to stop, but I have to break away and give up the feel of her body and the taste of her mouth. It's what our arrangement requires.

So I step back, creating a distance between us. "Good night, Rika."

My voice sounds rough, almost hoarse.

Before she can speak, I spin away from her and stalk down the hall.

Chapter Seven

Rika

I toss and turn all night, tormented by dreams of Dane kissing me, Dane's body pressed against me, Dane's hungry groans, the way he'd fondled my ass and my breast. Yeah, sure, I had hauled him into me. I can't blame Dane for how hot our kiss got, because I suggested a real kiss, I pulled him closer, and I ravaged his mouth like a sex-starved lunatic. Sure, I haven't had sex in a while, but sheesh. I should have more self-control, shouldn't I?

Not with Dane Dixon.

The man can barely speak to me during office hours, but on our date, he didn't stammer the way he usually does. He was courteous, respectful, sweet, and funny—and he even held doors for me and pulled my chair out for me. He behaved like the perfect boyfriend. But he's not my boyfriend. I want him to be. Last night I'd realized that. I should tell him how I feel, but he's made it pretty clear he wants nothing to do with actual dating.

The next morning, I walk into the office with dark circles under my eyes that no amount of makeup can cover up. Twice overnight I'd woken from a dream of Dane so turned on that I had to relieve my lust the solo way. My hair is still damp because my stupid hair dryer decided to break this morning, so not only do I look like I broke out the booze and had a massive bender after Dane said good night to me, but I also look like a drowned puppy.

At least my clothes and makeup look okay.

I've just sat down at my desk when the phone rings. It's Dane's extension.

"Hi, boss," I say, feigning a cheerfulness I don't feel this morning. "What can I do for you?"

"Come into my office, please. I need to speak to you."

"Sure thing."

I march into his office, and when he waves for me to sit down, I settle onto a chair across the desk from him.

Dane shuffles papers on his desk, head down, moving only his eyes to glance up at me repeatedly. He must notice my wet hair and my dark circles.

I clear my throat. "I'm so sorry about the way I look this morning. I know it's unprofessional to have wet hair at work, but my hair dryer broke and—"

He raises a hand to silence my babbling. "I don't care about any of that. Chance and I have found you another position."

"Already?"

It's been one day since he asked me to be his fake girlfriend. He already got me another job? Maybe the slutty way I'd dragged him into me last night has embarrassed him, so he quick found me a new job. Right. He got up at two a.m. to hunt for another PA position for me.

Well, with this guy, who knows?

Dane fiddles with his tie. "Yesterday, after our discussion about the…uh…fake orgasm—" He blushes. Really blushes. And he clearly remembers my joke about orgasms. "I meant the fat—the fake girlfriend issue. You aren't fat. N-not at, um, all. Or ever. Or—"

"Relax, Dane, it's okay. I know what you were trying to say." Jeez, he's even more nervous than every other time we've spoken. So I give him what I hope looks like a sympathetic smile. "This is all kind of weird for me too."

"Is it?"

"Yep. Take a breath and start over. This is business, right? There's no reason to be nervous."

He takes a breath and sets his palms on the desktop. "Chance has a mate who owns a home business, and he needs a personal assistant. His name is Eddie Masters. He films fitness videos that he sells on his website, and he also offers live classes over the internet."

"I love streaming exercise classes. It's more fun than doing it by myself in my living room, and I've never liked going to the gym."

"Neither have I." He picks up a sheet of paper and hands it to me. "These are the details about the job. You're to report there immediately."

"This morning?" I lean forward to take the paper, but an icy chill has washed over me. "I thought it would take longer to get a new job. This is so sudden."

"Yes, I know. I'm sorry, but considering our new relationship—" He freezes for a second, not even blinking, then clears his throat and adjusts his glasses. "I meant considering the business relationship we have. The dating business." He squeezes his eyes shut and hisses, "Bollocks."

I can't help smiling at his frustration. Every time he stammers or says the wrong thing, I want to hug him. "Take it easy, Dane. I know our dating thing is only a business arrangement. And it makes sense to get me a new position right away."

But the thought of not seeing him every day makes me a little queasy.

Which is so incredibly dumb. I've known him for a few weeks, but we hadn't spoken much until this week. I loved our lunch the other day and the kiss that came after it. I loved our dinner last night and the super-hot kiss we enjoyed when he walked me to my door. And that's one of so many things Dane does that no other guy would bother with these days. Walking me to my door. Picking me up at my door. Giving me flowers.

I read the laser-printed text on the paper Dane gave me. It's a printout of an email from Chance that outlines the details of my new job.

"Stamford, Connecticut?" I say. "That's, like, forty-five minutes away."

Or so I've heard, but then, I've never taken a train or driven a car from New York to Stamford.

"If it's too far for you to drive every day," he says, "I'll pay for you to rent a flat in Stamford."

"But being your fake girlfriend is my job too. How are we going to date when I'm way over there in Connecticut?"

"There are trains to and from the city. I checked." He offers me another piece of paper. "This is the train schedule for all the lines that go from New York to Stamford."

"Oh. Thanks." The way he seems so eager to get rid of me makes me feel like I'm shrinking into an ant-size version of myself. "I'm sorry if I embarrassed you last night. With that kiss."

And the way I forced you to plaster yourself to me.

He pushes his glasses up with one finger. "I wasn't embarrassed."

I believe him, which leads to one inescapable conclusion. He'd taken off so fast after our kiss because he'd been as turned on as I was. I'd felt his erection. His big, hard erection.

"Good," I say. "Thank you for finding me another job. This one sounds like fun."

"Chance told me Eddie is a decent bloke who will treat you with respect, not like that arse who harassed you at your previous job."

"Yeah, I don't think anyone else would act the way that jerk did."

Dane glances at the open door to the office. "Maybe we should say goodbye the way, uh, couples do."

I glance over my shoulder and suddenly get why he's suggesting that. A man has walked up to my desk—my former desk—and is sitting down in the chair I once occupied.

"That's your replacement," Dane says. "Not that anyone can really replace you. My new PA is here for a temporary position, with the potential to make it permanent later."

He's already replaced me. I know he had to do it, but still…I'm feeling queasy again.

Dane comes around the desk to me.

I get up too.

He pulls me into his arms and fuses his mouth to mine. It's not a steamy kiss. Our lips meet, and we hold our mouths like that for a moment without deepening the kiss. It feels wonderful anyway. I love having his body crushed to mine, so I can experience every single one of his muscles.

Dane lets go of me but doesn't back away. "Good luck at your new job."

"Thanks."

I let him take my hand and lead me out into the reception area. He introduces me to his new PA, Noah Smolak. The guy looks fresh out of college, dressed in khaki pants and a polo shirt. Did no one tell him how to dress for a big-time job like this one? When Dane gives the kid an assessing look, Noah cringes the tiniest bit.

"Good morning, Mr. Dixon, sir," Noah says, his spine ramrod straight. He even raises his hand like he might salute Dane, but he lowers it quickly. "Sorry about my clothes. I didn't have time to go buy a suit before work this morning. I only had two hours' notice."

Wow, this replacing-me thing really is a rush job.

"It's all right," Dane tells Noah. "I know this was last minute."

Dane kisses my cheek and wishes me a good day, then strides back into his office and shuts the door.

I hustle to the train station.

At least my hair will be dry by the time I meet Eddie Masters.

The train ride gives me time to collect myself. Walking into the office to find out I'm not wanted there anymore was like getting slapped in the face with a big wet towel. Dane still wants to date me, for show, but he doesn't want me around at work. I knew this would happen, but I didn't think he'd leap on the task of getting rid of me with so much enthusiasm.

The second I step off the train at Stamford, my phone rings.

"Are you there yet?" Dane asks when I answer the call.

"Yes, I'm in Stamford. But I haven't gotten to Eddie Masters' place yet."

"I forgot to mention Eddie is sending a car for you. The driver will have a sign with your name on it."

Glancing around, I spot a man holding a cardboard sign with my name scrawled on it in big red letters. I wave to the driver, who nods. "I see him. How's it going with Noah?"

"He keeps calling me 'Mr. Dixon, sir.' It's odd."

"At least he's being polite." I follow the driver toward a silver Lexus sedan and climb into the backseat. "I doubt you'd like it if he called you 'dude.' Noah seems nice. I'm sure you two will get along."

"Not as well as I got on with you."

I get a warm feeling all over when he says that. "You should take Noah to lunch. Make him feel welcome. The poor kid took the job with two hours' notice."

"All right. I'll take him to lunch." Dane lowers his voice to a husky rumble. "But I absolutely will not be kissing him in the hallway."

I smile with my lips sealed, holding my fingers to my mouth until the urge to laugh subsides. "Just buy him lunch like the good boss I know you are."

"Yes, I will." He pauses, like he's thinking about what he wants to say next. "I'd like to have dinner with you again tonight. For extra practice. The publicity campaign starts in earnest in ten days."

"Guess we'd better get practiced up, then." Practice making out with Dane. Oh, that sounds like exactly what I'll need after a long day of working for a fitness trainer and taking the train back and forth to New York. But there's a problem. I'm already tired from not sleeping well last night. "Um, I think I'll be wiped out after my first day at a new job, plus the commute."

"I'll order takeaway and bring it to your flat. It would be, ah, good for us to get it on—Uh, get in the habit of, you know, doing things together."

The Lexus is pulling into the driveway of a large house.

"Okay," I tell Dane, "we can meet at my place. Not sure what time I'll be home."

"Call me when you get off the train."

"It's a date." I decide I really ought to go all in on playing the part of Dane Dixon's love interest, so I add, "See you tonight, honey. Can't wait to snuggle with you."

Dane sputters, and I bet there's spittle flying. "Y-yes. God—Goodbye."

Click. Call ended.

The driver opens my door for me. Wow, another gentleman in the modern world. Of course, this guy gets paid to be polite to his passengers. I walk up concrete steps to the front door of a big, beautiful stone house that must have cost a fortune.

Seconds tick by after I hit the buzzer, then the door swings open. And I get my first look at my new boss.

The guy works out for a living, so I shouldn't be surprised by his ripped physique. But damn, he knows how to flaunt it. Eddie wears skintight blue shorts and a gray tank top, showing off his bulging biceps. His eyes are the color of coffee, his lips are thick and wide, and his face is angular. All of that gives him a ruggedly sexy look.

I should be hot for this guy, but all I can think about is Dane. What does he look like in workout clothes? Or buck naked?

"You must be Rika Solberg," my new boss says. While we shake hands, he keeps talking. "I'm Eddie Masters. So glad to have you here. I've needed a PA for a while, but it's hard to find someone who knows what they're doing. If Chance Dixon recommends you, I know you'll be top-notch."

"Thank you. You're very kind."

Eddie moves aside, gesturing for me to enter his house.

It's gorgeous, but I have trouble focusing on the interior design or on his explanations of the architecture. My mind keeps wandering back to my former boss, the one who kisses me like he means it, like he's not pretending, like we're dating for real. But we're not.

Maybe tonight, he'll change his mind about that.

I won't hold my breath.

Chapter Eight

Dane

I shouldn't have pushed Rika to let me go to her flat to-night. We could've waited until tomorrow for our next date, but I had an overpowering urge to see her. Knowing she's out there in Connecticut all day, every day, from now on… It makes me uncomfortable. I've gotten used to being welcomed by her smile and her cheerful greetings every morning. From this day forward, I'll hear "good morning, Mr. Dixon, sir" instead of Rika's lovely voice.

Why does Noah insist on calling me "Mr. Dixon, sir"? It's overkill. Either "Mr. Dixon" or "sir" would be more than enough deference, but he stacks on layers of it. Noah seems like a nice enough bloke, but his face is not the one I want to look at every morning.

After an entire day with my new PA, I need to see Rika again.

But she's exhausted. I can tell that the second she opens her door. Especially when she yawns.

"Hey," she says. "What's for dinner?"

I hold up a takeaway bag. "Chinese. I hope you like that."

"Sure." Rika yawns again. "Sounds good. Come on in."

"Maybe I should leave the food and go. You look knackered."

"Yeah, I am. But it'll be nice to have dinner with you." She moves to the side so I can walk into her flat. "I don't know how

Eddie has the energy to teach all those classes. I got wiped out just watching him."

She leads me to the sofa, where we sit down with the takeaway bag between us.

I bring out the cardboard containers that hold our food, along with plastic forks and plastic knives. "I hope you like sesame chicken. I also have Szechuan pork, kung pao chicken, dumplings, wontons, chow mein, and egg rolls."

Rika laughs while she opens the box of egg rolls. "You brought enough food for five people."

"You need nourishment after a long day at your new job."

She smiles. "You're so sweet, Dane. Thank you for bringing all this yummy food."

Her compliment makes me uncomfortable because I'm the reason she's so exhausted. I insisted she had to take another job, one that's in Connecticut. "I should've brought wine. Sorry."

"You don't have to apologize for not bringing wine." She plucks an egg roll out of the box. "Besides, if I drink wine tonight, I'll be asleep in five minutes flat."

"What's wrong with that? You need rest."

She bites off a chunk of her egg roll and chews it slowly, then she gestures at the many boxes of food. "Aren't you going to eat?"

"Yes, of course. But I think we need plates." I get up, glancing around. "Ah, where's the kitchen?"

"I'll get the plates."

"No, you will not. Point me in the right direction."

She waves toward a door on the other side of the living room. "In there. Plates are in the cabinet right next to the sink. So are the glasses."

I hurry into the kitchen and get two plates plus two glasses of water. When I return to the sofa, Rika is still working on her egg roll, biting off small chunks of it and chewing them like she's in no hurry to finish.

"Here," I say offering her a plate and a glass.

"Thank you." She sets the plate on her lap and the glass on the table. But when I try to move away, she grasps my hand. Her pale-brown eyes focus on me. "You really are so sweet. That's why I can't understand this fake dating thing. Why don't you get a real girlfriend?"

"Well, I—uh—" Fuck, I'm tongue-tied again. I use sitting down and putting food on my plate as an excuse to take a moment to get hold of myself. Not that I ever have much luck with that. Not when I'm in the same room with Rika. Or the same building. Or the same world. "Does it really matter why?"

There. I spoke five unbroken words.

Rika studies me for a moment while she finishes off her egg roll. "I can't believe you have trouble getting dates. I mean, you're gorgeous, smart, sexy, and super nice."

She thinks I'm sexy? Of course, she's not saying she wants to *have* sex with me. Or have a normal relationship with me. A woman of her caliber deserves better than a man who talked her into engaging in a fraud.

"I don't have room in my life for a real relationship," I say. "The re-launch is…complicated and time-consuming."

"You do seem stressed."

"There's a lot to do. Frankly, I have no bloody idea how to do most of it."

"But you ran your own company before signing with Bonsoir."

"That's true, but…" I focus on my plate and shift food around on it with my fork. "I had one small factory with twenty employees, and I was in charge. I hired Reese to do a single marketing campaign with online advertising. It was Chance's girlfriend who made my business a success by talking about it on her blog. Now I work for the second-largest cosmetics company in the world and have to do whatever Celeste tells me to do."

"Reese says you underestimate yourself and give everyone else the credit even when it's you who really made your company profitable."

I stare at her. Reese said that? I love my brother, but he's normally sarcastic and never says anything like that to me. The closest he ever came to giving me a compliment was when he slapped me on the shoulder and said with a smile, "Well, congrats on not cocking it up." That had been on the day I sold my ten thousandth device.

But he's told Rika I underestimate myself. I have no idea what to make of that.

"In those wedding videos," Rika says, "you were laughing and grinning. You even made a toast in which you said lots of words without a hiccup. So I know you can be well-spoken and charming. I don't buy that the only reason you don't want a real girlfriend is because you're too busy."

Should I tell her the actual reason? It's not a complete lie that I don't have time, but mostly, I got so bloody sick of women telling me I'm boring compared to my devices. The last girl who said that was not the first to criticize my bedroom skills. I couldn't stand it if Rika reached the same conclusion about me. *Why can't you be as exciting as your toys?*

"Maybe there is another reason," I say, "but we don't know each other well enough to talk about that."

"Okay, you're probably right." She consumes a bite of sesame chicken, eying me with curiosity. "It can't be a problem in bed. You're way too hot for that, a fact I can attest to since we've kissed twice."

She'll probably change her mind about that if we ever do have sex. Which is why we won't. Not ever.

We eat our dinner and talk about inconsequential things, like Rika's favorite places in New York and what Eddie Masters' house looks like. She describes his video recording studio in great detail. She's clearly excited about her new job and enjoying the challenges of working for a fitness guru.

I work out, but not as much as I'm sure Eddie Masters does. I've never seen the man, much less spoken to him, but I can tell Rika thinks he's impressive. Especially when she says those exact words right after I've thought them.

"Eddie is one impressive guy," she announces. "An entrepreneur who turned his life's passion into a successful brand." She pokes my chest with her finger. "Just like you."

"I don't have a brand yet. Celeste explained to me how a brand is different from a line of products, but I honestly can't remember half of what she said. It's all too bloody complicated." I grumble and, I suspect, make a petulant face. I don't mean to, but this re-launch and branding rubbish makes me feel like a child being led around by his mother. "Apparently, a brand involves my face on the sodding package."

"Celeste will give up on that idea, trust me."

"What makes you think that?"

"She's a good person, but sometimes she goes overboard. I've gotten to know her over the past six months, since I became good friends with her granddaughter. Eventually, Celeste will realize she needs to give you some space."

I hope she realizes that soon. Tonight would be brilliant, but I'll have to wait until Monday to find out if she's seen reason yet.

"I like Celeste," I say. "But you're right. She can be a bit too… enthusiastic."

"You mean bossy. Go on, you can say it." Rika leans toward me, her face so close to mine that I can feel her breaths tickling my skin. "Celeste Arnaud is a bossy, bossy woman. Repeat it with me. Celeste is—"

"Why would I want to repeat that? You're being ridiculous."

"Maybe. But you need some serious stress relief. Why not spend the weekend at a spa?"

"A spa? Only if you come along to help me relax."

The second those words come out of my mouth I know I've made the biggest blunder yet.

"Sorry," I rush to say. "I didn't mean—That wasn't—Ah, bollocks."

Rika smiles, like she doesn't mind my faltering speech. "Don't panic. I know you weren't suggesting we go to a spa together for a weekend of Reiki and hot sex."

I stare at her for several seconds, and my eyes start to burn because I've stopped blinking. She can't mean she wants to… No, she's making a joke. Because, obviously, the idea of her sleeping with me is ludicrous.

She pats my chest and leans back. "How about dessert?"

"I didn't think to buy dessert. Sorry."

"That's okay." Her mouth opens on a big yawn. "I've got some Oreo truffles in the freezer."

She starts to get up.

I hold up my hand to stop her. "Let me get it. I think I can manage to find the Oreo truffles on my own. I imagine they're round?"

"Yes. Round, white balls with chocolate streaks on them. They're in a plastic bag. I made them myself. The insides are full of crushed chocolate chips and white chocolate, mixed with cream cheese. Totally decadent and delicious." She licks her lips. "I love feeling those big, succulent balls in my mouth. Mm-mm-mmmmm."

"All right. I'll find them." I hurry into the kitchen because her description of how good those truffles are has roused my cock. Why on earth would she describe candy as "big, succulent balls" that she loves to feel in her mouth? Is she trying to drive me insane?

I rummage in the freezer until I find the large, plastic bag full of big, white balls. My balls will be blue in thirty seconds flat if Rika describes these truffles to me again.

After dumping the truffles onto a plate, I go back into the living room. I've just sat down on the sofa again, and I'm about to speak, when I notice her eyes are closed. She still sits sideways on the sofa, angled toward me, but her cheek rests on the back. Her breathing has become even and shallower.

Rika is asleep.

I pop a truffle into my mouth and chew it. The flavors of the semisweet chips and white chocolate merge on my tongue, and the cream cheese makes the truffle, well, creamy. It tastes delicious, like Rika said it would.

After returning the truffles to the freezer, I hunt around until I find a fleece throw, then I lay it over Rika's shoulders. She looks so beautiful sleeping, her mouth curved into the faintest smile, her face and body completely relaxed. I envy her for that. When was the last time I felt at peace? Or took a day off? I can't have a spa day or do anything else that might in the slightest resemble relaxation.

I'm too fucking busy.

Chapter Nine

I wake up after midnight and realize I'm still on the sofa, but someone has put a blanket over me. Though the floor lamp is still on, I don't see Dane anywhere. Rubbing my eyes, I yawn and sit up, looking around like I think Dane will be waiting in the armchair or something. Of course he's not. I fell asleep, so he left.

But I see a piece of folded paper that stands upright on the coffee table like a little tent. My name is written on the paper in Dane's handwriting.

Yes, I recognize his handwriting. Though I only worked for him for a few weeks, I memorized a lot of things about him. He has elegant, crisp penmanship. I envy him that because my cursive absolutely sucks.

I pick up his note and read it. Sleep well, it says, we can have those truffles another time.

A yawn overtakes me, so I carry Dane's note into my bedroom and set it on the nightstand where I can see it, then I crawl into bed. I'm gazing at the note when I fall asleep.

The next day, I decide I really ought to make sure Dane isn't holed up in his big hotel suite all alone, like the creepy loser our fake relationship is supposed to ensure nobody thinks he is. Yeah, that's the reason I wind up at the Four Seasons Hotel at ten o'clock in the morning on a Saturday. I'm making sure we keep up appearances. It has nothing to do with the fact his sweetness last night gave me a warm glow all over.

I take a private elevator all the way up to the penthouse suite. When the car stops and the doors open, Dane is standing right outside the elevator waiting for me.

"Rika, what are you doing here?" he asks. "I saw you on the camera, but you didn't ring me first to say you'd be coming."

"Um, what camera?"

"This suite has three elevators and cameras in all of them."

"Wow, that's a little spooky."

Naturally, he's wearing dress slacks and a dress shirt. At least he isn't wearing a tie, though he does have shoes on. Shiny loafers. And he has a belt too.

I remember Elena telling the story of how, the first time she visited Chance in his big hotel suite, he answered the door wearing nothing but a towel. Why couldn't Dane do that? I'm in serious need of man candy. But no, he looks like he's about to hold a meeting with foreign diplomats.

"Shouldn't you be happy to see your girlfriend?" I ask. Leaning in, I whisper, "Even if it is a sham, we should make sure everyone sees us together. Don't you think?"

"I suppose you're right."

Dane steps aside so I can walk past him.

Holy moly. I've never seen a hotel room like this one before. We're up on the fifty-second floor, with a fabulous view of the city and its skyscrapers with a blue sky as the backdrop. I wander through the huge suite, taking in the jaw-dropping views from the four glass balconies. I stop in what looks like a library. I mean, it has books on shelves, so yeah, it must be a library. The room has gorgeous golden-brown paneling, two sofas, and two chairs, not to mention a baby grand piano—and one of those glass balconies.

Dane comes up beside me, his expression neutral, like none of this opulence affects him in the least. "What should we do? To show the world we're a couple."

"Hang out, I guess. If I stay here for a while, everyone will probably assume we banged each other all day long."

"I'm not sure—That's, ah—" He scrubs a hand over his mouth. "Do we really want to give people that impression? You're not my mistress."

"Sure I am." I turn toward him and wave my hands at my body. "Arm candy here, remember? I'm just an ornament to help you prove your manliness."

"I don't like that description."

"Neither do I, but that's the deal. Right?"

"Yes, but—" He scrunches his whole face in the cutest expression of frustration and annoyance. "I don't want the world to see you that way."

"Ugh, Dane." Now I sound frustrated and probably look it too, like he had a second ago. "You can't have it both ways. I'm your fake girlfriend, but you don't want to use me as a body ornament. That's the point of this charade, isn't it? I mean, you told me this would be a business arrangement because Celeste insists you must have a woman on your arm at public events."

"You remember exactly what I said? That sounds verbatim."

"It is. I have an excellent memory."

"Yes, I can tell." He shoves his hands into his pants pockets and ambles over to the glass balcony. While he gazes out at the view, he sighs and removes his glasses. After staring at them for a minute, he puts them back on and slumps his shoulders. "This sounded like a good idea when I suggested it."

I approach him, slipping my arm under his. "Well, you can always fake dump me."

"Would you mind not making jokes about our…arrangement?" He hunches his shoulders, his gaze veering down to the floor. "I don't like to think about it."

"But you have to. We're in too deep to back out. You got me a new job and everything."

Maybe I'm secretly afraid I won't see him again if he calls off our phony relationship. I work in Connecticut now. Dane has a new PA. He won't need me anymore if we're not pretending to date. I love spending time with him, like last night when he'd brought me dinner and we sat on the sofa talking. He even put a blanket over me when I fell asleep.

He groans. "I know we can't back out of it. The wheels are already in motion. I told Celeste first thing yesterday that you and I are dating and that's why I needed a new PA." He scrunches up his face again. "I'm sure Celeste has already told Reese to start a new marketing campaign all about you and me and a lot of bollocks about how well I satisfy you in bed."

Maybe he would satisfy me—if we had sex.

Not maybe. He absolutely would fulfill my every desire. Those two make-out sessions heated me up in all the right ways. No man who kisses like that could be anything less than stellar in bed. It's not "bollocks."

"If you're so miserable," I say, "you should talk to Celeste. She cares about keeping her employees happy."

He leans against the glass balcony, his eyes aimed toward the view but his focus clearly on something much farther away. "I'll think about it."

"Okay." I'm pretty sure that when he says he'll think about it he means he's never going to do it. He seems shy about telling anyone how he's really feeling. So I decide to distract him from his worries. "Let's do something fun, like order room service. A whole bunch of totally fattening, cholesterol-laden goodies."

He eyes me sideways. "Is that meant to make me feel better? Getting nauseous from eating too much doesn't appeal to me."

"Who said you have to eat too much? Let's order everything on the breakfast menu and try all of it. No overeating unless you feel like it." I nudge him with my shoulder. "What do you say?"

"All right."

Dane makes the call to order our late breakfast. I already had breakfast when I got up this morning, but I ate light, so I've got room left for a decadent brunch. Besides, Dane needs cheering up. And I want to make him feel better. Want to so much. I would hug him, but I'm afraid that might embarrass him.

Dane says he needs to take a shower while we wait for our food. He looks clean to me, but I figure he needs some alone time. He emerges from the bathroom about a minute before the elevator doors open and a hotel employee wheels a cart full of our food through the suite and out onto the spacious balcony. The polite young man sets our food on a table. Dane gives him a tip and sends him on his way.

We don't talk much while we eat, but we do feed each other. He surprises me by starting it, holding a forkful of pancake to my lips, then slipping it inside my mouth when I open up to accept the food gift. I never would've expected Dane Dixon to do something like that. He acts so serious most of the time, but feeding me pancakes and French toast and eggs Benedict doesn't jibe with that. He knows how to relax. Huh.

When I take a sip of milk, I get clumsy and wind up dribbling some down my chin.

Dane grabs a napkin and wipes the milk off my skin, then he rubs his thumb over the corner of my mouth.

I feed him too, but he doesn't dribble anything on himself. I kind of wish he would so I can lick it off. Seeing him this way, at ease and enjoying our brunch, makes me want him even more than I already do. Okay, pretty much everything he does makes me hot for him. Yeah, I'm still massively crushing on him, and it's still pathetic.

After our meal, Dane tells me he has work to do. I point out that it's Saturday, which means it's the weekend, but he dismisses that with a shrug and a grunt. I let him have his alone time, only because he fed me breakfast, literally, using his own hand and fork.

On Sunday afternoon, I call his suite instead of just going there like I did yesterday. He informs me he doesn't have time for a visit because he has tons of work to do. Jeez, will he never take an entire day off? I don't ask him that. We're not a couple, so it's none of my business.

Why do I have to keep reminding myself of that?

Sunday evening, I'm in the middle of cleaning the toilet, elbow deep in the bowl, when the doorbell rings. I jog through my apartment and pull the door open, realizing too late that I'm still wearing big rubber gloves. At least I remembered to put down the toilet brush.

Celeste Arnaud smiles at me. "Good evening, Rika darling. We need to have a chat about Dane."

"If you've got a problem with Dane, why not talk to him?"

"Because you're the only one who can get through to him."

Me? If she knew about our make-believe relationship, she wouldn't say that. Celeste believes Dane and I are a legitimate couple and that I have some kind of sway over him.

"Come on in," I say, moving out of the way so Celeste can walk inside. "My apartment is messy right now. I'm in the middle of cleaning up."

She walks past me, turns around, and glances at my gloved hands. "Yes, I can see that. If you still worked for Bonsoir, I'd make sure you had a cleaning crew to take care of those jobs for you. Hasn't Dane offered to do that? I pay him enough that he could afford to hire you an entire team of cleaners, housekeepers, cooks, and anything else you need."

She pays him that much? I have no idea exactly how much it is, but I get the picture that it's a lot. My fake honey has no obligation to pay for anything for me. I wouldn't want him to even if we were a couple because it would make me feel weird.

Celeste and I sit down on the sofa, and I take off my big gloves.

"Dane is very stressed," she says. "I called him an hour ago, but he didn't pick up his cell, so I tried the direct line to his suite. When he answered, he sounded...rough."

"What does that mean?"

"He said he hadn't slept much last night and he's too busy with work to talk to me. I asked what work he has to do on the weekend." She smiles a little, like what she says next is almost funny. "He growled at me, then said he's working on the 'bloody devices' that I 'commanded' him to create."

"Did you command him?"

She waves a dismissive hand. "I asked him to create two new devices. That should be easy for a smart, talented man like Dane. But he's clearly more stressed than I realized." She touches my knee. "He needs your tender loving care."

"Me? I have no idea what to do to help him." But yeah, I've noticed how stressed he is too. I did my best yesterday to make him feel better. What else can I do? We're not actually dating.

Celeste doesn't know that.

Should I tell her? Oh no, not in a million years. Dane would freak if I did that.

"I told Dane I'm sorry," Celeste says, "if I put too much pressure on him. But honestly, he should've told me he was struggling. Since he's not comfortable discussing the problem with me, you are the only one who might get through to him."

Can I? No idea. Should I try? Not sure.

The clock on the wall tells me it's nine p.m., which is way too late for me to dash over to Dane's hotel and do...whatever. I need to go to bed so I can make my early morning train to Stamford. For my new job. The one Dane insisted on getting for me. He made a few passing comments yesterday that suggested he and his new PA aren't exactly hitting it off like a house on fire.

After what Celeste has told me, I'm positive the friction between Dane and his new PA isn't Noah's fault. Dane is simply too anxious to get along with anyone.

Except me. We hit it off just fine.

"Okay," I tell Celeste, "I'll talk to him. But it'll have to wait until tomorrow. I need to sleep, or I'll be useless at my new job. I will stop by Dane's hotel after work."

"Perfect." Celeste pats my knee and gets up. "I know you'll straighten him out. Every woman understands how to help her man relax."

She winks.

"Uh, sure," I say, pushing up off the sofa. "Somehow I'll relax him. Maybe a massage will help."

Celeste slants in to stare straight into my eyes from inches away. "Maybe I wasn't clear enough. Dane needs sex. Relieve his stress with an orgasm, darling, not a massage."

Then she walks out the door.

Sure, the idea of getting it on with Dane makes me tingle all over, but I can't do that. Our "relationship" is a business arrangement. I want us to give each other fantastic orgasms, over and over, like Celeste thinks I should do. I want it so much that my sex is getting slick and hot just thinking about it. I want *him*.

Maybe a good night's rest will help me figure out what to do. Give in to my lust and seduce Dane, or talk him down off that emotional ledge—then rip his clothes off and ride him until we're both sweaty and satisfied.

I give up on cleaning and relieve my own stress the Celeste Arnaud way while I fantasize about Dane Dixon.

Chapter Ten

Dane

For the entire weekend, I hide in my hotel suite and struggle to come up with ideas for the new devices I promised Celeste I'd create. I made that promise months ago, and I still have no ruddy idea what I'm going to do. I used to excel at creating sex toys that would make women feel good, but now I can't think of even one thousandth of an idea.

Why can't you be as exciting as your toys?

Those words still echo in my mind on Monday morning when I head for my office. The call I received from Celeste yesterday keeps replaying in my thoughts too, and I wonder if I am as pent up as everyone seems to think. I never used to be, but the re-launch is fraying my every nerve.

"Good morning, Mr. Dixon, sir," Noah says as I walk past his desk. He smiles too. "Can I get you some coffee?"

"Yes, please. One sugar, no cream."

While he retrieves my coffee, I shuffle into my office and drop onto my chair. My shoulders sag. I brace my elbow on the chair's arm and rest my head in my raised palm, which forces me to slump to the side. I have no energy whatsoever, not for what I need to do today. Meetings, meetings, and more meetings.

Noah brings me a cup of coffee, setting it on my desk in front of me. "Anything else I can get you?"

"No, that's all. Thank you." I sit up and glance down at my desk. "Where's the agenda for today? Rika always has it on my desk waiting for me."

"Oh, gosh, I'm sorry. I didn't know. Let me print that out for you."

He leaves, shutting the door.

And my phone rings. Will I never get a moment's peace?

I snatch up the phone. "What is it, Noah?"

Maybe I sound a touch irritable. And maybe I should apologize for that, but Noah speaks again.

"Your brother Reese is here to see you."

"Send him in, please."

I hang up the phone and wait for Reese.

He walks through the door, a casual smile on his lips and his eyes bright and clear, unlike mine which are bleary and bloodshot. Not sleeping well doesn't agree with me. My new position at Bonsoir doesn't agree with me. Noah certainly doesn't agree with me.

Rika does. Always.

"What do you want, Reese?" I ask.

He sits down in one of the chairs across the desk from me. "I hear you have a problem with the new packaging. Celeste asked me to talk to you about that."

I groan and let my head fall back against my chair. "Go on, then. Talk to me about it."

Reese sets his ankle on the opposite knee. "What's your bloody problem with the packaging?"

Though his words suggest he's annoyed, his tone of voice contradicts that. He's still smiling too. My cheerful, smiling brother waits for me to respond.

"Well, uh, I…" Now I stammer when I speak to my brother? Christ, I need a tranquilizer or…something. "I don't want my picture on the ruddy box. Or my name on it either."

Reese keeps smiling at me, though he tips his head to the side like he's trying to figure me out. "You didn't complain when Chance's girlfriend promoted you and your devices on her blog."

"That was different. She didn't show my face on the package with the words Dane's Delights printed next to it, and she didn't label me 'the man behind the O's.' She didn't order me to get a girlfriend either."

Reese chuckles. "Celeste told me about that. But you're with Rika now, aren't you? So that's one problem solved." He angles toward me and smirks. "Get Rika to shag your brains out, mate. That'll relieve all your stress."

I clench my jaw. Celeste suggested yesterday that all I need is "one good night in bed with Rika, alone and naked." Now Reese tells me the same thing, as if sex will cure all my problems.

I can't tell either of them Rika and I are only pretending to date.

So I scowl at my brother. "You always claim sex solves everything, but it's not the panacea you say it is. And I do *not* want my face or my name on the sodding package." I slam my fist down on the desk. "Do you understand, Reese?"

He raises his hands, palms out. "Take it easy, Dane. We'll remove your picture from the package, but I'll have to talk to Celeste about whether we can change the name. She won't agree to Bedroom Buddies, but if you came up with an alternative—"

"Get my name off it, Reese. Now. You're the vice president of advertising, so come up with a new name yourself."

"All right, all right. Let me work on that." Reese stands, then bends over my desk to look me in the eye. "You need a good shag, Dane. Trust me."

My brother leaves my office—while humming cheerfully.

What is wrong with me? I never yell at anyone. Certainly not my brothers. Yet here I am acting like a wounded wild beast, snarling and gnashing my teeth at anyone who gets too close.

I rest my arms on the desk and stare down at the surface. Maybe I do need a good shag, but I can't ask Rika to give me one. She doesn't really want me. She's doing me a favor by acting like my girlfriend.

What have I gotten myself into?

Groaning, rather loudly, I drop my head onto the desktop.

"Are you okay, Mr. Dixon, sir?"

Noah's voice makes me groan again.

I wave a hand in the air but keep my face on the desk. "Fine, thank you."

He doesn't leave, despite my assurance I'm fine. It's a lie, but he doesn't know that. Does he?

"Uh, I have the agenda for today, Mr. Dixon, sir." The shuffling of feet on the carpeting tells me he's moved closer. "Here it is."

I force myself to lift my head, and I see the paper he's set on my desk, just above where my head had been lying. "Thank you, Noah."

He turns to leave.

Groaning yet again, I mutter, "I need to get pissed."

Noah stops halfway to the door, turning toward me. "You're really mad, huh?"

"What? No, not really. I said I want to get pissed."

His eyes flare wide for a split second. "Oh, I get it. Sorry, I don't do that."

"You don't do what?"

He gestures toward his groin with both hands, flapping one hand with his fingers curled like he's cupping his dick. "You know, the golden shower thing. I don't do that."

For a moment, all I can do is stare at him. Then the meaning of his statement hits me like a snowball lobbed at my face.

I growl, and that's not a metaphor or an exaggeration. I literally growl at him. "I don't want you to piss *on* me. I want to *get* pissed. Which means I have a strong urge to get drunk."

Not that I think it will help. Can't hurt, can it?

"Oh, sorry," Noah says. "I don't do that either."

I brace my elbows on the desktop and cradle my face in my raised hands. "That will be all, Noah."

His footsteps assure me he's left my office.

After several minutes of sitting here with my head in my hands, I realize what I need. Not sex. I just need to see Rika. Why, I have no bloody idea. But I need it so badly that once I think of the idea, I find myself getting up out of my chair and stalking out to Noah's desk.

"I have a dentist appointment," I say, lying much more convincingly than I'd thought I could. "I'll be back this afternoon."

Noah glances down at his desk calendar, and the corner of his mouth crimps. "I don't see it on the agenda."

"That's because I made the appointment myself on Friday, after Rika left. I forgot to tell you."

"Okay, sure. Have a good dentist appointment."

Does anyone have a good time at the dentist?

I hurry out of the building and drive all the way to Stamford, breaking the speed laws the whole time. I don't get pulled over by a policeman, thankfully. By the time I park in Eddie Masters' driveway, I'm beginning to feel odd about this. What will Rika say when I turn up at her workplace? She'll probably think I've lost my mind.

Which I have.

The door opens seconds after I ring the bell.

A middle-aged woman dressed in a maid's uniform smiles at me. "How may I help you?"

"I'm here to see"—I swallow hard—"my girlfriend, Rika Solberg. She works for Mr. Masters."

"Oh sure, hon, come on in."

The woman leads me through the house to a set of sliding glass doors that access a large patio. I thank her, and she leaves.

Out on the patio, Rika stands in her bare feet with one foot on the ground and the other leg raised behind her, with her arms outstretched. One arm is horizontal to the ground while the other is perpendicular to it. She wears only leggings and a tank top, with her hair tied up in a ponytail.

And Eddie Masters has his hands on her.

My fists clench all on their own. I can't think clearly enough to fist my hands on purpose, because that man has one hand on Rika's thigh and the other on her hip. He says something that makes her laugh, then he pats her hip.

I storm out onto the patio and stop just past the glass doors. "What the bloody hell is going on here?"

Rika's gaze swerves to me, and all the happiness floods out of her expression. "Dane? What are you doing here?"

"The better question is what is that tosser doing with his hands all over you? You're my girlfriend."

Eddie Masters backs away from Rika, holding his hands up. "Hey, relax. Nothing's going on here."

Rika stomps up to me looking like she wants to throttle me with both hands. She seizes my arm and tows me into the house. As we cross the threshold into the living room, she tells Eddie, "Sorry about this. Gimme a minute, okay?"

"Sure, no problem."

We make it halfway across the living room before she forces me to halt and slams her palms onto my chest. "What is your problem? Showing up at my work to snarl at my boss? What the hell, Dane?"

I've never seen Rika angry. She's always polite and happy.

But I'm behaving like a sodding arsehole. Of course she's angry. I deserve whatever she wants to do to me.

"He had his hands on you," I say. "That looked like sexual harassment to me. Since you had an employer treat you that way once before, I don't want to see it happen again."

Maybe that is a small part of it, but mostly, I hated seeing another man touching her when I can't do that.

The anger seems to flood out of her, and her shoulders slump. She sighs and rolls her head in a circle, like she's working out kinks in her neck. "Okay, fine, I can see how you might think that. But I don't believe concern for me was the main reason you shouted at Eddie."

Maybe I should be honest, but I can't make the words come out of my mouth. "I—well—it, uh—"

She holds up a hand. "Please stop. I forgive you, it's over, we're cool."

I glance at the patio, where Eddie seems to be doing tai chi. "I'm sorry. It's just that every man who sees you wants you. You're beautiful, sexy, and clever. I wouldn't blame Eddie Masters if he did make a pass."

She snorts, clearly trying to contain her laugher. "You don't need to worry about Eddie."

"He's a man, and you're a beautiful woman."

Rika smiles and lays her hand on my chest. "You're so cute, but you really have nothing to worry about. Eddie's gay."

"Are you having me on?"

"No, he's really gay. And he's way too nice to sexually harass anyone." She leans in closer. "For the record, Eddie had his hands on me because he was giving me a yoga lesson."

"Oh. Maybe I should, ah, apologize to him."

"Let me handle that. Don't you need to be at work?"

"Yes, I do."

She waves her hand. "Then go."

I go, and I violate the speed laws again on my way back to work.

Noah almost cringes when I step out of the elevator, heading toward his desk and my office. I pass him without glancing at or speaking to him. What can I say? *Sorry I made you think I wanted you to urinate on me, then I snarled at you.* I'd scared Noah. The bloke has known me for less than two days, and I've made a brilliant first impression.

Well, I can kiss that Boss of the Year trophy goodbye.

After fifteen minutes of glaring down at my desk and cursing at myself in my thoughts, I realize what I need to do. *One* thing I need to do, that is. Most everything else… I've got no fucking idea.

I approach Noah's desk.

He stops blinking and darts his gaze everywhere but at me. "What can I do for you, Mr. Dixon, sir?"

"Noah, I…" Scrubbing a hand over my mouth, I try to figure out what to say. "I'm sorry for the way I behaved earlier. You didn't do anything wrong. It's entirely my fault."

"Oh. Thank you, Mr. Dixon, sir."

"Call me Dane, please."

His eyes are large, but he sounds happier when he says, "Sure. Thank you, Dane."

The elevator doors open, and Rika steps out.

Before I can summon the brainpower to comprehend the fact she's here, she takes hold of my tie and leads me into my office using my tie as a leash.

When we cross the threshold, she says, "Close the door."

I kick it shut while I follow her around my desk to my chair. What is she doing? Her bossy tone when she ordered me to close the door made my cock wake up. What she's wearing wakes it up even more. She still has on the leggings and tank top, but now she's added running shoes and a long, open sweater that hangs down to her knees. Her ponytail bounces with every step she takes.

And I imagine grasping that ponytail while I fuck her.

She stops beside my chair and releases my tie. "Sit down."

"Why are you here? Don't you need to be at work?"

"I told Eddie I need the rest of the day off to take care of my boyfriend. He lent me his Corvette so I could get here faster." She wags a finger at me. "No more talking. I'm here to relieve your stress, Dane. So sit down and shut up."

Relieve my stress? If she means to talk me into meditating or doing yoga…

She grabs my tie again and hauls me closer, with only a hair's breadth between our bodies. "You'll want to be sitting down when I do this. Otherwise, your knees might buckle. For sure, your eyes will roll back in your head."

I sit down.

Rika kneels in front of me, crawling forward on her knees until she's wedged between my thighs. She undoes my tie and tosses it onto the desk, then she unhooks the top button on my shirt.

Suddenly, I'm having trouble breathing. My cock is hard. She can't mean to have sex with me here in my office. Why would she make me sit down for that, anyway? I want to fuck her on my desk, up against the window, on the floor, any way she'll let me have her.

Rika unfastens my belt, frees the button on my trousers, and slides the zipper down so slowly that watching her do it makes me breathe harder, faster, my mouth open and my whole body tense with anticipation. She bends toward me, her lips grazing my ear as she whispers, "I'm really good at doing this."

"Doing...what?"

She pulls back so I can see her face, and her lips curl into the sexiest little smile I've ever seen. "Prepare to have your mind blown." She glances down at my groin. "And other parts of you too."

No, she can't mean to—

Rika pulls my dick out of my trousers and shorts, cupping it in her soft, warm hand. "Oh wow, you're so big and hard and hot. Can't wait to swallow you whole."

Fuck. She means to do what I thought she meant to do. The thought of her mouth on me... I may not last long once she starts.

She strokes me with one hand, humming like she can't wait to consume me, and with her other hand she massages my inner thigh.

"Rika, I—"

Her tongue rakes across the head of my erection.

I jerk and gasp, gripping my chair's arms so tightly my fingers ache, but I don't care. Her tongue, it's velvety and warm and moist. When she flicks it out to tease me again, I let out a choked sound. My ears are ringing, and she hasn't even gotten to what I know will be the best part.

"Mm," she moans, licking her lips.

"You'd better hurry. I can't—I won't—make it much longer."

Rika closes her fist around the base of my cock. "Time to blow your mind."

She opens her mouth and does exactly what she said. She swallows me whole, taking me deep inside. Her soft moans vibrate my flesh while she sucks gently and moves her mouth up and down, up and down, flicking her tongue as she moves. Her hand pumps me too, her smooth palm so fucking arousing I've lost all capacity to speak, to think, or to breathe.

My back bows. The pressure builds and builds while she starts to suck me more forcefully, her moans turning into grunts while her eyes drift half closed like she loves doing this to me.

She won't swallow when I come. Women never want to do that, at least not with me.

"Fuck, Rika."

The orgasm rips through me, hot and hard and so bloody incredible that I squeeze my eyes shut and let out a long, rasping shout. When it's over, I'm breathing hard and so limp that all I can do is lie here slouched in my chair.

But I've never felt better in my entire life.

I gaze at Rika, probably looking dazed, because I am.

She slides her tongue over her lips like she's lapping up every last bit of what I spent in her mouth. "Mm, you're the best thing I've ever tasted. And I love the way you look when you come."

"Rika, that was…amazing."

"Do you feel more relaxed now?"

"I can honestly say I've never been more relaxed in my life." I cup her cheek in one hand. "You are the most wonderful woman in the world."

She laughs, the sound delicate and sweet. "You're adorable when you're satisfied."

As I gaze into her golden eyes, with those green flecks sparking in the sunlight that streams through the windows, I realize exactly what I need to do.

I bend forward to wrap my arms around her waist and lift her up with me. Once we're both standing, I pull her snug against me.

"It's your turn, Rika."

Chapter Eleven

Rika

Dane backs me up to the desk, slips his hands under my ass, and lifts me onto the desk so I'm perched on its edge. It's my turn, he said. Oh God, I hope he means what I think he means. I got so turned on when I had him in my mouth, and the look on his face only made me hotter for him. What I want most of all is for Dane to thrust into me and make us both come.

His slacks are still undone, and his dick hangs between our bodies.

I need that inside me. But I also want his mouth on me, and I can't decide which I want first.

Dane kneels between my thighs. He pulls my leggings down, and I lift my hips to help him, until they're lumped around my ankles, trapped by my shoes. He glides his hands up my calves, his skin grazing mine and setting off a wave of tingling heat in its wake. He places a soft kiss on each knee, then sweeps his hands over them and up my thighs.

He hooks his fingers inside the waist of my panties and drags them down too.

I spread my legs more for him. Oh God, I'm so wet and ready that it's almost embarrassing. I wanted him the day we met, but I've been desperately crushing on him since that day in the restaurant. It's become more than a crush, though. I might be kind of obsessed with his body.

Dane takes his glasses off, sets them on the desk, and lowers his head between my legs. The first touch of his tongue makes me gasp and grip the desk's edge. When he drags his tongue up and down my cleft, my breaths turn into sharp gasps, one after another after another.

"Oh yes, Dane." I clasp his head with both hands while he swirls his tongue around my clitoris without touching it. "Please, yes, please."

He laps at the slick skin just below my clit, his nose brushing that hard nub. When he finally closes his mouth around it, an electric current fires through my body, exciting every nerve. Holy shit, Dane knows what he's doing. I've had guys do this before, but none of the others got me so excited so fast. When he thrusts a finger inside me, I start panting and dig my nails into his scalp. He licks faster, sucks harder, thrusts that finger deeper, until I'm teetering on the edge. So close, almost there.

"Yes, Dane, more," I plead between panting breaths.

Dane pushes two fingers inside me now, while he keeps lapping and suckling me, and I bite back a cry when he groans against my clitoris, vibrating that most sensitive part of me. A coil inside my body winds tighter and tighter, and I get wetter and wetter, so desperate for release that I'm clamping my lips shut to muffle my frantic noises. A fevered flush sweeps over me from head to toe, and I go rigid, frozen in that blissfully torturous moment before I tumble over the edge.

"Dane!" I cry out, oblivious to the fact there's a stranger right outside the door to this office. I don't give a damn who hears me. The pleasure rolling through me consumes my focus, making me shut my eyes while my body bows inward, my knees draw up, and I let out a hoarse, wordless cry.

The orgasm fades gradually, but Dane and I stay frozen with my body curled around him and his head between my legs. After a minute or two, he kisses his way down my thighs and sits back on his heels.

He drags his tongue across his lips three times like he's savoring the taste of me.

"Wow, Dane," I say, still kind of breathless from what he did to me. "That was… I can't even think of a word that's good enough to describe it. I've never come that hard before."

"You gave me the same gift. This was reciprocity."

He's got to be joking, right? Reciprocity? It was so much more than that.

Dane rises, zips up his pants, and snags his tie from the desktop. While he works on doing up his tie, he says, "I feel much better now. Thank you."

I'm sitting here on his desk, my pants and underwear around my ankles, and he thanks me. What the fuck?

"Let's go to lunch," I say, because I have no clue how I'm supposed to respond to his gratitude for the blow job I gave him.

"I don't have time." Done with his tie, he buttons his pants and secures his belt. "I'm sure Eddie wants his Corvette back."

"He said I can bring it back to him tomorrow." I hop off the desk and pull up my leggings and panties. "I told Eddie I need the rest of the day off. That means we are spending time together. You go tell Noah you'll be out of the office until tomorrow."

Dane looks at me with a bland expression. "I don't have time for—"

I seal two fingers over his mouth to shut him up. "I get that we just had a very intimate encounter and you're feeling off kilter because of that. But I am not letting you get away with dismissing it as nothing."

"Have I called it nothing?"

"No, but you're acting like that."

"You said you were going to relax me, you did it, and I can't see what else there is to say. It was a casual thing."

Casual? Is he out of his ever-loving mind? The way he brought me to climax had been the single most intense sexual experience of my life.

His face has gone stoic, though, and he pats my arm like I'm a puppy he just gave a tummy rub. "This was nice. Thank you."

Then he waltzes toward the door.

"Hey!" I shout.

Dane freezes with his hand on the doorknob, turning only his eyes to look at me. His wide, stunned eyes.

I stomp up to him, stabbing my finger into his chest. "You do not get to walk away like getting a blow job in your office is an everyday thing."

He flinches the tiniest bit.

"We shared an intense experience," I say. "It wasn't casual. I get that you're terrified of that, though I have no idea why, but being your fake girlfriend does not make me your on-call plaything."

"You're not—I never said—That's—" He screws up his entire face, drops his head onto the door with a thump, and groans.

Oh jeez, now he looks so pitiful that I want to hug him. This man has more tension and angst inside him than I ever realized until this moment. And I feel for him. More than I should, probably. But I can't help it.

"You need a break," I say. "Celeste came to see me last night, and she's worried you're putting too much pressure on yourself. I'm worried about you too. Let's go back to your hotel, cuddle up on one of those big sofas, and order a bunch of decadent desserts from room service."

"I can't," he moans with his head still resting on the door. "There's too much to do."

"Come on, Dane. You need more than oral sex, and I want to help you, so let me." I bite my lip, studying him and his defeated posture. "Okay, I'm just going to do it."

He lifts his head, his brows cinched up tight. "Do what?"

"This." I throw my arms around him, resting my chin on his shoulder. "I've never met anyone who needs a hug more than you do."

"I..." He trails off like he has no idea what to say.

So I keep myself mashed to his body, my arms around his neck, and breathe in the scent of him. He's not wearing cologne, but he smells good naturally. He feels good too. I can't remember the last time I hugged anyone, and I think I'm getting as much comfort from it as I hope he will.

Little by little, his body softens. His head lowers, and his cheek brushes against mine. A breath gusts out of him as he links his hands at the small of my back.

We stand there like that for a minute or two, maybe longer. I lose track of the time because this is the nicest thing I've done in ages. Why do I love cuddling with Dane? I'm not sure, but I'm also not sure it matters. This feels so good and so right that I don't want to examine the reasons why.

"All right," he says on another, gustier sigh that flutters my hair. "Let's go to my suite and…do whatever."

I suppose "or whatever" is the closest he'll ever come to admitting he wants to snuggle with me on a big sofa. I'll take it.

Without letting go of me, Dane opens the door and announces, "Noah, I'm taking the rest of the afternoon off. You should too. I'll make sure you're paid for the full day."

"Thank you, Mr. Dixon, sir," Noah says. "Sorry. I meant Dane."

"Enjoy your afternoon."

Dane keeps an arm around my waist as he leads me to the elevator. The car is empty, and once the doors glide shut, Dane pulls me snug against his gorgeous body and kisses me. The second our mouths collide I hum with pleasure and excitement. I love kissing him, though we've only done this a few times before. I love the sensation of his mouth on mine, of his tongue diving between my lips to tease me and arouse me, and of his hands splayed over my upper back. He takes it slow like he's in no hurry, like we can do this all afternoon.

And I guess we can. He's taken the rest of the day off.

When we exit the elevator into the lobby, I feel so deliciously warm and relaxed and turned on at the same time. This desire is softer than a little while ago in his office. I want him, but mostly, I want to spend time with him. Get to know him. Find out what he wants and needs and feels deep inside.

Which sounds an awful lot like legitimate dating.

And yeah, that's exactly what I want.

But does he want that?

Chapter Twelve

Dane

What am I doing? Taking an afternoon off during the most critical time in my career? The re-launch of my brand of sexual wellness devices is coming up sooner than I'd like, sooner than I can handle. Celeste has hammered it into me that these next weeks will make or break the re-launch, but then she tells Rika I'm stressed out and she's worried about me.

I can't blame Celeste for all my stress. I've done this to myself, haven't I? She warned me what it would be like if I signed a contract with Bonsoir. She never glossed over the downsides or what I would be expected to do. But now… I have no bloody idea how to deal with all of this.

Maybe that explains why I talked a clever, sweet, beautiful, sexy woman into pretending to date me.

When we get to my suite, Rika takes my hand and guides me into the library where we do exactly what she suggested. We snuggle on the sofa. I take off my jacket, tie, and loafers while she kicks off her shoes. She tucks her legs under her and leans against me, so I put my feet on the table and drape my arm over her shoulders. She's warm and smells like powder or…something. It's a pleasant scent. She always smells good, a fact that makes me want to shag her all the time.

I haven't done that yet. Why not?

Because it would be wrong, that's way. I want to smack my forehead with my palm, but I don't. Rika will think I've gone completely insane if I do that. But I am an idiot, to say the least, for thinking for even one second that I deserve to sleep with this woman. She should have a real boyfriend, not an arse like me who tells her it's only for show.

"What are you so afraid of?" she asks, not sounding at all irritated, despite the fact I hurt her feelings earlier.

I open my mouth to tell her I have no idea what she's talking about, but I stop short of saying it. Am I afraid? If I am, why is that?

Why can't you be as exciting as your toys?

My head falls back against the sofa like it's transformed into a granite ball and I can't hold it upright anymore. I should tell her the truth, shouldn't I? But I can't make the words come out, so instead I say, "I'd rather not talk about myself."

"That seriously limits the conversation." She wriggles until she's turned partway toward me, though she stays under my arm and nestles against me. "Tell me about your family, then. Please."

"You know my brothers."

"Not well."

I shrug my shoulder, the one she's not tucked up against. "Reese is incessantly cheerful and irritating. Chance is mature and irritating."

"Oh come on, I know you get along with your brothers. Why are you calling them irritating?"

"Because they both insist on telling me I've lost my sense of humor and I've become..." I grimace. "Uptight."

"That's because you are uptight. I'm not criticizing, but remember, I've seen the wedding videos. You were smiling and laughing, dancing with all the ladies. You even told jokes during your best man speech for Chance. Funny jokes." She nudges me with her elbow. "I know the way you are now isn't how you usually act."

"Maybe it isn't, but I can't change the way I am."

"Because you're completely stressed out."

I drum my fingers on my thigh. "Fine, yes, I'm stressed out and uptight and not any fun at all anymore."

"Admitting you have a problem is the first step to recovery."

"This isn't an AA meeting."

"No, it's a private session with your personal counselor." She points at herself. "That would be me."

"We're not actually dating, which means you aren't required to counsel me."

"I want to help you, Dane. If you'll let me."

"And what is it you think you can do for me?" I grunt and shake my head. "Even my parents think I'm on the verge of a nervous breakdown. They told me so in an email because I've been avoiding their calls."

"You need to talk to your family, not avoid them. You work in the same building as your brother Reese. Talk to him."

I clear my throat while I avoid looking at her. "I can't. I sort of, ah, shouted at Reese earlier today. Told him I don't want my face on the sodding package for my devices. And I might also have slammed my fist down on the desk when I said it."

"Reese isn't mad at you, I'm sure. He looks up to you."

"Are you sure you're talking about the same Reese? Maybe you've got my brother confused with someone else."

She laughs, and it sounds almost affectionate. "I've met your brother, in person, with his wife. Arden wouldn't hang on anyone else's body. And Reese told me, face to face, that he admires and respects you and wishes he could be more like you."

"He wants to be an uptight arsehole? I rather doubt that."

"The way you were before Bonsoir gobbled up your company."

Celeste's company gobbled up mine because I served it to Bonsoir with garnish and red wine sauce. What had I been thinking? I want to rewind the months to that moment and say no this time when Celeste offers to make me an instant billionaire.

But I can't. I'm trapped.

Rika places a hand on my cheek and touches her lips to mine.

The kiss is soft and sweet, but the feel of her skin on mine makes me want to deepen the kiss, to taste every millimeter of her mouth and explore all the ways I can excite her. I want to hear her moan and feel the vibrations of it through our fused mouths.

I can't move, though. I can't do anything except relax my lips and let her kiss me.

She pushes her tongue inside, flicking it until her teasing compels me to dive deep into her mouth and do what I thought of doing seconds ago. I devour her. And when she moans into my mouth the way I wanted her to, I feel the vibrations just how I'd imagined I might. The sensation is even better than I expected, even more arousing. I thrust a hand into her hair and pull her even closer so I can plunge deeper into the hot, silky depths of her mouth. Christ, that sounds idiotic. Hot, silky depths? But that's what she feels like. I've never loved kissing any other woman as much as I love kissing this woman.

Rika pulls away, but only enough to look me in the eye. She slides her tongue across her bottom lip. "Let's have sex, Dane."

"What? I, uh… What?" She can't mean it. I must have misheard her, or she must have misspoken.

"I said let's have sex." She swings her leg over me so she's straddling my lap, then she wraps her arms around my neck, her mouth so close I could take her bottom lip between my teeth and suck on it. "You want me. I want you. We've proved we have chemistry. We're adults, and there's no reason in the world why we shouldn't go all the way."

"But—"

She seals my lips with one finger. "You'll feel lots better when you stop fighting this attraction. Do I have to be blunt about it? Well okay, I will." She moves even closer, her breasts crushed against my chest and her lips skimming mine when she speaks. "Fuck me, Dane."

Chapter Thirteen

Rika

I can't believe I said that. *Fuck me, Dane.* I've never spoken those words to any man, but I calmly told Dane Dixon that's what I want. Okay, yeah, it is what I want. I've craved this man since the day we met, but I'm not the kind of girl who asks a man to have sex with her in such bold, explicit terms. I really hope I haven't scared him because I want to sleep with him.

And I don't care that it's afternoon and we won't fall asleep once we're done. I want Dane. Right here, right now, no more waiting. So what if our relationship is a sham? We can still have earth-shattering sex.

What happens when an uptight man lets go? I've never been with anyone like Dane before, so I have no idea. But my gut tells me sex with him will be fantastic.

"All right," he says with a sigh. "I'll do it."

He sounds…resigned.

Oh yeah, that's super sexy. *Not.*

"What's wrong?" I ask.

"I need to get—" He sighs again, shakes his head, and frowns. "One moment. Stay here."

He pushes me off his lap and gets up, walking out of the library.

Ohhhh-kay. What just happened? He agrees to having sex but says it like he's preparing for a root canal, then he leaves the room.

Dane comes back a minute later holding a plastic grocery bag full of things I can't make out.

"Everything okay?" I ask.

He shrugs one shoulder and drops onto the sofa. Offering me the bag, he says, "This is what you want."

I gingerly accept the bag, taking it by the plastic straps, and peer inside. It contains a selection of vibrators. "What is this?"

"It's what you want."

"You said that a second ago, but I still have no idea why you're giving me vibrators."

"Because you want me to fuck you."

For several seconds, I stare at him with my mouth open. Vibrators? I asked him to have sex with me. Why does he think I want toys? Something else is going on here, but I know I won't convince him to tell me what that is until after we get it on.

I set the bag of toys on the table and crawl onto his lap again. "We can play with those later if you want, but I need *you* inside me, Dane, not your toys."

He watches me, his eyes shifting this way and that like he's trying to determine if I'm telling the truth. "You mean that?"

"Yes, I do." I let my entire body sag against him, my lips ghosting over his. "I don't care where we do it as long as we do it *right now*."

He clasps the back of my head and kisses me. It's rough and hot and so damn good that I moan and rock my hips into him, desperate to have him inside me.

Dane flips me onto my back, spread lengthwise across the sofa with my feet on his lap. He doesn't even bother unbuttoning his shirt. He tears it off over his head and flings it away. Then he gets rid of his pants and underwear, his socks too. On his knees, naked and aroused, he rakes his hooded gaze over me from head to toe.

His steamy appraisal makes me so wet and achy for him that a tingle sweeps over my entire body. I'm about to get what I've wanted since day one. I bite down on my lip while I admire the view of him. Dane has muscles—oh yes, lots and lots of delicious muscles that I want to explore with my tongue—but the part of him that robs me of breath hangs between his hips. That beautiful, thick, long cock is hard and ready for action, its tip rosy and glistening.

Oh yes, please, give me that.

I've had his dick in my mouth, but I didn't get a good look at it earlier today. I'd been too obsessed with making him come to take the time to admire that gorgeous cock.

Dane removes my socks and hooks his fingers inside the waistband of my leggings and my panties. He tugs both down to my ankles. "Think I'll leave you like this for now."

The fact that he wants my ankles bound by my leggings, like he had earlier in his office, makes me even wetter. I have no idea what he plans to do to me, and I don't care.

He crouches over me on his hands and knees. "Take off your shirt and bra."

I get rid of them faster than I've ever stripped before. Yeah, I want him like crazy, remember? I've wanted him for what feels like forever, though it's only been a few weeks. Lying naked under him with that beautiful hard-on dangling between our bodies, I'm so damn ready for this.

"Bend your knees," he commands.

And I do it. Bending my knees forces me to spread my thighs. With my ankles caught in my own clothes, I can't wrap my legs around his hips the way I want to, but it doesn't matter. Any second, he'll take me. He'll fuck me. He'll do whatever the hell he wants to do to me, and I'll love it.

He freezes, not even blinking. "Bollocks."

"What's wrong?"

"Condom. I didn't—we need—I, ah, don't, um, have—"

"My pants pocket."

His brows squish together. "What?"

"Check my pants pocket." I've kept a condom on hand ever since I met Dane. Eternally hopeful, that's me.

He fumbles with my leggings, since they're lumped around my ankles, and finally extracts the item we both want.

A condom packet.

Dane looks so adorably relieved and gets the condom on in a matter of seconds.

Then he's over me again, his hands at either side of my head, his gaze locked on mine. He thrusts into me, consuming my body with one long, slow, sensuous stroke that makes me gasp and arch my back. Oh God, this feels even better than I'd imagined all those times when I fantasized about Dane fucking me while I got off with a vibrator. He's so firm and hot, and when he's buried himself as deep as he can go, he pauses there so we can both revel in the sensations of our bodies joined at last.

He kisses me tenderly, then he dips his head to latch on to my nipple, loving it with his lips and his tongue until I'm squirming and clutching his head. The heat of his intimate kiss robs me of breath. I grasp his biceps, gazing into his blue eyes and letting them lure me down into a warm pool of liquid desire.

Releasing my nipple, he begins to move, pulling his hips back and lunging them forward in a powerful rhythm, and I abandon myself to the moment. Since I can't grip him with my legs, I grip his arms even harder and let him do whatever he wants. My sex gets even slicker and molds to his length, creating a wet sucking sound with every thrust. He hisses in a breath every time he pulls out, until only the head of his cock brushes my entrance, then the air gusts out of his lungs when he plunges inside me again, over and over and over.

"Oh yes, Dane, yes," I gasp. "You feel so good, so incredible, don't ever stop."

He lowers onto his elbows, dropping his head to my shoulder.

And he keeps going. Every lush stroke ramps up my need, and I sling my arms around him, determined to hang on to him until the very end. But I never want this to end. I need him filling me up forever, so I'll never stop experiencing the sensations he evokes in me with every little movement. When he shoves a hand under my ass and lifts it, his strokes become slower, more sensual, though he's driving even deeper into my body.

"Rika," he groans into my ear. "I need you, Rika."

"I'm here." I turn my head just enough that my lips touch his ear. "I'm not going anywhere. Please, Dane, please don't ever stop."

He groans, and the sound is so husky, so intense, that my clit throbs. "Have to—ah. Can't wait—"

"Then don't wait. Do it now, please, make us both come."

Dane slips his fingers between our bodies to separate my folds, and suddenly, I feel him even more with every stroke. He rubs that aching bud, the one that makes me writhe and cry out, and he keeps rubbing until every muscle in my body tenses in anticipation of the release I feel coming, like a train barreling straight toward a cliff, faster and faster every second, about to plummet over the edge.

At the instant I go off, he hoists himself up on his straight arms and punches into me so hard and so deep that I come even more fiercely, my body clenching his length in rolling waves of pleasure. While my nails sink into his flesh, I scream his name and squeeze my eyes shut, overwhelmed by the power of my climax, and I feel him come apart inside me.

"Rika!"

His hoarse shout echoes in the library.

I peel my lids open, still gasping for breath.

Dane is crouching over me, though his arms are shaking like he's too exhausted to hold himself up anymore but doesn't want to crush me with his body.

"Lay yourself on top of me," I say. "I want to feel you all over me. Please."

His brows do that squishing-up thing again, but after a couple seconds, he lowers his body onto mine.

The weight and heat of him feels heavenly.

With his head on my chest, he caresses my arm with his fingertips.

I comb my fingers through his hair. "That was so unbelievably spectacular. You are one incredible lover, Dane Dixon."

He tenses up, like I've told him something bad instead of paying him an awesome compliment.

"What's wrong?" I ask. "Most guys would love to be told they're fantastic lovers."

"It's, ah…" He lifts his head, searching my gaze. "You mean that, don't you?"

"That you were incredible? Hell yes, I mean it." I run my fingers over his lips. "Why does that surprise you?"

"I've, uh, been taken—been told—" He buries his face between my breasts and groans miserably. When he looks at me again, he's got the cutest befuddled expression on his face. "You really liked being with me?"

"No, Dane, I *loved* it."

He pushes up off me and sits back on his heels near my feet. "You're the only woman who has ever told me I'm spectacular and incredible. The others had…less-kind words for how sex with me made them feel."

I sit up and get rid of my leggings and panties, then I scoot closer to him. "What do these other women tell you?"

"Why can't you be as exciting as your toys. That's what they say."

Chapter Fourteen

Dane

I slump into the corner of the sofa, my legs hanging off the edge, while I watch Rika and wait for her to say she agrees with the idea that I'm not as exciting as a vibrator. She already said she loved being with me. The way she came, it was the most beautiful thing I've ever seen, and her expression evinced wonder and joy and total satisfaction. She loved it. So why am I still convinced she'll change her mind?

Rika climbs onto my lap again, her hands resting on my thighs. "About these incredibly stupid women you've been with…"

"They weren't stupid. I failed to live up to their expectations, and that's my fault."

"Bullshit." She shakes her head. "After what we just did, how can you still believe you suck at sex? Those brain-dead twerps are obnoxious, rude, and completely wrong for you."

Nothing with Rika feels wrong, despite the fact I keep insisting we're not really dating. Our fake relationship feels more real than anything I've had with other women, even the ones who didn't tell me I'm not as exciting as a sex toy.

"Maybe you're right," I say, "but I can't get over being uptight because we had one fantastic shag."

"No, it'll take lots and lots of shags." She clasps my hands to her breasts. "You need to do me several more times. And we should order a big dinner with dessert, because we are going to be burning some serious calories."

This woman wants me—again and again and again.

And fuck, I want her too. All day, all night, for the rest of the week, the month, the year.

Can we have sex nonstop for an entire year? If we take the occasional break to eat…who knows?

Rika grins.

"What's so funny?" I ask.

"It's not funny. It's a miracle." She cradles my face in her palms. "You're smiling, Dane."

"Am I?" I touch the corners of my mouth like I'm checking for a smile. "Look at that. I am smiling. Let's order champagne to toast the occasion."

Her grin gets even wider and brighter. "I knew you had a sense of humor underneath that uptight shell."

"You knew because my brothers told you."

"No, I knew because I saw through that shell."

Her words send a chill through me. She saw through me? For a moment, the idea makes me uneasy—until I realize it's not a bad thing. Rika is getting to know me. Maybe she understood me, at least a little bit, from the start. No other woman bothered to do that.

The chill gives way to a gentle warmth as I look into her eyes and tell her something I thought I'd never admit to anyone. "I don't have a problem getting dates, but everything after that point has always been…troublesome."

"In what way?"

"Women are usually disappointed in me, either because being a mechanical engineer is too boring for them or because I'm not as exciting as the devices I design."

She slides off my lap to sit beside me, her head on my chest.

I hold her close and tell her the rest. "Women don't want to hear about mechanical engineering. But what else can I talk about? It's my job, my life. If I don't say anything about that, all I have left to talk about is my family. Women don't like to hear me banging on about that either. Over the last couple of years, since my company became somewhat successful, women only want to talk about my devices."

"And then these moronic women decide they like your toys but not you."

"Yes. The problem will only get worse once the company relaunches as a branch of Bonsoir."

"Why do you think it will get worse?"

I sit forward, my elbows on my knees, while I remember the past six months. "It's already gotten worse. Every woman I've tried to date since I signed the Bonsoir contract only wants my sex toys, not me. I can't have a real relationship."

"Of course you can."

"You don't understand—"

"I get that you're convinced it's true, but that's a big old armful of hooey." She scoots forward to sit beside me, laying her head on my shoulder. "You already have a real relationship."

"Have you not been paying attention? The only woman I've been with is you, and that's all for show."

"Yeah, I know." She straightens and clears her throat. "Our relationship is not fake. Maybe we both convinced ourselves it was, but it's not. I am your girlfriend, Dane. For real."

I glance at her, unable to form any words in response. My girlfriend? Rika? I've kept telling her it's fake, that I don't have time for more, that this is strictly for publicity. Except I haven't taken her out in public more than twice. I've treated her like an employee, not a lover. Haven't I?

We had a romantic dinner at a posh restaurant. We gave each other mind-blowing climaxes in my office. I've kissed her, even when no one else was there to see it. I got jealous when a waiter spoke to her in French and when Eddie Masters put his hands on her. We hardly know each other, but maybe...

Maybe I do want more with her. More than a farce. Maybe I want her, full stop—as my lover and my girlfriend.

"I want to have a genuine relationship with you, Rika," I hear myself saying. "But I couldn't stand it if one day you tell me I'm not as exciting as my sex toys."

She slides off the sofa to kneel on the floor between my legs. "I would never say that. First of all, I haven't used any of your toys. Second, there is no way on earth any mechanical device could do better than you. The way you made me come, on this sofa and in your office, those were the best sexual experiences I've ever had." She taps her finger on my chest. "And you did that, not your devices."

"Yes, but—"

"No, Dane. You do not get to downplay what we've done together. It's real." She takes my face in her hands again. "I want you, not your devices. To prove I mean that, I'm ordering you to fuck me repeatedly until you believe it."

I laugh, and I can't remember the last time I did that. "You're ordering me to fuck you? Again? I can honestly say that has never happened to me once before today, much less twice." I smirk when I add, "Well, Reese did tell me the cure for my problems is to have you shag my brains out."

"Reese is a smart man." She unfurls her voluptuous body, which places her groin directly in front of my face, and offers me her hand. "Come on, let's get naughty everywhere in this suite. It's got, like, a hundred rooms. By the time we're done, you won't worry about which I prefer—you or your devices. You'll know the answer for sure."

"The answer will be me."

"You got it."

I stand up and look straight into her eyes. "You are my girlfriend, Rika. There's nothing fake about us."

She smiles and kisses me. "I knew that already, but I'm glad you said it."

And I let her lead me off to another room, then another, and another. We do everything two people can do together with only their bodies and various pieces of furniture. Rika and I don't need toys. She's the most inventive woman I've ever been with, and I discover I can be awfully inventive too when I have her body as my inspiration.

And yes, Rika shags my brains out.

It feels bloody incredible.

Chapter Fifteen

Rika

I spend the next several weeks watching Dane Dixon open up and bloom like a big, sexy flower. Maybe that's not the best metaphor, but the facts are irrefutable. Dane still gets stressed out sometimes, but he lets himself relax and enjoy life too. Every time we go out on a date, he smiles and tells jokes that make us both laugh.

Sure, we're doing this for publicity. And yeah, the occasional photo of us shows up on social media or in the society section of a newspaper. When someone on social media names him The Dirty Dixon, my boyfriend seems uncomfortable with the title, but he quickly decides to roll with it. Chance and Reese get mentions too, but only as The Dirty Dixon's brothers. Their names are rarely mentioned.

Dane and I might have told each other in words that we're a real couple now, but our actions speak everything we don't say about the depth of our feelings for each other. We hold hands in public and in private, like in the elevator that takes us up to his suite. And my uptight Brit now loves to make out with me in all three of the suite's elevators. He shocks me, however, when he seduces me in one of them. It's so hot and fun that I beg him to do that every time we go to his hotel.

And he always gives me what I want.

We haven't used his toys yet, not even as foreplay. I insist we don't, though he keeps suggesting we should, because I'm not sure if he's over his fear of me liking his devices better than I like his body. Maybe in another week, we can play with his toys.

About ten days after we first had sex, Dane and I are in his office taking a coffee break. Yes, Dane takes breaks now. But for us, a "coffee break" means I sit on his lap in his chair and we kiss. A lot. Dane also loves to tickle me in places where I had no idea I was ticklish, like behind my left ear and in the centers of both palms. He's blowing a raspberry against my throat, making loud giggles burst out of me, when Celeste Arnaud marches into the office.

Well, we had left the door open. Noah has gotten used to our antics, and Dane even tells jokes that make Noah laugh.

Celeste stops on the other side of the desk, plants a hand on her hip, and raises her brows at us. Her lips kick up in a self-satisfied smile.

Dane peels his lips away from my throat but keeps his arms around my waist so I can't get off his lap. Not that I want to.

"Good afternoon, Celeste," he says, sounding so cheerful that it seems to knock her off kilter for a second or two, based on the way her mouth falls open a touch. "What can we do for you today?"

Her surprise melts into a delighted little smile. "I knew you two would hit it off. Am I a matchmaker or what?"

"What are you talking about? Rika and I found each other on our own."

"But I hired her to be your personal assistant. I knew she'd be an excellent match for you professionally, and I hoped she might turn out to be your perfect match in love too."

Dane's expression goes blank as he stares at Celeste. After a moment, he grins. "You do have great taste, in everything. I suppose I shouldn't be surprised you picked the right woman for me even if you didn't set out to do that."

"A happy accident." Celeste winks. "Or was it?"

Did she seriously hire me because she thought Dane and I would make a good couple? No, even Celeste isn't that sneaky. We do have to give her credit, though, for bringing us into each other's lives.

Celeste sits down across the desk from us. "I'm glad to see you happy, Dane, but you need to prepare yourself for what's coming. The buildup to the re-launch kicks into high gear next week. That means public appearances—and I don't mean just having dinner with Rika at a fancy restaurant."

Dane groans and slumps in his chair, with me still on his lap.

At least Celeste and Reese took Dane's face off the packaging and changed the brand name so it no longer says "Dane's Delights" on the boxes. But I know Dane is not looking forward to press conferences or whatever it is Celeste and her marketing team have in mind.

"What do you want me to do?" Dane asks, sounding like he's about to be arrested instead of about to become filthy rich.

Celeste vowed she'd make him a billionaire, but twice he told me he's not sure he wants that.

"Haven't you checked your email?" Celeste asks. "Reese sent you an itinerary half an hour ago."

"Oh, I, uh—" Dane squirms like he's trying to sit up straighter, but my body is holding him down. "I've been…distracted."

Celeste glances at me. "I can see that."

Dane reaches around me to bring up his emails on the computer on his desk. He seems to be trying to print the one from Reese, but once again, the fact I'm on his lap is complicating the task.

I shoo his hand away from the keyboard. "Let me do that."

A few clicks later, the printer spits out the itinerary. I lean way over to grab the sheet out of the printer, then I hand it to him and loop my arms around his neck. Sure, this has become a business meeting, but I know Dane wants me to stay right where I am. He loves cuddling, especially when he's about to get news he won't like. I didn't mean to peek at the itinerary, but it was kind of inevitable. What? I had to look so I could make sure I printed out the right email.

Dane scans the list of events. He groans and shuts his eyes. "A fashion show? Why do I have to go to one of those? It's not like the models will be demonstrating my devices." His eyes fly wide. "Please tell me you're not having them do that."

Celeste laughs in her usual boisterous way. "Dane darling, you are so charmingly suspicious. No, your devices will not be featured at the fashion show. You will attend, with Rika, to show how hip and stylish you are." She eyes him with her analytical gaze. "I'd better send you over to Armani to get a decent suit. You can't show up to a fashion show wearing a suit from a discount store."

He glances down at his suit. "What's wrong this one? I got it at Marks & Spencer."

"Which is a department store in the UK." Celeste clucks her tongue while shaking her head. "Honestly, my dear, you need to dress that gorgeous body in the proper clothing. Rika will help you choose a suit. Won't you, darling?"

"Uh, sure," I say. I know nothing about designer duds, but what the heck, I'll give it a try. I think Dane looks hot in anything, so I may not be much help. In my opinion, though, he looks best in nothing at all.

We chat with Celeste for a few minutes, then she goes back to her office and Dane lets me drive the sports car he rented so I can get back to Eddie's house faster than the train can get me there. Eddie doesn't mind if I take a very long lunch once a week so I can hang out with Dane more. I make up the lost time by doing website maintenance for him on Saturday, from home. Eddie is one of the nicest people I've ever met, but Dane is my favorite person on earth.

Every weekend, we do something fun—like going to the zoo, which was Arden's suggestion, or visiting Chance and Elena in New Hampshire. Dane likes to sleep over at my apartment several times a week, and I think it's because he's used to a homey place instead of a luxury hotel suite. He grew up in a small town, after all. I'm from Chicago, but even I find that suite kind of off-putting. I mean, it's gorgeous and amazing, but it's not a home.

Our trip to the Armani store results in Dane buying three new suits and a tux. I buy a few dresses too. We both wince at the price tags—discreetly, so we won't offend the store employees—but Celeste insisted we should both have designer threads. She's paying for all of it, so we can't say no.

I have to admit Dane looks extra super yummy in an Armani suit. Am I drooling when I ogle him in that suit? Maybe. Who cares? My boyfriend is hot, hot, *hot*.

We survive the fashion show. I enjoy it, but Dane tolerates it. We get our picture taken by various members of the press, and the next day, we see ourselves in those ultra-chic clothes in various newspapers and magazines, plus some websites. More events follow, including a charity fundraising ball and a photo op at a store that's going to sell Dane's devices. It's a dizzying whirlwind of appearances that leaves us both exhausted.

One night, in Dane's opulent hotel suite, we reach another milestone. We've just made love, and the afterglow is pure bliss.

He turns onto his side and pulls me snug against him, our noses bumping. "I love you, Rika."

"I love you too, Dane."

A glow inside me suffuses my entire body. It's the glow of happiness, a kind I've never experienced before. I get the feeling he experiences the same thing, since his eyes have gone soft and warm, and he kisses me with a sweetness that triggers a dull but pleasant ache in my chest. Then he makes love to me again, infusing the act with all the emotions neither of us can fully express in words. I love this man, and he loves me. My crush has matured into the best thing that's ever happened to me.

The next morning, it's time for the hammer to drop.

It's re-launch day.

Chapter Sixteen

Dane

I stand on a temporary stage set up in the cavernous lobby at the global headquarters of Bonsoir Beauty Incorporated with a microphone on a stand positioned in front of me. Well, not me specifically. Not yet, anyway. Celeste will make her speech, then I will be required to speak. To a large audience. Full of reporters. With flash bulbs firing off like machine guns.

Bloody hell, it's hot in here. I'm starting to sweat, but when I glance around, no one else seems disturbed by the sweltering heat. Maybe it's just me. I don't want to do this.

Celeste begins her introduction, smiling and sounding as confident as ever. She gives a brief overview of Bonsoir and its subsidiaries, then she starts to talk about my corner of the Bonsoir domain. Any minute now she'll introduce me.

I resist the impulse to scratch under my shirt collar. Why do I feel like tiny insects are crawling all over my skin?

When I scan the crowd, I don't see anyone I recognize, so I turn to look at the people standing in the wings, behind a curtain. Reese is there. He gives me the thumbs-up sign and grins. Rika stands beside him. When she notices I'm looking at her, she smiles and mouths, "I love you."

I stand up straighter, lifting my chin. She loves me, and I won't let her down by stammering like an idiot in front of the international press.

"And now," Celeste says, spreading an arm toward me in a grand gesture, "may I introduce the genius behind our new line of sexual wellness devices—the gorgeous, charming, and talented Dane Dixon."

Christ, why did she have to give me an overblown introduction?

I glance at Rika again. This time she mouths, "You can do it."

So I do it. I walk up to the microphone and start my speech. Reese wrote it for me, but thankfully, he didn't include any racy jokes. What he wrote for me sounds like me, not like my little brother. I shouldn't be surprised. I've always known that Reese is cleverer than he used to let on and that he has a way with words. It's why he was successful as an advertising copywriter and why Celeste made him her vice president of advertising.

And I'm even more thankful that he kept the speech short.

"Thank you for coming today," I say, surprising myself with how composed I sound. "I'm proud to present our new line of sexual wellness devices for women—Bonsoir Delights, designed by me and manufactured by our extraordinary teams in the US, UK, Canada, the European Union, and a dozen other locations around the world. Soon, we'll be selling these devices everywhere from Boston to Beijing, and from Norway to New Zealand." I pause for a second, but not because I'm nervous. Not anymore. I'm following Reese's instructions in the script he gave me, which tell me to pause for dramatic effect. "Now, let me walk you through the products we have."

The rest of my speech goes by in a blur. I say all the words I'm meant to say, I hold up each device while I discuss it, and I don't stammer or choke on my own tongue. Not once. Not even when I have to say the name of the most embarrassingly titled device—the Jackrabbit. No, I am not going to explain why it's called that, not to this audience or to any of my friends or family, mostly because I have no idea. Reese came up with the name. He says his wife, Arden, gave him the idea. I don't want to know how or why she did that.

It's one of the two new devices I created. The second one won't be unveiled quite yet. I'm planning a private reveal for one person, the woman who inspired it. When I told Celeste I wanted to delay the announcement, she didn't complain. She said, "Yes, Dane darling, whatever my favorite employee wants."

"Shouldn't Reese be your favorite employee?" I'd asked. "He is your grandson-in-law."

"And I adore Reese, but I adore you even more." She patted my cheek. "Let's not tell Reese that. It's our little secret."

I've wrapped up my speech, so I walk behind the curtain. Celeste assured me I wouldn't need to answer questions from the press. She'll handle that. I hear her voice, projected by the speakers, as I pull Rika into my arms and hold her tight.

"So fucking glad that's over," I groan.

Reese chuckles. "You really aren't built for the public life, are you?"

"No, I'm not." I pull back enough to see Rika's face. Her smile is bright and loving. "Can we talk alone? I want to discuss something with you."

"Sure thing."

Reese winks at me. "Yes, Dane, you drag your girlfriend into a closet or whatever and have her shag you until you can't see straight. That'll make you feel much better."

"Piss off, Reese."

I don't drag Rika into a closet, but I do drag her out to the limousine Celeste hired to take us to and from the headquarters. We kiss for the entire ride back to my hotel, and that kissing involves plenty of groping as well as Rika's hand inside my trousers. I want to get my hand under her skirt, but it's the sort that's so bloody long and narrow that I can't get any part of me under it.

Once we get inside my suite, I strip off all her clothing and mine too, then I lay her down on the bed.

"I have a surprise for you," I say as I crawl up the bed to crouch over her beautiful body.

"You said you want to talk about something." She clasps her hands above her head, smiling in that subtle, sexy way I love. "But we're naked, so I'm thinking a conversation isn't tops on your list of things to do."

"We can talk after." I pull open the drawer in the bedside table and bring out a velvet bag. "Your surprise is in here. I made something just for you, because of you, and you're the first human on earth to see it. I made the prototype myself."

"Is this a new device?"

"Yes."

She cradles my face in her hands, the desire in her expression softened by a tenderness that always sets off a pang behind my ribs. "I told you before, I don't need your devices. I want you, Dane."

"But we can play with my devices. I know you'd like that." I tug the velvet bag open, reaching inside it. "I know you want me, without any mechanical aids, and I'm not worried about that anymore. But I want to play with you, Rika."

Her smile gets bigger, and her eyes sparkle. "I'd love that."

I knew she would, and I can't wait to do that. Pulling out the item I'd kept inside the velvet bag, I slip it onto my hand.

"That's a glove," she says, her forehead crinkling along with her brows. She's so fucking adorable when she's confused and aroused. "It looks soft, and I love that, but—"

"It is soft. It's made from the finest microfiber on earth." I spread my gloved hand over her belly and squeeze a tiny button on the inside of the glove's cuff. It begins to vibrate, not as much as other devices I've made, but with a gentle vibration meant to tease her. "How does this feel?"

She stiffens for a few seconds, then her entire body relaxes, and she hums with satisfaction. "That feels soooo good."

While I glide my gloved hand over her belly, I watch her enraptured expression, and blood starts to rush down to my cock. "I thought about making the glove from silk, but that would drive up the price. I want every woman to have the opportunity to feel the way you look right now. You're gorgeous, Rika, and I want to shag you until you're half out of your mind."

"Yes, please." She writhes and moans when I cup her breast with my gloved hand. "You really are a genius, Dane."

I flick my thumb over her nipple.

She jerks and cries out. "Oh God, do that again."

"Like it, do you?" I flick my thumb again, then brush my fingers over her areola in slow circles. Her throaty moan makes my cock twitch. "Time to come for me, love."

I drag my hand down her belly, pausing over her mound only long enough to make her squirm and gasp, then I push my hand between her folds. Naturally, I made the ultra-soft material waterproof. When I whisk my finger around her clit, she goes off.

"Dane!" she shouts while her body goes rigid and her fingers clench the sheets.

Once I've made her come for as long as she can stand to, I turn off the glove and toss it onto the table.

And I make love to her for an hour.

While we enjoy the afterglow, we talk about the future.

"This isn't the life I want," I tell her. "I thought I did, but I don't. I'm not meant for a public life."

"Yeah, I figured. You were amazing at the press conference, but I know you don't like doing that kind of thing."

"Would it, uh, disappoint you if I, um, sort of…quit my job?"

She kisses me. "I want you to be happy. Quit, if that's what you need to do."

"I'd much rather go home to England and start designing different kinds of devices. No more vibrators. Maybe I can help people with physical therapy or something. Haven't decided yet."

"Whatever you decide to do, I know you'll be a genius at it." She dances her fingertips over my chest. "And I'll go anywhere with you. England, the South Pole, wherever. Besides, England is a lot closer to where my parents live in Sweden."

God, I love her.

The next day, we break the news to Celeste. She's not upset about it. In fact, she doesn't even seem surprised—and she offers me a severance package so generous that I can take my time figuring out what the next phase of my life looks like. Our life. Rika and I will do this together, whatever "this" turns out to be.

A few days later, Chance and Elena pick us up at the airport in the jet they chartered, and we all fly to England. When we get to my parents' house, everyone is there, including Reese and Arden as well as Arden's parents, Elena's brother, and Rika's parents. I had them flown in from Sweden since I know Rika hasn't seen them in quite some time.

One of the guests has stayed at the periphery, glancing around like he's uncomfortable.

"Who's that guy?" Rika asks.

"That's my cousin, Grey. He's a bit shy around strangers, and this is the first time he's met you, Arden, and Elena."

"Couldn't his parents make it? You invited everyone else."

"I let Chance and Elena do the inviting." I slip my arm around her waist. "But Grey never knew his mother, and his father died several years ago. We're all the family he has."

"That's so sad. We should adopt him. Not literally, of course."

"Let's talk about that later." I move in front of her and drop to one knee, pulling out a small box and flipping its lid up. "Fredrika Maria Solberg, I love you more than anything or anyone in the entire universe. You changed my life and showed me everything I'd been missing. I owe you my happiness, a debt I want to spend the rest of my life repaying. Will you marry me?"

She bursts into tears. "Yes, Dane, of course I will. I love you so much."

I slide the ring onto her finger.

Reese whoops. Chance whistles. Their wives shriek and jump up and down. Rika's mother cries while her husband grins. Kyle Linwood pumps his fists in the air and grunts like a gorilla or…something. My mother and father rush up to us to hug me, then Rika, then me again. My mother is crying too.

Grey shuffles up to us after everyone else has gone off to arrange some sort of celebration that I'm sure will be embarrassing. My cousin shakes my hand and kisses Rika's cheek. "Congratulations. And welcome to the family, Rika."

"Thank you." She kisses his cheek. "I hope we'll get to know each other a lot better."

"I'd like that."

My fiancée wants to take Grey under her wing. I love that she cares so much about a man she's just met, simply because he's my cousin. Rika is wonderful in every way.

A few more people arrive for the party, but most of them are mates of Reese and Chance. I don't have any close friends, but I plan to change that.

Rika sidles up to me and whispers, "Who's the hottie talking to Chance? Another cousin?"

"No, that's Richard Hunter. He and Chance have known each other since university. Richard owns a publishing company that he inherited from his father."

"Hmm. Is he a nice guy?"

"Seems to be, yes."

"Is he married? Or does he have a girlfriend?"

"Not that I know of."

She lifts onto her tiptoes to peer across the room at Richard. "You know my sister, Maddie, is coming to visit us next week. And she's single too."

"No meddling, Rika."

She bats her eyelashes at me with fake innocence. "All I want to do is introduce them."

I don't get the chance to order her not to meddle, because Reese approaches me. Rika leaves us alone while she wanders over to Richard.

Reese grins and slaps me on the shoulder. "Told you, mate. I said you'd be next, and here you are volunteering for the ball and chain."

Being chained to Rika doesn't sound like torture. I never want to let her go, so if a wedding ring shackles me to her, I absolutely do volunteer for it.

"That's right," I tell Reese. "I'm signing up for that ball and chain, as long as it's attached to Rika for the rest of our lives."

And if my fiancée has her way, Richard Hunter will be next.

Dane's Version

One Hot Crush
Chapter One

I am an idiot. I know this, but I can't seem to do anything about it. Only an idiot would develop a speech impediment that only manifests itself in the presence of one woman. A woman who works for me. The sexiest, most beautiful woman on earth. I want to get her naked and kiss, lick, nibble, and fondle every inch of her body.

So naturally, I can't speak a complete sentence when I'm talking to my new personal assistant, Rika Solberg.

Today is no different. I exit the elevator and see her—that chestnut hair, those striking hazel eyes, that sensual body. I dream about her breasts every night, and in my dreams, I don't stammer.

But this morning, I do. Of course.

Holding a magazine so I can pretend I'm reading it doesn't help.

"Good morning, Miss Solberg," I say. I make the mistake of glancing at her for half a second. Her lips seize my attention. I want to suck the bottom one into my mouth and—*Fuck.* I swallow hard and resort to staring at the magazine again. "Do I have any pointers—uh, I mean, appointments today?"

"Yes, Mr. Dixon. Today's agenda is already on your desk."

I knew that. She puts it on my desk every morning before I arrive.

"Oh. Of course," I say, swallowing again. If I keep doing that, my throat will get raw, especially since my mouth has gone completely dry. "Let me know when—if I, uh, have…calls or whatnot."

"I will." Rising from her chair, she tugs her jacket down. "May I get you a cup of coffee, Mr. Dixon?"

"Yes. Thank you, Miss Solberg. One sugar, no cream."

I knife a hand through my hair, trying very hard not to stare at her breasts. Or her legs. Or her mouth.

The fact that I'm thinking about those parts of her means I'm failing to not look at her body. *Bollocks.*

"Do I have a meeting with Celeste today?" I ask because I suddenly can't remember what the fuck I'm supposed to do today.

Well, at least I spoke an entire sentence with no hiccups.

"Yes, sir," Rika says. "Ms. Arnaud is coming at ten."

I nod, bowing my head. *Don't look at her.* "Thank you."

Before I can do anything else stupid, I rush into my office and shut the door. Sitting at my desk eases some of my anxiety. Why I get anxious around Rika, I have no bloody clue. She's pretty and clever and desirable, but I've been around women like that before. Something about this woman turns me into a complete idiot.

Once I've sat down at my desk, I turn my computer monitor on, intending to browse my emails. But my mobile makes that irritating noise that means I have a text message, so I dig it out of my pocket to check for texts. I do have one, from my brother Reese.

He asks, *How do you like your personal assistant?*

She's fine, I type. I cock it up four times before I get it right. Texting has never been my strong suit. My fingers are…uncooperative. Though telling Reese "shit's phone" might make him laugh, that's not what I meant to say.

Fine? Reese responds. *She's sexy as hell.*

Yes, she absolutely is. But my little brother is being sarcastic and trying to annoy me, so I reply with Rika is my employee, you daft arse. Yes, I insult my brother. He knows I'm just reciprocating his attempt to irritate me.

Go on and shag her, Reese replies. *If she sues you for sexual harassment, Chance will defend you.*

You're not as funny as you think.

He sends me a series of emojis, most of which I don't understand. One is what looks like a laughing face with tears pouring from its eyes. The rest are too bizarre to comprehend.

I'm hilarious, Reese tells me in words since he seems to be done with the moronic emojis. *You are an uptight arse.*

Thank you. Bugger off now.

See you Thursday.

He ends that statement, and our conversation, with an emoji of a winking face.

At least I understand that symbol.

Reese and his wife, Arden, are flying in from London late Wednesday. Reese travels back and forth between England and New York for his job as vice president of advertising at Bonsoir Beauty Inc., and I'm positive the CEO, Celeste Arnaud, ordered him to stay in New York for the duration of the re-launch nonsense.

I have to admit it will be nice to have both my brothers on the same continent with me. Chance is in New Hampshire with Elena.

But why did I ever agree to merge my company with the second-largest cosmetics corporation in the world? What do sexual wellness devices have to do with makeup, anyway?

Someone knocks on the door.

It's Rika, of course. So I call out for her to come in, and she waltzes into my office, setting a cup on my desk

Naturally, I do the worst thing I could possibly do. I glance up at her. And immediately avert my gaze. She's too perfect to look at, which is barmy. But if I let myself drink in the sight of her, my cock will do things it shouldn't be doing in the office.

"Thank you, Miss Solberg," I mutter.

She leaves, and I stare at the papers on my desk.

Rika Solberg, the most enticing woman I've ever seen, will be my right hand for the entire ordeal of this bloody re-launch business. I'll work closely with her—and her body. She doesn't seem to notice me in the same way I notice her, which only makes the problem worse. Unrequited lust might drive me insane.

I drink my coffee while I try to figure out how to survive nearly two months with Rika.

Go on and shag her, Reese said.

Yes, that sounds like the perfect solution. But I can't. I won't. She works for me, and I have never and will never violate the employer-employee relationship or compromise my ethics. No, never.

Absolutely never.

Unless she sashays into my office again.

Rika's Version

One Hot Crush
Chapter Two

On her way out of Dane's office, Celeste gives me marching orders. I'm supposed to print out some stuff and take it to him so he can review and approve it. As soon as Celeste leaves, I print the documents and knock on the door to Dane's office.

"Come in, Miss Solberg." His sexy voice makes me horny even when I hear it through a wood door.

I summon all my willpower and walk into his office, straight up to his desk, and offer him a folder. "Celeste wanted me to give you the latest projections for sales in the first month after the re-launch of Dane's Delights."

"M-Miss Solberg," he stammers, "please—I mean, thank you. It—yes, I needed this."

He snatches the folder from me and squints at the papers inside it like he's poring over them.

Jeez, I feel bad for the guy. And I wonder for the umpteenth time if he struggles to speak to other women or if it's just me. Would Celeste have brought him into her company if he couldn't hold a conversation? Not even an itty-bitty one?

"Can I get you more coffee?" I ask.

"No. No, I—" He swallows visibly. "I'm fine, thank you."

I should leave. Shouldn't I? But my feet seem to have gotten stuck to the carpet, and I can't tear my gaze away from him. As usual, his glasses obscure his eyes, leaving me to imagine what they look like without those lenses in the way. I fixate on his kissable lips and imagine nibbling on them, then I wonder what they would feel like pressed against my lips.

He pretends to study the papers I gave him, but he keeps glancing up at me without lifting his head. Every time he does that, he swallows hard again.

"Celeste told me to stay until you've gone over those numbers," I tell him. "Then I'm supposed to get you to sign off on it and send all of it back to her."

"Oh." He flips through the pages, seeming not to pay attention to what's printed on them, then he signs the last page and hands the folder back to me. "Here it is."

"You looked at the numbers so fast. Are you sure you don't want to take more time?"

He waves like he wants me to leave. "It's fine. Thank you."

"Okay, if you're sure." I bite my lip, and he stares at my mouth when I do that. Which makes me look at his mouth. At those sexy, sexy lips. "Is there anything else I can do for you?"

Dane freezes, not looking at me or anything, but seeming to stare into a distance no one else can see. He compresses his lips, scratches behind his ear, and clears his throat. But he's still focused on something I can't see—something inside his mind, I assume.

"Are you okay?" I ask.

He straightens his glasses, which don't need straightening, and aims his gaze directly at me. "Actually, there is one more thing you could do for me."

"What is it?"

He opens his mouth, but the only sound that comes out of it is a soft croaking noise.

Oh God, what if he's having a stroke? Or a panic attack? A seizure, maybe?

I lean over his desk, peering into his eyes. "Are you sure you're okay? Should I call a doctor?"

"No, I'm all right." He takes a swig of his coffee. "No need for a doctor."

"Okay." I keep leaning over the desk, and his attention flicks down to where my blouse has fallen away from my chest, revealing a hint of my cleavage. "What did you want to ask me?"

"Uh…" He tugs at the collar of his shirt. "Would you have lunch with me? I need to discuss some business matters with you."

"Lunch?"

"A business lunch," he says. "Nothing untoward about it. I'd like us to get to know each other a bit, strictly to improve our working relationship."

Yeah, of course he's not asking me out on a date. Duh. Maybe I'd thought that for a second, but no, he doesn't want anything of the sort.

I straighten. "Okay, sure."

What the heck? At least I'll get a nice meal. He's paying, right? I can't ask that, but I really hope he doesn't want us to split the bill. I mean, he asked me to lunch. And he's my boss. Shouldn't he pay? It's a business expense.

Dane stands up. "You should choose the restaurant. I don't know the area."

"Um, it's nine thirty," I say. "I guess you're still on UK time?"

"Oh. Yes, I suppose I am." He doesn't sound sure of that. "You settle on a restaurant, and we'll take our lunch at one o'clock. All right?"

"Sounds good."

I walk out of his office and sit down at my desk, then I consider the options for lunch. Does Dane like fancy places? Or homey diners? Maybe he's into ethnic cuisine. Is there such a thing as British cuisine? No idea. Maybe I should ask Elena or Arden. They're married to Brits, and they know Dane, so they ought to have some pointers for me.

When I call Elena, Chance answers her phone. He tells me she's out doing research for one of their clients. They own a law firm, with Chance as the attorney and Elena as his paralegal, so she's often doing stuff like that. Next, I try Arden. She and Reese are in England until Wednesday evening, when they'll come back to New York for a while. But I get her voice mail, and I don't bother to leave a message.

Okay, I'll have to guess about what my smokin' hot boss likes. Not me, that's for sure. He might've ogled my boobs a little bit, but he clearly doesn't like being around me. Which means lunch ought to be a blast.

I grab the bag of chocolate-covered almonds I'd hidden in my desk, tear it open, and start stress eating.

And I fantasize about Dane's lips.

Anna Durand is a bestselling, multi-award-winning author of contemporary and paranormal romance. Her books have earned bestseller status on every major retailer and wonderful reviews from readers around the world. But that's the boring spiel. Here are the really cool things you want to know about Anna!

Born on Lachland Air Force Base in Texas, Anna grew up moving here, there, and everywhere thanks to her dad's job as an instructor pilot. She's lived in Texas (twice), Mississippi, California (twice), Michigan (twice), and Alaska—and now Ohio.

As for her writing, Anna has always made up stories in her head, but she didn't write them down until her teen years. Those first awful books went into the trash can a few years later, though she learned a lot from those stories. Eventually, she would pen her first romance novel, the paranormal romance *Willpower*, and she's never looked back since.

Want even more details about Anna? Get access to her extended bio when you subscribe to her newsletter and download the free bonus ebook, *Hot Scots Confidential*. You'll also get hot deleted scenes, character interviews, fun facts, and more! Plus you'll receive the short story *Tempted by a Kiss*, two bonus chapters for *One Hot Chance*, and a bonus audiobook chapter narrated for you by Shane East.

Visit AnnaDurand.com to sign up.

9 781949 406375